What's it about!

Three best friends. Two crumbling estates. And one trip that changes everything.

When three barn besties escape for a girls' trip to Ireland, they expect a lot of fun. They don't expect to want to stay... forever.

Natalie was always the responsible one, the organized one, the together one. But when she inadvertently leaves one day early for their vacation and comes home pink-cheeked with embarrassment, the last thing she expects to find is her husband. . .in their bed with another woman. Luckily, they don't notice her, and she takes the trip as a time-out to figure out what to do.

Samantha's marriage has never been full of fireworks and trips to Cabo, but they were making it work. At least, she thought they were. When an unreasonable ultimatum sends her into a tailspin just before the trip, she takes the time to reevaluate what matters and what she wants out of life and love.

Vanessa's husband passed a few years before, and she's been soldiering on. Moments away from her job and responsibilities as a mother of three have been rare, but she has no plans of uprooting their life in Colorado. At least, not until someone she trusts betrays her in a big way. That wound makes her question everything about her own value and her family's future.

Can these three friends help each other find firm ground in a world that seems to be unsafe, unsteady, and unhappy? And can found family really be what they all need when the going gets tough?

The Crumbly Old Castle

THE IRISH ESCAPE

B. E. BAKER

Purple
Puppy
Publishing

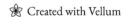 Created with Vellum

For Elana, for Anna, and for my sister Emma

You're the three women I'd drag along to Ireland if my world was burning.

Because I know you'd pull me out of the ashes, brush me off, and help me pick out a new, soot-free outfit that would kick-butt.

Author's Note

As usual with my books, I contemplated taking the "easy" route and making up a fictitious place for our three friends to visit. I could set their transformation in a small town, and that would allow me to make up anything I liked.

But I obsess.

I also love blending reality with fiction, and so as always, I chose a real place. As I researched, I soon decided that I had found the *perfect* place. You see, there was a graceful and elegant estate, privately owned, near another, fancier old castle that was owned by real people, and it was FOR SALE, and it was currently being rented as well.

That meant I could book a trip to visit it myself, and I could stay on site! How exciting was that!? The more I learned, the more I truly fell in love with the rich history and the beautiful scenery of the Fortwilliam Estate. I hope you'll fall in love with me—along with the characters, too—with this little slice of Ireland.

One last note on how I research. I keep all the facts about families and estates true, right up until the current LIVING people. I always make up new names, often lifted from a few generations back as families are wont to reuse. So when I talk about the Duke of Devonshire, if it's about the "current" duke in the book, it's not real. I made it up. If it's about the family history, such as horse racing or the history with Adele Astaire, it's all true.

I hope that helps you enjoy this book as utter fiction, but based on real life histories.

CHAPTER 1

All my friends had braces when I was a teenager, and boy did they whine about them. Food got caught around the brackets and made them look bad, or worse, gave them cavities. Their teeth ached. They looked stupid. It gave them sores on their gums and inside their mouths. The only thing they liked was missing school for the appointments, but I'm sure their parents were as annoyed about the hassle as they were about the expense.

I never went through any of that.

My dad was a dentist, so one Friday afternoon, he drilled off all the weird edges on my various snaggleteeth and by Monday, I had permanent veneers in place that gave me a beautiful smile. *Voila*.

Perfection on the first go.

It was the week after I got my perfect smile that Chad McCormick, whom I'd had a crush on for months, finally asked me out. That was my first lesson in the importance of presenting yourself well. Now, twenty-five years later, when I meet someone new, the first thing they ask me is *how on earth* I can keep track of everything. Because as I aged, I managed to present myself even better than I did back then, both because I hide the bad and because I highlight the good. I like to joke that I'm like a fine wine —I just keep improving—but really, I just keep presenting myself better.

Not that I'm an embarrassment at a baseline.

I'm a mother of five who's been president of the local food bank—twice. I manage social media for several local companies. I volunteer at the nearby animal shelter once a week. I work out every morning, and I ride horses four days a week for a local barn. I'm paid for that, but I also love it. I keep my house clean, my closets and car organized, and I haul my kids to all their various activities and events every day. I stick to our family budget religiously, and we're always dressed and ready for church at nine a.m. on Sunday.

I'm never late.

Because an organized life is a happy life.

It's missed bills, forgotten appointments, and late fees that tumble all the other dominoes into disarray. When you have a schedule and you stick to it, you're rarely surprised, at least, not in a bad way. Which is why it's so terribly embarrassing when my Uber drops me at the airport and I wheel my luggage over and scan my credit card only to discover. . .

My flight doesn't leave today. It's *tomorrow*.

I whip out my phone, aghast. This can't be right. It just can't. I've pre-paid Clara's teenage friend to ferry Blaire to her piano lesson. Clara's taking Hannah and Amelia to their horseback lesson. Mason's assistant's picking up Paul and taking him to my friend Tiffany's house after school, where Mason will pick them up after work. I've prepared all the meals they'll eat while I'm gone and put them in the freezer with tags.

I text my bestie, Tiffany, even though she'll tease me more than anyone else.

> You busy? Or can you call?

I wait to see if she'll respond, on the off chance she might be free. She gets a little irritable when I leave on these girls' trips. She never wants to come, because she doesn't know Samantha and Vanessa, but she's still sore to be left out. She also doesn't ride horses, and that's where we all met—it's what we all have in common. I did invite Tiffany to come several times, but my bestie said if she came, it would be awkward.

She's probably right.

Samantha, Vanessa, and I all rode together for a decade—third grade until twelfth—before we graduated from high school, and we've done these trips almost once a year since then. Adding someone that only knows me would throw off the whole dynamic, but I hate upsetting Tiffany. Usually we kind of hit pause for the week I'm gone, not talking much, and I sort of avoid bringing up the trip in conversations with her until it all blows over.

I've just ordered a new Uber when she finally responds.

> On a conf call that won't end. Everything ok?

My fingers are itching to confess, at least to her, but before I can do it, I remember something—an earlier text. When I climbed into the Uber on the way here, I messaged my old barn friends. What did I say? I scroll down and breathe a sigh of relief.

> Ready to travel. Can't wait to see you both!!!!

Thank goodness my departure text was vague. They probably assumed that I'm already packed, not that I was *en route* to the airport a day early, like a dummy.

Ugh.

My second Uber of the day arrives, and as I get in, I panic. Is it possible that I got *all* the dates wrong? I scroll through my emailed reservations in a cold sweat, but thankfully, the only day I had wrong was my departure. What I thought was a nine-day girls' trip is only eight, but all the other dates, tours, and hotels are correct.

That's something at least.

But, oh, how Mason's going to laugh when I confess over dinner tonight what I did. It's times like this I wish I wasn't quite so judgmental of others. I mean, if I hadn't—gently—mocked our neighbors about things just like this, it wouldn't feel quite so lousy.

As I stare out the window of the black sedan on the way home, I can't help thinking about the time my friend Tina *slept through* our kids' piano recital—oops. Or a month ago, when my mother-in-law called to wish me a happy birthday. . .ten days late. Or the time Tiffany was *so upset* when she brought her dog in to get it spayed and discovered the office had charged her a hundred dollars for missing her appointment the day before—an appointment she thought she was right on time for.

Only, now *I'm* the idiot.

3

If I'm lucky, my friends—and the rest of the world—won't ever need to know.

I'm really glad I didn't get the other dates wrong, because if we missed our horseback ride, it would break all our hearts. Samantha's still in Ocala and rides daily, but Vanessa moved to Colorado, and I'm in Austin, Texas. Even though we still love horses, Vanessa and I can't ride daily any more. Vanessa's lucky to ride a few times a month, and I mostly just do exercise rides at the barn where I work. We've been meaning to do a ride together for years, but something always comes up to get in the way. Canceled tours, illnesses, inclement weather, and injuries have all conspired against us.

But it's happening this year.

In fact, the ride I booked is in the southern part of Ireland, and it's a ride that goes past an honest-to-goodness castle and a monastery. They even offered us a discount coupon for being in the off-season.

I shoot a quick email to each of the places we're staying, just to confirm that everything's fine. After today's mess, I feel like it's better to be safe than sorry. That's when I identify the discrepancy that caused all my woes. Leaving as we are in the afternoon of one day and arriving the morning of the next, I must have gone backward instead of forward in my head—that's how I wound up being off by a day.

Rookie mistake.

As the Uber driver drops me off, I think of ways I can bribe Mason to convince him to keep this secret. He really enjoys teasing me, and I'm sure he'll be keen on telling Tiffany and her husband at the very least. But. . .he *loves* the monster cookies I make, and they're tiring to make. Ever since he gave up gluten a few months ago, there aren't as many sweets he really loves. He insists that gluten-free bread tastes like crackers, and I can't really disagree with him there.

I think I have all the ingredients for monster cookies at home, but the recipe size is so massive. . .I might need to grab more oatmeal. I'm glancing at my watch, preparing to message my teenage fill-in to cancel today's pickup, when our sprinklers kick on. I hop out of the way and walk around to the back gate on my way to the back door. Without my garage door opener or car keys—Mason was going to pick me up, so I left everything with him—I don't even have a way into my own house.

Luckily, we have a keypad that will let me in. With kids, you get locked out a lot. I type in the numbers and open the door, but then I freeze. There's a strange noise, some kind of talking or mumbling.

Someone's *inside* my house.

Our cat, Fiona, pads her way over to me, meowing lightly. "You're useless," I whisper. "You don't even look worried, and someone's *here*."

Could it be Clara, cutting class?

I glance around the room, whipping out my phone to prepare to dial 911, and grabbing a tall, flat vase from the end table with my other hand. Then I inch closer to the sounds, which are coming from my bedroom. I'm still several feet away when I hear a murmur I could recognize anywhere. It's low, husky, and masculine, the very thing that drew me to him in the first place.

It's my husband, Mason.

We were high school sweethearts, or at least, sort of. He asked me to Senior prom, and we've been together ever since. I know every single thing about him. I know he's O positive. I know he likes to doodle on napkins, no matter where he is. Bar, restaurant, hotel. The napkins will be covered with tiny Eiffel towers, cartoony humans, and puppies with their tongues lolling out.

The one thing I didn't know, apparently, was that he's a cheater.

Or maybe he's not.

Maybe the laughing and moaning I hear from some woman he probably met on a business trip isn't what I think. I ball up one hand and prepare to march into the room, all the angry words I'm ready to say buzzing around in my head. But then I trip on something—a shoe. A bright, hot pink shoe. I lean over and pick it up.

What kind of woman would wear something this tacky—a sparkly, hot pink, platform stiletto? My rage only grows. I'm prepared to rip Mason a new. . .something. Only, when I turn it over, I notice the designer name: Valentino.

Valen-friggin-tino.

He's not with a gold-digger—she has money, whoever she is. And somehow, knowing the brand of her shoe makes her feel *real*. It makes this whole thing, which felt like an out-of-body experience before, feel *real*, too. Painfully real. Achingly, soul-wrenchingly real.

The moans and sighs that only seem to grow louder aren't helping.

The worst thing I could imagine's actually happening to me, and I suddenly have no idea what to do about it.

I thought Mason and I were happy. I thought we were fine. Just like I thought I was leaving on my girls' trip today, I was totally clueless about the truth. Clearly we weren't fine. We must be *profoundly* broken.

Which makes me think about what everyone will say.

What everyone will think.

How my children will look at me once they know.

Fiona brushes up against my leg, and I realize she may be the only living thing that this betrayal doesn't really impact.

Only, even that's not true.

When we get a divorce, which feels like a forgone conclusion, she'll have to move into an apartment with me, which will be all I can afford on child support. I won't be able to ride anymore, because the eighty bucks a day I get for riding a horse for five hours won't pay for *anything*. I'll have to either get a real job or dramatically expand my social media marketing business, and I'll start missing kids' activities and events just so I can make rent.

From the sudden quiet that has overtaken my previously noisy bedroom, I'm guessing they're *done*. And that means at any moment, they're going to discover I'm here, and I'll have to face the hurricane.

It'll wreck my girls' trip.

It'll wreck *everything*.

I'm not the kind of person who hits pause. I don't bury my head in the sand like a clueless ostrich or flamingo or whatever dumb bird does that. Everyone who knows me would tell you that I have *never* hit the pause button in my life, not on anything. They'd tell you that if I realized my husband was cheating on me, I would deal with it head-on. I'd bite his head off, chew him up, and spit out the resulting goo.

Only, those same people would tell you that I'd never be a day early for a trip. They'd tell you that I would never in a million years completely botch the dates on something so important.

And they'd be wrong, on all counts, apparently.

I feel as fake as my teeth—a flimsy resin polish on top of something raw and imperfect.

In that moment, I realize that I'm not who I thought I was either. Instead of pushing past the mostly-closed door and confronting Mason and his rich, probably sophisticated and thin girlfriend, I duck back out the back door as quietly as I can and walk three blocks in my own boring, serviceable, black high heels. They're heels I spent just enough on that they'll last a decade, but not enough that anyone will ever notice them. I pull my perfectly serviceable rolly bag behind me before summoning my third Uber of the day. Then I pay cash for a single night at the Holiday Inn near the airport.

I *am* going to have to face this.

I'm going to have to smash my life to bits and somehow put it back together again. I'm going to have to watch everyone I know judge me, and judge Mason, which he totally deserves, and I'm going to have to try and find a new world to live in.

One that makes sense.

But I'm not going to do it today.

In fact, I'm not going to do it this week.

This week, I'm going to fly to Ireland, and I'm going to ride horses with my childhood friends, and I'm going to buy any stupid, expensive thing I see that I like, and I'm going to let Mason's eyes bug out when I show him just how much money I spent enjoying myself. I'm going to buy myself Valentino *something*. Heck, maybe I'll buy two somethings.

And then I'll tell him that I'm filing for divorce.

But not. Right. Now.

Right now, I'm going to do something for myself. It may be the worst week of my life so far, but by golly, I'm going to try and enjoy it anyway, because I refuse to let Mason take anything else from me. He's taken more than enough already.

CHAPTER 2

Samantha

I'm not a complete moron.

I know that all the heart-twittering you feel when you watch a romantic comedy isn't real.

And the absurd passion people write about and depict in movies—the sweaty bodies, fingernails clawing against skin, moaning, and screaming and writhing and whatnot?

That's not real either.

In real life, love means picking up someone's shoes without going all Lorena Bobbitt on them. Love's your husband gritting his teeth as he fishes fifteen Amazon boxes off the porch, all full of more of the throw pillows he hates. Love's mopping up muddy footprints for the nineteenth time, when he could just take his darn shoes off in the garage. It's taking out the trash when it's cold, even though you want to leave it for him to do. Love's pretending it doesn't enrage him that I bought a twentieth saddle pad, when I didn't need more than two.

Given the reality of love, I think Brent and I are doing alright.

We've been married for sixteen years, and I've never cut any part of him off. He hardly ever yells, even when I've buried him in Christmas tree throw pillows. He rarely even grumbles when I leave on my annual girls' trip.

In fact, this year, he stood by and helped me pack.

"Do you think you'll be warm enough?" He pulls another knit cap off the shelf.

His mother makes them like it's some kind of compulsion. Unfortunately, with the way I wear my hair—short with a little mohawk on top—they make me look like a cancer patient. Once, at a church party, a woman came up and told me she'd be praying for my speedy recovery. Chemo's hard, she told me, but it's worth it.

I haven't worn one of those knit caps since.

"Uh, no, I think the two I have packed will be fine."

Because I love him, I don't mention that there's zero chance I'll wear either of the ones he already handed me.

And *that*'s real love.

"I just don't want you to freeze. I'm still not sure why you're going to Ireland in April instead of July."

"The girls have kids," I remind him. "They can't just go anytime—it's easier for them to go during the off-season. Since their kids are in school, they're easier to have someone else take care of."

He compresses his lips and nods. "Right. Right, I remember."

"Well." I zip the top of my suitcase closed and reach for the handle.

Brent practically body checks me to pull it off the bed before I can. "Here. Let me get that for you."

It's not normal behavior.

Something's wrong.

I press one finger against his chest. His not-very-impressive-but-not-super-squishy-either chest. "What are you doing?"

"What?" His eyes widen, and his breath hitches, and I just know.

When you've been living with someone for a long time, you develop your own sort of language. It's not spoken—it's entirely nonverbal. I'm one hundred percent fluent in Brent.

"Out with it." I cross my arms. "What do you want?"

He releases the handle of my suitcase. "Why would you think I want something?" His voice isn't exactly deep in any situation, but it's not usually this high and squeaky either.

"You haven't tried to carry my suitcase for me since we were *dating*," I say.

"When you had that shoulder surgery," he says, "I—"

9

"But I'm fine right now, so just tell me what's up." I lean forward and grab the handle of my own bag.

"Are you angry?" He frowns. "Because if so, we can talk later."

"It's big," I say. "You want something big, or you'd already have asked." I narrow my eyes. "Just tell me."

"It's not big." He huffs.

"What is it?" I'm quickly losing patience. "My flight leaves in three hours, and it's international."

"Fine," he says. "I just wanted to check, before you left, if you could sign some papers for the house we're selling my brother."

"Oh." I roll my eyes. "Why would that make you nervous?" I drop the bag and cross to the kitchen table. I saw a manila envelope there earlier. "Is it this? This is what you need signed?" I point.

He nods, but his mouth's still tight, and his eyes look nervous.

I open the paperwork and skim it. It all looks the same as the paperwork for every house close, really. In fifteen years of buying and flipping houses, I've read a *lot* of closing docs. Usually Brent's the one who barely reads it, and I handle all the paperwork, pointing so he can sign, but it's all just fine. . .

Until I see the settlement pages. "What exactly is this?" I spin the pages around and hold them toward him. "Did you even look at them?"

Brent's brother has been a total mess until very, very recently. He's an alcoholic who never had much interest in cleaning up his act, and he's almost five years older than Brent. I've lost track of all the mean things he's said and the hurtful things he's done, but in the past year or so, he's gotten a tiny bit better. I think he's almost three months sober. Brent said he was having trouble finding a house, so he wanted to sell him Oak Tree Lane.

Our first home.

Right after we got married, we bought a small three-two, which is now in a great, redeveloping area. We cleaned it up a year or so ago, and we've been renting it out, but the lease on Oak Tree Lane expires in three weeks. We paid less than two hundred, and now it's worth close to five.

"I looked at all of it," Brent says. "What's wrong with it?"

"It says we're selling Oak Tree Lane to him for twenty-four-thousand dollars, which won't even cover our closing costs, much less the remodel we did last year. We'd lose. . ." I glance down at it and laugh. "Seven thousand six hundred and forty-four dollars for the pleasure of giving it to him. I think the amount due's missing a few zeroes."

"You said we could give him a good deal," he says. "You agreed."

I can't help spluttering. "A *good deal*?" I shake my head. "Brent, you must be kidding. A good deal would be four hundred thousand. A *screaming* deal would be three hundred and fifty. We paid two, and then we put another fifty or maybe even a hundred into it. I'd have to look." I step closer. "This is *paying* to *give* it to your insane brother."

"Insane?" His eyes flash. "*Insane*?"

"What would you call him?" I'm still laughing, but only because this whole thing's so absurd. "He vandalized that house—don't you remember? He painted a picture of male anatomy right under the front windows! Then he wrote Brent is a d—"

"So what?" He snatches the papers from my hand. "So *what*? He's trying now, and he needs some help. This is what family does."

I can hardly believe what he's saying. "That vandalism thing was one of like a hundred awful ways he's attacked us over the years. Selling it to him for a steal would have been hard for me—but this?" I point at the papers. "I will *never* give your brother a house. Not any house. Not even a *doll* house." I cross my arms. "Am I being clear enough?"

"So it's fine for you to go on these lavish girls' trips every year, and it's fine for you to buy new furniture for our home, furniture we didn't even need. You can buy saddles, and more saddle pads than any human could ever even use—heck, you can even buy your sister's kid a horse, but you can't sell my brother an old house we don't even live in anymore, because he's *my brother*? Is that it?"

"First of all, I didn't buy my sister's kid a horse. I trained that horse, so we got it for a screaming deal, and then I kicked in a few grand to pay the referral fee, but her mom paid for the rest—you know what? It doesn't even matter. I make twice what you do and always have. We flip these houses together, so it's not like that income is just yours either. And you waste at least as much money on computer crap as I do on horses. You don't get to tell me that I have to give your brother a house because of how you're undervalued and mistreated. We jointly own that house—and a 'deal' is not even close to the same as *free*."

"You know, I was afraid to talk to you about this." Brent's nostrils flare. It's a sign that he's mad—as mad as I've ever seen him. "I was nervous you'd react just as you have, but that's not my fault. That's yours —you're the problem here. You've always been a cold, heartless bitch who only cares about herself."

In all the years we've been married, he has done a lot of things to hurt me. He's been inconsiderate and unkind and downright disconnected at times, but he's never said anything like this.

Never.

"If you really think that, I'm surprised you're still married to me." I hate how much my voice wobbles as I say the words.

"So am I." His hands are clenched at his sides, and his voice is hard.

I wait for a moment, and then I wait for another, but he just glares at me. No apology. No softening. Nothing at all.

My hands are shaking as I grab my suitcase and wheel it out to my car all alone. As I drive off, though, I realize this isn't the first time I've been relieved to fly away from him—away from my entire life, really.

The flight from Florida to Ireland is long and exhausting.

And even so, it feels like an escape.

CHAPTER 3
Vanessa

It's always sad when someone dies, but I've learned in the past two and a half years that good can come from it, too.

Of course, if someone had told me I'd say that right after Jason died, I'd have smacked them. And blocked their number. I'd probably also have muttered curses about them. After my husband died unexpectedly from a heart attack brought on by complications from COVID. . .I wasn't seeing the silver lining on *anything*.

But with the benefit of a little perspective, I've recognized a few miracles.

The biggest and brightest one is standing in front of me—my husband Jason's useless brother Jeremy, or, his formerly useless brother, has *transformed*. Years ago, when Jason's father passed, Jeremy said he wanted nothing to do with Heavy Lifting, the equipment and heavy machinery rental company their father ran with Jason.

That was fine with us—Jason even took out a loan to buy his brother out of his half of the value of the company. It was hard to repay it, but between the money I made at my accounting job, and the hard work Jason put into the company, we always managed to pay the note. When Jason died a few years after his dad had passed, I was nervous. Terrified, really. I hadn't been involved in running the company, what with working all day at my own nine-to-five. I had no idea what to do with the daily management. Jason wanted our son Trace to take over eventually, but Trace was barely a teenager when his dad died.

I couldn't keep my job and take over. I was going to have to sell it.

The timing couldn't have been worse. When COVID hit, Jason and I took out a home equity line of credit to help several of his friends who didn't have any savings to survive the shut-down. Jason assumed the notes on all kinds of equipment they couldn't afford so they wouldn't go under after months and months without work.

Of course, when Jason died, we were up to our eyeballs in debt, and the business wasn't worth a bean. Selling just meant declaring bankruptcy. Jeremy stepped up, for the first time in his life, taking over the daily chores and calling all the people he knew through years of intermittent work for his dad and brother. People who had no faith in me managing things believed in Jeremy, because he was a man. I didn't care *why* they believed in him—I was just relieved they did.

With his help, we managed to hold things together.

Then, when the economy surged back, demand for new building was at an all-time high. Heavy Lifting rebounded in a huge way. Jason's gamble with helping his friends stave off bankruptcy buoyed the whole enterprise, but only because of Jeremy's surprise support. My brother-in-law's talking on the phone when he reaches my house, but the second he hangs up, he turns toward me with a smile. "Alright," he says. "Where's the list?"

He hasn't watched my three children often, but after Jason died, he insisted I still leave on my annual girls' trips. My mother isn't about to spend a week of her vacation to fly out here and help me. Sadly, Jason's mother's health hasn't allowed her to help anymore. Most of the time, Trish isn't even sure who I am, and she rarely knows the kids for more than an hour before becoming confused again. Jeremy's my only real option for childcare, and by now—his third time watching them—he knows I'll have a detailed list of all the activities planned for each day I'll be gone. "Here." I hand it to him with a smile. "You'll notice that on Friday, there's no dinner listed. That's because—"

Jeremy frowns. "Do you really think I don't remember pizza Fridays?"

"Fine," I say. "I'm sure you'll do great, and I really appreciate you doing this."

"Are you sure you don't want a ride?" He glances at my car, already backed out of the garage and parked in the driveway. "It's not a big deal, and then you won't have to pay for parking."

"My return flight comes in the middle of the day," I say. "I wouldn't want to show up when you'll have work to do."

"If you say so," he says. "But you could have at least let me load your suitcase into the trunk."

"It's a small suitcase," I say. "It was fine." I'm about to awkwardly wave goodbye—the Littlefields aren't huggers—and head for my car when my phone rings.

My heart sinks when I see that it's the high school.

It sinks even further when Cherry Creek's principal's the one who says, "Mrs. Littlefield?"

I can barely force the words out. "Are you calling about Trace?"

"Unfortunately, yes." His voice is flat.

"But he did graduate from rehab," I say. "He graduated with honors, basically." Which sounds really dumb when I say the words out loud. It's not like you can really *ace* rehab. "He said he was really done with all of it this time."

"I caught him not just using," Principal Jones says, "but selling to other students in the bathroom."

So much for my girls' trip. "I can come pick him up in about twenty minutes." Just long enough for me to cry, unload my suitcase, and drive around the corner to the school.

"He'll be suspended for the rest of this week, and I'd recommend another rehab facility. Maybe one that will help him stay away from pot for more than a week."

I start to cry—not because of my girls' trip, though that's part of it—but because this is happening again. Every time I think we're moving past this, he just circles back around. I swipe at my cheeks as I hang up.

"You won't pick him up." Jeremy's staring. "I'll do that. You need this break, and if this had happened tomorrow, you'd already be gone."

"I shouldn't have booked this at all," I say. "I should've known—"

"You've been dealing with this for a year now," Jeremy says. "You can't put your life on hold indefinitely."

Trace has apparently been smoking pot for more than a year, but it was last year around this time when I came home from work earlier than Trace thought I would and caught him doing it—with some friends,

15

behind the house. Since then, we've tried three rehab facilities and count-less other programs, counselors, and therapies. What he insisted was casual use was far more frequent than I could accept.

Input from family and friends has varied widely.

Some people insist that smoking pot is no big deal—twenty percent of the population of Colorado does it regularly, after all. But when I did more research, there's a *lot* of uncontested bad stuff that accompanies the use of weed. Precancerous lesions, cognitive impairment, memory loss, and development of psychotic disorders, to name a few. That doesn't even get into the havoc it has wreaked on his already mediocre scholastic performance.

"You don't have kids." I sigh. "That's why you don't understand. Parents don't get time off, not even for good behavior, and I'm not sure I'd qualify for that, even if we did."

"He lost his dad," Jeremy says. "Then all he had was football, and when he lost that, too. . ."

"I know," I snap, and then I regret it. "I'm sorry. You're right—I know all of that. I've cut him a lot of slack, believe me, but the problem is that everyone has cut him slack, and they're all losing their patience. He needs to figure out how to process his disappointment, and fast, or he's going to start ruining things we can't glue back together." I open the trunk and move to pull out my suitcase. "If he hadn't been fired by four therapists already, I'd say something like that might help."

"They all just told you he needed rehab anyway," Jeremy says. "None of them had lost someone, and none of them were athletes."

"You know, finding a therapist with room in their schedule was hard enough. I didn't have the luxury of looking only for former athletes who had a dead family member."

"No one's blaming you," Jeremy says.

I'm blaming me. I'm pretty sure everyone else is, too. Who else would they blame? Jason for dying? Trace's shoulder? I reach for my suitcase again.

"You have to go." Jeremy moves to block me. "Vanessa, I mean it."

"Jeremy Littlefield, I appreciate the sentiment, but—"

"But what?" He frowns. "If you stay, you'll yell at him again, then you'll apologize, and then you'll tell him all the reasons he needs to stop using, and then you'll do research and call and call and call places until you find *another* rehab facility to try, and then you'll get him all checked in. . .and we'll sit back and watch your money disappear again as the cycle restarts."

It all feels *so* futile—I burst into tears.

Jeremy nailed it.

That's exactly what I'll do, but he forgot one thing. Trace will be a little older, and a little harder, and the people at school will write him off a little more. I've been watching the same thing a lot of mothers of teenagers watch with pain and sadness—my son turning into an angry, frustrated man I don't even recognize. But in my case, I'm not sure he's going to pull out of the anger.

Plus, I'm pretty sure Trace blames me. He's so mad every time I put him into rehab. He's so angry every time I tell him that he can't keep living like this. He feels like I should be supporting him, not attacking him.

He doesn't get that I'm supporting him *by* attacking him.

"This time, V, just let me do all of it." Jeremy pulls me in for a hug, which I can tell he hates by the way he stiffens, and then he pats my back awkwardly. "You shouldn't always have to be the villain."

I *really* miss having a partner who could be the bad guy sometimes. But. . . "I just—I can't fly off on a trip during all this, Jer. Surely you can see that."

He shakes his head and sighs, releasing me from the obligatory hug. "If you didn't have me lined up to step in, then yes, you'd have to stay. But I'm an uncle—I'm family too. I'm Jason's brother, and you can trust me when I tell you that I can yell, and I can apologize, and I can call rehab places just as well as you can." He softens. "And Vanessa, you deserve a break. In fact, it might even help. Give him some space. Give you both some space."

Is he right? I don't even know anymore. "Well."

"Take this week to talk to your friends. Ask them what they think and what they would do. Maybe one of them will have an idea, some insight, something that can help you get through to him."

I can't tell them about it. I can't talk to anyone about it. That's one of the hardest parts. I don't want them to judge Trace—or me. The more people who know, the more permanent it all feels. I just want this all to go away so he can live a normal life again. "Maybe."

"Not maybe." He points. "Get in the car, and drive to the airport.

Breathe in and out. I'll go get Trace. I've offered to talk to him before, and you've always said no. It's time for you to let me try."

It is one of the few things I haven't done—enlisted the aid of someone else. "Fine." My anxiety spikes as I say the word, as I step away from my responsibility to do this task that I truly abhor. "I mean, I can fly right back home if you tell me—I'll come back right away."

"I know you will." Jeremy seems *so* sure.

I miss having someone to talk to about big decisions. I miss having someone else to bounce ideas off of, and someone else to discuss hard things with. It's nice to have someone tell me what to do, and maybe that's why I'm waffling. I'm worried that I'm happy because he's saying what I want to hear, but does that mean what he's saying can't also be right?

"Just *go*, Vanessa."

I close the trunk, and I circle around to the driver's seat.

"Oh." Jeremy smacks his forehead. "I almost forgot—the power of attorney."

"For the refinance on the power tools," I say. "I signed it already. It's on the kitchen table."

"It had to be notarized," he says.

I nod. "It was—at the bank."

"You're awesome," he says. "Always so on the ball. Now go take a break, and have a little faith in me. I can help, I swear."

He may not know what to say to get through to Trace, but honestly, I don't either, clearly. It's been like, ever since the physical therapist told him he'd never get his throwing arm back to a hundred percent, he's just *given up* on life. It kind of hurts that he thinks that without a dad or foot-ball, he has nothing else to care about.

Bryce and Trina are struggling with him too.

I roll down my window.

Jeremy's smirking. "You're going to remind me that this will be hard on Bryce, and that I need to make sure he's alright and has someone to talk to."

I close my mouth. Then I narrow my eyes. "Not *exactly* that, no. I was going to say maybe you should go get some Crave Cookies. They always help everyone feel better."

"I'll get a dozen." Jeremy bites his lip, clearly suppressing a smile. "I'm guessing Trace will be hungry."

Now I'm scowling. "No cookies for him. Not a single one!"

But I can't help smiling a little as I drive to the airport. For the first time since Jason died, someone else is doing the most miserable part of parenting, and I'm just ducking out and letting him.

I should feel guilty, but somehow, I just feel relieved.

Of course, when my plane lands, I have a bevy of text messages to return, including approving the rehab place that Jeremy found. It's not cheap—they never are—and it's relatively far away. We've already done AspenRidge, CeDAR, and Sandstone. I suppose I should've expected to have to drive an hour or more to find one with space. But perhaps going all the way to NorthStar in Boulder will make Trace think twice about this —there's not much chance he'll make more local drug buddies there, either.

> That's fine, do it. Glad you have the power of attorney.

> Don't stress. We'll be fine. Try to have fun.

Trust Jeremy to text me back in the middle of the night. It feels like Jason would have said the same thing, so for their sakes, and for my own sanity, I'm sure going to try.

CHAPTER 4
Natalie

I've just discovered that learning one new piece of information can make you revisit every single thing about your life. I've found myself obsessing a lot in the twenty-four hours since my simple mistake uncovered my husband's big betrayal.

I'm an obsessive person.

It's really hard for me not to obsess at a baseline.

In this instance, I'm stuck on a plane headed for another country, and I know my husband isn't missing me at all, so I'm not sure how to break out of my obsession. All the small things about our relationship that I always chalked up to "So what? Every couple disagrees..." start to bother me in a way they didn't before.

For instance, last month, I told him that I either had to lose the fifteen pounds I'd gained or buy new clothes, and instead of telling me I looked amazing, Mason suggested that I could hire a personal trainer and still save a bundle if I didn't have to buy new clothes.

Then, last week at the girls' horse show, I teased him for always being on his phone, even during the girls' runs. He glared, told me someone had to pay for the show, and kept right on tapping away. I felt guilty when he said someone had to pay for them. I mean, horse shows *are* expensive, but now I can't help wondering. . .was he even working?

Or was he talking to her?

Was it even a *her,* singular? Or has there been more than one woman he's been unfaithful with?

Does it even matter?

Bigger things bother me, too.

We have five kids, and to everyone else, that's already a lot. To me, some days, it feels like too much. Even so, I always wanted more. I never felt *done* at five. But when I mentioned it a few months ago, that we weren't really past the point of no return yet, Mason bit my head off. "You just think you're not done, because you have nothing else in life to care about. Stop talking about having another kid and get a real job."

It hurt at the time.

Now? It makes me want to cry. I should have seen he wasn't happy with me. I should have known he was unimpressed.

And I can't help wondering whether he's right.

Is that why he found someone new? Am I empty inside? Do I fill my life up with children because I'm not anything special on my own anymore?

Or did he snap at me because he felt guilty? Had he already moved on from *us,* so the idea of another child felt like yet another shackle, tying him down to a family he no longer wanted?

The more I think about Mason, the sicker I feel.

None of this is the reason I came on this trip though. I didn't come to escape from Mason and those hot pink Valentinos. I planned this whole thing so I could have fun and reconnect with my friends. I think the reason that I flew out in spite of the discovery is that I'm hoping to heal my battered, brutalized heart enough to face it. That means I need to be thinking about this week, not about every slight or injury from the past few months or years.

As my plane prepares to land, I mentally calculate how many girls' trips I've done with Vanessa and Samantha over the years. I come up with twenty-one. If our friendship was a person, this year, it could finally drink. I must be really tired, because that thought makes me laugh out loud, to the great dismay of the older woman next to me.

Our first group vacation was right after we graduated from high school—we drove to Miami and stayed at a place called the "Bikini"

Hostel, which probably should have been our first clue it was going to be a dump. It was only twenty-one bucks a night, and they were overcharging.

But we all got beautiful suntans.

Thanks to the three-dollar margaritas at the bar next door, and a bartender who didn't even bat an eye at our horrible fake IDs, we had so much fun that we were already planning another trip for the next year by the time we were sober enough to start our drive back. In those days, none of us thought we'd ever live in separate corners of the country.

Vanessa was only going to Colorado for school to make her grandma —who was paying—happy. She thought she'd move back to Florida before we all knew it, and I never even imagined I'd meet Mason and move to Austin, Texas of all places. As we set up our households in far flung areas of the United States, our vacations became more and more important. Sometimes we made it somewhere exotic and exciting, and other times we went close—once we went to Disney World for three days. Often one of us was pregnant or had a newborn that tagged along.

But whatever the plan, we always had a good time.

At the beginning of every single trip, there's an awkward moment when we first see each other again after so long. It's like putting on a bra you haven't worn in a while. You have a brief moment of worry that it's too tight, or that maybe your boobs changed shape, before you shimmy around a little, and voila. It fits.

Familiar. Easy. *Right.*

When I walk off the plane and head for Belfast baggage claim, I'm nervous. I know Vanessa and Samantha are landing forty-five minutes after me. I'll see them soon, and unlike past trips, I *need* to feel right around them.

I don't like needing things.

What if that awkward moment stretches? What if this isn't the healing trip I need? What if I should have just stayed home and confronted Mason right away? What if I'm a wreck all week and ruin this for both of them, and then they hate me after today?

I've barely clocked the "Welcome to Belfast International Airport" sign before my phone rings.

It's Tiffany—I texted her earlier, but she was in that meeting. It's just like her to call the second I land. Not because she's that aware of my schedule, but because she has good luck like that.

"Hello?"

"You finally there?" Tiffany sounds exasperated. "I swear, I've called you ten times. I thought you landed, like, a million years ago. Having too much fun for me already?"

"I'm not. In fact, with flight delays, I've barely done anything yet." I don't even have to fake my groan. Even though I wasn't delayed at all by the airlines, I was *delayed,* at least compared to what I planned.

"You're kidding." Tiffany groans. "Natalie, that's horrible. I'm so sorry."

"It's fine," I say. "Because I'm in Ireland!" I spin around in a circle, see my suitcase as I straighten, dive for it, lug it off the jetway, and then fall in with the line of people heading out before I realize I'm not leaving yet. I have friends to meet up with first.

"You sound out of breath. What are you doing over there?"

"Not all of us run every day."

"You're invited to join me on my jog any morning you like."

"I'd rather die," I say.

Tiffany laughs. It's such a normal sound, such a familiar sound, that I relax a little. My entire world may have turned upside down, but not her. Tiffany's unchanging, like the tides.

"Is everything okay? That was a pretty weird sigh."

I think about telling her, but I'm standing in the midst of a hundred people. If I break down and start bawling. . . Even I have some dignity left. "I'm fine," I say. "I'm just happy to hear your voice."

"Are you being weird because you know I get jealous of your sacred, girls-trip bubble?" She sounds a little miffed—probably because she *is* a little miffed. "I'm sorry to call, but at least I'm not interrupting much, if you're still all jet-lagged, right?"

I've been so caught up in my stuff, I didn't even think about why she called. She usually half-ignores me when I go on these, sending me a few texts and not much more. "I assumed you were calling me back from yesterday, but is something wrong?"

"Yes." Her voice sounds so wobbly, so unsure, that my stomach ties in knots. Could she have—did she—she works with Mason. She lives down the road. Did she catch him? Is she about to ruin my trip a second time?

"What is it?" I swallow. "Tiffany, just spit it out."

"You're never going to believe this. I mean, I could hardly believe it myself."

Now I'm positive. My best friend in the world's about to tell me my husband's a skunk, and I'm going to have to pretend not to know. What would I do if I really was shocked? What would I say?

"Nat, Harriet asked *me* to take over as PTO president. She said the whole board talked about it already."

Harriet. . .what? I can't help spluttering.

"I *know*!" I hear the whush whush of her slacks as she paces on the other end of the phone line. "It's insane, right?"

It takes me a second to pull out of my crazy nose-dive, but luckily, Tiffany interprets my slow response as shock. "So crazy." I can't help the high pitch of my laugh. "That's bad. Like, really bad."

"I told them they should find someone who doesn't work. Someone like. . ."

Like me, that's where she's heading. "But I do work."

"I know your online posts and stuff are work, but—"

"There's no but," I say. "It's not just posting. I manage the social media marketing of quite a few companies now, and I've been billing almost thirty hours a week most weeks. It took me a lot of long nights to get all my posts scheduled before this trip. I may not bill the same for my time as you do for yours, but we can't all have MBAs from Cornell."

"That's my point," Tiffany says. "I know you work too. I know it's not just internet posts, and I know the horseback riding's also work. Believe me, I wish I could get paid for my workouts, but I *might* have suggested you would have a little more time than I do when she kept bugging me about it."

"Tiffany, you have two kids," I say. "I have five."

"Oh, I know, and believe me, it's not a contest. It's just that with business going well for ClockSpeed, I've been working more than forty hours a week, always. Sometimes more than fifty. It definitely doesn't leave me time to run the PTO."

I'm probably being way too ragey, thanks to my misery yesterday. At least I can blame jet lag. "I'm sorry if I sound crabby, but I have *zero* interest, and they have a lot more options than just you and me. I hope you didn't really push them my way—I only joined the PTO because you badgered me into it. Remember?"

24

"But Paul has years of school left, and Amelia and Blaine are going into fifth. It makes sense for you to step in for their last year." The way she says sense, all sing-songy, even after I've been quite firm, irritates me.

"Look," I say, "I can't tell you what to do, but it's a hard no from me."

"Oh, fine." Tiffany sighs, and I realize she was always planning on doing it. It's the kind of thing she excels at. No one can get more done in less time, and now she can tell everyone she tried to get out of it. "Fine."

"You can just tell them no," I say. "They'll find another sucker to get dragged up there for hours each day."

"But this year's fundraiser was a disaster—Harriet ruined everything. I could fix a lot of stuff." I hear Tiffany tapping her lip with a pen. "If I do it, you'll at least help, right? Maybe you can be the VP or something."

"Did you call me so I could talk you out of it? Or so you could get preapproval for a minion?" If she didn't work so hard at everything, she'd be supremely annoying.

"Look, if you're doing it too, my boss can't get too mad at me for missing work for PTO stuff."

"As if Mason would ever get mad. If I have to hear *one more time* about how you saved their supply chain woes, I might puke." Tiffany's a brilliant MBA whose potential was utterly wasted when she first married her rich, old man husband, David. But a few years ago, I suggested that Mason talk to her about some of the management stuff, and she cleaned up everything within a few months. It gave him so much free time that until yesterday, I'd have credited her with saving our marriage.

Clearly having free time for me wasn't enough to save us.

"Hey, I need to go." From all the way across the room, I see two very familiar specks, one wearing her signature massive hat—it *has* to be Vanessa. "Text me and tell me whether you get stuck doing it so I can extend my congratulations and condolences, but I am *not* going down as Vice President. You hear me?"

She's laughing as she hangs up. I have a feeling that's exactly what's going to happen.

Now that they're closer, each of them dragging a dangerously large suitcase behind them, Vanessa and Samantha are waving. They shared a flight from Heathrow—I was the oddball on a Virgin flight that came in through Amsterdam.

"You made it." Samantha always manages to look like a very hip Miss

America. I tell myself it's because she didn't have kids, but a large part of me thinks that even if she'd had children, she'd still have shiny hair, a perfectly toned body, and no wrinkles. She hugs me like her life depends on it, and as always, I forgive her for making me look dumpy and old.

Now that she's close, I can finally see Vanessa's face under her floppy hat. "How was your flight? Ours was so long." She yawns.

Then I yawn.

Samantha yawns next, and we all start laughing. "Jet lag," I say.

"You know, the biggest advantage to picking a place like Disney World," Samantha says, "is that there's no jet lag."

"True," I say. "But does Disney World have Irish accents and creamy, foamy stout?"

Vanessa grunts. "Probably at Epcot."

We must all be really tired, because we laugh even harder at the ridiculous notion that visiting Epcot might be better than flying to Ireland.

"I'm glad we're all here," I say.

As I say it, the truth of it sinks into my bones.

My daughter Blaine was obsessed for a while with something called Naraka Bladepoint. It's a fighting game where you have different attack levels: normal, blue focus, and red focus. She spent a *lot* of time talking to me about them, so I know that red focus is a special attack that disarms the attacker so that your damage goes right to their heart, basically.

I didn't realize it until just now, but I was hit yesterday with a red focus attack. I was unprepared, and I've been reeling ever since. If you get hit hard in a video game, you can run and hide to recover your health. In life, we don't usually get chances like that, but this is my equivalent. For the first time since I walked into my own house and got broadsided, I almost feel safe, and it's all thanks to these women. We may not have lived in the same place for more than two decades now, but they're still home to me.

I didn't know how much I needed them until I got hit with that stupid red attack.

Thanks to Vanessa's goofy straw hat, and Samantha's slap-your-face good looks, I can finally breathe for the first time in more than a day. I force a smile that almost feels real. "Let's take our bags and our hats and go pass out somewhere nice."

26

"Did I mention how happy I am we aren't staying in a hostel?" When even Samantha looks tired, that's saying something.

"Oh my word, me too," Vanessa says. "Do you remember the Bikini Hostel?" Her eyes are already crinkling. "I thought we were going to get hepatitis from the toilet."

"You can't get that from a toilet," Samantha says.

"Someone should have told those toilets that," Vanessa says. "They were really trying."

This time, my smile isn't even forced. "Do you remember that hotel clerk who kept asking you out? His beard was so strange."

"The weird guys always like me. His beard looked like it was trying to drip its way off his chin," Vanessa says. "Like a goatee that never got trimmed and just kept growing. I haven't thought about that guy in—so long I don't even know!"

"Let's have a contest," Samantha says. "Whoever can get hit on by the most creepy guys on this trip wins."

"What's the prize?" Vanessa asks. "I'll win for sure—creepy guys are the only kind who like me. Plus, I'm the only single lady here."

That's a sobering thought, especially since no one knows, but I'll probably be joining her soon. "I'm not about to let you hog all the glory." I wrap my hand around my bag handle. The bright red suitcase with the distinctive beige leather stripe is so new it practically shines.

"Whoa," Vanessa says. "That's a fancy bag. Is it. . ." She squints.

"I just bought it," I say. "In Amsterdam. My old one looked. . ." I shrug. Mason had bought it for me, and in the last twenty-four hours, I've thrown out and replaced every single thing I packed that he gave me. "This one's Coach."

"And what about your coat?" Samantha tilts her head, narrowing her eyes. "Is that—"

"The night before I left, I realized I had no warm clothes—I live in Austin, for heaven's sake, so I found a Nordstrom and bought this." I twirl in a circle to show off the new black wool coat. It has gorgeous leather trim on the hood, the belt, and the pockets. "I'd never even heard of Mackage, but now I'm obsessed."

"And, apparently, so am I," Samantha shakes her head and whistles. "You look *amazing*."

I know that's a lie—I've gained at least ten pounds since I saw them last, but it's nice to hear it even when it's not true. Mason should have known to say that too. He should've known a lot of things that he didn't. "I thought it was time for a bit of a wardrobe upgrade." I want to tell them that I was rage-shopping, but I can't quite bring myself to say it.

Maybe for now, in this moment, that's okay. Maybe being with them and feeling safe is enough. There's always tomorrow to face my demons— today is for recovering my health enough to survive the confrontation.

CHAPTER 5

Natalie

New boots on my first day of vacation might have been a mistake. I looked and looked for a Valentino store, but I had to settle for something a little less posh. Apparently even $800 Stuart Weitzman boots cause blisters.

"Wait up, guys," I say. "I'm coming."

"You okay?" Samantha's eyebrow's raised, and she's peering suspiciously at my left foot.

It's the one that's throbbing the most, but compared to the pain I felt when I walked in and heard Mason with that woman, it's an inconvenience I can ignore.

So I do.

"I underestimated how much walking we'd be doing at the Giant's Causeway, but it's fine." I force a smile, but not for long. Pretty soon, it's not forced anymore.

This place is well worth a small amount of misery.

Giant's Causeway used to be the site of a volcanic eruption, but now all that's left is forty thousand basalt columns that all interlock. They kind of poke up in these funny little towers all over the place like some kind of gameboard straight out of Minecraft.

"It's more walking than I expected, too." Samantha whips out her purse. "But I'm prepared." She pulls out a Ziplock bag that, I swear, has everything a normal first aid kit would have and then some, all swimming around in a massive Ziplock bag. It makes sense, given that she's a medical provider. "See?" She brandishes a little piece of fuzz at me.

"How's a tan Kleenex going to help me?"

"It's not a Kleenex," she says, shaking her head. "It's moleskin. And once I use my tiny scissors to. . ." She frowns. "Shoot. I think they took those away from me when I got on the plane."

This is *so* how my life is going right now. I drop a hand on Samantha's arm. "It's fine." I toss my head. "He's moving again." Our Irish guide's as entertaining as I've ever had.

"As you'll remember, Old Finn McCool's the Irish Giant who created this causeway so he could get across the Irish Sea to face his rival. Well, that eejit, the Scottish giant Benandonner, was at least smart enough to realize that if Finn returned, he'd be defeated for sure. Some legends say Finn loved the same giant woman as Benandonner, and everyone prefers an Irishman to a Scots, so you can see the Scots dinna have much choice."

We finally stop in front of a strange sort of J-shaped stone. It's large— as befits the stories of giants, I suppose.

"When that great brute, Benandonner, destroyed Finn's fine causeway once and for all, it knocked poor Finn back so hard he lost his boot." The guide points. "And it's petrified, still resting here for all to see." The stories of Finn McCool and Benandonner are pretty entertaining, and the Irish accent just makes them better.

As with all good things, the tour finally ends. Then we're free to take photos, and once even Vanessa's obsession with snapping photos for a scrapbook has been satisfied, I finally sit with an exaggerated exhale. I'll be ready for the return hike as soon as I've rested just a bit.

"Are you alright?" Samantha's voice startles me. I thought she'd gone ahead, toward the coast with Vanessa.

"Fine," I lie. "Totally fine."

"I'm sure someone has scissors, and—"

I laugh. "Trust me. My little blistered heel isn't a mortal wound."

Samantha, instead of laughing, frowns. "I used to think I knew what mortal wounds were." She sighs, dropping down to sit next to me on the hard but flat top of a column.

"Uh-oh," I say. "Sounds like someone had a bad patient."

She shakes her head and sighs. "I did have one, just last week. She came in with the usual, run-of-the-mill type of symptoms. That's why she was assigned to me instead of a doctor."

"What's run-of-the-mill?" I ask. "I always hear about people with headaches who have brain cancer, and people with a cough who have lung cancer."

"It's early in the year—still cold and flu season. People complaining of coughing and congestion are about as basic as it gets." She blinks. "That's why I decided to become a nurse practitioner, you know. The doctors get the scary stuff. I take care of things that can be fixed."

"But not this time?" I don't even know this woman, but now I'm worried about her. "This is why I could never have gone into medicine. You wouldn't have brought her up if it wasn't something worse than a cold, right?"

"I guess you wouldn't be surprised, since you said you've heard about it. But I see a lot of patients, so finding one with lung cancer by a cough. . ." Samantha's entire face scrunches up. "She's young. She had hardly any symptoms, and no risk factors, but she's got stage four cancer. Two kids, and she'll be dead by the end of this year."

"That's horrible." For some reason, it makes me feel better. Probably because I'm a sick, sick person. At least I'm not dying. "I'm sorry."

Samantha shrugs. "I think sometimes we don't really know what the mortal wounds are. Sometimes we think our heel's just bugging us, or our cough's just annoying, and we ignore it." She stares out at the ocean. "We ignore it, and we carry on, and we have no idea that we're already dead."

I tear my eyes away from the varied columns and the beautiful blue of the ocean behind them. "Are *you* okay, Samantha?"

She shrugs. "Oh, you know. It's always the same thing with me. I wonder whether I should've had kids. I wonder whether my life's all been a waste. I move on to the meaning of our existence, and then I lather, rinse, and repeat."

I laugh and sling an arm around her. "Well, one thing you don't have to worry about?" I point. "My blister. It's for sure not foot cancer. I've already identified the cause."

"The boots?"

I shake my head. "My pride. If I hadn't wanted to look nice for all Vanessa's photos, I wouldn't have worn these today. If I'd worn my old, battered Doc Martens, I'd be fine."

"We can get a cab and go back to the hotel and get your battered shoes."

"Stop," I say. "It's fine."

And it is, at least, until we reach our next destination. After sitting on the tourbus for almost an hour on the drive from the Giant's Causeway's Visitor Center cafe steps to the parking lot for Dunluce Castle, my blister seems to have swollen. It's way more tender than it was before. I'm kind of proud that I don't cry when I first start walking on it again.

But after taking photos of the castle from the road, then tromping down the lawn, across the bridge, and around most of the castle, it feels more like a stabbing pain than I'd have guessed any blister could. "Well, that was fun." I force a smile that I worry looks more like a grimace. "But I guess that's everythi—"

"Wait, look." Vanessa spins, one hand holding her purple felt fedora on her head, the other firmly pointing at a sign that reads: Lower grounds —Admission free. "That sounds so fun."

I want to cry.

The sign even goes on to warn of lots of stairs and rough terrain. I'd kept my mouth shut—I didn't want Samantha to worry about my blister, and I didn't want to slow them up. But there's no way I can walk another step. Before I have time to express my concern, our tour guide claps. "Absolutely. All of you who have an interest, let's walk down and explore the area below the castle. We can't walk into the Mermaid's Cavern, but you shouldn't miss the story of Maeve and how she met her lover and escaped her father."

Vanessa and Samantha are already following him, and I realize that if I beg off, they'll feel obligated to skip it, too.

So, I lie.

I whip out my phone. "Oh, hey, Mason. No, it's fine. I can spare a minute." I cover the bottom of the phone and wave them on. "I'll catch you after. You can tell me the story."

They both stare at me for a moment, but then they nod and move down the steps without complaint. There are too many people milling around by the edge of the castle, including what looks like another small tour group showing up, so I hobble toward the prettiest view that's not too far away.

I nearly drop my phone when Mason *actually* calls. I answer by accident.

"Hello?" The tinny sound of his voice from where I'm holding the phone in my hand snaps me back to reality. Without even thinking, I lift the phone to my ear. "Nat?"

I swallow.

"Hey, are you there?"

"Yes," I say. "What?"

"Oh. I hope you're having fun—sorry for interrupting, but the school's calling."

"About?" My voice sounds strange even to me.

"There's some kind of field trip form they wanted for the zoo. They left a message, but I'm not even sure which school—"

"It's for Amelia and Blaine," I say. "They're going to the zoo next week, but don't worry. They'll accept the forms late, even if they say they won't. They're in the blue folder on top of the microwave."

"Thank goodness," he says. "I don't know how you keep up with all that stuff."

For a brief moment, listening to him talk, I can almost forget. So many calls, just like this. He has a question, and I have the answer. A surge of raw emotion bubbles up inside me. A feeling I can't even place. "Happy to help," I say lamely.

"I hope you're having fun."

"I'm at a castle overlooking the ocean right now," I say. "But I have a horrible blister. It's really too bad that one small thing can totally ruin everything else, isn't it?" Talking to him on the phone, my hand pressing it against my ear, is making my hands freeze in the wind. It's not just my cold hand that's upsetting me, though.

Talking to him is ruining the day more, even, than the blister.

Betrayal.

That's the feeling I couldn't recognize. His voice brings all the familiar emotions of family and home and safety, but they're all ruined now.

Because everything he says is a lie.

Our whole life, it's all a lie.

"Sorry about the blister, but don't let something small, something stupid like that, wreck everything. Okay?"

"Right," I say. "Small. Stupid."

"Exactly. Have fun. That's what life's about—having fun." Those words are rich, coming from him.

"Is that what life's about?" I ask. "Is it really?"

"Isn't it?" he asks. "I mean, that's why we do everything we do—so we can be happy and have fun."

"Are you happy?" I ask.

"Of course we are. Why are you asking that? Aren't you on vacation?"

"I wasn't asking about me. Are *you* happy?"

"What's going on, Natalie?" Did I really think he was going to just confess on the phone? Why am I disappointed that he doesn't?

Because I want it to be a one-time thing. I want him to be riddled with guilt. I want to see a way back to him, to us, to our beautiful life.

"Natalie, are you okay?" Him asking me if I'm okay—that's my limit.

"I have to go, Mason. The girls are waiting."

"Okay, well, don't worry about the field trip forms! I'll get them handed in tomorrow."

I hang up.

I slide my hand in my pocket and drop my phone, but my hand snags on the wool of my new coat, and I look down at the problem.

It's my ring.

My wedding ring—it's a marquise diamond in a yellow-gold setting. I never liked it, but Mason's mother helped him pick it out. If I'd said anything about it, it would have been rude. She'd never have gotten over it. Mason would probably have been upset, too. That's why I kept my mouth shut. I suffered in silence, just like I'm doing with my blister. Just like I always do. No one made me be a martyr; I did it to myself because I wanted people to like me.

But apparently no amount of suffering makes people truly like you.

I sit down then, right on the edge of the stupid, weathered rocks of this crumbly old castle, and I rip my boot off, and I peel off my sock, too. It's cold, and it's windy, and I don't even care. My poor white sock is bright red on the heel where the blister popped and my heel started bleeding.

I reach into my purse to rummage around for a Band-Aid—as a respectable mother, I always have at least one of those on hand—my ring catches on the lining. It must have a prong that's damaged.

It's now caught on my new coat, and my purse liner.

Mason's ugly ring, his damaged ring, is now snagging and pulling and damaging the coat and the purse I picked out and bought for myself. My hatred for this ring I allowed myself to be shackled with rises up, and it overwhelms me. I tug and I yank and I pull on the ugly thing until it slides free, and I stand up, my foot bare on the slick, cold ground of the Irish battlement, and I rock backward and I hurl it as far and as fast as I can.

It sails up, up, up, and out toward the ocean, and it flashes once.

And then it's gone.

"Well, I hope you don't need whatever that was ever again." The voice behind me is deep and almost scratchy, and it startles me. I stumble forward, my arms slamming into the guardrail at the edge of the crumbling rock walkway.

"Whoa there." Strong arms grab my shoulders and yank me back. "You don't want to follow that rubbish out into the ocean. It's just as rocky out there as it is right here. It wouldn't be fun."

I spin around, shoving the hands away. "I don't need any help."

The man's tall—much, much taller than my five-foot-five frame. His large, blue-gold eyes widen. "I'm so sorry. I shouldn't have interfered." He nods sharply, his eyes darting down to my bare foot. "Clearly you're quite capable and doing very well on your own." His lips are compressed, and it looks like he's about to laugh at me.

"You're rude," I say. "You don't know me or anything about me, and —" When I slip this time, I'm not falling forward. I'm sliding backward, and I have no idea whether I can catch myself, not while holding one very expensive designer boot.

Luckily, the debonair, tall man grabs my right arm with his vise-like grip, and my entire body shudders to a stop. "Let me apologize once more for interfering, but the miserable Irish spring weather makes it hard for Americans, I think. We can't have you sliding to your death, can we? It would be plastered all over the news."

"It might be." I want to glare, but I can't help myself. I smile. "I'm sorry. You caught me in the middle of a nervous breakdown, and apparently I'm crabby when I'm having a breakdown."

"I did hear the bit at the end." He looks almost chagrined, like he was caught snooping through someone's office.

"At the end?" I can't help noticing he hasn't released my arm yet.

"You said you had to go—the girls were waiting, but there's no one

35

here waiting. That's what caught my attention." He shrugs. "Then you sat down on the ground, started yanking your shoes off in the mud. . ." His sideways grin is irritatingly charming. "So when you pulled something out of your pocket and threw it?" He's wearing what I just learned is called a classic Irish flat-cap. It's grey plaid, just the exact color of the grey in his suit and his overcoat.

"My wedding ring," I say. "I threw my wedding ring."

The poor man blinks. "Oh." He releases me, stepping back. "Well, I'm sorry. I imagine you'll want that back at some point."

I shake my head. "I really think not."

He lifts his eyebrows. "No?"

Slippery wet ground or no, I slide back down to my bum. I've probably ruined my beautiful new coat, but I have to put my sock back on. My foot's so cold now that it's moving from a stinging feeling to being almost totally numb. That can't be good.

"Maybe don't tell your husband you threw it."

"I don't plan to tell him anything about it at all." I huff. "The day before I left Texas to fly out for this girls' trip, I walked in on my husband with another woman."

His eyes widen. "Oh."

"He was busy enough that he didn't even notice me, so he doesn't even know I know." I shove my toes into the wadded up sock. "Actually, *no one* knows I know, except you, I suppose."

"Sounds like a pretty bad two days, and now it looks like your heel's not doing great." He pulls out his wallet and starts fumbling around.

"I threw away my other boots, because he gave them to me," I say. "Blisters are just a hazard of new boots, you know."

He crouches beside me. "Maybe this will help." In his large hand he's holding a small, rectangular Band-Aid. "I know it may not do much, but it has to be better than nothing."

"I was looking for one of those when my ring caught on my bag." I take the Band-Aid carefully, very conscious of the heat from his hand. "I guess that distracted me."

He sits down next to me.

In the mud.

"Oh, no," I say. "Your suit looked pretty nice. I hope you didn't just ruin it."

"I always wonder about that in movies, especially when people get truly upset over a stain. Mud doesn't ruin most clothing items, especially quality ones. Haven't people ever heard of dry cleaners?" He smiles. "Some situations call for a little mud. I think hurling wedding rings off the overlook of a crumbling castle is one of them. In fact, on a day like today, sitting in mud's probably just the thing."

"You're not Irish," I realize. "You're—are you British?"

His smile broadens. "You're such an American. You're just realizing that now, are you?"

I shrug. "An accent's an accent to us, alright? I should get credit for noticing at all."

He laughs. "Noted."

"Well, strange, chivalrous British man, I think I'm locked in, now."

"Locked in?"

I slide my foot into my boot, trying not to let it show that my heel hurts just as badly with the addition of the Band-Aid. "If you told me a year ago, or really even a week ago, that I'd catch Mason cheating on me, I'd have told you that I'd have set him on fire and walked away."

"You have kids."

I nod.

"And it's complicated."

"I'm—I'm not the person he married." I sigh. "It might be partly my fault that he started looking elsewhere."

"That's the biggest lie humans tell ourselves before we get married, I think, that it's a sort of *contract* we're entering. It's pretty restrictive if you think about that, the notion that we are who we are and that it can't and shouldn't change, and if it does, they don't have to love us anymore." He shakes his head. "I always hated that. When you marry someone, you should be saying you have loved all the iterations of them you've seen, and you'll do whatever it takes to love every iteration of them they find while you're by their side."

I blink.

"People aren't objects, and that means we're all in a constant state of flux. We all know it, but then we act terribly surprised when other people change." He looks me right in the eye, and he pauses. "No matter what else you do today or on this trip, you should know this. *It's not your fault* he cheated on you."

"I think part of the problem is that I've grown *outward* a little too much, if you know what I mean." I gesture toward my midsection, which has taken the largest hit. "You probably can't tell with my coat and sweater and whatnot, but I'm not nearly as trim as I once was, and well. . ." I sigh. "I can't blame him. I wouldn't be attracted to me, either."

He shakes his head. "Please. That's the easiest, and the hardest, thing to change sometimes." He leans closer, his voice dropping. "Let me say it again, since you didn't seem to have heard me the first time. It's not your fault. I barely know you, and I can already tell."

It's nice to hear the words, even if he doesn't know me and has no idea whether they're really true. "Thanks."

"Look at this castle." He waves his hand at Dunluce. "It was built almost a thousand years ago, but by 1513, it was owned by the MacQuillan family. They had it for quite some time before it was seized by the MacDonnell clan, the MacQuillan's enemies, in 1550 something." He shakes his head. "The MacDonnell family had it for even longer, but eventually chunks of it, reputedly the kitchen, fell into the ocean. After that, the owner's wife didn't want to live here anymore."

"I've been through the castle tour," I say. "I know all that."

"This castle has changed hands over and over," he says. "And now it's being run by the Northern Ireland government."

"It's a little depressing," I say. "Don't you think?"

"Is it?" He shrugs. "Things have to change. Your husband should have celebrated the ways you changed and grew, or at least come and talked to you about whatever it was he didn't like. Betraying your trust wasn't *your* fault. It was his."

"Sometimes things change too much," I say. "And you need to just let them go."

"Look, you're a good person. If you weren't, you'd have set him on fire already." He's smiling again. "So if you think you should let the marriage go, do it. But don't ever feel like it was your fault that he did what he did."

"I guess." I can't help my smirk. "People talk about setting the cheater on fire or whatever, and I get it. I never would have thought I'd just tuck tail and run away. . .on a vacation."

"Most of the world makes jokes about how the British are cold," the man says slowly. He's staring off at the ocean ahead, nonthreatening, his expression serene. "They think we're cold because we don't shout and yell and express every feeling we have, like the French or the Italians. But that's not it—we're just aware that there are a lot of consequences to our actions. We've made so many mistakes in the past that we want to do better in the future."

"We?" I can't help laughing. "Well, since you're speaking for all the British, I will say that we—the Americans—appreciate your desire to do better."

He rolls his eyes. "All I'm saying is that discretion sometimes is the better part of valor. Your angry tirade would have created a very distasteful experience for your children. They deserve better, and so do you. I wouldn't look at this as running away so much as taking a beat to decide how to proceed with grace."

"Thanks." I look around. "I can't help feeling like my marriage is like this castle. Crumbly. Old. Doomed."

"I don't know," he says. "Sometimes even crumbly, old things are worth saving."

"So you think I should try and fix things?"

He shrugs.

"What would that even look like? I'd, what? Tell him what I saw, ask him for an explanation, and see whether I can accept it?"

He braces one hand against the rocky outcropping next to us. "I can't tell you what to do—I just don't know. When my wife cheated on me, I begged her to stay. I begged and begged and begged, and you know what?"

I can hardly believe what I'm hearing. "Your wife—I'm so sorry to hear that."

"She didn't stay." He shakes his head. "I'm not sure what would have happened if she had, but I know that I tried in every way I knew to try, and I needed to try that hard, so I could walk away and be okay with it."

I don't even know this man's name. I know he's handsome, British, well-educated, and chivalrous. And I know that both of us have been cheated on by our spouses. "I really am sorry."

"When I saw you throw that ring—"

"So you knew it was a ring all along," I say.

"Of course I knew." He chuckles. "I watched you wrench it off your hand. I was trying to be polite."

"How did I not immediately know you were British?" I ask.

"I'm quintessentially British," he agrees. "But losing your ring isn't

39

definitively the end. That's all I'm saying. Tell him what you did and why. Or lie and say you lost it, or tell him it was stolen. Who cares? The ring isn't really what matters." He turns slowly. "The real question is whether you can ever trust him again. Because any castle can be repaired, but will you ever feel safe living in it? You can't live somewhere that might fall into the ocean at any time."

He's right. That's the question.

I wish I knew the answer.

"Why are you here?" I stare at him. "You're here by yourself?"

He nods.

"You're. . .what? A tourist?"

He snorts.

"Not a tourist, then."

"I have my own crumbly old castle," he says. "I'm trying to figure out what to do with it."

I wonder whether he's talking about a situation or a relationship, and I'm surprised that I even care. "If you tell me about your castle, maybe I can keep you from hurling your ring into the ocean."

He laughs.

"Natalie?" Samantha and Vanessa are standing a few feet away, both of them gape-mouthed and wide-eyed.

"I'm sorry." I scramble to my feet, my back and boots slick with mud. "I slipped, and this nice man helped me, but then—"

"I fell myself." The man stands, inclining his head. "But now that your women-in-arms have returned, I'll leave you to it." He winks at me. "And best of luck working out how to handle the crumbling castle."

And then he's gone, marching down the path of the tour, while my dear friends splutter and gasp. "What on earth just happened?"

"Nothing," I insist. "Nothing at all."

I refuse to explain what just happened to my very nosy friends, because discretion, as it turns out, really is the better part of valor.

CHAPTER 6
Natalie

Every year, as we share one bathroom between three adult women, we swear that *next year* we'll get three rooms. Every year, we make the same vow. And then as time rolls on, we don't care about whether someone heard our stomach when it was upset, and we don't care that we tripped over one another getting our hair ready. We don't care that we're late for half our tours.

And again, we book one room to share.

But I swear, every year I forget that Samantha snores. "This year," I say, as I hop my way back to the tour van, "I brought you a present."

"What is it?" Vanessa asks.

"Not for you." I roll my eyes. "It's for Samantha."

"Hey, why does she get one and I don't?" Vanessa's a shameless pout.

"It's a snore-guard," I hiss.

"You're just trying to change the subject," Samantha says. "Away from you and that *guy*."

"Yeah, who on earth was that?" Vanessa asks.

"He was nobody." I shake my head. "I don't even know his name."

"Oh man, I'd like to meet me a nobody. Or three," Vanessa says. "'Nobody' was *hot*."

"He *was* hot, and Natalie Cleary, don't even think about trying to change the subject again. We aren't letting this go until you spill."

I grab the handrails and hop up into the bus, bouncing my way down the aisle to the seat I blessedly have to myself.

Two minutes later, the other two have caught up, and they're hanging their heads over the seat like dogs.

"Just tell us already," Vanessa says.

"Yeah, what on earth happened while we were tromping around below hearing sad-sack stories about mermaids and daughters who died for their father's dumb old pride?" Samantha's eyes sparkle. "Meanwhile you were up top, flirting with some hot, rich guy."

Vanessa frowns. "Our goal was supposed to be to make weirdos fall for us, not hot, rich men." She frowns. "Why was that our goal, anyway? We should change it. I want to meet a hot, rich Irish guy."

"Uh, me too," Samantha says.

"You two are beyond ridiculous." I jab at Vanessa, who's strangely being the most aggressive. "Knock it off."

"Hey." Vanessa snags my hand, her eyes narrowing. "Where's your wedding ring?"

I latch on to the stranger's suggestion that I just make up an excuse. "It caught on my coat, and I didn't want it to tear it. Must have a loose prong. I tucked it into my purse pocket."

"Oh, oh, oh," Vanessa's excitement ratchets up yet another notch. "No *wonder* Mister Debonaire was chatting you up! He thought you were available!"

I let them hoot and holler most of the way back to the hotel. Luckily, it's not very far. We'll have most of our driving to do tomorrow morning. I figured it would be smart not to be responsible for driving on the first day, while I'm still jetlagged, and now I'm thinking that was wise. The second we get to our room, I change out of my boots. . .into another new pair of boots that are almost as bad.

"Voila." Vanessa's just coming back through the front door when I emerge from the bathroom, and she's brandishing a very large, very shiny pair of what look like sheep shears. "The front desk didn't have scissors, but the maintenance crew did." She nods. "With these, Samantha's going to save your foot from amputation."

She's joking, as usual, but Samantha's weird fix actually does help. "When we get back, I'm buying stock in—what is this stuff?"

"Neatsfoot," Vanessa says.

"No," Samantha says. "That's what you put on basketball gloves. This is called moleskin."

"You mean *baseball* glove oil." I chuckle. "We're a mess—but are you really saying the company's called MOLE-skin?" I can't help cringing. "They need a new marketing director."

Samantha laughs. "It's not a brand name. That's just what the stuff's called, like, tissues, or like socks. The brands are Dr. Scholls, or, I don't know. There's probably generic moleskin too. It's not patented, or I don't think it is."

"Well, that's a shame." I frown.

"Not really," Vanessa says. "When things are patented, they cost the consumer way more."

"Oh, shut up." I point at the door. "I'm starving, and I'm not talking any more until you guys feed me."

"Do you promise?" Samantha's beaming.

I don't punch her shoulder, but only because I'm a good person, and also I'm not a fan of physical violence. Not for moral reasons, but because I'm not very coordinated. I'm far more prone to slip and fall while trying to hurt someone, like I did at Dunluce Castle today, than cause any damage.

Samantha searches on her phone for the best pub in Antrim and finds a pretty highly reviewed one less than three blocks away.

"The important question is whether our fair lady of the injured foot can make it through a three-block hike." Vanessa arches one eyebrow. "Our other option is to carry her."

"Or find her an eligible bachelor to do it." Samantha shimmies.

"Or how about an Uber?" I roll my eyes. "I think I can make it there, but I make no promises about the way back."

Samantha grabs her purse and twists a scarf around her neck. "You better make it back. If you can't get yourself home, I'm leaving you behind."

"Just because I've gained a bit of weight," I say, "isn't justification for you to abandon me."

"Ha," Samantha says. "You look great—you're not the problem. I'm just not a very good friend. I'd have abandoned you at any weight and any age."

Good friends are the best. They pretend all sorts of things aren't true when they are, and then they make you laugh about them. We manage to take two wrong turns and make three blocks into six, but eventually we stumble into the place Samantha chose. "Top in the Town?" I squint. "This place is pretty full of itself, huh?"

"Top *of* the Town," Samantha says. "Not common that one word matters, but here, it does."

"I guess," I say. "But the food better be good, or I'll call it slop of the town."

"Oh, it's good." A large woman with a ruddy face and a beautiful smile's walking past us. She points at the door. "You won't regret coming, you can trust me on that, pets."

"And what's the very best thing on the menu?" Vanessa never misses a beat. "I hate to miss out on it, and you sound like you know things."

The woman releases the arm of the man she was holding and sidles closer. "Dessert or main course?"

"Both," I say. "We like all food."

"Speak for yourself," Samantha says. "Dessert always comes first."

"Best friends since birth?" The woman glances around at the three of us.

"Close enough," I say. "Besties since we started riding horses, anyway."

She claps. "Yeo, but you ride, do ye?"

I blink. Samantha and Vanessa look confused, too. Is she happy we ride? Or. . .what's she saying?

"I love ponies too, but ever since I hurt me knee, I can't." Her date looks a little put out, but a little glaring never hurt me much.

"What kind of riding did you do?" I ask. "We all jumped."

She slaps my shoulder. "As did I, pet. As did I!" She nods. "Then ye must try the lamb tacos. Nothing more Irish for some champion tourists than that—America is it?"

"Texas for me," I say. "Colorado." I point at Vanessa. "And Florida." I point at Samantha.

"I always wanted to visit the States," she says. "But the closest I've gotten is McDonald's."

I can't help cringing.

"For dessert, you'll have to try one with the honeycomb in it. Yellaman honeycomb's a real treat." With that strange pronouncement, she spins on her heel and rejoins her crusty date.

"Did she say *yellow man*?" Vanessa asks. "Because that sounds. . ."

"It's not racist," the host says as we walk through the door. "It's not honeycomb either—more of a candy, named for the bright yellow color." He grabs a few menus and waves for us to follow him. "She's not wrong—anyone who likes sugar's sure to like yellowman honeycomb."

With that endorsement and a wink, the way-too-young host with the shaggy hair and the adorable smile leaves us at a cramped booth in the corner. Thanks to some reasonably decent live music, it's hard to hear every word my friends say, but one Black and Black later and we're all roaring.

"I forgot how good this was." Vanessa sets her empty glass down on the table and waves for our waiter, pointing at our empty glasses. Then she raises three fingers. He nods.

"It was good in London," I say. "But this is better."

"Either that, or we forgot how good it was then." Samantha shrugs. "That bartender was right, though. The shot of blackcurrant eliminates the porter's bite *perfectly*."

"I hate when one little thing ruins something that was otherwise perfect." I take the last sip of mine. "There aren't many perfect things in this world, so I try to appreciate the things that are."

"Says Miss Perfect herself," Vanessa says.

"Right?" Samantha sighs. "What exactly in your life falls short of perfection?"

"Plenty," I say. "Believe me."

"I'd like to," Samantha says, "but, I don't." She's smiling, but she almost sounds serious.

"Me either," Vanessa says. "Because I don't just follow you on social. I talk to you on the phone—and I know that for you, 'imperfect' means you were five minutes late." She sighs. "Five minutes late feels like twenty minutes early for me lately."

"Oh please," Samantha says. "The two of you run circles around me. I don't even have kids, and I'm always messing everything up."

"Is it hard for you?" I ask. "Winning the grand prix so often that you can't fit all the trophies in your office?" I arch one eyebrow. "Or were you talking about saving another horse and turning it into a prize show jumper?"

"Most of them don't even have trophies," Samantha says. "Just cash."

"That must be really hard," I say.

"I bet she's talking about how she's just not very good at gutting and remodeling houses and then making a killing when she flips them. In her free time around being a doctor, of course." Vanessa practically lunges as the waiter shows with the next round of drinks. "You two make me feel terrible about myself, I swear."

"I'm not a doctor," Samantha says. "I'm a nurse practitioner."

"Yeah, yeah," I say. "Whatever."

"No one gets the real story." Samantha stares at the drink sitting in front of her. "Even your best friends, I guess."

"What?" When I look at her, I realize she looks. . .upset. "Are you alright?"

"I'm fine." She wraps one hand around the base of her drink. "By the time we get back, I'm guessing Brent will have some papers all drawn up."

"For another house sale?" I ask. "Or are you guys buying a place with a big old barn like you always wanted?"

Samantha picks up her drink, her voice flat when she says, "Neither. Divorce papers." Then she drains her entire drink in one go, slamming it down on the weathered wooden tabletop.

I catch myself staring at her, my jaw dangling, and I snap it shut. I'm a complete dunce in situations like this. I have no idea what to say. I want to pat her back and cry and blurt out that I probably am getting divorced too, but all those thoughts slam into me at the same time. So instead of saying or doing anything at all, I just keep staring, my eyes wide, my brain blank.

"Samantha, I'm so sorry." Vanessa hop-slides her chair closer and wraps one arm awkwardly around Samantha's farthest shoulder. Then as Samantha leans in, Vanessa starts to sob. Not Samantha sobbing against the person consoling her—*Vanessa's* the one crying. "I'm a total fraud," our widowed friend wails.

The people at the table behind them are staring at us. It's times like this it might have been helpful to be in Italy or France where they might not understand us as easily. Although, as Americans, most people can understand us wherever we go. Stupid American television.

"What are you crying for?" I ask, still dumb as a wood post. "A fraud—at what? Are you not really a widow?" I blink. "Did Jason leave you?"

"No, he's really dead." She sobs *harder*.

Ugh.

Samantha, eyes totally dry, straightens, staring at Vanessa. "What's going on?" Her voice, instead of being annoyed, is kind. Soft. "Tell us."

"I—" Vanessa cough-clears her voice. "The thing is—it's been really hard since Jason died. And I haven't talked about this to, well, to anyone really. It's so embarrassing, but Trace. . ."

Trace is her football star son who's just a year younger than Clara. He has a face that was made for television. Seriously. "Is he alright?" I ask.

"He got into drugs," Vanessa whispers. "We've tried three rehab places, and they 'graduate' him, but none have worked. On the day I left." She shakes her head.

"What?" I reach across the table, my hand dropping over hers. "Is he okay?"

"The school called to say he was using *again*." She drops her face on her hands. It's hard to make out her next words, but it sounds like she says, "I shouldn't have come, but Jeremy told me to go."

"Of course you should still come," Samantha says. "That all sounds really hard. You clearly needed a break."

Vanessa lifts her head. "I'm really sorry about your divorce, and I'm sorry for lying to you guys about this. It's not just you—only the school administrators, my brother-in-law Jeremy, and my mother-in-law, when she's lucid, know."

"Wait, your mother-in-law's not lucid?" Samantha asks. "When did that happen?"

"In the last six months or so," Vanessa says. "She'd been confused a little here or there for a while, but about six months ago, we had to put her in an assisted living facility. It's been rough."

"You weren't lying to us," I say. "You just didn't tell us about everything, and that's okay."

"It's basically lying," Vanessa says. "I didn't tell you because I'm embarrassed. I can't manage my life without Jason, clearly."

"You're not the only one who can't manage your life, and I don't even have any kids to take care of. Things have been bad with me and Brent for a while," Samantha says. "I didn't say anything to anyone either—I didn't even admit it to myself."

"I think it's hard to accept when things aren't going well." I release her hand and straighten. "And sometimes you think things are going well, and then you find out how stupid and blind you were."

"Yeah, Brent wanted me to sign some papers *giving* our old house to his brother. He practically shoved them at me on my way out the door, and when I wouldn't sign them away, he called me a cold-hearted witch, except not with a 'w,' and said he wasn't sure why he was married to me." Her shoulders slump. "I just. . .*left*, so I'm not sure what I'll be going home to, but I doubt it's anything good. It was the worst moment of our marriage, so far. I keep hearing him call me a cold-hearted witch over and over. How can the person who's supposed to love you most call you that?"

It feels, for just a moment, like I've stepped outside of my body. It feels like the world's narrowing to a tiny point, and all the sounds and smells and sights around me aren't real. And then everything sort of slams back into me, and my mouth just opens and words pour out. "I thought we were leaving on our trip a day earlier than we were, and I even got an Uber and got out at the airport before I realized I had the wrong day."

Samantha and Vanessa are both staring at me.

At least the people at the table behind them aren't watching us anymore.

"That's a terribly embarrassing blunder," Samantha says. "It's right up there with forgetting and leaving the oven on all night. Your electric bill's bad when you do that." Her eyes are sparkling, so I know she's amused. "But don't worry. We'll take your dirty little secret to our grave."

Vanessa looks mildly annoyed, like I've just told them I had a hangnail.

"When I got back home—my second Uber for the day—I found Mason in bed with another woman."

Vanessa, who was reaching for her beer, startles, knocking her glass over and dumping dark liquid all over the table.

"Oh, shoot." Samantha's nearly as fumbly as Vanessa, knocking the specials sign over as she tries to blot at the spreading mess with her already-soiled napkin.

Luckily our waiter's paying attention. He shows up seconds later with a towel and starts blotting up the mess. "You ladies doing alright over here?"

"Well, out of our three husbands," Samantha says, "one's a greedy, demanding mess, one's a philandering sack-of-crap, and one's dead. I'd say we're going to need another round."

The waiter blinks, picks up the soggy towel, and turns on his heel. Two seconds later, he's back with a tray. "This one's on the house."

"Thanks," I say.

Vanessa's laugh-cry makes me laugh, too. "We're a pathetic bunch, but somehow I think I love you ladies more for it."

We spend the rest of the night exchanging details and for some reason, I finally feel. . .better. By the time the sticky toffee pudding with yellowman honeycomb ice cream arrives, I feel happier than I would have thought possible, given the circumstances.

I guess misery really does love company.

Or maybe it's the Guinness I should thank. Either way, I might be a disaster. It might be my fault that Mason cheated, but Vanessa and Samantha are the best people I know. If their lives suck too, if their kids are a mess and their husbands are awful, then maybe—just maybe—it's not all my fault that my marriage is falling apart. Maybe we've all just hit a really, really hard patch, and maybe if we stick together, we'll all survive it.

Most importantly, for the first time in days, I don't feel utterly alone.

CHAPTER 7

Vanessa

The next morning hits hard.

I haven't done much drinking in my life, and this is why. As I open my eyes against the harsh rays of the sun, I wonder for just a small second, whether this is how Trace feels when he's dragged awake after getting high the night before.

The difference is that I rarely drink, and he gets baked daily.

Also, he's sixteen.

There's a funny little plinging sound coming from the nightstand. "Shoot," Natalie says. "We have to be packed and out of here in the next thirty minutes."

It's a rush of jostling and flying clothing as we all dart into the bathroom and stuff our things into our bags, but we manage to check out a mere fourteen minutes late. For three women in one room, I'm rather proud of us.

I'm relieved not to be the one driving, however, especially as we approach our third round-about. "What's wrong with these people?" I brace my hand across my eyes. "All this spinning is not making my stomach happy."

"I hear the cafe at Kilkea Castle's wonderful, and they have afternoon tea today," Natalie says.

"Afternoon tea?" Samantha's almost annoyingly excited. Normally I'd find it cute, but everything's annoying when you're this hungover.

"Remind me not to drink this much ever again," I say.

"We deserved last night," Natalie says. "We've all had a bad year."

"That's an understatement," I say. "It's been a *terrible* year."

"Today we're going to turn that around." Natalie's even peppier than Samantha. Their hangover reactions must be broken. "I've never stayed in a castle before, and this one's supposed to be amazing. When I was planning the trip, I ran across an article about the guy who bought it. He's an American, actually, and he's a business mogul from Boston or something. He spent three hundred million dollars renovating it."

"Euros?" I ask.

"Huh?" Natalie's brow furrows as she turns my way.

"I'm guessing it was three hundred million *euros*, since it's in Ireland."

Samantha rolls her eyes and snorts. "Even hungover, you're one of those people."

"What people?" I ask.

"We're on vacation," Samantha says. "You probably email authors to complain about tiny incongruities in their books too."

"No." I fold my arms and huff. "I wouldn't let stupid things like that bother me, and if they did, I'd never email them about it. But I was just—" She's right. I'm being annoying. "Why are you two so peppy? You don't feel crabby and irritable today, like you're about to die?"

Samantha and Natalie both laugh.

"We do," Natalie says, "but I'm guessing we both drink a little more often than you, so we're better at hiding it."

She's probably got me there. "I don't have anyone to go out with." I hate how pathetic that sounds.

"Well, chin up," Samantha says. "In another two or three months, neither will Nat and I."

"No, no, no," Natalie says. "We are *not* moping. We're in *Ireland*, going to stay at a fabulous castle that a brilliant and rich American remodeled into a four-star hotel. We are happy and posh and brilliant, and we'll act like it."

She's right. This is a cool experience, and I won't rain on it. I rummage around in my bag for some aspirin, pass them out, along with a water bottle, and throw on my sunglasses. "Now I'm ready to be fabulous," I say.

"Hey, I'm going to ask again what you were talking to that hot guy about," Samantha says. "Because you sure seemed chummy, and after what Mason did to you. . ."

Natalie rolls her eyes, but keeps them on the road. "Nothing. I mean, he saw me throw my wedding ring into the water, and I think he was just a good Samaritan or something. He wanted to make sure I wasn't headed over next myself."

"What?" Samantha sputters.

"I can't believe you did that," I say. "You could have sold it."

"Yeah, I wasn't exactly thinking through my options," Natalie says. "I was—I was just so mad."

"Good for you," Samantha reaches forward from the back seat to clap her hands on Natalie's shoulders. "I should've done that, too."

"Don't you think Brent might cool off?" Natalie asks. "I mean, sure, he was mad, and who knows? He may push you more, but he won't really divorce you because you won't just give his horrible brother a few hundred thousand dollars, right?"

"If he doesn't, I may file myself," Samantha says. "I don't want to be married to a man who calls me horrible names, and I don't want to be in a relationship where he's threatening to leave me if I don't do what he wants. I think it's all a symptom of other problems that have been there for a long time." Her voice is sad, but resolved.

"I'm sorry," I say. "If I'd been more honest with the two of you in the past year or so, maybe you'd have confided in me, too. Then you wouldn't have felt so alone."

"We all know everything now," Natalie says. "So I expect you guys to keep telling me how you're doing. How you're *really* doing."

"That's enough depressing talk for now." Samantha turns on a girls' trip soundtrack she made, and we spend the rest of the drive singing. Neither of them seems to care that I'm always a half-note off-key—they never have, even though they both sing like Celine Dion, if she were less annoying.

Our vocal disparity is kind of symbolic of our entire relationship. They're fabulous, and I'm always just a little off.

But they love me anyway.

As we drive through the gates of the estate, marked Kilkea Castle, I'm not sure what to expect. Will it be old and moldering, dark and cold? Or will it be a large, palace-looking castle? After driving past a million tiny sheep farms and little bush-hedges, I'm guessing it's on the humble side. But as we cross the small, one-lane stone bridge, the view opens up and I see it. All of us stop singing, leaving poor Taylor to mournfully sing on about her latest heartbreak alone.

"Wow," I say.

"I think this one night will definitely be worth the amount we paid," Natalie says. "I know it was the costliest place we're staying, but. . ."

A large sign boasts the finest spa in Ireland. "We got the spa package, right?" I ask. "Please tell me this is where we got the spa package."

Natalie laughs. "We did. They have falconing and horseback riding and a spa, and they were all. . .not cheap, but we decided to do our horseback riding down south and the spa and the falcon experience here."

"Oh, good," I say. "We chose right." The reason I voted for the spa was actually that I didn't want to try and come up with an excuse not to ride twice, and doing it near the end of the trip seemed easier.

For a split second, I consider telling them about my fall and confessing that I haven't ridden in years. They were great when I told them about Trace last night. . .but this feels different somehow. Apparently they were both dealing with family stuff, but I know they both ride—daily. Horses have always been the bedrock of our friendship. If I tell them I don't ride anymore. . .

Will they start to realize all the other ways I don't measure up?

I focus on the spa and my excitement and gasping along with them as we drive past a stunning, manicured garden, breathtaking grounds, and a stately castle that looks just like I imagined it would. A massage will be just the thing to release all the stress from Trace and lying about horses and just life in general.

"They had a room that would accommodate three?" Samantha asks.

"Not exactly," Natalie says. "Remember, you guys agreed that we should book the castle rooms, not the lodge."

I have no idea what she's talking about, but sometimes our group chat flies so fast that I miss things.

"Right," Samantha says. "Because who comes to a castle to stay in the lodge rooms?"

"They all have special names, the castle rooms. They're all different, so they're named after some important person who lived in the castle."

As we lug our big bags out of the back of the car, Natalie fills me in on what I either didn't read or forgot.

"We got a luxury suite—we were assigned the Sir Thomas de Rokeby room—and they're going to bring in a cot." Natalie pauses. "I think we can decide who gets the cot by deciding who has the least pathetic life." She beams. "So I'm sure to have the bed."

"I'm pretty sure Samantha's getting the cot," I say. "She and Brent may be fine." I hold up one finger. "She's smoking hot." Another finger. "And she has loads of money and horses." I hold up a third. "Plus, her husband didn't *die*."

As we roll our way toward the front of the gorgeous castle, Samantha defends her position. "But I couldn't have kids, and my stupid husband refused to ever adopt. I have a knee that aches all the time, in spite of two operations, and my husband's just *good enough* that I've been miserably shackled to him for twenty years." She blinks as if she's surprised by the truth of her statement. "Other than finding her husband shagging another woman, Natalie has the best life. And who knows? Maybe he has some kind of explanation." She grimaces, like she feels bad for even saying that.

"Oh ho ho," Natalie says. "I've gained fifteen pounds, and I have five kids no new guy will want to deal with. Plus, on top of that, I'm the only one who doesn't really have a way to earn money. Once I divorce my loser husband, I'll be poor as a church mouse."

"Are church mice really poor?" I ask. "Where did that phrase come from?"

We've just walked through the massive, metal studded castle door, which was opened by a man in white button-down shirt and black pants, who looks just like I imagine a butler should. For someone who spent years watching *Downton Abbey*, it sends a tiny thrill down my spine.

The woman behind the counter's chipper, kind, and very Irish. I have a little bit of trouble understanding her, but I'm pretty sure she's delivering some bad news. "Yer rooms aren't ready—the cleaning staff is up to ninety right now," she says. "I'm sure you're knackered and wanting to check in, but dinna fear. We can hold yer bags for ye, and you can do your falconry activity a wee bit early." She beams.

For some reason, I just want to make her happy. "Oh, okay, sure," I say.

"We might want to grab a bite to eat first," Samantha says. "Or I might try to eat the falcon."

The woman behind the counter's eyes widen. . .and then she howls with laughter. "We can't be having that, can we? Fergus Fitzgerald loves those birds more than he loves his own mam."

"Okay," I say. "Could you hold our bags while we eat, or do we need to wheel them back out to the car?"

"Of course we can," the woman says. "Though—I did just get a notification from the system. The room you booked, the Rokeby, is still being cleaned, but the one next door, the Earl of Kildare, is available now. . .and it's only a tiny upgrade."

"Wait," I say. "Could we get *both* rooms?" I raise my eyebrows. "And how much more would it be to get that one *and* the Rokeby?"

The woman blinks, but to her credit, she pivots fast. "Yes, that's smart. I don't think the Earl of Kildare room accommodates a cot. I'm not sure what I was thinking." She shakes her head. "But yes, we can add the Earl of Kildare room for just another two hundred and forty-seven euros, tax included." She looks up. "Would you like to do that?"

Something about the sum makes me a little nervous—it's not a cheap trip, and I'm hardly rolling in money. "Let me check something really quick." I have no idea, with the exchange rate, how high my credit card balance has already climbed. I tap on my bank app and wait while it logs me in.

And then I very nearly drop my phone.

"Are you alright?" Natalie asks. "Vanessa?"

"I'm. . .I'm fine." I blink and focus again, not even looking at my credit card balance. I'm too gobsmacked by the checking account balance on the top line of my summary page.

When I left a few days ago, I had nearly eight thousand dollars in there. My normal two thousand dollar reserve, and the fifty-eight hundred or so dollars I have in the budget for the next month.

"Hey, is everything okay?" Samantha walks toward me.

"We'll take the room," Natalie says. I'm only vaguely aware of her handing her credit card over.

"Wait." I lunge toward the counter, fumbling to pull out my credit card instead. "I'll pay. It's fine."

The woman at the counter has gone extremely quiet as she processes my card, but her smile's just as kind as she hands me an old-school key. "We're happy to hold luggage, of course, but you can also stow it in the room right away if you'd like."

"Yes," I say. "We'll do that."

"Both your rooms are on the second floor." The woman hands Natalie a key. "The Rokeby's just two doors down, and it should be ready in the next hour and a half. I trust you can hold the key but not use it until the cleaning staff are through?"

Natalie nods, but neither she nor Samantha say anything else.

At least, not until we reach the elevator.

"What's going on?" Vanessa asks.

"Are you alright?" Natalie shakes her head. "I wish you'd let me pay. I'm sure Mason can afford it." Her voice only sounds a little bitter, so that's an improvement, I think.

"It's almost two p.m." I say, "which means it's only seven in the morning back in Colorado." I sigh. "I'll have to call my lawyer later and figure out why Heavy Lifting just transferred two and a half million dollars into my personal checking account—or how we even had that much to begin with."

"Whoa," Natalie says. "If you don't want it, I'd be willing to give them my account information." She frowns. "Although, maybe not. Let me set up an account that's just mine, and *then*, I'd be willing to take it." She's smirking now.

"Do you really have no idea where it might have come from?" Samantha asks. "Check your email—usually there's going to be some kind of transaction record or something, right?"

Duh. I'm such a business dunce sometimes, especially for an accounting major. "Right. I mean, yes. There should be." Except, there wasn't anything like this on the horizon. "I just—I can't imagine where it would have come from."

"Nothing going on with Jason's company that would have—maybe a loan for new equipment?" Natalie's always so sensible.

Could it be something to do with the refinance? Like, somehow they dumped the money into my account, but really it was supposed to go to the bank?

By the time the elevator doors finally open, I've pulled up my email and I'm waiting for it to update. It's slow—everything's slow here, though —so I'm at the end of the hallway, standing in front of a room with a little placard next to it that reads, "Earl of Kildare," by the time my email finally refreshes.

The big, bold words from my lawyer's office at the top of my email read: For Your Records, Heavy Lifting Sale Sheet and Final Files.

Sale Sheet.

I fumble to insert the solid brass key in the lock, but my brain isn't working right. How could I be getting *sale* paperwork on a company that isn't for sale? Sale sheet. . .for what? Did Jeremy *sell* the equipment instead of refinancing it?

That can't be right.

It would take more than half our equipment to be worth even close to *that* much, plus, if we sell our equipment, what would we rent? That's the whole business. We rent stuff.

It finally hits me—I can't call my lawyer, but I can call *Jeremy.* Surely he'll have some idea of what's going on. It must be a bank glitch or a paperwork mix-up. Or maybe they transferred someone else's funds into our account. Gosh, I hope I didn't do something wrong—something that caused this to happen. Did I sign the wrong form? Or check the wrong box?

As I wheel my way into the extravagant room I just paid for, I have a tiny panic attack. I should *not* have paid for such a pricey room. What was I thinking? But at least the room's stunning. It's spacious, with a round wooden table and upholstered armchairs set in front of two tall, arched, and inset windows. The bed's large, white, and fluffy with several gold pillows, one massive wine-colored pillow, and a bright golden-and-wine-colored blanket lying across the base that matches the drapes.

In addition to the beautiful view of the garden below, the walls are a soothing, darkish blue—cerulean's cousin, almost—except for the parts that are creamy white with lovely molding. There's a tiny plaque on the nightstand, and I bend over to read it, somewhat grateful for the distraction.

* * *

Lord Gerald FitzGerald was the eighth Lord of Kildare. None that went before or came after him could quite compare. He defied the King of England and still managed to rule for nearly twenty years before being sent to the Tower of London for punishment.

But that was not the end for him. Not even close.

No, after being accused by one of the King's close confidants of burning up the Archbishop of Cashel's cathedral, Lord Kildare told the king, "I would not have done it if I had not been told the Archbishop was inside."

His raw honesty delighted King Henry VII, who married Lord Kildare to his cousin and sent him back to rule Ireland. The king famously said, "All Ireland cannot govern this Earl, then let this Earl govern all of Ireland."

Kildare was open, hot-tempered, and honest to a fault, and people loved him for it. He was the first truly charismatic ruler of Ireland, according to the records. His leadership forever changed Ireland and Castle Kilkea, where he died. This was his favorite room due to the view of both the gardens and the stable, and although he used it as an office, we've repurposed it to honor him and the history of this fine castle.

* * *

One of the most fascinating things about Ireland, or really most of Europe, is the weight of history that just permeates everything. In Colorado, most of our records only date into the mid-eighteen-hundreds. It's hard to find many artifacts or much in the way of old buildings, since the settlers kind of destroyed whatever was there before. Here, there's a thousand years of castles and fighting and struggles. Princes and other dignitaries stayed in rooms that we're renting now.

As the girls wheel their bags across the plush, ornately shaved carpet of my fancy room—the heavy smell of clean linens, lemon-verbena disinfecting supplies, and something else I can't quite pinpoint washes over me —I decide I'm sufficiently buoyed up.

I'm ready to channel my inner Lord of Kildare and force answers out of the people in my life who might have them. I can't hide and just hope things work out. I have to be honest and brave. It may be a little early yet, but I pull out my phone and dial my brother-in-law anyway.

"Hello?" Jeremy sounds surprised to hear from me. "Vanessa?"

"Oh, you're awake early."

"It's seven-thirty. Wicket's been waking me up every single morning at seven, and I haven't killed her yet." He snorts. "If she wasn't such a cute dog, I might have."

"You can get up, let her out, and go back to sleep," I say. "For the record. But listen, I just found out there's been some kind of terrible mistake at the bank or something. Instead of refinancing the equipment, somehow they deposited way too much money into my checking account. You need to call once they're open and make sure the bank fixes it so they don't come take anything away."

"I was wondering when you'd notice." For some reason, he sounds delighted. Smug, even.

"Notice?" My voice has become quite shrill. I wonder if they'll bill me if my high-pitched tone breaks the thick, old-castle-window glass. "Notice what?"

"I've been working on this surprise for quite some time, you know."

"Surprise?" My stomach starts to ache. "What surprise, Jeremy? Is Trace okay?"

"Trace is fine," he says. "He's doing amazing, honestly. We all are. There's no reason for you to worry whatsoever."

That's a relief. I exhale slowly. "Then what do you mean, 'surprise'?"

"You know how, after Jason died, both of us were scrambling around, panicked?"

"Mm."

"And neither of us *wanted* to run his company, but we didn't have a choice. Because he'd helped all his friends with buying their equipment before they defaulted, and we had way too much that we needed to rent out in that market?"

"I was there," I say. "I'm the one who used all the life insurance money we got after he died to keep things afloat."

"Right, right," Jeremy says. "Supply chains being what they are, we're some of the only people with equipment in the area. It's why we've been doing such good business, and now we finally get to benefit from it."

"Benefit?" The sick feeling's back in full force. "What are you talking about?"

"I found a buyer—you know them, actually. It's the Fox Rental Group. Remember? You sold them a few of our front-end loaders when they were in a bind on that bank project."

"Jeremy, tell me what's going on."

"I got that power of attorney from you, and I used it to take care of everything so you didn't have to—my dad's stupid company's finally sold —and we made a killing."

"We?" I can barely breathe.

"I mean, I've been running it since Jason died. Without my help—"

"Jason and I bought you out," I say. "Before your dad died, we took out that loan—a loan it almost killed us to pay off."

"Oh, don't worry about that," Jeremy says. "I made sure the documents reflect my repayment for that. You got four hundred thousand more than I did, the exact amount of the loan."

"Why did you get anything from the sale of *Jason's* company?" My hands are shaking. "Why did you sell my company without even telling me about it? You had to know that company's meant for Trace and Bryce to run. You had to know."

"Look, Vanessa, you're on a nice vacation right now. It's a vacation you needed badly. Let's talk about this when you get back, okay? I'll keep taking care of your kids here, and when you come home, I'm sure you'll be in a better state of mind to discuss the details."

He hangs up.

He *hangs up* on me.

I'm utterly filled with rage, right to the top of my head. "I'm—I'm going to kill my brother-in-law," I say, "but not before I get this whole sale reversed."

I leave two messages for my lawyer—irate, rambling messages—and then I finally turn to face my friends, who have surely pieced together most of what's going on.

"I can't believe he'd do that," Natalie says. "I thought Jeremy was helping you."

"If I've learned anything in the past few months," Samantha says, "it's that we can't really trust the men in our lives at all."

It's terribly sad, but I'm afraid she's right.

CHAPTER 8
Natalie

Before I met my husband, Vanessa's husband Jason tried to set me up with his little brother Jeremy. I went out to Colorado for a weekend to visit her, and we went on a double date. After Jeremy mansplained the difference between stew and soup, the way men can never compete with women in strength thanks to fast-twitch muscle fiber growth, and the way all women have been duped by male marketing into believing that a discount's somehow saving them money, I knew he was wrong for me.

I didn't know he was a *total* dirtbag, though.

He's lucky I'm not in Colorado right now—I could hear how patronizing he still was on the phone. I don't have a lot of patience right now, and I'm full of Mason-generated rage. I'm not sure I'd be able to keep from explaining to him how guns can level the playing field between the sexes. Being a Texas woman, I know my way around a shooting range—I figure I know *just* enough to set things right.

Stealing from a widow? There's a special place for someone like that.

To keep Vanessa from obsessing when there's not much we can do from here, we go down for our falconry experience.

"Our falconer's on his way over and should be here in the next fifteen minutes or so," the peppy front desk woman says.

"Thank you so much for changing our time around," Samantha tells her. "We could use some fun today."

Her eyes light up. "Oh, yer in for a treat then. Fergus has the best manner with those sweet birds."

"The birds of prey are sweet?" I ask. "Do they apologize before eating the mice?"

"Sweet might not have been quite the right word." Her lip twitches.

"You've been so helpful," Samantha says. "I'd love to know your name."

The woman beams. "I'm such an eejit sometimes. I forgot my name tag at home—it's Fiona."

"I love that name," I say. "Thanks for all your help."

Fiona waves at someone behind us. "I've had the kitchen bring over a light tea for you ladies to enjoy while you wait."

Her definition of a 'light tea' service and mine are clearly not the same. Two women wheel a cart with two large pots of hot water and a little box of tea to choose from for the three of us, as well as a three-tier tower of tiny sandwiches and cakes.

As the women with the cart are transferring it all to a small table with four little chairs set up around it, I nearly fall on the cakes like a wild dog. My stomach actually growls—loudly—as the women are turning to leave. The shorter one hides a giggle with her hand.

"Sorry," I say. "It was a longish drive this morning, and we were running a little late."

"Plus she's been starving herself," Samantha mutters.

The short one shakes her head. "Don't starve yourself in Ireland. We want you to love our country."

After they're gone, I can't help raising my voice and calling to Fiona. "Do you do this for all your guests?"

"We have the chance to be a little more attentive in the off-season," she says.

I'll make sure to leave a tip on the table—people in the UK almost always seem surprised when I do that for some reason. I think they must not tip here as often as we do back home. Lately, we have to tip for every-thing. If someone hands me an ice cream cone, they expect a twenty percent tip for it.

As I reach for a cucumber sandwich, I notice they have three of everything. They must've made this little tea service just for us. Samantha must notice the same thing.

"This was so kind," she says.

Fiona shakes her head. "Really, it's no bodge. It's just a tray of sandwiches and cakes they'd have had to throw away in an hour."

"I may never leave Ireland," Vanessa says. "I swear, the people here are so nice."

"It helps that we're in a really fancy place and we're paying them a fortune," Samantha grumbles, but I notice she eats every single sandwich as well, including the egg salad. She usually hates egg salad.

"I figured I'd get your egg sandwich for sure," Vanessa says, mock-glaring at Samantha.

"It sounded crunchy," Samantha says. "I wanted to try it, and then it wasn't boggy and rubbery—it was great."

"It's got crisps in it," Fiona says, eavesdropping as naturally as if she was part of our group. "I love watching Americans try our crisp sandwiches."

"Crisp?" I ask.

"Chips," Vanessa says. "They call chips 'crisps' here."

I nod. "Right. Well, that's brilliant, adding a little bit of crunch to the egg-salad."

"It has lettuce too," Vanessa says. "It was great."

Before we can thank Fiona again, an old man with crazy white hair barely contained under a dark brown cap strides toward us, a smile on his craggy face. "You the ladies here for the falconry experience?"

I stand. "That's us. Thanks so much for moving it up."

"You're helping me, really. I'm Fergus." He motions for us to follow him. "I just have some paperwork for us to fill out and some rules to go over, and then we'll go into the courtyard to meet the birds."

Samantha bites her lips and shivers. "I'm so excited."

"Have any of you ever had a falconry experience before?"

Vanessa and I shake our heads. "Nope. Not ever."

"Me either," Samantha says. "But I had a blue jay that adopted me when I was a kid. Wild animals always love me."

"Adopted you?" I ask.

Samantha laughs. "That's what my mom called it. One day, it just flew over and sat next to me. I gave it some goldfish. From then on, any time I went outside, Jay joined us. He would sit on my shoulder or on my arm, and when I had food, I'd share it with him. He must not have migrated, because I saw him all the time—until I was about eight."

"How have I never heard about this?" Vanessa asks.

"When he disappeared, I didn't handle it well," Samantha says. "My parents kind of stopped talking about it."

"Some birds, even wild ones, do take a real liking to certain humans— usually just one," Fergus says. "It's a phenomenon we rarely see, but it's fun when it happens. Often, however, a bird that acts like you're describing is actually sick, so you're lucky that wasn't the case."

"Fergus is a bit of a buzzkill," I whisper.

Samantha snickers as we follow him over and work our way through the rules and forms. It boils down to four things: don't touch the birds without permission, don't feed the birds anything unless directed, don't make loud noises, and listen to Fergus.

Check.

"Now, before you meet your first bird, you all need to put on a falconry glove." Fergus hands them out—they do *not* look very good. They're all weathered and off-color. "The important thing here is to protect your hands from the razor-sharp talons meant to catch and gore prey while also allowing you to feel the bird. Your hand will be a large part of how you communicate with the birds today."

"We're communicating with them?" I can't help my widening eyes. "I was *not* informed, or I'd have studied bird in DuoLingo."

Fergus frowns.

"She's kidding," Vanessa says. Then she turns her head and hisses, "Stop being weird. He doesn't speak Natalie."

At least my friends are fluent.

Fergus tells us a few more basics, like how to hold our hand in a closed fist with our thumb up toward the sky, but finally, he opens a crate on the back of his big van and a grayish-brown bird with a striped chest and yellow eyes pops out, fluttering quickly up to his outstretched hand.

I can't help my gasp.

The bird's head tilts and he stares right at me for a moment before making a high-pitched chittering sound.

"The sparrowhawk's the single most common bird of prey in Ireland. They're small, as you can see, but very agile. In fact, they often fly along the small hedgerows you've likely already seen around Ireland on your way here." Fergus carefully takes one wing in his non-gloved hand and spreads it out. "As you might already have guessed from these short, broad, blunt-tipped wings, Ronan's a gliding hawk. We'll see a kestrel in a moment, which is our only Irish bird of prey that hovers. The sparrowhawk tends to dart and dive instead, always moving. It mostly eats other small birds, but it'll also catch mice, rats or other small mammals."

"It eats other *birds*?" Vanessa's eyes widen.

"It's kind of in the name," I say. "It's called a *sparrow*-hawk."

Vanessa laughs. "I guess so. It just feels. . .cannibalistic."

Fergus continues like he can't hear us—or maybe he's intentionally ignoring our bizarre side commentary. "Hawks can be a little more aggressive than most falcons around food, and when they're growing, they'll start to associate whoever feeds them with prey. For that reason, people almost never hand-raise hawks—a hand-raised bird's called an imprint. Generally you're better off letting hawk parents raise the fledglings and then placing them with a handler after it's time for the parents to abandon the fledglings."

"They call them imprints?" Samantha frowns. "Like, the plaster molds of people's feet?"

He chuckles. "Falcons will literally imprint on whoever has been helping care for them. Hawks will too, but it's not a great thing. Their parents abandon them around a year for a reason—they'll start attacking their parents for food if they don't. Sometimes you can also catch a young, wild bird. When a falconer does that, the young bird's called a passager."

"Passenger to what?" I ask.

"No, not passenger," he says. "Pass-a-ger."

Weird. This guy must be a leading expert on all things predator-bird.

After showing us how Ronan chases and retrieves a lure—a fake prey thing that he doesn't have to kill, but does get to eat—Fergus is clearly preparing to put him away.

"Why does he have bells on his feet?" Samantha asks.

"Losing a bird's pretty devastating," Fergus says. "The bells helped trainers find them before GPS tracking was possible. I like to do bells *and* GPS, just to be safe."

"And do you hunt with yours?" I ask.

Fergus looks smug. "Most of mine, yes."

"Most of them?" I can't help pressing, since that sounds almost ominous.

"I have a dozen different birds, some of them my own personal birds, some of them rescues. Notably, of the three you'll meet today, I don't ever hunt with the owl. Owls aren't great for falconry, but ever since J. K. Rowling gave Harry Potter an owl familiar, they've become extremely popular."

"Ooh, you have an owl?" Vanessa asks. "I love owls."

"See?" Fergus asks.

"Not because of Harry Potter, though," Vanessa says. "We had barn owls back when we were kids. Remember?"

Samantha's smile says it all.

"You liked them," I say. "Because your horse Adonis was a saint. But Royal hated them. He flipped out when they flew out of the top of the barn a few times. I can't say I was a huge fan." Those stupid owls got me chucked out of the saddle at least twice that I recall.

A few moments later, when Fergus gets the kestrel out, I immediately know which bird will be my favorite. A gorgeous, speckled bird that hovers?

Yes, please.

Fergus asks for a volunteer to hold Niamh. Since Samantha got to hold the sparrowhawk, I volunteer right away. She weighs almost nothing—but even such a tiny bird has a pretty tight grip. I'm grateful for the thick glove.

"Niamh was my very first imprint," Fergus says. "She's been a delight to train, and I catch more small game with her than with any other bird." He's beaming—clearly besotted with this bird. "She's the only bird I ever fly with just the bells."

"Why would you ever forgo the tracking technology?" Samantha asks. "Isn't there a bigger risk you'll lose your bird—and this is one you seem to love?"

Fergus nods. "But if you're like me and you got into this hobby in order to spend more time outside, staring at your phone the entire time to follow the tracking kind of ruins it. I think that's why Niamh and I get along so well. With her, I don't worry as much that she'll come back—she always has. I do regulate her weight, so I keep her hungry when I'm flying her, but even so, she's special. A bond like ours is rare, honestly. Many of my birds I catch myself and keep for just a season or two. Passage birds—the birds we catch and train—aren't usually with us for very long."

We ask a million other irritating questions, and he answers them all with a good attitude. At the end, he lets us stroke Niamh's back. It's pretty exciting—and she's a champ for the photos.

"Our last bird today's a little difficult," Fergus says. "She's a barn owl, which are usually not kept for falconry, as I mentioned. They don't have crops, like the falcons and hawks, so they fill up quite fast when you fly them. As you'll hopefully also recall, we rely on the birds' hunger to bring them back to us when we fly them. A bird that immediately eats and is full. . .it's a risk. But she wasn't raised in the wild, so if she escapes or I release her, she'd quickly starve."

"Sad," Vanessa says.

"Indeed." He frowns. "You can see why we're all a little annoyed that owls have become so popular. People who should never have gotten one do because they think they're cute. In any case, Eilidh was an imprint, which is actually quite bad. Her owner didn't properly socialize her with other owls, and she's not safe to release. We took her in after her owner suffered a heart attack. Poor little Eilidh has been grieving the woman's loss quite a lot. It's not common for birds of prey to refuse food, but she's gotten quite thin." He sighs. "We're not sure what to do."

"Poor thing."

"She does actually like people, or at least, she's not scared of them at all. Her former owner socialized her quite well around other humans. She went to a lot of renaissance festivals and whatnot with her. Often, after meeting a group of humans, we can get her to eat, so we've started bringing her to meet people quite often." When Fergus opens her crate, a tiny, mostly white owl with a heart-shaped face and brown feathers on her back pops out. She swivels her head around. . .and flies straight at Vanessa.

Fergus calls her, his arm extended, but Eilidh's not having it. She lands right on Vanessa's shoulder.

Fergus harrumphs and crosses toward them, but Vanessa shakes her head. "She's not digging her claws into my shoulder. It's fine with me if—"

"It's not safe," Fergus says, slowly approaching and gesturing at Vanessa's glove. "Hold your arm out away from your body like I showed you, thumb up, to make a proper perch."

Vanessa's staring right at the small owl. "Does this mean she likes me?"

"She certainly seems to," Fergus says.

Vanessa lifts her hand and brings it closer to her shoulder and almost immediately, Eilidh flutter-hops right over to her wrist, fluffing her feathers and then settling them again. She swivels her head, this time focusing on Vanessa and tilting her head to get a better look.

"She thinks you're pretty," I say.

"Actually, they can't see very well close-up," Fergus says. "Which is probably good. You are quite pretty, and her owner was *not*, but she clearly can't tell the difference." He sounds annoyed, but he's smiling.

Eilidh tilts her head, and hops an inch closer, making a sound that's somewhere between a coo and a chitter.

"What does she want?" Vanessa asks.

"She wants you to scratch the feathers around her neck," Fergus says.

Vanessa's eyes widen. "Will she bite me if I do it wrong?"

His smile's slow. "No, I really doubt it."

When my poor friend reaches out her bare fingers, I can tell she's half-terrified, half-in-awe, but when she starts to scritch the feathers around Eilidh's head, the bird closes her eyes and makes a little squeak that sounds a *lot* like delight.

We're there, watching and photographing, as Vanessa plays with this bird and scratches it, for a very long time. Eventually, though, Fergus asks her to feed Eilidh. I can hardly believe my eyes as we watch Fergus demonstrate holding the bits of raw meat right under the edge of her thumb. . .and Eilidh digs in.

Fergus is beaming when the little owl finishes her second piece, and he's quick to clip a small wire to the ankle cuff she's wearing. "She's eaten more than she normally would, so we'll need to keep her secure or she might fly away and not return."

"I doubt she'll ditch Vanessa here," Samantha says. "She looks twitterpated."

"Twitter what?" Fergus arches one bushy eyebrow.

"I'm just kidding," Samantha said. "I'm sure she's not in love."

"Actually, lots of people say that with owls, the imprint is either a mimic of a parent or a mate, so she very well may see Vanessa here as her new mate." He shakes his head. "Too bad you're just passing through."

"And also that I have no earthly idea what to do with an owl." Vanessa looks amused.

"You figured it out with the blue jay, didn't you?" Fergus doesn't look like he's joking at all.

"That was me," Samantha says.

"Whoops," Fergus says.

"Apparently we have a new bird-whisperer," I say.

Vanessa's cheeks turn pink, and I realize she looks happy. Really, really happy.

"Birds of prey can be aggressive," Fergus says, "but the falconry bond's a special one. They need us, and if we let ourselves, we sometimes find out that we need them, too."

In the end, it almost hurts to watch Vanessa pass poor Eilidh off to Fergus. The little owl just looks so distressed, and the noises she makes are heartbreaking.

"I feel like I'm betraying her," Vanessa whispers.

"If you email me." Fergus hands her a card. "I'm happy to keep you updated on how she does." His smile's kind.

And I can tell it healed something inside Vanessa, having something want her. Between Brent caring more about his estranged brother than Samantha, Mason cheating on me, and Vanessa's brother-in-law basically stealing from her, I think all of us feel a little betrayed.

One of the things no one talks about is how betrayal makes you feel.

Small.

Inconsequential.

Entirely and utterly worthless.

I keep thinking about it all day, during my massage and my facial, and right through a lovely dinner. As they bring us the check, I pick it up before anyone can toss their credit card on to split it. "I'm paying tonight, and you know, I've been thinking about something." The waiter takes my card and walks off. "Men are aggressive, and they mostly just care about food. They have to be tamed, and they're great at attacking things. Sometimes they're even cute. But I wish men could be as honest as those birds."

My friends freeze.

"I'm sorry." Vanessa drops a hand on my wrist.

"Me too," Samantha says. "Really sorry. Mason's an idiot."

I sigh. "And Brent, and Jeremy. They're all just monumental morons."

Vanessa laughs, and Samantha joins her, and as I scrawl my name on the receipt, we all look a little insane. I don't even care. Like little Eilidh needed some scritchy scratches, I needed this. Time with my friends. Time with people who *do* like me.

So I can like myself again, too.

To keep me from wondering whether I'm even likable.

When I drag myself back to my room, I'm a little jealous of Vanessa. She gets to go right to bed in her private room.

"I'm going to email Fergus about Eilidh." She yawns. "And then I'm going to sleep. I have to be ready to talk to the lawyer tomorrow."

Meanwhile, I have to wait on Samantha to shower before I finally can. Once I get into the bathroom, I realize I won't be showering at all. "We only have a tub?"

Samantha hands me a little metal plaque.

"What's that?"

She lifts her eyebrows.

I read it.

* * *

Sir Thomas de Rokeby was one of the first rags-to-riches stories of Ireland. He started out life as a poor Englishman, and wound up in prison in Scotland. Shortly after his release, he managed to warn the king of England of Scotland's impending attack, and he won himself lands that generated a hundred pounds a year, a great sum in 1327.

Later, after waging quite a few battles against the rebellious Scots, he was made the High Sheriff of Yorkshire. After seven years of solid service, King Edward III of England made him the Justiciar of Ireland—the ruler, basically. People were shocked. He was not more than a soldier, and this was a sensitive political appointment.

He served carefully, and paid no attention to the existing power structure. Drinking only from wooden cups, adorning himself not at all, he cleaned up all the bribes and embezzlement in Ireland, and he set things right. All the wicked people hated him, but the people of Ireland quite liked this particular foreign ruler. Not enough to quell their desire for freedom, but more than usual. For a time the king recalled him, but he thought better of it and sent

THE CRUMBLY OLD CASTLE

him back, where de Rokeby ruled until his death, here at Kilkea Castle.

We don't know what room he might have used, or indeed, whether this room was even around at that time, due to extensive remodeling in the fourteen hundreds. We do know, however, that de Rokeby enjoyed a soak in a very long, very wide tub. In his honor, this bathroom features the one tub still remaining from that time period, just as long and just as wide as de Rokeby demanded for himself.

Please wash yourself like a rags-to-riches ruler and think about how much your life might change, if only you were willing to fight for it—and betray anyone who plots to go against the king, of course.

* * *

The Kilkea Castle people aren't kidding. The tub must be at least seven feet long, and it's more than three feet wide. I'm not sure how they can handle the water bills. . .until I remember what we paid. By the time it's finally full, I'm dozing off. Once I've finished and I'm toweling off my hair, I check my phone. It's almost one in the morning here, which means it's seven p.m. back home. I'm more than ready to crash for the night.

I'm surprised when my phone rings, and I think about ignoring it. I am on vacation. But then, with a groan, I check who's calling. It's Fortress, one of my premium clients, so I hit talk immediately. "Hello?"

"Natalie?"

"Yes, it's me."

"I'm sorry—I know you're on vacation, but can you take a look at the social media posts? The wrong posts went live today. They were supposed to go live tomorrow, and it caused a big mess—I had to rush to the shop and key in the codes a day early, and we didn't have enough of the strappy sandals put out yet. I had to inventory them and rush them to the front."

I must have mixed up some of the days. My stomach ties in knots. "I'm so sorry. I swear, Donatella, this isn't the norm with me."

"Nat, I know. You've been doing this for over a year, and it's your first mistake. I just wanted to make sure it didn't happen again tomorrow since you aren't here."

"Absolutely," I say. "I'll check it right now and make sure everything else is right."

It's a nightmare—made worse by the fact that I wind up having to throw on a bathrobe and hike to the end of the hall to get decent internet. I crouch by the ice machine, rearranging the three posts I screwed up, but I manage to get them all set to the right times, I think. Time zones are complicated from Ireland, and my brain keeps rejecting whatever it is I need to make them simple. I'm back in the room, pulling the door shut behind me, and I'm about to call my best friend Tiffany to beg her to log in to my account and verify the times aren't screwed up from scheduling them here when I notice something.

Something disturbing.

Something my brain refuses to accept.

I was about to close out of Instagram when Tiffany's latest post popped up. It's a shot of her long, lean, tan legs on a beach chair, her hand wrapped around a tropical drink—maybe a colada—and the caption says, "Take your breaks when you need them. #Staycation."

She doesn't say she's at the Commodore, but I'd recognize her favorite local getaway from even the smallest, most-cropped photo. The canary yellow beach chairs, the white and yellow umbrellas, and the full, sun-drenched live oak trees in the background all scream out where she went.

We've been there together a dozen times at least for an overnight.

But I'm not with her, and Tiffany never goes anywhere alone.

Most importantly, she's wearing fabulous new shoes. Shoes I've never seen her wear, but that I *have* seen before. Strappy, fabulous, sparkly, hot pink, platform stilettos that I know are Valentino, because the last time I saw them, they were on the floor of my house, and I could read the label, plain as day.

I can't stop seeing them—just outside my very own master bedroom.

I was upset when I caught Mason, but catching Tiffany has me well and truly *wrecked.* Broadsided. Completely, sock-me-in-the-jaw flummoxed.

And I feel smaller than I ever have before.

Nothing prepares you for the discovery that your own best friend, your ride-or-die, is in fact a sparrowhawk of the worst order, willing to eat her own kind.

It's a red-focus attack if I've ever been hit by one, and I may never recover.

CHAPTER 9

Vanessa

When I wake, I feel better than I did the day before. It helps that I slept on the most comfortable bed of my entire life. I have no idea who this Earl of Kildare was, other than what that plaque said, but if the man had anything to do with my mattress, I'll praise his name all week.

Even after a great night's sleep, I'm still not very happy. I still can't believe Jeremy *sold* Jason's company and kept half of the proceeds—behind my back. At least we have paperwork to document this whole thing. Anything that's done on paper can surely be undone, right?

I pull up my email, hoping for a 'just kidding! What a joke,' email from Jeremy. Or some kind of email from my lawyer, saying they didn't know I had no idea, and they'll unwind the whole mess.

No dice.

I do have an email from Fergus Fitzgerald. That makes me smile. The subject line is *Eilidh*.

* * *

Vanessa,

I'm so glad you checked in on Eilidh. She ate even more when she got back to her enclosure yesterday. It's too bad you're not a resident of

Ireland. I'd try to convince you to adopt her. Here's a photo of her, fluffed up, and happy after eating.

You may not know this, but barn owls mate for life. Like humans, they often mourn the loss of a mate or family member. If any of your circumstances ever change, please let me know. Otherwise, keep checking in and I'll update you on her progress.

Cheers, Ferg

* * *

That makes me smile. I really hope she keeps doing better and better. I do have a voicemail from my lawyer telling me to call him back as soon as I can. I pick up the phone, check my reception, which looks alright, and call him.

"Vanessa," he says.

"Matt!" Somehow, after hearing his voice, my panic comes back. "How could you sell my business without me even knowing about it?"

"I assumed you *did* know," he says. "I represented the company, and Jeremy had signed powers of attorney that specifically allowed him to sign on your behalf, *and* he had letters testamentary from the estate filing."

"From the—what?"

"He probated your father's will—not through me. Another lawyer's handling that. Apparently he was right up against the limit on time there, but he has a lot of documentation showing that he owned half the business—I actually processed the corporate documents after he gave me the probate forms."

"I don't understand—how could he do that?"

Matt makes me walk him through what we did—how, before my father-in-law died, he asked if Jeremy would ever want to work in the business. At the time, Jer was obsessed with skiing and was working as a ski-instructor. He told his dad that all he wanted was money to compensate him. We had the business valued, and Jason and I took out a loan to buy out his share. Jason's dad promised he'd redo the will to reflect it.

"The problem's that your father-in-law either never updated the will to leave it all to you, or if he did, we don't have a copy of the new one. The will that's been probated shows that the estate should be split evenly among the two sons, and the corporate documents are still in Jacob Little-field's name."

After another half an hour of back and forth, Matt basically tells me that I could contest the will, and I could sue Jeremy. . .but I'd have to do both. And, both of those things would only really—at best—get me money back from the company. The purchasers bought in good faith, so no matter what, I can't get the company back.

The company I owned three days ago is gone.

It's like a nightmare.

Only I'm not dreaming.

And I'm never going to wake up.

I have to decide whether I'm willing to sue my own brother-in-law when it's just money on the line. No matter what, we can't unwind the transaction itself and make things right again.

"And remember that, since Jeremy has documents showing your payment to him was just a loan, and since he repaid that with the sale proceeds, and since the will supports his position. . .it would be an uphill battle. He's pretty likable in person."

He's very likable in person.

I'm not. Not really. Not like that.

He's a bereaved brother to my widow. He's a handsome single guy to my middle-aged woman.

Something occurs to me, now that I've looked over the documents with a clearer mind. "But he didn't pay the loan back," I say. "He just made sure I got four hundred more than him in the final transaction. I should have gotten eight hundred more, right? Even by his own interpretation, he should have split the proceeds evenly, and then he should have taken four hundred and interest out of his share and given it to me."

"Instead, they made sure you received four hundred more," Matt says.

"That's true. I should have thought about that. We could, possibly, get that fixed, at least."

So he stole from me, and then he stole from me even more. Why would he do that? It all just makes me so angry to contemplate. Which is why I'm pacing when the girls knock on my door.

Pacing in my fuzzy plaid pajamas.

"Oh my gosh, you're so stinking cute," Samantha says.

Bless her. "Uh, sorry I'm not ready. I just got off the phone with my lawyer."

I thought I'd composed myself. I thought I was fine. I hate that tears are welling up, even now.

"And?" Natalie steps forward, her eyes flashing. "What are we going to do? Sue Jeremy? Sue the lawyer? What's the plan?"

I burst into tears.

They wait while I get dressed, and then they drag me down to the cutest breakfast spot *ever* so we can hash and rehash the situation.

"I think you sue the pants off him," Natalie says. "I'll fly out and testify about—well, about everything. You told me about all of it as it happened. I knew about the loan, and I knew about the will, and I knew about the company and how you ran it."

"I don't think any of that's admissible," I say.

"I know a private investigator." Samantha nods slowly.

"Who lives in Colorado?" I can't help my smirk.

"Well, no. I'm sure he lives in Florida, but I bet he knows people who live there." Samantha clenches her hand around her knife like she's preparing to stab someone. "We're not letting this go."

I sigh.

"You can't let it go," Natalie says. "Is that what you meant when you said, 'if it's even worth doing'?" She shakes her head. "You *can't*, Vanessa. He just can't get away with this. It's too... Disney villain or whatever."

"But even if I did sue him, could I even win? Or would I just create all sorts of family nastiness—"

Samantha drops the knife and covers my hand with hers. "*You* didn't create anything. Don't forget that. *He* did this. You did nothing. You gave him money when he didn't want to work hard. You were a great sister-in-law, and you took amazing care of his brother and his niece and nephews. You're a rock star—he's the snake."

"Okay, but the point is that he seems to have been planning this for a while."

"Since the business took off, I'm sure," Natalie says. "But before that, before *you and Jason* took the risk to help Jason's friends, he did nothing. He took no risks."

"He did help me a lot after Jason died," I say. "It might have gone under without him and then there wouldn't have been any sale proceeds at all."

"And you paid him for his time—and it's his job as your brother-in-law to help."

"Still," I say. "He's going to make me look like a liar, and like a greedy, manipulative woman." I can't help it. I start crying again. "I hate this."

"I hate *him*." Natalie's eyes are gleaming.

"Me, too." Samantha sighs. "But now that breakfast's over, I vote that we head for Waterford. We've wasted enough time on him today."

"Oh, no," I say. "I can't go." I clench my fists. "I need to change my ticket and head home."

"Vanessa Littlefield, I forbid you to go home early because that *jerk* stole your company," Natalie says. "There's nothing you have to do right away. You can enjoy yourself—don't let him ruin this—and then go home after a few days' contemplation and decide what to do."

"You *do* have two and a half-million dollars," Samantha says. "And by the time we're done with him, you should have another million or so at least, right? It won't return the company you and your husband built to Trace and your other kids, but it's something."

It would be something. They're right.

"Let's go to Waterford," I say.

"I have *just* the playlist for this."

Natalie's playlist's pretty heavy on Metallica, Evanescence, and Alanis Morissette, but I'm surprised by how much better I feel after a few hours of terribly belting angry music. When Natalie parks the car in the parking lot of the Waterford Crystal factory, I half-smile.

"It's cathartic," Samantha whispers.

"The singing?" I shrug. "I had no idea it would help so much."

Samantha leans closer. "The singing's fine, but it's the friends that help. Friends you know would *never* betray you."

"Speaking of. . ." Natalie shoves the rental car key in her purse. "I guess I've been processing, and when I saw this last night, Samantha was already asleep, but. . ." She turns her phone outward and cringes.

I have to peer over Samantha's shoulder and squint at the small screen. "What are we looking at? Did you buy more shoes?"

Samantha's jaw dangles.

"What am I missing here?"

"That's your friend Tiffany's account, right?" Samantha's eyes slowly rise to meet Natalie's stricken ones.

"Guys!"

"She said that other woman had hot pink Valentinos," Samantha says. "I'm guessing *those* are the Valentinos?"

Natalie's mouth tightens. That's all the confirmation we get.

"No," I say. "No way. Your best friend?"

Samantha shoves me with her shoulder. "We're her best friends, idiot. Clearly Tiffany sucks."

"Majorly sucks," I say. "I'm so sorry—I blathered on and on about money for so long that you couldn't even tell us."

Natalie shakes her head. "Not at all. I could have—but you needed some time, and I was plenty angry to go all in on the singing." Her smile's small and crooked. "It helped me, too."

"Well," Samantha says. "At least now you have all the information."

"Are you kidding?" I ask. "Not even close. How long has it been going on? How did it happen? Are they in love? There's a *lot* more to know."

"I did make one decision last night, as I lay on the bed next to a snoring Samantha." Natalie looks utterly serious.

"Do I really snore?" Samantha looks panicked. "Are you serious?"

"She's kidding," I say. "I'd have noticed for sure."

"Dude, you definitely snore," Natalie says. "Not a lot, but you for sure make this little wheeze-rattle sound."

"Oh please," I say. "I thought you were kidding. That doesn't even count. When Jason snored, it rattled the bed frame."

"Just shoot me," Samantha says. "I thought the snore-guard was a joke. My mother-in-law snored, and I hated it so much."

"For the record, I usually find it cute," Natalie says. "It was almost comforting, knowing someone was there. The reliability of the tiny, repetitive little sound was not that bad." When the wind blows past, whistling, she shivers. "You know what's not comforting?"

"The wind?" I ask.

"Yep. Let's go inside." Natalie tosses her head, and we all start walking. "I did decide last night that there's just no way I can stay with him. No matter what he says, no matter what he does, I just can't. It's over. Like, *over*, over."

"But between the two of them, that's like everything in your life that's ruined," Samantha says. "You should pack up the kids and move back to Florida."

"My parents are there," Natalie says. "At least I'd kind of have help."

"Forget your parents," Samantha says. "Your *best friend* lives there. I'll give stupid Brent and his brother Frank our old house and we'll keep my nice, big one. You can move the kids in with me."

"You'd be pushing us back out in less than a week," Natalie says. "My kids are noisy, messy, and *everywhere*. Did you forget that I have five?"

"Crap. I did. I thought you had three," Samantha says.

"That's Vanessa," Natalie says.

Samantha rolls her eyes, slides her arm through Natalie's, reaches her hand out for me, and marches us to the front of the very classy looking Waterford Crystal showroom where we're hoping to buy tickets. They probably don't get forty-something women walking arm-in-arm and crab walking toward them very often.

Or at least, the very neatly dressed women who are staring at us when we burst through the doors look pretty shocked—right before they burst into laughter.

"Welcome to Waterford Crystal," the woman with her hair in a neat bun says. "You look like good craic."

"I think that means we look fun," Samantha says, "and you're right. We *are* fun."

"Doesn't it mean you've been drinking?" I ask. "I think I read that— it's used for when you're going out at night."

The corner of the mouth of the woman with the bun turns up. "No, no drinking's required, although people are often good craic when they're a little tipsy." She winks. "I imagine the three of you are."

"We'd like to book a tour. Is there one soon?"

The bun-lady looks a little judgmental now. "You're lucky it's the off season, lass. Thanks to the time of year, we do have tickets for the tour starting in just twenty minutes. You can browse the showroom until then."

"A showroom where everything's for sale," I whisper. "Did you see this *stunning* carriage with four horses pulling it?" I point and hiss. "Look at the price."

Natalie peers closer to the glass cabinet and gasps. "Forty thousand euros?"

79

"When you take the tour," the bun lady says, "you'll understand more about why that piece is worth that much."

"I look forward to it," I say. Once we're not right next to the employees, I whisper, "Because right now, it feels like it's the benefit of good branding."

"I doubt they sell a lot of forty thousand euro pieces," Natalie says. "But look at these." She points at some glasses. "That one has the big dipper on it. I might actually buy. . ." She ducks her head to price-check the whiskey tumblers, and straightens rapidly. "Nevermind. Still over a thousand bucks."

"I think you're the only one rich enough to buy something here," Samantha says, looking at me.

"Yeah, right," I say. "I have to put all that money in savings, and now I have no income other than my accounting job income."

Moments before our tour's set to start, Natalie approaches the register. She talks to the bun lady, and then she hands her a credit card. They murmur for a moment, and then she joins us for the tour.

"What was that?" I ask.

Natalie just shrugs.

The tour kicks off right away. We meet master craftsmen, hear how long they work from apprentice until master. Then we see them blow the glass. It's amazing to me that not a bit of it's ever wasted. Even when they're training, the old crystal can be broken, melted, and reused.

The lead content—thirty-three and a third—combined with the intricate cuts done by hand make it the most stunning crystal in the world. Even I'm a believer by the end of the tour. In fact, even though we're in Ireland, I feel somehow patriotic when we finish the tour.

Maybe patriotic's not the right word.

I feel like I'm a part of it all, somehow. I'm semi-seriously scanning for the cheapest item I might buy when bun-woman approaches Natalie with a bag.

"What's that?" I ask.

"I bought three sets of the Lismore Diamond tumblers. That's six— one for each of you, and one for the men we'll surely find once we're ready." She smiles. "Like this crystal, we may crack or even break under tremendous pressure, but our composition's still thirty-three percent lead. We sparkle, because we're special. And once we get away from all the misery other people have pushed onto us, we're going to be like these tumblers." She pauses for dramatic effect, which is *so* Natalie. "Perfect."

"What were you whispering with that lady about?" Samantha asks. "You could've just grabbed those boxes."

"I asked her to find us the nicest ones they had." She smirks. "I told her what we were dealing with, and that we really needed each other this week. I told her the significance of the purchase."

"Why is that funny?" I don't understand. "Aren't they all the same— isn't that the point?"

"When I picked them up, she told me she made sure these glasses were made from glass that was broken and reformed—not stuff that was just right on the first go."

"Seriously?" Samantha asks.

"Actually, she said two of these three boxes have glasses that were made from re-melted glass. One of the sets was perfect from the start, no cracks, chips or errors." Natalie glances at the woman and smiles.

Bun-woman smiles back.

"How do we know which is which?" I ask.

Natalie whips one of the boxes out and removes two of the glasses, setting them on the counter. "See how gorgeous they are?"

"Were these the broken and re-melted ones?" I ask. "Or not?"

"That's the point." Natalie smiles. "There's no way to tell. They're all just as stunning in the end—and we will be, too. Thirty-three percent lead."

CHAPTER 10
Samantha

After the tour, Natalie insists she's spent more than enough at the Waterford showroom, but Vanessa and I force her to do a little shopping before dinner anyway. I find a cute pink skirt I may never wear, and Vanessa finds a scarf in some kind of Irish family plaid that she loves. I'm not sure what the protocol is there, which worries me.

"Dinna worry," the clerk says. "In Ireland, it's not family or cultural heritage that determines the plaid color, but the county of your birth."

"So it's fine for me to wear it, even if I'm not from here?" Vanessa strokes the soft, smooth wool and cashmere blend.

"It's not your average 90/10 or even 80/20 wool to cashmere blend," the clerk says, clearly eager for the sale. "Our scarves are forty percent cashmere, which is why they feel like a shaggy silk, but they aren't as delicate and fussy as straight cashmere."

"It's also why it costs so much," Natalie whispers with a smile.

The clerk shrugs.

Vanessa's favorite is mostly green, with wide bands of blue, and small, narrow bands of yellow and red interspersing the green. "What's this one?" She holds it up.

"That's Waterford county," the clerk says.

"Hey," I say. "We were just there."

"And Natalie bought us all glasses," Vanessa says. "So I'm going to buy us all matching scarves."

It's almost as expensive as the glasses, when all's said and done, but they are lovely. Vanessa hands us each a little bag with our scarf in it.

"Thank you," Natalie says. "That's such a generous gift. I'm not even giving you the glasses. They're staying at *my* house, for when we all get together."

"What?" Vanessa snatches the bag back. "I need a refund!"

I laugh, but Natalie looks a little concerned.

"I'm kidding." Vanessa shoves it back at her. "I knew you were keeping the glasses—it'll be symbolic. We can use them when one of us gets remarried or something." She beams. "I call being the first." She drops her voice to a whisper. "I've been waiting the longest, you know."

We're all in a pretty good mood as we put our scarves on and walk back to the car. Vanessa looks five years younger with a scarf around her neck. Or maybe she just looks happier than she did last night. Who knows?

As we take turns showering at our Waterford hotel, I realize that including my travel day, I've already been gone for four days.

Brent hasn't texted or called once.

I've texted him every day with selected photos and details about our itinerary. He hasn't so much as liked a single message. I'm not sure whether he just needs time to cool off, or whether he's going to stay angry, or whether he's just *done* with us.

I've showered, and my hair's drying, and Vanessa's on the phone with her boss outside about some kind of discrepancy on some kind of boring accounting report, and Natalie's showering. I decide it's time to try calling, now that we've both cooled off, but then I do the mental math in my head. It's eleven at night here, and they're five hours ahead of us. That means it's—wait. I think *we're* five hours ahead. So it's six p.m.

It's the perfect time to call.

I hit talk, and then I wait.

For a moment, my heart leaps into my throat—surely he'll pick up. He'll apologize. He'll explain he'd had a bad day. He felt guilty that his dopey brother Frank's such a mess, and that he never helped him get his life back together. Brent'll tell me that he just wanted to do something—anything—to help Frank get back on track. Maybe someone on social he knows lost a sibling. Maybe he's just worried, because we're all getting older. Who knows? But he and I have so much—maybe he wanted to be Christlike or something. That would be nice.

Our marriage isn't perfect, but we've been together a long time.

I've forgiven him for a lot of things.

He's forgiven me for plenty of stuff, too.

It's what married couples do. There's a click on the line, and I say, "Hey, it's me." For some reason, my hope surges.

But then I realize, it's just going to voicemail. "Hi, you've reached Brent North. I'm either busy, or I'm at work. Leave me a message, and I'll call you back."

I inhale and exhale slowly, and then I hang up.

He's going to have a voicemail with the sound of me breathing. I wonder what he'll make of that. It feels pathetic, somehow. My own husband isn't answering my calls, and I'm the only one making an effort. I spiral a little then, my anger rising up to cover for my own sadness.

When Natalie finally finishes in the shower, Vanessa's just coming inside the hotel room again. I can barely make out their small, quiet conversation, but the words wash over me like soft rain. As they chat, I drift off to sleep.

The next morning, I check—pathetically—but Brent didn't reply to my texts or call me back. He didn't tell me why he couldn't take the call. He didn't ask me to call back today.

But it's fine.

Everything's fine.

I wake up energized, because today we're finally going for a ride together. It's been five days now since I saw Brent, but more importantly, it's been almost a week since I've ridden a horse. I haven't gone more than a week between rides in almost a decade, and each of my week-long droughts has been during one of these girls' trips. We've had the worst luck for the last five years—something has come up to keep us from riding every single trip.

Not today, though. I need to go for a ride.

I'm not sure if it's really the size of a horse's magnetic field like people say. Maybe it's something about their eyes, or the way their heartbeat can go from a billion beats a minute to resting in ten seconds flat. But whatever it is, nothing helps soothe me like being around horses.

Singing helped me when I was upset, just like it helped Natalie and Vanessa. This whole trip has been tremendous, really. Spending time with my best friends always makes me happy, but from the time I was a little girl, horses have been my happy place.

They're my home. My center. My safety.

Natalie put the whole trip together, but she updated us and checked in pretty often. When she sent me a link to the Fortwilliam House Hotel, all I noticed was the stable. Its cobblestone courtyard with robin's egg blue stall doors looks exactly like I imagined the barns for posh lords and ladies of the past would look. We're staying in the newly refurbished cottage house, and it's supposed to be right around the corner from the stable.

"I hope you all have your boots packed at the top of your bags," I say as I climb out of bed. "Because today, for the first time in more than five years, *we're going for a ride!*"

Horses brought us together, and for some reason, it feels like without horses, we aren't quite complete. Maybe I should've pushed harder for a week-long equestrian excursion, but the ones Natalie sent were both really pricey, and I worried that for Vanessa, who rarely rides now, they'd also be too grueling. Unlike Natalie and me, she can't ride a horse every day. She's lucky to get in a ride once a week.

A whole week of riding might kill her, or so she said.

"We have to grab a quick breakfast," I say, "because the map says it's an hour to the Fortwilliam Estate, and our reservation for the trail ride says we need to check in at ten sharp." I'm practically bouncing. "I mean, if you wanted to, you could just change into riding clothes now."

I practically live in them back home. When I get my turn in the bathroom, I go ahead and change into my Sync, lined, winter riding pants—magenta—and my stone LeMieux polo shirt. Last year, I grabbed a knee length LeMieux waterproof riding coat, the Anya, on closeout. Sadly, I've never found an occasion to wear it. I do live in Florida, and with the World Equestrian Center so close, I almost never travel anywhere colder to show.

For some reason, wearing it for the first time today feels fitting. I'm going to look fabulous in the photos we take, and I plan to take *all* the photos. I'm going to make Vanessa look like a photo-hater, with the photos I plan to take of our ride.

"Did you guys bring boot warmers?" I lift my eyebrows.

"Uh, no," Natalie says. "I didn't even think about it."

I grab a packet and toss them to her. "You can thank me later."

"I guess I'll put my gear on now, too." Natalie's grinning as she ducks into the bathroom.

I bend over to zip up my boots.

"Whoa." Vanessa sits next to me on the edge of the bed, still in her plaid pajamas. "Those are the fanciest boots I've ever seen."

"They're Kingsley boots. If you think these are nice, you should see their dressage line. They're so gorgeous that I almost picked dressage up just so I could wear them instead." I can't help my smirk.

There's no way I'd stop jumping to do horse-dancing, but it makes a funny joke. There aren't many people in the world who would even realize I was making a joke, but my two favorite people will.

"Let's make bets on what color horse we'll be riding," I say.

"Sorrel," Natalie shouts. "I pick sorrel."

"For which of us?" I ask.

"Uh. . ." Natalie fumbles with the door and finally bursts through. "You. I think you'll get a ginger, and then I bet Vanessa gets. . .are there many roans here?"

I shrug.

"Hm, well, I'm going with roan." Natalie nods. "I love a good roan."

"What kind of roan?" I ask.

She shakes her head. "Nuh-uh. Roan's specific enough. And for my trifecta, I think that I'll get a bay."

Vanessa rolls her eyes. "I think you'll get a paint."

Paint's Natalie's least favorite color pattern, and for some reason, almost every time we go ride somewhere, she gets a paint.

"And what about me?" I ask.

Vanessa taps her lip. "A gray."

"And for yourself?"

"I think I'll get the bay." Vanessa stands. "But you didn't answer what we get if we're right."

"I haven't picked yet," I say. "I think I'll get a fat bay with a blaze. I think you'll get a nearly-white-old-gray, and I think Natalie will get. . ." I smirk. "A paint. I mean, some things are beyond our control."

Natalie glares at Vanessa. "Are you planning to ride in those pajamas?" She claps. "Get a move on, sad sack!"

It works, and because Natalie used her mom-voice, Vanessa didn't even get offended. That's the one thing I really wish you could somehow manage to have without being a mom, but apparently it's impossible. When I try to use a mom-voice, I just sound officious. "Do you want boot warmers?"

Vanessa ignores me, ducking into the bathroom and shutting the door in my face.

"She's crabby today," I mutter.

"I'm not sure." Natalie plops next to me, her boots in her right hand. "I have a conspiracy theory."

"Ooh, I like these." I rub my hands together. "Share."

"So, five years ago, the morning we got ready to ride, Vanessa got sick. You and I had to go alone—she insisted we not miss it."

"Right," I say. "She was puking the whole time we were gone."

"But not a single time while we were in the room. The bathroom didn't smell." Natalie narrows her eyes, and I wonder if it's the same look she gets when her kids are telling her a sketchy story.

"Okay, go on."

"The next year, we got all the way to the riding place, but then when she went to mount, Vanessa pulled a hamstring."

I remember that. We had to skip two of the things we had planned afterward because they didn't accommodate wheelchairs. "And?"

"Then the next year, Bryce had some big emergency and she had to spend all morning on the phone with him, so she made us go ride without her."

"Yeah, that was sad—she said Bryce hadn't made that sport team or something."

"But Bryce is a total computer geek," Natalie says. "I'm not sure he's ever played a sport of any kind."

"So of course he wouldn't make the team." I frown.

Natalie rolls her eyes and drops her voice even further. "I think she might have made it all up."

I gasp. "How did she make up the one two years ago? That trail ride got rained out."

"But when they offered us a ride in their covered arena instead, she said no."

"Her husband had just died," I say. "Everything disappointing was a no that year."

Natalie shrugs. "And last year?"

That was strange. "They canceled on us last minute," I say. "But how does that have anything to do with Vanessa?"

"Instead of going on the official cruise ship excursion, she found the other one. *She* set that outing up," Natalie says.

"Because it was cheaper," I say. "The official ones way overcharge you." I can almost hear her saying that.

"Yeah, but Sam, I'm not sure they *did* cancel."

Okay, *that* blows my mind. "Are you saying that she—"

But right then, Vanessa comes out, wearing her riding gear. If she really doesn't mean to ride, why would she bring all of that? Why would she change into it at all? "Ready?" She arches one eyebrow.

We load up quickly after that, stop at a bakery and grab some croissants to go, and then we're on the road.

"Why can't they make pastries this good in the United States?" I ask.

"We regulate our food," Natalie says. "You have to have less butter than flour."

I start to argue with her, and then I realize she's teasing me. "Oh, stop. I'm serious."

"Just enjoy the delicious and fattening food," she says. "Some of us are trying to watch our calories."

Somehow, even though I got the front passenger seat, I didn't notice until that very moment that only Vanessa and I bought croissants. Natalie's eating another of her gross protein bars. She's had one every morning.

"Dude, you can't eat protein bars on vacation," I say. "That's lame."

"You know what else is lame?" Natalie asks. "Being single and fat. That's what."

"You're not fat," Vanessa says. "Saying you are ticks me off."

"I'd never say it in front of my girls," Natalie says, "but it's how I feel when I look in the mirror, so that's my truth. Breakfast's my least favorite meal of the day, so I'm replacing it with a two hundred calorie protein bar so I can justify eating nice stuff for lunch and dinner."

"Fine," I say. "But for the record, your truth is dumb. You look great."

Natalie rolls her eyes, but she mostly keeps them trained on the road, so I don't argue further.

"You probably already know this," Vanessa says, "but that's not why he cheated on you."

The only sign that Natalie even heard her is that her hands tighten on the steering wheel until her knuckles turn white.

"Or if it is why he cheated on you, he's a bigger lowlife than I ever imagined he could be," I say. "Either way, that's not on you."

"Can we talk about something else?" Natalie asks.

"Sure," I say. "Did I tell you guys I'm shopping for a new horse?"

"What?" Natalie asks. "Are you kidding?"

"Varius turns twenty next year. I'll never sell him, but I've been letting some of the juniors at my barn ride him, because he just can't jump quite as high—or he shouldn't, I don't think. I want to spare his legs for a long and full retirement."

"He still loves jumping?" Natalie asks.

"I'd never turn him toward a jump if he didn't," I say. "You know that much, surely. But I hear him grunt when we clear a jump now, and I think it's time for me to think about my next show jumper ride."

"It's sad," Vanessa says. "Watching them age and die while we just keep right on going."

"It's terrible they really only live twenty to thirty years," I say. "I agree. I hate it."

"Better than dogs and cats," Natalie says. "But not by much."

Her phone starts to ring then. I can't help it—it's a reflex. I glance down at the screen to see who's calling.

Tiff.

As in, Tiffany.

The pink, trashy-Valentino-wearing tramp.

I reach for the phone and then ball my hand into a fist. "Sorry. Reflex. I swear, I want to answer and just yell at her."

"Me too." Natalie's voice is so quiet I can barely hear her.

"Then do it," I say. "What's stopping you?"

"I need to do some things before I confront them," she says. "I don't trust Mason at all anymore, so I want to get screenshots of our investment accounts and stuff. They're both smarter with finances than I am, and I want to be smart about this."

"My business faux pas notwithstanding," Vanessa says, "I am an accountant. I'm pretty good at numbers. I'm happy to help."

"You just trusted the wrong people," Natalie says. "I know you're good with numbers." Her smile's kind.

The call finally cuts off. . .and then Tiff calls again two seconds later.

"I'm going to have to answer," Natalie says. "We're five hours ahead, which means it's only five in the morning there. Something's wrong."

"Hello?"

My stomach flips when Natalie answers.

"Hey, lady! It's like ten or something where you are, right?" Tiffany's voice is shrill and high, and I want to slap her. Hard.

"Yep," Natalie says. "But it's ridiculously early where you are. What on earth are you doing up?"

"I woke up to pee," Tiffany says, "and you know me. Once my mind gets spinning, I can't stop."

"Is everything okay?" Natalie's voice sounds weird. I wonder if her so-called bestie has noticed.

"Am I on speaker?" she asks.

"I'm driving, Tiff. What's up?"

"So, I happened by that shoe place you love yesterday, and the owner mentioned there was a problem with the social media. I thought I better check and make sure the other posts looked right, so I logged in with your profile, and I just saw something weird."

"Weird?" Natalie sounds like she's half-choking. I drop a hand over her thigh.

"Breathe," I whisper.

"What was that?" Tiffany asks.

"Just the map," Natalie says. "What did you notice?"

"Your social media account had those photos of Waterford—which looked really cool, by the way. But then I counted how many days you'd been gone, and you're a day short. Was that because you really did get that delayed on those flights? Or are you posting late? Or did I miss something?"

Natalie's laugh sounds almost like a bark. "You're too smart for me, I guess. You caught me."

"What?" Now it's Tiffany who sounds nervous.

I love it.

"Well, I've been lying to you—to everyone really," Natalie says. "I was hoping you wouldn't find out." She drags it out, still not clarifying.

Tiffany's quiet, too.

"Did I lose you?" Natalie's knuckles are white again, and her mouth's set in a grim line.

"No," Tiffany says. "I'm here—I'm just not sure I understand."

"As my very best friend in the whole entire world, I'm sure I can trust you to keep this secret for me," Natalie says slowly, seriously. "But here's the thing. The day I left. . ."

I hear Tiffany inhale.

"I had the dates wrong. I went to the airport, and I realized I was a day early, so I thought about heading back home."

"What?" Tiffany's exhale's loud and strong. Any doubts I had about whether those pink shoes were hers are gone. I wonder whether that's what Natalie's checking on too. "So what did you do?"

Natalie's glorious. Magnificent. She continues to drag it out.

Painfully.

I'm so proud.

I half-expect her to spring it on Tiffany—call her out. Accuse her. Hang up. Rant. Anything at all. Everything.

But then Natalie just says, "I didn't want anyone to find out what I'd done, so I paid for a Holiday Inn by the airport with cash and hid, hoping no one would discover my *dirty* little secret. I'm not so organized after all." She snorts. "But now, since you work with him, I'm sure you'll rat me out to Mason."

Tiffany's laugh is high and forced. "Not at all. I would never—*you're* my best friend. Duh." One more forced-chuckle escapes. "I can't believe you didn't tell me right away."

"You know, I almost did," Natalie says, "but then I got nervous. I wasn't sure how you'd react. I mean, how well do you ever *really* know someone else?" My dear, devoted, smart old friend just pauses then. She doesn't fill the awkward space with some kind of platitude. She just waits.

Punishing Tiffany.

Not nearly enough, but it makes me happy to see Natalie getting some of her—well, her Natalie-mojo back.

"Now that I know the truth, I can get back to my massive to-do list," Tiffany says. "I knew something was off, but I swear, I'll take your secret to my grave."

"Which might be the day Natalie gets back," Vanessa mutters.

"What?" Tiffany's voice sounds sharp. Nervous.

Natalie frowns.

And I realize that she wasn't baiting Tiffany. She wasn't trying to punish her. I should've known that—it's not who Natalie is. I would do that, but she never would. No, she was hoping, praying probably, that Tiffany would come clean. That she'd tell her the truth and have some kind of reason, an excuse, *something* Natalie could use to forgive her.

But Tiffany disappointed her again.

And then she hung up.

"I'm sorry." I pat Natalie's shoulder awkwardly, but I'm relieved when the GPS chimes that we should turn, and I realize we're only a mile away. I had no idea what to say, no idea how to comfort my dear friend, not when the main leg of her support system has betrayed her so terribly.

Of course, that's when the GPS cuts out.

"Just a mile to go," Natalie says. "I'm sure we can find it from here."

I fumble with my phone and pull it out, but I was looking at my email late last night, and that's still up when I unlock my screen.

Which is why I see the email from Brent at the very top of the list.

The title of the email is rather ominous: Decisions.

My mouth goes dry, and my fingers feel slow and clumsy as I tap to open the message. He dodged my call. He's ignored my texts, but still, maybe he needed a simpler way, a longer space to tell me how he feels. Apologizing has never been Brent's strong suit. I usually have to read between the lines to realize he's sorry.

I prepare myself for him to say he's 'decided' to sell the house to Frank for a fairer price. Or maybe he'll ask me how low, exactly, I'm willing to go. He could ask me to rent it to Frank for a hundred a month for a year or something.

I'd do it.

Any olive branch he offers, I'll take.

It makes me feel pathetic, but the idea of Brent not being there, not having my back, it's terrifying. He's been by my side for twenty years. Who am I without Brent? I wouldn't even be Samantha North anymore —he's literally my true north.

But as I read the words he wrote, my lips moving silently, my heart stutters. My blood chills.

* * *

Samantha,

You know my brother's struggling. My family isn't great, which is why he needs me so much. I've always made more money than you, and you spend more than me. Horses, horses, and more horses.

I rest my case.

The fact that you refuse to sell our old, rundown house to my brother for a 'family' price tells me just what a cold-hearted monster you really are. I can't be married to someone like that. Looking back, I realize that I never should have married you in the first place.

If I'd married someone else, someone who didn't have pelvic inflammatory disease, I could have had kids. Real kids—my kids.

I can't get the twenty years we've wasted back, but since you're not capable of changing, I can cut my losses. I've attached the paperwork for the house sale to Frank again. If you won't sign it, the next papers I'll send will be divorce papers. I already had Jay's friend draw them up—that's what took me so long.

I'm sure you don't care how long it takes, since you're busy spending more money in Ireland with your friends.

Brent

* * *

A monster.

He thinks I'm a monster if I don't agree to do what he wants. I think that makes him a *dictator*. I should probably sit on the message. I should think about it. Ruminate. Talk to the girls.

But I can't do it.

As Natalie drives our car down a picturesque, tree-lined drive, as we rocket our way toward the bestie-horse-ride I've been so looking forward to, my thumbs fly over the teensy keys of my phone.

* * *

Brent,

I will not negotiate with a terrorist. Send my liberation papers, stat.

I'll be delighted to sign them, but let this be your warning. Your delusions about our income won't convince a judge. I've made as much or more money than you for the entirety of our marriage, and we've spent almost the same thing—I should know. I'm the one who balances the budget, pays the bills, puts money in savings, and files our taxes.

I plan to take every single dime I'm entitled to or more, as any good monster should.

Soon-to-not-be-yours-anymore,

Samantha

* * *

"Everything alright?" Vanessa asks.

My head snaps up, and I watch as the most beautiful stone mansion I've ever seen comes into view through the opening between the trees. "Please, *please* tell me that's the Fortwilliam Estate where we're staying."

From the corner of my eye, the stables appear, and my entire body orients itself toward them. Their light blue doors look just exactly as I remember from the property photos, and all the darkness in my heart lifts. It's not gone, but it's not nearly as oppressive.

Brent may have tried to kick me in the teeth, and the blow may have hurt. I might even be broken, but Natalie was right. Even broken crystal can be repaired, and today, I intend to sparkle my monstrous little heart out.

CHAPTER 11
Natalie

Last year, we went to Cabo. The year before that, we had a five-day cruise out of Galveston. So when we started planning this trip, all of us agreed that we wanted to do something *amazing*. After years of prioritizing our families and everything else in life, we wanted to really go somewhere epic. Thanks to the shocking revelation the day before I left, I really needed to do some fun stuff. I needed time to think, and this trip has been exactly what I needed in so many ways.

But it's also been kind of a mess.

I mean, if you told me that I'd throw my ring off the side of a cliff, or if you told me I'd sit down in the mud and bawl next to a complete stranger, or if you told me I'd hit my life's low point on this most epic of girls' trips?

I'd have called you crazy.

But between my heel blisters, and finding out all my girlfriends were struggling, and finding out that Tiffany was the owner of the pink Valentinos, it hasn't exactly been perfect.

Until this moment.

When we drive up the beautiful, serene drive and then, through the stunning old trees, a fabulous stone mansion comes into view, I'm just suffused with a sense of peace. This is *exactly* what I needed. I'll spend the day riding horses with my best friends, and I won't think about the misery back home at all for the next few hours.

Samantha's been a little preoccupied with her phone, which is abnormal for her, but as we reach the house, her gaze snaps up too. "Please, *please* tell me that's the Fortwilliam Estate where we're staying."

"It is," I say. "It *is*." I can't help beaming. "Doesn't it look just perfect?

"I mean, it does," Vanessa says from the back seat, "except for that." I stop the car and glance behind me. I follow her finger to the far side of the house and then my eyes widen.

"A 'for sale' sign?" Holy cats. "If we'd come a little later, we might not have been able to stay here. I can't believe they're selling it."

"Good thing we came when we did," Vanessa says. "And let's hope that trying to keep it looking good for any showings doesn't ruin our trip."

"I just love that old stone barn." Samantha's staring. "Look at those sky-blue doors. They even painted the upper windows."

"It is really cute and also somehow classy," I say. "But, like, where do we check in? Did anyone see a sign or some kind of front office designation?"

We drive past the big house and down the road toward the farm, barn, and cottages, but we still don't see any signage.

"I get wanting it to stay classy," Vanessa says, "but for heaven's sake, at least let people know where to go."

We finally drive back around and head for the main house. Even if that's the wrong place, surely someone there can tell us where to go.

"Should we check the email again?" Samantha asks. "Maybe it'll say something about checking in."

I shake my head. "I pulled it up to read it again this morning, right before we left. We got one single confirmation email, right after I booked, and it said nothing, basically."

Vanessa sighs. "I don't see any other cars parked here either."

"Maybe the crew lives onsite," Samantha says. "Their cars could be in garages or around back. It's not like we're here during peak season."

"I guess," I say, but the general lack of signage and personnel's making me nervous.

"I'm just going to call the real estate agent, that Cillian Doherty guy." Samantha points at the sign. "Surely he'll know how to reach the property manager. They'll have to coordinate for showings and whatnot."

"I'm going to walk over to the barn," I say. "We're supposed to be going on our ride in thirty minutes. Someone should be over there, getting things ready, right?"

But Samantha's already tapping keys on her phone.

I do notice that, as I walk, she and Vanessa follow me like baby ducks. I've just swung around the corner toward the barn we saw earlier when I nearly plow into a woman with her hair pulled back underneath a little white cap. What wisps I can see flying free are almost as white as the cap. Her brilliant cobalt eyes, in a nearly unlined face that's at odds with the white hair, widen. "Begging your pardon."

"A person!" I can't help being excited. "Surely you can help us."

"Help you with what?" The woman's short—quite short—and fairly round, but she looks sturdy and not at all off-putting. "Tell me. I'll certainly do my best."

"I'm Natalie Cleary, and we booked and prepaid for a three-night stay here months ago. Do you know where we're supposed to check in?"

The woman's eyes widen.

I plow ahead, doggedly. She may not be used to handling this, but when no one else is around, she'll have to step up. "Is the normal check-in office not open until three or something? And if so, where do we check in for our scenic horseback tour of the Blackwater Valley?"

The woman's eyes have grown rounder and rounder, and now she takes a step back. "You—you booked and *prepaid*?"

"Yes, for lodgings at the Fortwilliam Estate Hotel. See?" I swivel my phone around and show her.

"Uh, Natalie?" Samantha's gesturing at me, like she can't *clearly* see that I'm already talking to someone.

"Ma'am, I'm not quite sure what to tell you. We don't have a hotel here, and anyone who tells you that we do is lying to you."

If she'd slapped me, I couldn't have been more shocked. "You—there's no hotel?" I blink. "But this says the Fortwilliam Estate Hotel, and the address brought me here."

"And this is the Fortwilliam Estate," the woman says. "But I've lived here my whole life, and I've worked here on this estate since I was fourteen years old, and there's never been a hotel. It's a private residence."

Which we've been driving back and forth through and now tromping around on like we own the place. I feel idiotic, and sick, and a little panicky, too. Where are we going to stay? And what happened to the thousand plus dollars we prepaid for three nights here?

"You're saying. . .we were scammed?" Vanessa asks.

The woman wrings her hands. "I'm not sure what happened, missus, but I know that—"

Samantha's now shouting, one arm waving around like she's swatting at flies. "Well, let me tell you something, Mister Doherty, it hasn't exactly been a wonderful trip for us *at all*. In fact, my friend just found out her husband of twenty years is having an affair, with her best friend, and my other friend's husband died, and her stupid brother-in-law just stole her company from her and her bereaved children, and I just agreed to sign divorce papers to end my marriage of twenty years, so I suppose this is about what we should expect. But when you're on your way home today, if you see a little grey Volkswagen parked on the side of a windy, stupid, Irish road, and three women sleeping in it, you'll know *why*."

She's crying. My big, brave, gorgeous friend Samantha's crying.

Brent asked her to sign divorce papers? And she agreed? When did that happen?

I feel sick.

It's my fault—I'm the one who booked this place. I should've done more vetting, I guess. I feel really stupid. On top of the thousand plus we paid on rooms, we prepaid for a horse experience that's clearly not happening either. As if on cue, one of the horses in the barn around the corner lets out a loud and seemingly distressed whinny.

"We feel your pain, lovely animal," I mutter. "Believe me, we do."

"Alright, well, we'll wait for that, then." Samantha hangs up, shoving her phone in her pocket.

"Wait for what?" I ask. "Because I really don't want to sleep in the car."

"I bet we can find something else," Vanessa says. "I'll pay for it, alright? It's going to be fine." She's looking at Samantha with the same soft eyes I probably am. Poor Samantha sounded a little broken on the phone, and I can certainly empathize.

"No, I'll pay." I whip out my phone and start tapping. "May as well really stick Mason with a painful credit card bill before I get home and unload on him."

"If you have any recommendations of something else that's close to here," Vanessa says, glancing at the poor woman who's still wringing her hands. "We'd be glad of any suggestions."

"You can stay with me for free," the woman says. "I have a little cottage just around the corner, and it's not very large, but one of you can have the sofa, and I bet my friend Maude has an air pad we can borrow."

"A—an air what?" She must mean an air mattress. My heart expands at the thought of this woman's kindness. There's no way we're going to impose on this poor lady, but I appreciate the generosity of the human spirit when it chooses to show up.

"Let's wait to book something," Samantha says. "The real estate guy says he's coming over to talk to us. He says his office is close—in Lismore."

"Cillian's coming?" the woman asks. "Right now?"

Samantha nods. "He said to hold tight."

"Aww, father above, I better go." She reaches out and squeezes my hand. "I was running a titch late, but if he sees I haven't even unlocked the place yet, he might have a word." She's smiling as she ducks around the side of the house and skips away. "You come find me after if you'd like to stay with me. I make an excellent pudding for breakfast."

She hasn't been gone long when I see what looks like a blue Audi A3 tearing down the drive. For a real estate agent, he sure drives like a demon. I'm guessing the homeowner isn't around today to watch and criticize, or he'd moderate his speed a bit. When the car door opens, I'm not expecting such a handsome guy to step out.

"He looks like Bradley Cooper," Vanessa hisses. "Did you have to shriek at him like a banshee?"

I can't help the smile that's tugging at my mouth when the man straightens his athletic-cut suit and strides toward us, his chin high, his eyes flashing.

I decide to spare poor Samantha. She's clearly had a bad enough day already. I circle around the other two women and intercept wannabe-Irish Bradley. "I'm Natalie Cleary," I say. "I'm the one who booked this hotel—

or, you know, tried to book it." I cringe. "The housekeeper already told us that there's no hotel here. We know we were scammed. I'm sorry we freaked out on the phone and basically pushed you into racing down here. We aren't insane; it's just been a really long week."

He surprises me by smiling and extending his hand. "Cillian Doherty. Believe me, I know that when you're on holiday and things go wrong, it always causes an inordinate amount of stress. It sounds like you ladies have already had quite the week. Are you the widow, or the one with a cheating husband?"

Samantha's trained her eyes on the ground, her riding boot attacking a completely innocent clump of flowering weeds beside the driveway.

"Cheating husband," I say with a half-grin. I'm not sure why it strikes me as funny that he knows us only by the nightmare of our life at the moment, but I suppose I should be happy that I want to laugh instead of cry. I take his hand and shake.

He has a big, warm hand, and he's got a good, firm grip. "Listen, this isn't a hotel. It doesn't have the things a hotel would have, like fresh washed white linens and a coffee maker or snack bar in your room."

"Believe me," I say, "we know. And the unbelievably kind housekeeper—"

"Mrs. Murphy," Cillian says.

"Yes," I say. "White hair?"

He nods.

"She already offered to let us stay with her." I sigh. "It was touching, but believe me, all evidence to the contrary, we aren't actually insane. We'll be able to find something else close by, and we can afford to pay again. You didn't need to come down here. We won't be smashing windows or anything else distressing, I promise."

"But if you have any recommendations for where we could go on such short notice," Vanessa says, "that would be great. You look like someone who might know the area well."

"Real estate agent and all," I say. "Or especially any place that offers horseback rides. Sadly, like idiots, we also paid for an all-day riding tour of the Blackwater Valley."

"I'll admit that I did rush over here to make sure you wouldn't set something on fire or break windows." He looks a little chagrined. "But after having met the three of you, it's quite clear you were just a bit overcome. To be honest, I feel guilty on behalf of my country. Ireland should be an amazing place to visit. I hate that visitors are dealing with this kind of nonsense."

"It's fine," I say. "It wasn't your fault. We know that."

"As I mentioned, this isn't a hotel," he says. "But—"

"We know," I say. "We'll be going."

He grabs my arm. "It's not a hotel, but it *is* vacant. We don't have any immediate showings, so I don't see why you can't stay here for a few days, if you don't mind the lack of normal amenities or the eclectic furnishings and whatnot."

Vanessa's brain appears to have short circuited. "You—we can—"

"We can't possibly impose like that," Samantha says, finally finding the use of her voice. "I'm sorry I yelled at you. It's just been a weird few days, and I think I went temporarily insane."

Even Cillian's chuckle's pretty hot, and the look he's giving Samantha makes me think he finds her not-insane-to-look-at either. "It's alright. In Ireland, we like our women fiery."

Whoa. Is he flirting with her?

Samantha's smiling back, and I feel my jaw drop.

"It's a very kind offer," Vanessa says, seemingly oblivious to the chemistry between Samantha and Mr. Irish Bradly Cooper, aka Cillian Doherty. "But we would never consider getting you in trouble with your client."

"Actually." Cillian shrugs. "On this particular property, I'm the client."

"You're the—what?" Samantha's eyebrows draw together. "You own this?"

"Well, to be more precise, my great-aunt owned it, and then left it to me when she passed five months ago. Having done absolutely no tax planning whatsoever, I have a massive amount of estate taxes to pay, so I don't have much choice. The property had to be listed."

"I'm so sorry for your loss," I say.

"Me too," Samantha and Vanessa say at virtually the same time.

"Oh, I was sad to lose her, but it was for the best. Her body was hale, but her mind had started to check out for long periods. I was trying to figure out how to get her out of this massive pile and into a smaller, more modest home, but she was not having it. I think she left this earth just the way she wanted."

"How did she leave?" I ask.

His green eyes widen.

"I'm sorry," I say. "Is that a rude question?" I shake my head. "Americans are brazenly curious."

He exhales. "It's fine—she was down by the river fishing when she slipped and fell. She cracked her head quite hard on a rock. The gardener heard the fall and rushed to help, but by the time they got her to the hospital, she'd already gone."

"At least she was active to the end," Samantha says. "My biggest fear is lying in a hospital bed for weeks or months on end."

"Same," Cillian says. "*Same.*"

They're staring at each other again. I'm not quite sure what to make of it. In all the time I've known Samantha, I'm not sure I've ever seen her flirt. She and Brent acted like an old married couple almost from day one.

"Again, it's a generous offer," I say finally, "but we'd never impose like that."

"Speak for yourself," Samantha says. "I want to stay here." She spins in a circle, stopping with her eyes on the barn. "But what's the situation with the horses?"

Cillian sighs. "Bollocks if I know. Aunt Clara turned this place into some kind of preserve for donkeys. It took me months to get the herd of them all rehomed before I listed this place. No one would ever possibly want it with all the incessant braying. But she loved horses too, and sometimes people gave her horses along with the donkeys. I know one of them's an absolute lunatic the undergardener's son said would just be here a week." He sighs. "Selling them off's next on my list to deal with, but I'm pretty sure they won't be capable of providing the easy afternoon ramble down the Blackwater Valley like you were promised, and trust me when I say I'm not a decent tour guide on horseback."

"Did someone say 'tour guide on horseback?'" A kid with a long mop of thick, wavy black hair and sky-blue eyes rounds the corner. "Because that's basically my calling." He pops a cap on top of his head and smiles. "I'd be happy to take you ladies out on a tour of the Blackwater Valley."

"Rían, if I find out that you were the one who put up a listing for this place as a hotel, or that you scammed these ladies out of money, I swear—"

The kid throws his hands up. "I would never do anything like that, but I do have some of the finest horses in Ireland right here." He gestures. "In fact, to show you that I had nothing to do with any of it, I'm happy to guide your tour on horseback, free of charge." His grin's practically devilish, but in a street-urchin way. He could've walked right off the set of *Newsies*. He's even wearing a little cap and a slightly dirty shirt. I was obsessed with *Newsies* as a kid, so I'm not complaining, even if this kid can't be more than twenty-five.

"I won't tell you ladies what to do," Cillian says. "But I wouldn't trust my life to Rían's judgment. He's not a bad kid, but his version of a ridable horse and mine. . .let's just say they aren't the same."

Rían rolls his eyes. "I'm not talking about them riding Scout."

"Who's Scout?" Samantha looks legitimately excited.

Now Rían does, too. "He's a thoroughbred I won playing poker, and let me tell you something." He leans closer and drops his voice, like it's a big secret. "He's the fastest horse I've ever owned."

Cillian rolls his eyes. "Stay well away from Scout, and you might not die today."

"We have a stable full of excellent trail animals," Rían says. "Trust me —I've been working with them regularly."

"All evidence to the contrary," Cillian mutters.

"I might come to work a bit later than you'd like, but I stay long enough to make up for it." Rían smiles. "A man my age with dimples like mine, I sometimes stay out a bit too late at the pub, and the horses don't mind having breakfast a mite later than they're used to. Believe me."

"I'm not at all sure that's true," Cillian says. "But so far, none of them have died, more's the pity."

"You don't mean that." Rían scowls. "And I'd never harm any of them, I swear."

Cillian glances at his watch. "I have to get back, but I'll call Mrs. Murphy on my way and see that she gets you all settled in. Feel free to use any room you fancy, with my apologies from Ireland." He winks on his way out, and I begin to wonder whether all the winking is contagious. It looks like Samantha wants to wink back.

"Careful," I whisper. "You're not divorced yet."

Samantha's head snaps toward me, and then her eyes widen. "I— you—"

Vanessa bursts out laughing, and Rían joins her.

"He's not bad looking for an old fellow," Rían says, "or at least, that's what me mum says."

Samantha's cheeks have now turned bright pink.

"Why don't you show us these allegedly docile horses," I say. "Before we can change our minds."

"Actually," Vanessa says, "if it's all the same to you two, I'd rather not risk riding horses that aren't really—"

"Cillian's bollocks on horseback," Rían says. "Fell off when he was a wee lad and never really got back on properly."

"That's Cillian's reason." I fold my arms. "Now how about you tell us, Vanessa, why you never want to ride on our trips anymore?"

My poor friend splutters.

Samantha looks like she's going to choke.

"Because I've been thinking about it," I press. "Something isn't right. I can't decide whether you've switched to Western and the English saddle scares you, or whether you just don't like riding anymore." I pause. "We'll love you, even if you don't like horses anymore."

"Speak for yourself," Samantha says, but I'm pretty sure she's kidding.

"I—" Vanessa swallows. Then she squares her shoulders and plows ahead. "Just like Cillian, I fell off, and I haven't been back on since."

CHAPTER 12

Vanessa

The first time I ever fell off a horse was on my fifth birthday.

Since five-year-olds are made of equal parts rubber and Red Bull, I sprang right to my feet and scrambled back into the saddle. The second time I fell, I was almost eight. It was a little frightening, but mostly because instead of a pony, I was on a massive, seventeen hand appendix.

It was a long way to the ground from his back.

I sprained my wrist, but that healed up quickly. I made it to my lesson a week and a half later. Using the brace while riding was hard, but I pushed past the discomfort.

I loved horses enough that I didn't even mind. Or at least, I loved my friends, and they loved horses that much. It took me a little while to understand the distinction. Samantha would have cut off her hand to keep riding. Natalie got antsy and itchy and grumpy if she didn't ride for more than a day or two.

Meanwhile, *I* was always fine when things were rained out, or when a horse pulled up lame and I had to take the day off. I like horses, and I've always considered myself a horse girl, but it wasn't who I was at a molecular level. Once I realized that Samantha and Natalie were fundamentally different from me in their heart of hearts, I worked my hardest to keep them from figuring out that I was a fraud.

It's probably been my biggest life secret.

After I had kids and got married, riding got harder than it was back then. It was also expensive—money I just didn't have as a newlywed and then as a new mom—and it was time-consuming. Plus, I wasn't someone who was willing to try and ride while pregnant, and between the birth of all three of my kids, I was pregnant or nursing for a lot of months. Once I had three small children, things became even harder. Who would watch them while I rode? Why wasn't I spending the money I had on them instead of on myself?

I went from riding once or twice a month to not at all.

Seven years ago, after Trina was born, Natalie came to visit to help me out. She heard that I almost never rode, and she was aghast. "It's hard to find time and energy, sure," she says. "But you have to make time." She had five kids. She'd been pregnant for longer, and she was busier than me. She somehow made time, because she *had* to—without horses, she felt like she was dying.

I didn't. "It's not just finding the time," I had explained. "It's allocating money to that, too."

"I totally get that." She nodded. "You need to find a barn that's looking for an exercise rider, and at first, you can do it for free," she says. "Trust me—you can always find a way."

She was right. I could find a way. The second time she followed up with me via text, I decided to try. It took a few emails and two calls, but I found a barn that needed a rider. I even *liked* riding again. It felt great!

The trainer at the barn I found, Brooke, made money in two ways. She taught lessons to kids, like Samantha, Natalie, and I had been. The second way was buying horses for cheap, cleaning them up, and selling them to one of her kids or a lesson program with another barn. Sometimes it worked perfectly. I helped her calm, train, and educate several horses, and it was actually pretty fulfilling, giving poor, neglected, and abused horses a second chance to shine. Other times, the horses she found were in terrible shape, and some of them had significant past trauma. Turning those horses around was *difficult.*

One of her prospect horses, Noodle, was an utter disaster.

If you didn't use crops or spurs while riding him, he would slow down, stop, and then lie down—rolling over you in the process to make sure you got off. But on the other hand, if you *did* use either a crop or spurs, he bucked. I swear, that horse was terrifyingly hard to ride from the start. But one afternoon, Brooke's blind Welsh pony had just given birth to a filly, and some horses go nuts when there's a baby horse around.

Noodle was clearly one of them.

Unfortunately, we discovered that while I was riding him. When Brooke's husband walked past with the filly on a lead behind her mother, Noodle lost his already very small mind and made it his mission to hurl me off and chase that baby. I wasn't easy to defeat, but he was determined. He slammed me against the side rails of the arena, bucked, reared, and then bucked again.

On that last buck, I went sailing over his head, and he ran me over, one cloven hoof catching my already bruised shoulder. After breaking my arm and bruising my shoulder, my inner thigh, and my head badly, I didn't have the heart to get back on the proverbial—or the literal—horse.

I haven't ridden since that day.

With time, instead of lessening, my panic about getting in the saddle again only seems to have worsened. When I so much as think about riding, I'm filled with panic. The only thing more terrifying than riding was telling my friends that I don't ride anymore. I've managed to keep the embarrassing truth from them for almost six years.

This is why.

Now that the truth's out, they're staring at me like I've just told them Jason died all over again. To them, I'm sure it's nearly as bad. A horse girl who doesn't ride?

I feel like such a phony.

"You fell?" Natalie blinks. "Why didn't you tell us? Was it bad? Are you okay?" She's looking me over like I might have been hiding a prosthetic limb all this time.

"I'm fine," I say. "There wasn't any permanent damage."

"Then why. . ." Samantha tilts her head, her lips parted.

I exhale. "I guess I kind of lost my passion for it."

Both of them freeze, their eyes widening.

"You lost. . ." Natalie's frown deepens.

"I don't understand." Samantha sounds broken.

"I knew you wouldn't," I say. "That's why I didn't tell you until I had to."

"You lied, you mean." Natalie says. "You've been lying about it for years, I guess." Her shoulders slump.

"Not because I wanted to," I whisper. "I was scared you'd be upset."

"I said we'd love you, even if you didn't like horses anymore," Natalie says. "And we meant it, but you have to at least help us understand."

"It was hard," I say. "Riding when you have kids is really hard."

"And as a widow, I'm sure it's even harder," Samantha says. "We get that part, or at least, we're trying to."

"I never even tried to ride after Jason died," I say. "I fell off years before he passed, and for a while, I couldn't ride with a broken arm, and after my recovery, I just..." I shrug.

"So will ye lasses be riding today?" Rían looks confused. "Or not?"

I can't blame the poor guy for being lost. "Yes," I say. "They both will ride. I'll stick around here and see whether I can lend a hand to poor Mrs. Murphy who can't really be delighted we've been allowed to stay on the estate."

"She'll be happy for the company," Rían says. "There's not a nicer woman in County Waterford." His smile's jovial, but also a little rascally. He reminds me of Trace—before his dad died and he started smoking pot.

"Wait, what about your mother?" Natalie asks. "Surely she's nicer than Mrs. Murphy."

Rían laughs. "Not even close. Me mam would gut me faster than you could say 'it's grand' if I offered to let strangers stay with us. She's not much like Mrs. Murphy, more's the pity."

"Well, at least he knows his mother," Natalie says.

"At least come meet the horses." I should've known Samantha wouldn't just let things go. "Or are you not even into touching them or being near them anymore?"

I worry that going with them will just encourage her, but I can't really say no to visiting the barn. I did want to see how many horses were here and I love looking at them—who doesn't? Horses, when they aren't completely covering themselves in mud or tooting as you put them to work, are quite majestic. "Fine," I say. "Sure."

"Mighty craic," Rían says.

I make a mental note of how he's using it. Craic isn't a word I'm really confident enough to use yet. I'm sure I'd use it wrong, and then I'd become the craic. I feel like a total fraud as I walk toward the barn, trailing Samantha and Rían.

Natalie drops back into step beside me.

"You couldn't tell me?" she whispers. "I mean, I get not wanting to tell Kathy Kusner up there."

"Who?" I can't help my frown.

"The first woman to win an Olympic gold for show jumping? No?" Natalie sighs. "Sorry. My nerd's showing. I'm just joking about Samantha." She snorts. "She's super intense, so I get not telling her. But me?" Her brow furrows. "I barely ride."

"What?" Samantha turns, and I realize we've reached the edge of the barn. If we turn left, it looks like we can walk into the back of the barn, but if we shift a little right, we'll walk through the inside courtyard, paved with small, weathered cobblestones. Six horses have their heads hanging out of the stalls, and I wonder whether they're always stuck inside. It seems like quite a shame if they are, with all this gorgeous property.

"We have ten horses on premises right now," Rían says. "But one of them's my Scout, and another one's so old his dark legs and face have started turning grey. They're over in that pasture." He flings his hand outward, and when I follow it, I see them.

As if the pointing somehow alerted Scout that he was being discussed, the black horse whinnies at us, ears pricked. Even from here, I can see the bay beside him's moving slowly, his head finally dropping down over the same fence line.

Scout screams his displeasure that Rían hasn't gone to see him. I remember that noise.

"Not now, Scout," Rían says. "I have work to do." He's smiling at the big, black horse, and it's clear he enjoys his work.

"The eight who're in stalls now are the ones we'll be meeting for today." Rían walks forward. "Although, this one won't be a good fit for any of you, either." He reaches out and rubs the face of an absolutely beautiful bay with his head hanging over the first stall opening.

"Why not this one?" Samantha asks, peering around Rían. "He looks stunning."

"You're welcome to try riding him, but Liam came here a few months ago, just before Clara passed. He's only five years old, and not at all broke.

110

You can halter him, and that's about it. I tried lunging him last week, and the idiot nearly ran me into the treeline."

Samantha sighs, but she nods. "Fine."

Rían keeps walking, and we follow him along. I notice that Natalie and Samantha both pet Liam as we pass, but I just nod at him and keep walking. The last thing I need to do is try and bond with one of these horses so I'll feel even worse about not riding any.

That's probably Samantha's plan.

She's probably hoping that, like that weird owl, one of these horses will somehow fall in love with me, act strangely, and I'll be convinced to get on.

Not likely.

Rían moves ahead to the next stall. "This pony's named Orla. She's a Cob, and probably our prettiest girl." The mare tosses her head and whickers, like she knows she looks like sunlight on shining wheat. I've always loved palominos. "They say these little feather-footed horses are the best rides for grandmas or nervous riders alike."

Everyone looks back at me, and I barely avoid scowling.

"Orla's fourteen years old, and she and her sister came to us as a pair a few years back. Their owner had three or four donkeys, and when they got surrendered, so did the two of them. Clara meant to sell them and never got around to it. They're both great rides, but they aren't used very much." When Rían stops petting her nose, Orla tosses her head.

"You do look like a sweet girl." Samantha takes Rían's place, and she moves her hand back to scratch Orla's nose. The little mare stretches her head out farther than I'd have thought possible, turning her head sideways.

In spite of myself, I can't help noticing that she's pretty cute, especially with the dapples all across her back and rump. "I'm still not riding," I say. "Especially not a horse that's been basically ignored for the last few years."

"I didn't say anything," Samantha says.

"You didn't have to," I mutter. "I know what you're hoping."

"This one's Riona, Orla's red roan full sister. She's twelve, and a little zippier than Orla." Rían seems to be reading the room, because this time he moves on faster. "Both of them would be good choices for either of you to ride." He bobs his head at Samantha and Natalie.

"If I wasn't five-foot-eleven?" Samantha asks. "These little mares don't look a bit taller than fifteen hands."

Rían shrugs. "Then you definitely won't want to ride Foxy."

"Who's that?" Natalie asks.

"Our Connemara," Rían says. "They say they're practically born broke, and I think that's almost true, but she's also our tiniest ride at just fourteen one."

"Where's she?" I ask.

Rían tosses his head. "Other side of the barn, but you'll know her when you see her." He moves ahead. "This boy here is Drew. He's our Irish Draught, and he was retired a year and a half ago from the Garda Síochána."

"The what?" I ask.

"You'd know them as the Guards, I guess," Rían says. "They're our version of your police." He sighs. "Drew had a stress fracture in his front leg here, and he could barely walk. Clara was saving some donkeys—she was obsessed—when she saw that he was about to be sold for slaughter. She fell in love with his sweet face, and she bought him instead. After a year of hobbling around in the pasture, what do you know?" Rían laughs. "One day, the old boy started running around, and then he never stopped. Clearly he was as surprised he felt better as all of us were."

"You're kidding." I can't help my delight. "Really?" I reach past Rían and pat Drew's nose. "What a great story."

"Apparently there's a surgery they could have done, but giving horses an entire year off in the pasture has about the same recovery rate. Now Drew seems to be entirely sound—fourteen years young and happy as can be."

"I want to ride him," Natalie says. "Do you think he'd be safe for me?" Instead of looking at Rían, she glances at me.

"Of course," Rían says. "He's almost bombproof, thanks to his past career. You could ride him through the middle of a parade in town and he wouldn't mind."

Natalie and Samantha are both looking at me now, and it's starting to irritate me. "I can like a horse and be happy he recovered without wanting to ride him."

Both of them turn away, their heads down a little. For heaven's sake, they're annoying—they're even making me feel bad for being annoyed.

I mean, they *are* just trying to help.

"Our last two stalls on this side are occupied by another set of siblings," Rían says. "The first one's Conor, who was Clara's favorite mount right up until. . ." He clears his throat.

Two large chestnuts, judging by the height of their heads, are looking at us all with a lot of curiosity. The one in the last stall's tossing its head.

"Conor and Dara are Irish Sport Horses. They're feisty rides, and they really like to move. Conor was so forward that Clara threw her spurs away." Rían's smiling. "She adopted him when his owner had their property taken for unpaid taxes, and she loved him so much that she tracked down and bought his sister."

Conor's a handsome horse with a sleek, rich coat and a mane that's slightly lighter than his red coat, which I believe makes him a sorrel, technically. He has a huge star on his face, and it really has five points—the one on the right side a little bigger than the others, making it look crooked. When Rían steps aside, I realize that his sister's even prettier than he is. She has a gorgeous face, with a big, flashy blaze, and her coat's covered in almost-shimmery dapples.

"Dara's the only horse here that Clara paid money to buy. Based on principle alone, she only adopted animals, but for Dara, she made an exception."

"Did she ride Dara, after she bought her?" Samantha asks.

Rían shakes his head. "Dara turned out to be even more forward than her brother, and Clara was aging. . .Dara was a little too much horse for her new owner."

"Who rode her then?" Natalie asks.

"For all intents and purposes, for the past year or two, I'm the only one who's ridden any of them."

"What does that mean?" Natalie asks, *"For all intents and purposes?"*

Rían sighs. "There's a neighbor who comes into town sometimes who's an excellent horseman, and Clara gave him carte blanche years ago, but he hasn't come around much lately—maybe twice or three times in the last two years. He's busier with his work than before, I guess."

Natalie and Samantha both look like they want to ask more questions, but neither of them presses.

"Do you really not mind taking them for a ride?" I ask. "Because you don't have to do that, you know. If you have tasks to do, we don't want to get in the way."

"Cillian's been planning to find new homes for these horses," Rían says. "It'll be good if we can tell the soon-to-be-owners how riders other than me did with them. And if you don't mind me taking some videos of you, that might help us place them, too."

"Of course," Samantha says.

"You *are* experienced riders, right?" Rían arches one eyebrow.

"Samantha was number eighteen in the FEI Longines rankings last year," Natalie says, "and she was number six a few years ago. She's been in the top twenty for almost five years." She shrugs. "I ride almost every day back home in Texas, but I rarely show."

Rían smiles. "That's just what I wanted to hear."

"Didn't you say there were eight horses?" I ask. "That's just six."

"Ah yes," Rían says. "Our Connemara pony and our little Kerry Bog are both around the corner sharing one of the big stalls."

"Sharing?" I ask.

"Neither of them likes to be alone, overmuch," Rían says. "They pace when they're inside, and in Ireland, with all the rain we've had, they've been in a lot." His half-grin says it all. "It's called the Emerald Isle for a reason—it's always raining."

"And?"

"I took out the divider on the two stalls across the way about six months ago so the two little ones can share. It made them both way happier." Rían shrugs. "They'd probably have been fine in one regular stall, but I feel better with them having more room."

We follow him around to the front, where Liam's now vocally asking for more attention with loud whinnying, and through the main barn entrance. Even with the lights on, it's a little dark inside. It's clear this barn has been around as long as the manor house. Still, it's a beautiful space, and you can feel the weight of the years and years of horses that have lived here. It feels almost. . .sacred. Which sounds crazy, but it still feels true, somehow.

Two tiny heads immediately pop over the edge of the stall door, one orangey-dun with a bright and fluffy mane, and the other a little bay paint, even smaller than the dun, but with big, expressive eyes. Its mane is almost evenly measured stripes of white and dark brown—like a zebra's mane, almost, but thicker stripes.

"How big is that paint?" I ask. "It looks teensy."

"The Kerry Bog ponies are quite small," Rían says. "I never ride her for very long. She's quite sweet though."

"I didn't think bogs came in paint," Samantha says. "Or maybe I'm misremembering."

"They're all rescues here. We think Teagan's a bog, but yeah, they're not usually paints, so who knows exactly what she is? She's barely twelve hands, so she's small enough to be a bog."

"And the dun?" I ask. "Which one's that again?"

"Foxy's our Connemara—the breed that the Irish joke is born broke. She's about the sweetest mare ever."

As I step closer, I notice something odd. "If she's super sweet," I ask, "then why's her stall gate *padlocked* closed?"

Rían doesn't get defensive—he laughs. "Ah, well, ye see, the Connemara are very sweet, but they're also very smart. She's been able to open every latch we've tried within a day or so, and not only that, once she gets free, she walks from stall to stall freeing all her friends, like she's engineered a prison break." He shakes his head. "The chaos this one causes."

I'm in love.

Foxy and her bright eyes and her miscreant mind—I adore it. "You just don't want to be stuck in a box," I say, stepping closer. "Who can blame you?"

"Certainly not me," Rían says, "but we have to think about the state of their feet and what they'd do to the pastures if they just ran amok. With nonstop mud, they don't do well. So." He gestures at the lock.

"While you go on your ride, could I just lead her around? Maybe getting out to graze would make her happy." My hands tremble a bit as I ask, but for the first time in years, I *want* to touch a horse.

"Aye," Rían says. "You're more than welcome to let her walk around in the paddock on a line. You just have to keep her away from the far end—that's where the swampiest parts are."

"Maybe her friend could go out there," Samantha jokes.

"Pardon?" Rían asks.

"It's a bog pony," I explain. "You said that part of the paddock is soggy—like a bog?"

Rían stares for a moment, and then he smiles. "Ah, yes, but that doesn't mean that—"

"I'm kidding," Samantha says. "I know it still has hooves."

"Natalie already called riding that big brute of a police horse," Samantha says. "What do you think? Could I ride Conor or Dara?"

"Either one," Rían says. "They love each other, so maybe I'll ride whichever you don't. But if you ride Dara, just know you're in for a *ride*."

Samantha's smile is bright. "Dara it is."

"Great," Rían says. "Let's get them ready, then."

"Are you sure it's fine?" Samantha asks. "I do feel a little bad, still."

"You're helping me work them all in less time," Rían says. "Truly, it's not just fine. It's welcome."

"Oh." Natalie's pulled her phone out, and she's staring at it. The screen's lit up, and I faintly hear buzzing.

"Who's calling?" I ask.

Natalie looks up at me. "Tiffany. Again." Her nostrils flare, and she hits talk.

CHAPTER 13

Natalie

When I walked into my own house and realized that my husband was with another woman, it felt like I was sinking. Life got darker, darker, darker. My world changed in an instant. Up was suddenly down. Light was dark. The axis of my beliefs tilted in a way it shouldn't have, and I wasn't sure what to do or who I was anymore.

But I kept breathing.

Because that's what you do. And the more I inhaled and exhaled, and the more I put food in my mouth, and I chewed and I swallowed, and the more I plonked my credit card down and bought pretty things, the more the bleeding from what felt like a fatal wound began to stanch.

I realized I was going to survive.

I felt like I might even heal, one day. Eventually.

And then I saw those shoes.

Hot pink Valentinos. The trashy-classy high heels owned by the woman Mason was with. Maybe it makes me a complete moron, but it honestly never even occurred to me that I might have been betrayed by both of the people I trusted most in the world.

Somehow, the second betrayal hurt *worse*.

Mason wasn't supposed to do what he'd done. It's right there in the wedding vows. Sickness and health, as long as you both shall live. I'm not dead, Mason, so keep things together. Be faithful. But I knew spouses cheated. It happens all the time. It's on the news. It's in books. It's in movies. Everyone knows someone who did it—it's a total cliché.

Plenty of people are probably hiding that *they* cheated.

We all change as we age, and when we grow too different from the person you're married to. . .it's not shocking for them to look elsewhere. But Tiffany and I haven't grown apart. I talk to her every day. I tell her everything. She's my biggest cheerleader, and my greatest confidante.

In fact, I almost told her about Mason.

It was on the tip of my tongue.

The only thing that kept me from blabbing was how pathetic and small I'd feel if she knew. The entire time we've known each other, she's been the winning friend. You know, the friend who is prettier, smarter, better educated, makes more money, has a richer spouse, has a more 'together' life, and just sparkles more. I'm not sure why, exactly, but it never occurred to me as a possibility that she might want anything I had.

To have her violate our friendship the way she did—she works with Mason, for heaven's sake. I'm such an idiot. I can't help wondering whether they laugh about me, about what a dupe I am. How unsuspect-ing, how stupidly trusting. Finding out that Mason was cheating on me *with her* made me feel smaller than anything else ever has.

Now that I know, I'm shattered inside.

Or maybe I'm a hollowed-out gourd.

Or an empty soda can, clattering down the road, buffeted by wind.

But that's not quite right either, because even old, used soda cans have a surrender value for recycling, and I feel like I must be worth absolutely *nothing* if the two people in the world who loved me the most could do what Mason and Tiffany did to me.

When I see that Tiffany's calling me again. . .I panic. I barely got through the call the last time, and only because of the element of surprise. I'm so full of rage and misery and self-loathing that thinking about Mason or Tiffany makes me want to sob. But I'm also chock full of *questions*. I have so many questions that they're bubbling up inside of me, clamoring their way out. They trip over one another, all of them vying to be first in line.

When did they first touch?

Who started it?

Was it just physical?

Or was it emotional, too?

Does he love her?

Does she love him?

Are they planning to leave me?

Does she secretly hate me?

When did it start?

How did it happen?

What does she want from him now?

What do *I* want?

That's really the only one that matters, and Tiffany can't tell me the answer to that. Only I can figure that one out, but I worry I won't be able to until I know more than I know now. So before the call can go to voicemail, I hit the green circle.

"Hello?"

"You answered," Tiffany says. "I was worried for a moment you might be screening my call."

Why would she assume that? "Not at all," I say, my voice only a little strange. "I'm just about to get on a horse, so it was hard to fish the phone out of my pocket." She hates when I talk about horses. They're the one thing she and I don't share.

And now I'm realizing they really *are* the one thing we don't share.

Ugh.

"Well, I hate to interrupt, but I had some important news." She squeals. "Guess who the new PTO President for next year will be."

"If you say it's me, I'll kill you."

"No, silly. You aren't even in town. It's me."

I can't decide whether she's actually happy, or whether she really didn't want to do it at first, and she's just gotten on board to be a good mom. "Please tell me I'm not an officer or anything."

"It turns out, if you're not going to be present for the election, they won't let you run."

"What a terrible tragedy," I say. "I might miss my ride, I'm so sad about that." At least, once I start talking, it feels less awkward. I just sort of fall into old patterns—the way I'd always talk to her.

"Yeah, yeah, I know this isn't really your scene."

"I thought it wasn't really yours, either," I say.

"If you had seen the look on that Blair Hersley's face." With the way she's talking and the tone of her voice, even without seeing her, I know exactly what she's doing. She's squeezing her earth-ball squishy, and her eyes are sparkling, and she's shaking her head. "But I beat her by a landslide. I mean, no one's supposed to know, but Hannah showed me the numbers."

Of course she did.

"Anyway, you're throwing me a party when you get back to celebrate."

"Oh, shoot," I say. "I can't."

"Why not?" She sounds annoyed now.

"I'm busy when I get back," I say.

"I didn't even say when. How can you know if you're busy?"

"I picked up five new social media accounts in the last few days, and I'm going to be swamped. Maybe you can host the party yourself."

"*Myself?*" She harrumphs. "You must be kidding."

"Tiffany, I'm sorry, but I just can't, not right now."

"Fine," Tiffany says. "I'll pay for everything, but it has to be at your house. I would look ridiculous if I hosted my own PTO President party."

For the first time, I step back metaphorically from what she's saying, and I realize that a lot of the things Tiffany says and does are dictatorial. . .and ridiculous. A PTO President *party*? What does that even mean? "What would the refreshments at something like that be?" I ask. "Chick-fil-a nuggets? Juice boxes?"

"Excuse me?"

"I mean, that's not a normal party to throw," I say. "And I know you want one, but I just can't be the one to throw it. I have to go, okay? I have a horse to ride."

"You're being weird," Tiffany says. "Really weird."

Because I told her no for the first time ever? "Am I being weirder than a 'PTO Presidency' celebration?" I'm being a little too mean—she's going to know something's up. "Fine," I say. "I'm just tired from the trip, I'm sure. We can talk about it when I get back."

"Where did you say you hid for the night in Austin when you realized you had the wrong day?"

"Huh?"

"What hotel did you stay at?" she asks.

"Holiday Inn," I say without thinking. "Why?"

"Since when have you ever stayed at a *Holiday Inn*?" She sounds so snobby, it's unbearable.

"Lots when I was younger," I say. "But in this case, a few days ago. I had enough cash to pay for it, and I didn't want to have to admit to anyone that I'd made a mistake. For some reason, at the time, it seemed to matter."

"But now it doesn't?"

Why's she interrogating me? Where does she get off? "You know what, Tiff, I have to go. I'm sorry, but everyone's waiting on me."

That's actually true, but even Rían, who has no idea what's going on, seems entirely fine with waiting. In fact, I realize that he's pulled a few horses out and clipped them into cross-ties in the center of the barn. He's handing grooming totes to Samantha and Vanessa.

Unbothered by my proclamation, Tiffany's still yammering. "You showed up at the airport in the middle of the day, realized it was the wrong day, and then just checked into a Holiday Inn? And no one even knows about this other than me and your horse friends?"

"Yep," I say. "That's all right."

"Well, I guess if that's what you did, that's what you did."

"What else would I have done?" I huff. "Fine. I was bored, so I went shopping. I got new boots and a new coat, because everything else I tried on made me feel too fat."

"Natalie," she says.

"What?" I ask. "I really do have to go."

Samantha calls out. "Hey, Nat, we can't wait any more or we'll miss our tour."

"Nothing. I guess I'll see you when you get back," Tiffany says.

"Sure," I say. "See you in a few days." I finally hang up.

"That was weird," Vanessa says. "Was she really telling you to throw her a party?"

I nod.

"And then keeping you on the phone when you said you were busy?" Samantha asks.

I shrug.

"Has she always been like that?" Vanessa asks.

I don't want to shrug again, but I'm not sure. "Maybe," I say. "But it never bothered me before. Sometimes when you find out things, your perspective changes."

"Find out things?" Rían asks. "Who was that?"

Samantha and Vanessa exchange a glance. I'm pretty sure neither of them knows whether I want to share my personal life details with a twenty-something kid we barely know.

What could be more anonymous than a boy I'll never see again? It's not like I'm a celebrity. I'm not delusional enough to think anyone would want to attend a party to celebrate my appointment to a school position, but I'm also not even important enough to *get* that kind of appointment.

Exactly no one cares about the personal life of Natalie Cleary.

"That was my best friend from back home," I say. "The day we left on this trip, I found out that my husband was having an affair, and then I found out. . ." I pause for dramatic effect. "The affair was with my best friend."

Rían looks suitably shocked. "And she doesn't know you know?"

I nod slowly.

"You could really use a ride with your friends."

"I could." My head swivels around, and a smile creeps onto my face. "What do you say, Vanessa? For old time's sake?"

The blood drains from her face, and I don't have the heart to push, even though I think that once she got into the saddle again, she'd be fine. In some ways, riding a horse requires excellent conditioning and strength that you have to gain one ride at a time.

But in other ways, it's like riding a bike.

Vanessa would probably remember exactly how to move the horse. Exactly how to stop the horse. Exactly how to move *with* the horse. Sure, her balance would stink, and she'd get tired easily. She'd be miserably sore tomorrow, but otherwise, I think a ride would do her a world of good.

"You know, when I got on for the first time after being pregnant and having a baby, I was always nervous." I shrug. "But it always felt *just like* I remembered. It was the next day when I could barely move that I felt the regret over my long hiatus."

Vanessa's face darkens, and I sense that I've gone too far. Clearly, I don't know everything. That's been made painfully clear to me lately.

"Oh, no," I say, when I realize Rían and Samantha have their horses tacked and ready, and now they're working on mine. But, like Rían said, Drew really does look like an angel.

Rían barely taps the back of his foot and he lifts his massive hoof. Rían darts around him like a squirrel, and Drew doesn't even bat an eye. In fact, the big old grey appears to be falling asleep while he's being groomed. I jog across to where they're swinging a saddle over his back.

"You should probably measure your own stirrups," Samantha says.

"They'll be a few holes shorter than yours would be, that's for sure," I say.

I'm average for a woman—five five—so Samantha practically towers over me at five eleven. Poor Vanessa's even smaller, at five two, and we also stand in height order for photos, which sticks me with the unflattering middle spot every time. Also, if the photo isn't taken from close, we look kind of like Samantha's children.

I slide the stirrup up under my armpit, shorten it a little and check again. Moments later, Rían has un-padlocked and haltered Foxy for Vanessa, and he's handing bridles to me and Samantha.

"Just stay in the pasture beside the barn here and you'll be fine," he says. "She's a big fan of grass, so she won't give you any trouble. If you get tired of leading her around, you can put her back in her stall, click the lock closed, and head to the house. Mrs. Murphy will have tea ready for sure. Cillian already texted all of us to let us know you'll be staying for a few days."

"Oh." Samantha slings the bridle over her shoulder and rummages around in her pocket. "Nat handed me the car key, but you might want it." She fishes it out and tosses it to Vanessa. She misses it, and it crashes into the ground and clatters along until it stops a few feet behind her.

Foxy's ears flatten, but she doesn't react otherwise—good horse.

"Throwing things?" Vanessa asks. "Really?"

"It's a Connemara," Samantha says. "I was testing her—she passed."

Vanessa's still half-scowling as we bridle. She's fully scowling as we tighten our girths, and as we walk out with her, she looks downright angry.

"Are you okay?" I ask softly.

She nods.

"You're not mad?"

"I'm a little nervous," she admits. "But it's fine. It's going to be fine."

I hadn't realized quite how scared she was after that fall. It must have been a bad one. "I think Foxy's going to take care of you," I say.

Vanessa smiles—she thinks I'm making a joke.

But I'm not.

Rubbing Drew's nose has already brought my heart rate down after my miserable call with Tiffany. Horses do a lot of stupid things—spook at blowing bags and waving flags, crash into stuff and hurt themselves, get stuck in ridiculous places, or slip in the mud and tear their bodies up.

But they've also healed me in ways nothing else could.

They ask so little of us, and they give so much. I can already tell that this big beast is like that. He's watching me with trusting eyes, and when we all mount, he stands steady as a big, white rock.

Not Dara, though.

She doesn't bolt, but she shies forward as soon as Samantha starts to swing up.

"Nope." Samantha takes it in stride, moves her back, moves her forward, eyes her, moves her back. Moves her forward again, holds her still, and then swings up in a fluid movement that even I envy.

Dara doesn't know what just hit her.

She's about to figure it out, though.

And Rían's smiling. He's realizing that he bet on a very good horse. . .trainer.

"I'll take the videos," I say. "You two look like quite the pair."

"Are you sure you don't want to stick around in Ireland?" Rían asks. "This area could use a great trainer."

Samantha laughs. "Sure, why not?"

He's beaming, but I can tell he knows she's joking. They wish they could be so lucky as to have Samantha.

"Ocala would flip out if you left," I say.

"They wouldn't even notice," she says. "Ocala's the only thing more conceited than your friend Tiffany."

"What's Ocala?" Rían asks.

Samantha and I are both laughing as we follow him down the path toward the Blackwater River.

"Ocala's a place in Florida, which is a state in the United States," Samantha says. "And the people there feel about the rest of the United States the same way that riders in Europe feel about all American riders."

Rían laughs. "Got it."

"It's basically the epicenter of anything hunter or jumper in the United States," I say. "And Samantha's their reigning queen, not to be confused with a reining queen, which is a Western discipline she would not be able to do at all."

"Stop," she mutters. "I'm a small fish in a relatively large pond there, and I could *totally* do reining."

I can't help rolling my eyes at both statements.

"Speaking of ponds and fish," Rían says.

We're nearing the edge of a pretty fast-moving river.

"This is the Blackwater, and if we head left, we can ride past the bend in the river, and come up alongside St. Mary's Abbey. It's the only Cistercian monastery for women in Ireland, and it's an easy ride." He's watching us for signs of interest.

"Sounds neat," I say. "Sure."

"Or if we turn right, we can go about the same distance, three kilometers or so, to Lismore Castle."

"Ooh, let's see the castle," I say, but at the same time, Samantha says, "I'd rather see the abbey."

I'm smiling, and so is Samantha.

"If you're not going to get sore, we could probably see both," Rían says.

"I'm pretty sure I'll be fine," I say.

As we move along, it's clear that no one has worked with Drew for a while. He's a good boy, but he's dead to my leg, and he's stiff and a little clunky. By the time I see the abbey drawing into view up ahead, the sun just behind it, shining brightly, he's starting to realize that I'm talking to him with my whole body, not just my hands.

When I press firmly on his right side, he sidles left as we move along. When I release that side and press with the other, he shifts right. "Good boy." I pat his neck. "You're such a smart guy."

When a flock of birds startles at our approach and bolts, winging their way up, up, and away, Drew merely jumps to the side. My heartrate accelerates, but it's no big deal.

Dara's reaction is another story.

Convinced the birds mean to kill us, she bolts. Rían and Conor take off after her. Samantha sits the spook beautifully, but it takes her quite some time to slow Dara down. I'm trotting along at a decent speed to catch them when another horse flies around the corner, barreling right at me.

I haul back on the reins, spinning Drew on his haunches, and we narrowly miss being smashed into horse-and-girl-confetti. "Good heavens," I shout. "Watch where you're going."

"Quite sorry," a voice calls from behind us. "There's never anyone down here."

Drew and I wheel around again, and I'm sure I don't look very forgiving when I round on the man. "Where's the fire?"

"Beg your pardon?" The man's eyebrows rise, and I realize that I know him.

Or at least, we've met before.

"Oh," I say. "It's you."

His full lips part, and his eyebrows climb higher still. "Oh, it's you."

"You?" Samantha has brought Dara around and she's staring from me to the gentleman who nearly ran me over. "Who is 'you' exactly?" She clears her throat. "How do you two know each other?" Now she's looking at me.

"He's the man I met up at Dunluce Castle," I say. "The one who saw me. . ." I cough. "When I *lost* my ring."

"Lost it?" Now he's smiling, and he looks even handsomer when he's smiling. "Is that the story?" His blood bay's breathing pretty heavily, even in the brisk weather, and he looks happy to be taking a break.

"You're the mud-sitting guy," I say.

"I didn't know you'd come back."

Back?

Rían's talking to mud-sitter. . .like he knows him.

"Do you live here?" Samantha asks. "I feel like I should at least hear your name." She's smooth. She knows I didn't get it before, and I wish I had. It makes for a better story if I can at least call him something other than 'mud-sitting guy.'

"You *know* him," Rían asks, "but you don't know his name?" He arches one eyebrow. "How is it that—"

"The pretty American and I go way back," mud-sitter says, his eyes still trained on me. "Don't we, er. . ." He frowns. "I'm afraid I didn't get your name, either."

Pretty American? Is he talking about me?

Mud-sitter smiles again, right at me. "I'm Richard Cavendish, and I'm delighted to meet both of you, officially this time."

"I'm Samantha." My friend's smile is enormous. "And the pretty American's my best friend, Natalie Cleary."

"Why were you in such a hurry, Mister Cavendish?" I ask. "Chasing a naughty fox?"

He chuckles, and when he does, I find myself even *more* impressed with his face. It's warm where it was merely aristocratically handsome before. It makes him. . .approachable in a way he wasn't. I'd have felt guilty even thinking that, before I found out about Mason. I haven't even noticed anyone was handsome for years until, well. Until right now.

Richard Cavendish shakes his head. "No foxes. I just needed a bit of a ride to clear my head."

"You did?" I ask. "Why?"

He shrugs. "Sometimes you just need some fresh air." He pats his horse's neck, and the horse turns around and bumps his hand with its nose. Clearly it's happy to be out and moving, too. It's a beautiful creature, a big, leggy blood bay with four perfect knee-high socks.

"We were heading for the abbey," Samantha says. "If you think you can control the speed of your diabolical mount, you could join us."

"Or you can carry on with your one-man race," I say. "We'll try and give you plenty of space."

"How do you know Rían?" Samantha asks. "And Rían, tell us, should we steer clear of this guy?"

Rían glances at Richard, seemingly unsure of what to say.

"It's fine," Richard says. "Go ahead."

"I told you someone helped me with the horses, someone who hasn't been around much," Rían says. "I was talking about Richard."

I scratch Drew's withers. "You're lucky if you've been able to ride this fellow. I quite like him."

"His recovery felt like a miracle," Richard says. "It was exciting to watch."

"So you live around here then?" Samantha asks. "Because your accent sounds—"

"British," I say, proud to remember. "I bet that's why Rían said you haven't helped much. You only visit here occasionally, right?"

Rían appears to be watching us in much the same way we watched the raptors on our guided tour. He's partially nervous, and very curious. I just can't figure out why.

Curious or not, he spills absolutely no information about the somewhat mysterious, British Mr. Cavendish. We do ride to the abbey together, and then we ride down toward Lismore Castle. Rían rides up ahead as the castle comes into view, chatting with Samantha. It could be that they're both riding forward horses, but it almost feels like they're giving Richard and me space, and that makes me feel vaguely guilty.

My husband may be a mess, but he's still my husband.

"I'm married," I blurt.

Richard's head whips toward me, and his smile is funny. "You don't say."

Of course he already knows that. He saw me chucking my ring into the ocean. I sigh—being a social idiot is tiring sometimes. "I'm not sure why Samantha and Rían keep riding up ahead," I say. "But I wanted to make sure you didn't get any strange ideas about them, I don't know, trying to give us space or something."

He laughs. "No strange ideas here, I assure you."

"Good."

"Are you going to forgive him, then?"

I snort.

"Or not?"

"Well, it feels a little bit like I'm on a soap opera and declaring myself, but here's the thing. The day after you found me chucking my ring into the ocean, I discovered who my husband was cheating on me with. It wasn't good."

"Don't leave me hanging," he says. "Is it someone I know?" He clucks and his horse shifts closer to mine, pulling just a bit ahead. "Was it. . .my cousin Beatrice? No, wait, Angelina Jolie?"

I roll my eyes. "He was with my best friend."

He looks around almost frantically. "Wait, there were three of you, and now there are only two." He lifts both eyebrows suggestively.

I can't help laughing, but then I explain about Vanessa being afraid to ride, and Tiffany the cheater being my best friend from back home.

"She works for your husband's company?" I don't like his tone, like I should've seen that coming.

"Plenty of people work with beautiful women," I say. "That doesn't mean that I should have—"

He cuts me off. "No, I'm not implying you should've figured it out. I'm saying she should be ashamed of herself, working for her friend's husband, and then betraying you like that." His brow furrows. "He should be equally ashamed of course. What a mess."

"I can't do it," I say. "I'm not going to be able to forgive them, but I still have so many questions."

"You're still reeling," he says. "That's natural."

Reeling. It's a good word for how I feel. "It feels like I'm tempest-tossed," I admit. "I'm up and down and. . .throwing my ring away and shouting and then crying." I snort. "Basically, I'm a mess."

"You're supposed to be a mess right now," he says. "How long do you have before your trip ends?"

"Not nearly long enough," I say. "Just a few more days, sadly."

He nods.

"I'm not sure what I'm going to do when I get home," I say. "I can't stay married, but I have nowhere to go. No plan. No idea how I'll support myself now that I have to raise all five of my kids alone."

"Five kids?" His eyes widen.

"Right," I say. "*Five* kids." I chuckle. "And what's funny is that I wanted more. I'd have had six, or even seven. But now, managing five kids on my own feels terribly daunting."

"You appear to be quite capable. I'm guessing you're a wonderful mother."

"Mother? Sure." I nod. "I think I'm good at that, but I certainly won't be dating again anytime soon."

"Too busy?" he asks.

I stare at him for a moment.

"What?"

"I'm pretty sure that any guy who hears that I have five kids will run screaming the other way."

"Not the good ones," he says. "And not once they've met you. They'll just be impressed."

"Sure," I say. "Sure they will."

"Well, I wish you the fortitude to withstand, and the nerves to hold strong."

"Oh, look." I point. "That's Lismore Castle." I can't help sighing. "It's so beautiful."

"You think so?"

That makes me turn entirely sideways. "Um, yes. I know you British and Irish people don't get excited about old castles and stuff, but we don't have awesome, historic buildings like this in the United States. It's always a little sad when places like that aren't open to the public, but it's almost good enough to see it on a ride. It makes it feel more. . .legit. Like even in this day and age, royalty and knights on white—er, blood bay—horses still exist." I can't help my grin.

"Would you even want to see the inside?" he asks. "Or would that spoil the magic?"

"You know, I was on a trail ride back in Texas once," I say. "My oldest daughter was only eight at the time. It was her first-ever trail ride, actually." I sigh. "We were passing this mansion. It was the biggest house in the entire neighborhood."

"And?"

"My daughter told me she really, *really* wanted to go inside it someday. I asked her why, and she said, 'because I want to see if their toilets and sinks are made of gold and silver.' Her eyes sparkled. 'And maybe the knobs are covered in diamonds.'" I chuckle. "She really thought the inside of the house would be as spectacular as the outside, and when I told her I really doubted it had gold toilets or diamond-encrusted faucets, she was pretty disappointed."

"Sometimes things look better from the outside." Richard nods. "You're a wise mother, as I thought."

"The world needs magical places," I say. "Even if they only exist in our hopes and dreams."

"Well, I'd love to see the inside." Samantha has wheeled Dara around. "But tomorrow we're going to see Blarney Castle," she says. "Since it's actually open for tours, that'll have to do."

"Blarney Castle, huh?" Richard asks. "I've heard kissing a stone there brings you good luck." He pretends to look around for something. "Know anyone who might need some of that right now?"

I roll my eyes because I know he's kidding, but he's kind of right. I'm definitely going to kiss that rock. Something that helps you say the perfect thing? I could really use that.

"You know, going back to face that jerk's going to be hard," Samantha says. "But there's something that might help." She arches one eyebrow.

"What?" I have no idea what she's talking about.

"You two move just a little closer together," she says. "And I'll snap a photo, and if that jerk Mason makes our devastatingly beautiful Natalie feel lousy about herself, I'll tell him that she's not a loser—a terribly handsome British guy *who loves horses* and has a lot of money was interested in her back in Ireland."

Heat floods my cheeks.

I'm going to *kill* Samantha.

"Sure," Richard says. "That's a good idea, actually. I'm happy to help."

When I turn to look at him, I'm absolutely floored. He's *smiling*. "You're kidding, right?"

He shrugs. "I am fairly rich," he whispers. "I do love horses, and I was disappointed when you reminded me you were married." He winks, and I swear, my ovaries contract.

"Samantha's just being stupid," I say. "Don't listen to her."

"After what happened to me," Richard says softly, "some days, I had a hard time remembering that I wasn't the loser I felt like." His horse side-passes beautifully, barely tossing his head at how close he's drawn to Drew. "When you have a day where you're not sure whether you're stunning, or whether brilliant men will want to date you, or whether you'll have a full, rich life again after this divorce, look at this photo, and know that you will." He turns then and smiles at Samantha.

So I do the same thing.

Samantha's ultra smug as she snaps the photo, and Rían looks like someone could knock him off Conor's back with a feather.

"Home for me is this direction," Richard says. "But thanks for joining me on the ride. It was much more pleasant than hacking out alone."

"It was a little like the first time we met," Rían says.

"Except you almost ran me over that time," Richard says.

"I remember." Rían's smiling, though, so he doesn't look too sore about it as the blood-bay rides away from us.

"Goodbye, Natalie Cleary," Richard says. "I'll be cheering for your success."

We start to move up-river, back to the Fortwilliam Estate, and I actually feel a pang of. . .something as the British man disappears from view.

"That was an *interesting* ride," Samantha hisses.

I'm blushing again as we move away. We're finally out of earshot when Rían says, "Now that he's gone, you *have* to tell me how you know the Earl of Burlington, and the future Duke of Devonshire, because I have *never* seen him look that jovial, not *ever.*"

CHAPTER 14

Vanessa

Foxy's as sweet as Rían said. She's eager to graze, but she's just as eager to interact with me. Every few bites, she turns back to bump my hand with her nose, as if to say, "thanks," or "don't you want any?"

I swear, if she could talk, I know just how her voice would sound.

Upbeat. Peppy. Kind.

Like an excitable but warm-hearted teenager who wants to be loved. Spending time with her feels healing in a way that riding along a trail wouldn't have been. The ride's for the riders. There's a conversation with the horse, sure, but it's not the same as standing with them, watching them eat, and interacting with their unique and calming push and pull.

Maybe all these years, I should've been volunteering at a barn as a groom. I'd have gotten the same sense of calm, my anxiety over life melting away, but I wouldn't have had the cost, the risk, or the fear.

I don't regret missing the ride even a tiny bit.

When my phone rings, I'm actually happy to hear from my mother-in-law. Some people don't adore theirs, and I hear jokes about them all the time, but mine was always a delight. She's been struggling with staying mentally acute lately, after losing both her husband and one of her sons.

"Hey," I say. "How are you?"

"I'm not calling in the middle of the night, am I?" she asks.

133

I try to calculate the time in my head—then I realize she's asking if it's the middle of the night here. It's the morning for her. "No, no, it's the middle of the day in Ireland." I can't help my smile. She was taking a shot in the dark, but she got lucky. She also remembered that I'm on my trip, which is great for her. "Are you alright?"

She sighs. "I'm most certainly *not* alright."

Uh-oh. "What's wrong?" I start thinking about what I can do from here—call her doctor maybe? Call Jeremy, though I might have trouble being polite to him over the phone right now.

"I just heard about what Jeremy did," she says, "and I'm not going to let him get away with it. I'm going to call the lawyer he lied to, and I'm going to make this right."

I have no idea how she found out, but my heart expands that she's upset on my behalf. "Oh, Trish, that's so sweet, but I'm not sure it can be fixed, not right now, anyway."

"Whyever not?" She splutters. "Jeremy had the audacity to act like the money you and Jason took out as a loan was a loan to *him*! He tried to lie to my face, and then when I argued with him, he told me I just don't remember." She huffs. "I know my memory's been a little disappointing lately, but I remember that like it just happened. Jeremy wanted nothing to do with the family business, and now he's *stolen* it from you." She sounds like she might be crying. "I can't believe my own son turned out to be a villain."

Even though most of what she's saying is correct, I can't really have my poor, sweet mother-in-law angry with her only son. "Trish, this is between me and Jeremy," I say. "Please try not to worry about it."

"But my testimony's what you'll need to fix it—otherwise it's your word against his. I was there. I can back you up."

I want to kiss her. "The only thing I can even get now is the money he kept—half the proceeds. The lawyer says we can't force the buyer to sell it back to us, because they were good-faith purchasers."

"I swear, I wish he was still small enough to turn over my knee. I must not have spanked him enough, probably because he was the baby." She sighs again. "I'm so sorry, Vanessa. I really am."

"It's not your fault," I reiterate. "Not. Your. Fault."

"Still, as soon as you get back to Colorado, come by and we'll make a plan together. I kept a lot of my documents and things, and I'm pretty sure I wrote about this in my journal when it happened. You can't ever let the bad guy win."

I can't help my smile. "Alright, Trish. I'll come see you just as soon as I get home."

As if she can tell the call was upsetting, Foxy gives up on the grass and swings her head against my face, rubbing my cheek with hers. I wrap my arms around her slowly—some horses hate being hugged—but she doesn't move, her ears still forward. I slowly tighten a bit, squeezing her until I feel better. After I'm done, I release her, and she goes back to grazing like it was no big deal at all.

Now that I'm calmer, I can think again, and I realize that Trish was right about one thing—the bad guy shouldn't win. Even if Jeremy succeeds in taking half the money from the sale, stealing from others isn't a win. I won't let him make me bitter and angry. That's the main thing I've realized on this trip, the power that anger and feelings of injustice have to drag us down.

I wonder whether that might help Trace, when I get home, to move on from the hurt he feels about his torn rotator cuff and the loss of his dad. I think he's spent a lot of time dwelling on how unfair everything has been, but life *isn't* fair. Fixating on it won't help anyone.

I'm reminded of how unfair life is when the girls ride back up, practically bubbling with excitement. "—no idea he was a duke," Samantha's saying. "Although, he was wearing a really nice suit that day, and he just plonked down in the mud in it like it was nothing."

"Who does that?" Natalie laughs. "I should've known something was weird then."

"Why's he here, though?" Samantha asks. "That's what I want to know."

"I'd like to know, too," Rían says. "Usually he comes for business, and he only spends a few days here before he goes back to London. He didn't say how long he'd be here or if he was coming over again to ride tomorrow."

Foxy's as curious as I am, trotting back toward the barn alongside me easily. "Who?" I ask. "What are you talking about?"

They fill me in, and I can hardly believe it. "He's a *duke*?" I try not to gawk, but it's hard. "From England?"

"Well, he's not a duke yet—his father's still alive." Rían says.

135

I wave my free hand. "Semantics."

"They do say he's worth a billion pounds," Rían says, "and I believe it. Did you get a look at Lismore Castle? That's his third or fourth residence. He has an art exhibit here that people pay to go look at, and all the paintings and sculptures that are on display rotate—their family's practically royalty."

"That's crazy," I say. "You just ran into him again, but on a ride? I'm sad I missed it."

"You should've come with us," Samantha says. "It was a lovely tour of the countryside."

"You know, we could take another round of them out," Rían says. "I don't have that much time before I have to report to the pitch for practice. We have a game tonight. It would help me if—"

"You two can't ride again," I say. "We're going to Dungarvan later, remember?"

"It's a cute town," Rían says. "And the castle there has free admission, though it's not nearly as nice as Lismore."

"Oh, oh." I bounce up and down. "Let's go see Lismore instead." I bite my lip. "Maybe we'll run into the duke guy and he'll take us on a tour!"

"Richard Cavendish, not the 'duke guy,'" Natalie says. "And Lismore isn't open for tours." She rolls her eyes. "Plus, I have to do some shopping at Dungarvan. I hear they have cute shops, and I've bought absolutely nothing for any of my five kids yet."

"If you finish your trip soon enough," Rían says, "you can come cheer for Lismore at the hurling match. We're playing Ballygunner, and usually that's a death sentence, but Shanahan's son's come home from Australia, and we think we might finally beat them."

Ballywhat? Shannawho? "I don't even know what hurling is," I say. "Do you guys?"

Rían splutters. "Don't even know—"

"That's what they call soccer here," Natalie says.

"Soccer?" Now Rían's entire face has turned red. "*Soccer?*"

"Sorry," Natalie says. "I meant lacrosse."

Rían's horse can tell how agitated we've made him. He's dancing around and tossing his head like he just saw a big, moving shadow or something equally terrifying.

"Let's get the horses put away, and you can explain what we got wrong while we do it," I say.

Rían has a lot to say—apparently we got it *all* wrong. Hurling's an exclusively-Irish sport that's nothing like lacrosse, rugby, or Gaelic football, which from what I can tell, is their version of soccer. It's run by a group called the GAA, and there are apparently big GAA clubs all over Ireland and in other places like Australia, too.

"Jack Shanahan's been on the team that played in Croke Park at the All Ireland Hurling Final the last two years, and now he's come back home to work, so he's playing for *Lismore* again."

I swear, Rían sounds, for all the world, like he's talking about LeBron James or Steph Curry. "I bet he's rich, then," I say. "Is he still polite to the little people?"

Rían's like a wind-up toy. Every dumb question we ask—and so far, they all seem dumb—works him up more. His arms are waving around, and his eyes are flashing. "He's not rich—the GAA players aren't paid, remember?"

"Oh," I say. "That's too bad." Not that I really care, but Rían seems to worship this guy. Then again, maybe it's good the kids here have role models who aren't rich. It's good to idolize normal people living attainable lives. I wish Trace had a few more healthy, average role models around. He's been obsessed with some body-builder on TikTok who made a gazillion dollars gambling for the last few months, and every time I hear another story about how he sold his car for three grand and bet on black before making it big, I want to cry.

"—actually, Jack's dad runs the GAA for Lismore." He's still rambling on, like we're going to retain any of this. "His dad's our manager, and he started the company that became TQS Integration."

Yet more words that mean nothing to any of us.

"Now Jack works for his dad, so he probably *is* rich, but not because he's so good at hurling."

"What time's the game?" Samantha's nearly done tacking down her sassy mare, and she looks like she's trying to placate poor Rían. "If we have time, we'll try to come watch. Sounds like we have a lot to learn."

"You do," Rían says. "The game starts at six."

Right when we'll be sitting down to eat and have a few drinks. There's no chance we'll go. "We'll definitely try to make it." I force a smile.

Once we head inside, a very animated Mrs. Murphy grabs not one, and not even two, but three separate room keys. "A lot of these old houses have special locks for the doors. They always welcomed a variety of guests, and when it was owned by the Duke of Westminster, lots of famous people came here." Mrs. Murphy whispers. "They say Coco Chanel never stayed here, but I'm pretty sure she did."

"Coco Chanel?" I ask. "Which room did she—"

Before I can even finish asking, Natalie cuts me off. "We don't need three rooms. We only booked one to share."

"You didn't book any rooms at all," Mrs. Murphy says.

"But if we occupy three rooms, you have to *clean* three rooms," Natalie says. "There's no way—"

"But if you're staying at the Fortwilliam Estate," Mrs. Murphy says, "you may as well experience it fully, don't you think?" She's beaming. "It's been terribly boring around here since Mistress Clara passed, so please humor me."

I can't summon the energy to argue with her, especially not when she dangles the prettiest key I've ever seen in front of me. Natalie and Samantha can't either.

Once we get them open, the rooms are absolutely exquisite. They're almost nicer than Kilkea Castle, but they feel less like a sanitized, stylized hotel, and more like a *home*. I can't quite figure out why, but it's definitely a different feel.

"Who decorated this?" I ask, as I spin around, taking in the large, bright, bay windows overlooking the courtyard below.

"The late Mrs. Clara Doherty decorated the house as it is now, but much of this was left by the prior owners. Her biggest task was bringing things all together in a way that preserved the past and still looked regal."

"You helped her, didn't you?" I ask.

Mrs. Murphy's shrug tells me that she did. "We kept very detailed records of where each piece came from, at least, to the best of Mistress Clara's ability to discover. There were quite a few letters and journals that passed with the house. She pored over them and flagged details that helped her figure out what time each chair, bed, and settee might have come from."

My room is bright, open, and airy. The carpet's sky blue, and there's a beautiful chaise lounge that coordinates, but is a few shades darker than the carpet. The wood in the furniture's dark and rich, which contrasts with the light carpet and upholstery. Even though we're on the second floor, the ceilings must be fifteen feet high. Clearly they didn't build this place when someone was paying an electric bill.

Thankfully, central heating was added at some point, because Ireland's too chilly for me to be satisfied with the fireplace in the corner, even with the jaunty fire that Mrs. Murphy clearly lit. The en suite bathroom's just as pretty as the room, with marble floors and stunning stone counters. It's been updated, too, with a shower and a tub. After I finish washing up, I change my shirt into one that doesn't smell of horse. When I head back out into the hallway, I notice Mrs. Murphy hovering on the landing by the grand staircase.

She looks. . .hopeful. Could she be worried we don't like it here?

"Mrs. Murphy, you didn't need to set up fires in our rooms. You worked far too hard, but this place is just delightful."

"When you've been managing a house for a year without anyone to tell you that you're doing a good job, it feels nice to have someone come visit, especially kind ladies like the three of you." She ducks her head and darts down the stairs, but I can tell she really is pleased to have us.

The girls emerge shortly after, and we walk down the stairs together.

"It feels like we should be wearing ball gowns," Samantha says. "Our hair should be curled, and we should be heading for a ball."

"I'm plenty excited to see Dungarvan," Natalie says. "From the internet photos, it's the cutest oceanside town, and there's a lot of fun shopping, too."

"Samantha's right about this place, though." I point at the fireplace in the entryway as we reach the bottom. "Fires in each room and the entry. These solid wood floors that look like they were designed by King Louis himself."

"King Louis?" Samantha asks.

"Louis the XIV?" I ask. "The most opulent monarch of all time?"

Samantha's brow furrows, like I'm speaking another language. "The point is that with the thirty-feet ceilings, the richly decorated sitting room in cream and gold. . ." I spin around. "This place is magical. It could be in some kind of historical romance novel for sure."

Natalie glances at the sitting room and nods. "With those beautiful sofas and the pale blue accents—those big, open windows." She sighs. "I could sit and read in that room all day if we didn't have a whole country to see."

"But we do," Samantha says. "Keys?"

I remember that I have them, and I fish them out of my pocket.

"Thanks," Natalie says.

On the way to the car, I can't help pointing out how well today went. "It could have been a real mess," I say. "We really could have wound up on the side of the road in the car."

"Thank goodness we didn't," Samantha says. "I'm way too long to sleep in a car."

"That scammer didn't post actual photos of the inside," Natalie says. "Or I'd have known there was no way we could have booked it for so little for all three nights."

As we're getting in the car, Mrs. Murphy catches us. "I'm headed home, so I'll be locking up."

We walk her through our plans to see Dungarvan and do a little shopping.

She gives us an exterior key for the side door and her cell phone number. "Call me if you have questions or anything comes up. Otherwise, I'll be back tomorrow around eight-thirty in the morning."

On the way to Dungarvan, we all agree that we're extraordinarily lucky.

"If you can call being scammed good luck," Samantha says. "But honestly, staying at the Fortwilliam Estate is cooler than if we'd booked a normal place and been welcomed in."

"It is," I say. "I can't believe how steeped in elegance it is. I feel like a princess in a story."

"We *are* sort of like princesses," Natalie says. "And like the princesses in stories, we're all kind of surrounded by choices forced upon us by villains."

"What are you going to do when you get back?" I ask. "Do you know yet?"

Natalie sighs.

"You always have a plan," Samantha says. "Just tell us what it is."

"I don't have a plan." Natalie's voice is small.

I hate it.

"You can't make a plan when your entire world's burning." She's frowning, but her eyes are still on the road ahead. "But I've decided—when I get back, I'm going to tell Mason that I know, and that it's the end of 'us.' I'm going to tell him I want to sell the house, and I'm going to immediately start looking for a new one—a smaller one. I'll try not to uproot the kids from school, but I may have to. I just have to go somewhere that every single person doesn't know me as Mason's wife."

"And Tiffany's best friend?" Samantha's in the back seat this time, but she seems to think seatbelts are optional. She's leaning forward, one hand on Natalie's shoulder.

"Dude," I say. "Buckle up."

"Our safety relies on this woman driving well." Samantha pats Natalie again. "I'm keeping her safe, therefore I'm keeping myself safe."

"She's driving on the wrong side of the road. Safe or not, we're all in constant danger here," I say.

At least they laugh at that, even if Natalie's mirth sounds a little forced.

"Don't feel too bad about the kids," I say. "Clara's old enough to drive, so as long as it's reasonably close, she can stay at the same high school if she wants. The others are young enough to deal with a move. Plenty of kids do."

"I agree—don't put yourself and what you need behind the kids. Not when you're going through this," Samantha says.

"But I can't really call myself a mother unless I do." Natalie's frowning.

"Are you worried he'll hide money from you?" Samantha asks. "Or about how you'll support the kids?"

"Really?" I hiss. "Don't stress her. She'll figure that stuff out."

"We won't be able to live in the same fashion we have been," Natalie says. "But Texas law says Mason and I will have to split everything we acquired during our marriage right down the middle, and that's everything." She nods. "He'll have to pay some child support, and I'll just have to figure out how to find more social media accounts to run."

"What do you make for doing that?" I'm not sure I want to know. I tend to worry too much about other people.

"Right now, two hundred bucks a month, per business. Two of them opted for premium service, and that's three hundred. I have eight clients. So, I make just under two grand a month, but it only takes me about ten hours a week. If I can find more clients, I can work more like twenty or thirty hours a week. I'd still be able to attend all my kid's activities. Things'll be tight, but with a few thousand a month for child support. . ." I sigh. "I'll just have to figure it out."

"What about your dad's estate?" Samantha asks. "Didn't you say you're his only heir?"

"My dad was a mess, though, remember?"

"He had five wives, or something, right?" I ask.

"Three, but two more serious girlfriends, so same thing, really. He was a dentist, and he did reasonably well, but all of those women made some claim to his estate. The lawyer thinks mine's the primary claim, but who knows how long it will be until I get anything, or what might be left after legal fees when I do. Dad liked to spend money as well, so I'm definitely not counting on anything there."

"Right, but once you get half of whatever you and Mason have, and after you get child support, and when you've grown your business some," I say. "You'll be fine."

"I hope so."

"What if Mason tells you that he's the father of your kids, and that he needs another chance?" Samantha's being annoying.

"Stop," I say.

"I'm not kidding," Samantha says, "What if Mason begs you not to throw away what the two of you have? You've spent twenty years together."

Natalie's frowning.

A quick glance to the back shows me that Samantha is, too.

"What's going on?" I can't tell what Samantha's getting at.

"It's hard to throw something away sometimes, even when you're mad," Samantha says.

"Are you talking about Brent?" Natalie asks.

"He sent me a pretty nasty message, and I emailed back and told him I was okay with a divorce," she says. "But now I'm feeling kind of weird about it. Am I being too hasty?"

"I'm the wrong one to ask," Natalie says. "I haven't even talked to Mason, but given the person he was cheating with, I can't imagine I'll change my mind."

"Maybe I should fly to Austin before I head home," Samantha says.

"It'll give me more time to think, and I can stand behind you with a base-ball bat and nod and thwack it against my hand in case Mason gets any aggressive ideas."

We all laugh.

For one moment, it feels good—like what a girls' trip should be. The shopping in Dungarvan isn't quite what I'd hoped, but I do find a cute green jacket with a shamrock on it. It's quite touristy and it says "Ireland" in orange lettering on the back, but I buy it anyway.

Natalie finds some candy for her five-year-old son, Paul, matching t-shirts for the nine-year-old twins who love to confuse everyone, and an adorable wool sheep with a little blue cap on its head for her fourteen-year-old daughter, Hannah.

"Whoa," I say. "I just realized your oldest daughter has the same name as the dead lady whose house we're at."

Natalie turns toward me slowly. "You just now remembered?" Her smile grows slowly. "It may have been too long since we got our families together."

"More than six years," I say. "I haven't even met Paul."

"I didn't realize that," Natalie says. "Trina wasn't even one yet."

Samantha asks, "Speaking of, have you found anything for Clara yet?"

Natalie sighs. "She's the hardest to shop for. Clara likes alternative music, and playing guitar, and not much else."

"I thought she liked horses, too," Samantha says. "No?"

Natalie shrugs. "She still takes lessons, but just one a week, and she hasn't shown in a year. Teenagers are hard. Our parents had it easy."

"I'm not sure horse girls could be called easy," I say. "But at least we weren't hard to shop for, and you could always find us at the barn." I'd give a lot to have that as my issue with Trace. I notice a book that's glaring at me from right beneath my elbow. "What about this?"

Irish Folk Ballads. I flip it around so she can see it.

Natalie nods her head slowly. "It's probably as good as anything else." She sighs. "When I talked to my kids this morning, Clara passed the phone off after two minutes to go work on her latest song. I'm sure she can make a punk version of all these songs and call them alternative or something."

"You could pick up some eyeliner for her at the airport on the way home," Samantha says.

Natalie shakes her head. "No, because makeup's another way the patriarchal system chains us down. Didn't you hear?"

"Seriously? Listening to the two of you makes me just a teensy bit less sad I never had kids," Samantha says. "I would be a terrible mother to teenagers."

"The good news," Natalie says, "is that we're all terrible at it. I'm not sure anyone knows how to deal with teenage mood swings."

Once we're done shopping, we head for Dungarvan Castle. It's both depressing and fascinating. It feels a bit like my life right now. It has an unusually shaped shell-keep castle, which is basically a bunch of stone walls and barracks created to protect Dungarvan Harbor. The structure itself was well built, but it still kept turning over from one group to the next. Most recently, before it was overrun with tour groups, the castle was the building that housed the local police force, the Irish Garda Síochána.

My favorite part of the tour's actually the beautiful southwest tower. At various points, it was where they displayed heads of criminals who had been executed—blech—but now, thanks to its beauty and shape, it's used for. . .wait for it. . .

Weddings.

"I can't even imagine having my wedding in a place where they used to put people's heads to dissuade the population from rebelling."

"I don't know," Natalie says. "There's something kind of, I don't know, cathartic? Is that the word? About this place being transformed. It endured a lot of misery and disgusting barbarism, but now it's a place of light and joy."

"Plus, we all got married in light and bright wedding chapels—or at the beach." She arches her eyebrow at me. "And look at us."

She's not wrong there. One miserable widow and two soon-to-be divorcees. It's a depressing thought. You can do everything right and still end up getting your teeth kicked in.

We're headed back to town, the beautiful afternoon sun shining over the green world all around us, and I feel strangely peaceful. No matter how bad our lives might feel sometimes, the nation's not at war. No one's threatening to kill us. All our problems are far simpler to solve than the issues that the average Irish citizen faced for most of the country's history.

"Ireland's a beautiful place," I say. "But I'm glad we're here now and not two hundred years ago."

"Same," Natalie says. "There are so many old things here. In America, the early nineteen hundreds feels old. Eighteen hundreds is ancient. But here, that's like, almost recent. You can soak up the history without dealing with the misogyny and danger."

"You two are getting boring and nerdy," Samantha says. "I think we should text Rían and go watch his lacrosse game."

Thinking of his face when I compared his sport to lacrosse makes me laugh. "Rickets," I say. "That's what it's called."

"*Rickets*?" Natalie asks. "Are you kidding? It's called *hurling*. I remember, because I thought, 'no, that's what your kid does when he's drunk bad milk.'"

Now we're all laughing. "It's one of the two main sports of the country," I say. "I think we should go see it as part of our Irish cultural education. Samantha's right."

"I've already texted him," Samantha says. "We have twenty minutes, so if it's close to here, we can make it."

I tap on my phone for one second, and there it is. "The GAA field's right by Lismore Castle, which is—"

"A mile from Fortwilliam Estate," Natalie says. "Do we need to change first?"

"I don't think we have time," Samantha says. "Let's just go, and if it's dumb, we can say we just stopped by, cheer for a minute, and leave."

"Good idea," Natalie says. "Hedge our bets."

"No one's eaten," I say. "Getting dinner can be our excuse."

I'm expecting a soccer field like the ones our kids play on back home, but when we pull up, I realize this one's both bigger and much nicer.

"Okay," Natalie says, "none of my kids have ever played soccer, so is it just me, or is this field *massive*?"

"It's not a field." Rían clearly saw us coming. He's smiling, so that's better than becoming apoplectic that we're talking about soccer again. "It's a pitch." He waves. "Follow me, and I'll get you seated on our side. Whatever you do, make sure you're cheering for the black and gold." He points at his uniform. "Do not, under any circumstances, cheer for the red and black team."

"Bally wagon's the devil," Natalie says. "Right?"

Rían smirks. "You can call them that. Might be funny, actually, but it's Bally*gunner*, and. . ." He drops his voice to a whisper. "They're the best team in our county." He narrows his eyes. "But if you ever tell anyone I said that, I'll call you a liar to your face."

"Got it," Samantha says. "We cheer for the bumblebees, and we boo at the red demons."

He smiles. "Exactly." He drags us over to aluminum stands that are nicer than I expected, and then he jogs off. A surprising number of men take the field—pitch—and they're all carrying sticks.

We're not sure quite what things to yell, and the game moves really fast, but it's clear we're sitting with the other Lismore folks, and one lady sitting right next to me's cheering really loudly. The two small children beside her are clapping and cheering just as energetically.

"How old are they?" I nod at the two kids, dressed head to toe in gold and black.

"They're twins," the lady says. "And they turn five next month."

"They'll be starting school soon, then," I say. "How exciting."

"Can't wait." The woman's smile says it all. Tired, excited, and proud.

"Who are we cheering for?" I ask.

"Lismore," she says. "Of course."

"Of course," I say.

"But you're American," she says. "So why are you cheering for Lismore?"

"It's kind of a long story, but we're here on—"

"On holiday, yeah?" the woman asks. "With your friends?" She tosses her head at Natalie and Samantha. "They look to be having a very nice time." Her half smile's conspiratorial, like we're in on a joke at our friend's expense.

They're both holding a Guinness and yelling rather loudly.

"Our tour guide from this morning's playing, and he told us we needed to watch a hurling match," I say. "But I'll confess, I have no idea what's going on."

The woman takes the next few moments, stopping only to cheer or jeer at the appropriate time, to explain the basics to us.

"They want to get that little ball, the sliotar, down the field, and hopefully get it in the small box, but they do get a point for getting it above, too." She points. "There are fifteen players on each team. One goalie, six defenders—full backs and half-backs—and six offensive players. The last two are mid-fielders who want to turn the sliotar over." She pauses. "Are you following still?"

I nod. "Sounds a little like soccer so far."

She laughs. "Not really, but there's a goalie, so I'll allow it."

The rest of the match is much more fun with her help. Natalie, Samantha, and I spend most of the second half cheering for Rían and for this woman's husband, Shanny. It's a weird name, but a lot of their names are strange.

By the end, I feel like I could almost explain it to someone else. Another American, anyway. I'm sure I'd make an Irishman choke on his own spittle. When the players finish, most of them pull their helmets off, stow their hurleys—the sticks they use for the sliotar—in bags, and work their way toward the stands. I realize that the tallest one's the man we were cheering for—Shanny. He's bald, or at least, he shaves his head, but it *works* for him. He's in great shape, and after all that running, the muscles in his arms are popping. . .

I remind myself that I've just made friends with his *wife.* She's a lucky woman, though, and I can't help thinking it when the children's faces light up as he draws near. He's clearly a good dad, too.

"Your babies clearly love their father," I say. "Their cheering was my favorite part of the game."

"Jack's their da." The woman smiles. "But I'm actually their aunt. I just agreed to watch my niece and nephew while he plays because Lismore needs him so badly."

"Oh," I say.

"And who exactly is my biggest cheerleader?" Jack turns to face me, and his deep blue eyes hit me like a sledgehammer.

I *never* stammer.

Or at least, I never have in my entire life, until this very moment. "It's —I wasn't—not the loud—loudest." I shake my head. "I mean, I was just cheering because she was." I point at his *sister.*

The woman laughs. "She did sound a little confused that your name was Shanny. I figured I'd let you explain that one." When the woman smiles, her dimples pop out even more. "I've got to get home—I have that paper to finish. I'll leave you with them, Jack *Shan*ahan."

Shoot.

Isn't Shanahan the player Rían was fan-girling over?

When I turn back, heartthrob Jack's staring right at me. "An American? What are you doing here in tiny Lismore?"

"They're on holiday, but I convinced them to come," Rían said. "I thought they might bring us luck, but I had no idea how well it would work." He pumps a fist in the air. "We beat Ballygunner!"

"You just might be my good luck charm," Jack says, still smiling at me.

"I fought I was your good wuck charm," the little girl says, banging her tiny hand on her dad's leg.

Jack bends over and grabs her, swinging her up to his waist. "You are, darling. You always will be." He smiles. "But wasn't it nice that Miss. . ." He lifts his eyebrows.

Oh, he's waiting for me to say my name.

Like a dope, I can't remember it. What *is* my name?

"Vanessa Littleton," Natalie says. "And I'm Natalie, and this is Samantha. We're staying at the Fortwilliam Estate around the corner for a few days."

Jack smiles. "I'm glad you could make the game—we have another one tomorrow. If the fates align, maybe you can come cheer us to another victory."

"You promised we could have apple cake if you win," the little boy says. "And you won!"

"You're right," Jack says. "It's time for me to pay up."

"Does your mom make the best apple cake ever?" Natalie asks. "I should ask for her recipe. I've never had it."

The little boy blinks. "My mom died when I was a baby. Ma-ma makes the best apple cake. Except when she burns it. But usually she doesn't."

"I'm so sorry," Samantha says.

"It's okay to talk about it," the little girl says. "It happened a wong time ago—I don't even wemember her."

"They're braver about me being a widower than I am," Jack says with a half-smile. He grabs the little boy's hand and ducks his head in our direction. "Don't forget—tomorrow night, same place, same time. We could really use another win."

I nod like the halfwit I've become.

"Earth to Vanessa," Samantha says.

I realize I've just been staring blankly in their direction as Jack Shanahan walks away. I snap my head back toward Samantha, worried they'll all realize that this Jack is the first man I've even *noticed* since Jason died.

But they don't appear to have thought anything of my awkward interchange. Am I always this embarrassing? My spluttering wasn't even noteworthy?

"This apple cake they were talking about," Natalie's saying to Rían. "Where could we find something like that?"

"Hmm, I'm not sure. Foley's might have one? Or Farmgate if it's open? Maybe Fuller's?"

"Is it some kind of law that every restaurant here has to start with the letter F?" Natalie jokes.

Rían frowns and shakes his head. "No, but—"

"I'm kidding," Natalie says.

"Oh, right." Rían leaves shortly after to celebrate with the rest of the guys, none of whom have two small children to care for alone, and we peel off to look for a restaurant with apple cake. For the first time since Jason died, I almost wish I could follow Rían and his teammates out. You never know. After Jack gets his kids put down, he could rejoin the guys. Or even if not, I might hear some extra information about him.

Because Jack Shanahan is *hot,* and I can't stop thinking about his smile, even though I know how ridiculous that makes me.

CHAPTER 15
Samantha

Some people are the glue.

I'm not.

In fact, if it had only been me and Vanessa at the barn when we were kids, I'm not sure we'd still be in touch. I liked her all along, of course, but I like a lot of people. I don't think Vanessa's our glue, either. She's smart, and she's talented, and she's funny and kind, but she's not *glue*.

Glue's what holds things together when other forces push apart.

It takes lots of small things and turns them into something bigger.

When we were kids, it was always Natalie who was planning parties, sleepovers, weekend trail rides, and birthday surprises. She organized things, and then in spite of hangups, bangups, and mishaps, she made them happen. I'm not sure what makes someone into glue, but I always wondered whether it was her family.

In her own family, I think Nat always felt a little left out.

Her mom married her dad and had her right away. . .and he turned out to be a jerk. It took her mom a while, but eventually, she left him. They were alone for a few years, but when her mom Patty met Marc, Natalie's whole life changed. Most of the changes were for the better. Marc had a son who was a pretty nice kid and almost the same age as

Natalie. But then Marc and Patty had a child together, a daughter. Mabel. I'm not sure Natalie ever felt quite like she belonged after that.

It wasn't that they were bad people.

They loved Natalie, but it was so easy for them to love Mabel, and things were so *hard* for Natalie. Not belonging in your own home must have been rough, and I think it forced Natalie to start making her own nest at an early age.

I think it made her into glue.

Well, that and some quality I can't quite define that makes everyone want to be her friend. I've wanted to get Natalie's approval for everything in my life since the day we met. When she smiles, it's like the world is warmer. When she's upset, I want to smash things. It's just something the glue can do. Impact the feelings of everyone around them.

Another thing about Natalie is that she always tackles every problem we encounter like she's the only one who can solve it and the world will crumble if she fails. Dogged determination was a phrase that must have been invented with her in mind.

Once the prize of a traditional Irish apple cake is dangled in front of her nose, nothing's going to stop her. Vanessa and I both know it, so we just sit back and wait. It takes Natalie ten minutes or so while we warm up in the car, but after a bunch of poking around on her phone, she says, "Aha!"

"Where are we headed?" I ask.

"The bakery's called Lizzie Brien's." She shoves the car into gear. "We better hurry, because it's closing in thirty minutes."

Clearly her half-starved-from-dieting-on-vacation self is motivated.

I grab the 'oh crap strap' prophylactically, because when Natalie's in a hurry, watch out. When Natalie's in a hurry *on the wrong side of the road*? It's better if you close your eyes and pray. We make it there with twenty-six minutes to spare, and no creatures of any kind are harmed in the process. It's a big win in my book, and it should be to Ireland as well.

"Let's get that apple cake." Natalie practically leaps from the car.

"Not excited about the apple cake?" I whisper to Vanessa, who looks a little less motivated to rush in than Natalie's teenager-lining-up-for-free-T-Swift-concert-tickets self.

She frowns. "I'm just a little more excited about the single dad who inspired it."

That makes me laugh out loud.

It's good to hear that Vanessa's noticing a man. Her husband's been gone for years. It's past time she started looking around. "Maybe he'll come here too," I say. "If his mom just burns that apple cake, Natalie was grumbling that there are hardly any places in Lismore to eat."

That perks Vanessa right up, and I'm surprised to see that she actually seems interested in the handsome, but quite young, rugby guy. What kind of future could she possibly have with a pretty-faced kid who must be a decade younger than her. . .and who lives in *Ireland*?

Or maybe that's the point?

I'm too old-souled to even think about something like a vacation fling, and I'm also far too preoccupied by my own failing marriage. But if it makes her happy, or if just the thought does, I'm all for it.

In the meantime, I'll just keep obsessing about my own life and the decisions I can't seem to stick to once I make. Do I want to let the house thing go? Or should I double down and fight? I can't seem to decide, and I suppose that's my answer. I wish I could tell whether I'm hanging on to hope out of stubborn nostalgia for what we once had, or whether I'm scared, or whether I still care about Brent somewhere deep down.

The twenty-something girl standing near the door of the cafe when we walk in looks a little distressed. "We close in twenty minutes," she says.

"We'll be quick," Natalie says. "But we heard you might have *apple* cake." Her eyes raise and her body shifts slightly forward, like she's going to live or die by this woman's answer.

As if the poor girl can sense Natalie's intensity, she steps back and blinks. "We do have apple cake—a crumble-style coffee cake with a custard sauce."

A smile spreads broadly across Natalie's face. "Excellent. We'll order so fast, your head will spin."

I'm not totally sure, but I think I hear the girl mutter, "Americans," as she walks away to wipe off a table.

I can't really blame her.

We're pushy, and we want things on our timetable. 'The customer's always right' is an ideal not often espoused in Europe, and I kind of wish it wasn't so endemic in American culture. The average customer that I've met lately is usually wrong, and that's the truth. But, the person who's paying has always had the upper hand. So here we are, pushing ourselves into a table just before they close.

"Stop looking all guilty," Natalie says. "We're paying them."

If *she* didn't feel guilty, she wouldn't be so snappy. "I'll have the mushroom soup," I say. "With a side baguette."

Natalie and Vanessa also order simple things, and the waitress who's apparently also their hostess looks a little less irritated.

"I bolt my food like a ten-year-old boy," Natalie says. "I swear we won't be here for very long." She smirks. "That's the good thing about Americans. We're in and out of your hair fast."

"My hair?" The woman blinks.

Natalie waves her hand. "Never mind."

The poor girl walks off, still looking a little confused by our American ways.

"This apple cake better be amazing," Vanessa says, "because otherwise, I'm going to feel a little bad about coming here and making them work—"

"Right up until closing time?" Natalie rolls her eyes. "You two have no *gravitas* at all. It's okay to take up space in the world, you know."

"I guess," Vanessa says.

"Speaking of taking up space," Natalie says. "I've been debating sharing this with you, but I figure if I were you, I'd rather at least have information." She half-cringes, which worries me. What on earth would my favorite loud-mouthed friend be unsure about sharing?

Vanessa looks even more concerned than I feel.

"I'm no expert, and to my knowledge, not a single one of my kids has ever done any kind of drugs, but. . ." Natalie frowns. "I heard a Ted Talk on addiction a few weeks ago, and it was *crazy*, because it was totally different than anything I'd ever heard before." She sighs dramatically. "And I know, I know, it's a *Ted Talk*, so how useful could it really be? But I swear, it made so much sense."

"Please do share," Vanessa says. "I'm at my wits end with Trace. I'm accepting any and all advice."

Natalie laughs. "I'm not sure I'd call this advice, but it was so opposite from everything we were always taught. Remember when we were growing up, all the D.A.R.E. classes? The videos of your brain—as an egg —on drugs?"

Even I find myself nodding along.

"Well, I'll send you the link to the Ted Talk so you can watch it your-self. The guy's name was Johann Hari, I think, and he was a British guy. He started by talking about how it's been a hundred years since England and the United States made drugs illegal, and he talked about how monu-mentally our war on drugs has *failed*." Natalie unfolds her napkin. "I think that's what caught my attention. I mean, I know it's a war, and we're the good guys. Everyone has always said that, but this Johann pointed out that a war on drugs is, like, a war on our loved ones, right?"

Vanessa's frowning.

"But then he says that in the UK, if you go into the hospital for a major injury, like a broken hip, you'll be given diamorphine, and he's right that it's commonly prescribed after surgeries there. He also said it's basi-cally heroin, and I looked into that, too. He was right."

Vanessa gasps, looking at me.

I shrug. "I heard they use that a lot here. But we use similar drugs that are just as strong. Mostly dilaudid."

"So doctors are basically getting all their patients addicted?" Vanessa asks. "Is it because of big pharma? Because Trace did have a surgery, but it wasn't until a few months later that—"

"Hold on," Natalie says. "It wasn't about that, but I did look into the United States, too, and they give morphine postoperatively, which is also an opioid, or like Sam said, they give dilaudid." She pauses. "It's important that the doctors can prescribe these, because when people break a signifi-cant bone, or when they have a major surgery, the pain during recovery can be really intense."

"But some of the patients do get hooked on the painkillers," I say.

"Sure, some do," Natalie says. "But why aren't *all* the patients coming out addicted, if the drug is the problem?"

I blink. I guess I always just assumed some patients are strong enough to quit and some aren't.

Vanessa looks just as confused.

"The Johann guy goes into the research behind blaming *drugs* for our addictions and where that notion came from. I guess the seminal studies were done on rats a hundred years ago. The scientists put them all in cages. Then they gave the rats two water dispensers—regular ones, and drug-laced ones. Once the rats in these plain glass enclosures tried the drugged water, they all drank nothing but that. Within days, they had all killed themselves—they overdosed. One hundred percent." Natalie's expression is grim. "After a rat tried the cocaine water, they did nothing but drink cocaine water until they just died, so that was our answer. The problem was the drug—eliminate the drug, fix the addition problem. Thus, the war on drugs."

Our waitress shows up then with a tray. "You said to bring the apple cake as soon as it was ready?"

Natalie straightens. "Absolutely."

Once it's been put down, we all kind of stare.

"It's even more beautiful than I'd hoped." Natalie smiles at me. "Now, if you don't think, after this display, that I'm addicted to sugar, you're wrong." She smirks.

"This is my son's life, though," Vanessa says. "It's not a joke."

Natalie's expression softens, but she doesn't look guilty. "Of course it is, and I'm not actually making a joke." She leans closer, her expression intent on Vanessa's face. "Because after that first experiment, we all blamed the drugs and the person who tried them. They were stupid enough to have been hooked by the evil drugs, and it was their job to either get away. . .or die."

Vanessa's brow's still furrowed.

"But that's not really right according to Johann," Natalie whispers. "He said that another researcher, many years later, redid the experiment. Instead of a boring glass cage with nothing but two water bottles in it, this research team put the rats into what they called Rat Park. The cages were big. They had varied food. There were other rats they could copulate with. It had places to play and toys and everything a rat could want. Games. Entertainment. Friendship. Mental stimulation of all kinds. Then they put the same two water bottles inside, but guess what?"

I shake my head.

Vanessa's staring, wide-eyed, like she's afraid to even guess. Somehow, in these rats, she seems to believe she sees Trace's future. Even I can see that much.

"None of the rats even drank the drug-water. They didn't want it. They had formed *connections* instead. Johann says that the real causal factor in whether someone struggles with addiction is whether they can bear to be present in their own life." Natalie stops, then, her eyes wide. "I didn't really want to say anything, because I don't want you to think I'm saying that any of this is your fault."

"But he did lose his father—I know they were close," I say. "And then he lost his chance to play varsity sports at almost the same time, right?"

"That was a year later," Vanessa says, "but yes. It was really, *really* hard for him."

"And then he explains that the way the United States and the UK usually handle drug usage makes things worse, because we tend to threaten the people who are addicted, and we tell them we'll punish them, or fire them, or be disappointed in them if they use—so the one thing they really need, a connection to us, a job to do, and a purpose in life, is what we're putting in jeopardy as our method of treatment."

Vanessa looks *wrecked*.

Natalie shakes her head. "V, I'm not attacking you, I swear. I think you've been loving Trace, and supporting him, and doing everything you can possibly do to take care of your son."

A tear wells up in her eye. "But maybe by sending him away to rehab, I've done exactly the wrong thing."

"Maybe." Natalie sighs. "But I really don't know. I'm not qualified to say, and I know that rehab centers are full of experts, and the places are run in a way that's specifically been shown to work, right?"

"Well, they told me their success rate over time is less than eight percent." Vanessa looks stricken. "They said it's a 'long haul.' And Trace has failed three times already. This next 'graduation' will be time number four." Vanessa pokes at her cake, breaking off one piece of crumbly, ivory-colored apple dessert. "I, um, I just have no idea what I'm doing." She looks up at Natalie. "But all of what you're saying sounds. . .right. Nothing else this whole time has made any sense to me. It feels like Trace hasn't wanted to be a part of his life anymore, not the way it is now, and instead of helping my little boy learn to fix things he doesn't like, I've been passing him off to other people and telling them to deal with it."

"No," Natalie says. "You've been loving him. You've been supporting him. I know you—you've *been there* for him. I'm positive of that. Some things in our lives are things we just can't fix. We have to endure with love, and that's what you're doing. You and Trace are surviving this together."

"But maybe once he starts to find things in his life that make him want to be present again," I say, "he'll be able to stop drinking the toxic water."

Vanessa nods slowly. "That would be amazing."

"For myself," Natalie says, "I know that I've turned to sugar a lot on days that have been hard. It makes me feel better when I don't feel happy in my life, and like Trace, that's been too often for me lately." She blinks. "I've been excusing Mason's behavior, at least in some ways because I've gained weight and he may not find me attractive anymore, but what if it's the other way around?"

I have no idea what she's saying.

"What if *I've* gained weight because I've been unhappy with him? What if my guilt is perceiving my reaction as the cause, when really it's a symptom of the way he's been making *me* feel?"

"He's the ultimate gaslighter," I say.

"We all need to start building lives we want to live in again." Vanessa's voice is soft, and I can't disagree with her.

"Coming on this trip with the two of you was step one." I lean my head against Vanessa's shoulder. "I needed you guys. Thank you."

When the waitress brings our meals, all three of us have tears rolling down our cheeks. It would be embarrassing if we didn't all need each other so much.

"Thank you," I say.

"You don't have to rush," the girl says. "Sorry I was being kind of rude earlier. I'm not in a hurry." Her smile when she walks off is very kind.

On the way back to the Fortwilliam Estate, we talk about our plans for the next day.

"I can't believe we only have three days left," Natalie says. "It feels like we just got here."

"Right?" Vanessa says. "Three days." She sighs.

"But tomorrow's Blarney Castle," Natalie says. "I hear it's amazing. And then we have that cheese tour and the farm tour. Those should be fun."

"I forgot about those." Vanessa perks up. "Yes, those will both be great. Especially the Cashel place, right? I love cheese."

Natalie laughs. "You've mentioned that."

"And we remember," I say.

Vanessa always had a cheese stick in her lunch—every single day.

"Oh my word." Natalie presses her hands down against the table top and looks at me. "Do you remember that time she left her lunch in my

157

car?" She makes a gagging sound. "My mom found that little brown sack like three months later, and the cheese stick—"

"Was totally fine!" I can't help shouting. "That was the worst part! It hadn't even molded. What kind of cheese is totally *fine* after months and months in the humid heat of a car in Florida?"

"It was shrink wrapped," Vanessa says. "Anything you shrink wrap would be fine." She's scowling, but just because it's her job in this story. She acts all annoyed and beleaguered, and we all howl.

It feels good to know my job.

And to be surrounded by people who make me feel safe.

It's in that tiny moment that I realize that I've been living in a marriage that's basically a plain, glass rat cage—nothing but a water bottle. If someone offered me cocaine water, I might've taken it.

I want to go to rat park and be surrounded by fun.

I'm sick of the constant, demoralizing comments. In this moment, I feel more sure of what I need to do. I need to hold the line. I know I'll wobble again, but shouldn't I do what I want to do in my happiest moments? I mean, it's the happy moments when we aren't acting out of fear that ought to guide our lives.

Or at least, I think so.

On the way back, my fingers fly across the keys of my phone as I write and delete and write more words in a message to Brent. I wind up rewriting it about five times, and in the end, I leave it in my drafts. It's more constructive than the last one, the one I actually sent, but I'm not sure it'll matter. My last communication was telling him I wanted a divorce, and telling him to go ahead and draw up the papers, so I guess I'll just leave it there. All night long, in spite of the massive, really comfortable old bed, I dream of rats and cages. When I wake up, I feel exhausted. I'm more than ready to get on the road and visit Blarney Castle.

Natalie's already eating her protein bar on the way downstairs, but Mrs. Murphy has made an amazing breakfast that Vanessa and I indulge in. Irish breakfasts are amazing. An entire basket of toasted bread, as if we could each eat five or six pieces. Strawberry jam, cherry preserves, and orange marmalade. Roasted tomatoes, sautéed mushrooms, baked beans, and my personal favorite, bubble and squeak.

"Where on earth did this name come from?" Vanessa asks. "Because this stuff is amazing, so if I can get my kids to start eating cabbage and potatoes for breakfast, maybe I'll feel like a better mom."

"The name alone might tempt them," I say.

"Thank you so much for breakfast," Natalie says. "I'm sorry I'd already eaten."

"That bar shouldn't count." Mrs. Murphy eyes the wrapper from Natalie's sad protein bar in the trash can. "You should have some real food before you leave."

"I should," Natalie says. "But I'm afraid I've been eating too much *real* food lately." She pats her belly with a sheepish expression. "It means I have to miss some things now that I wish I didn't."

"It feels brutal, but I should be minding the same thing." Mrs. Murphy's smiling when she bids us good day.

"Would you like to come with us?" I ask. "You'd be welcome, and you'd fit in the car easily."

"To Blarney Castle?" Mrs. Murphy laughs. "The Irish don't often go to the tourist places."

"Have you ever been?" I ask. "Maybe you'd like it."

She shakes her head. "It's not my cup of tea, but thank you for the invite. It's very kind of you."

"Thanks again for breakfast," I say. "It was amazing."

On the way to Blarney, we talk about the next few days. Other than the farm tours and the Cliffs of Moher, we don't have much else planned. That bums me out a little—I can hardly believe it's almost time to go home.

Natalie's phone pings, and I pick it up for her. "It's from Rían. He wants to know if we'll ride again today."

"Tell him we won't be back until later," she says. "I'd like to go out again if he's alright with waiting until the afternoon."

Rían's keen—I think he liked having some help. "Alright, we're on for later today, around three."

"Capital," Natalie says, clearly in a good mood. "A castle tour and another ride."

I glance back at Vanessa, hoping maybe she'll have some interest, but she ducks her head. Once we get to Blarney, she seems happy enough. She actually knows a shocking amount about the castle itself. In fact, it's Vanessa who points out that with the way the fifteen-foot walls slope outward, anything the defenders threw down would bounce and crash into the attackers below. She also shows us the murder hole once we walk inside the castle, a circular cutout right above the entrance where the defenders could drop tar, weapons, or rocks on people that made it through the gate.

"This would've been a scary place to attack," I say.

Vanessa, Natalie, and our guide Edward all agree. The other tourists with us, a French family of four, seem a little lost.

When Vanessa gets in an argument with our tour guide about whether the Blarney stone was brought back from the Crusades, or whether it was half of the Scone Stone on which Scottish kings were coronated, Natalie and I step back and exchange a glance. Vanessa's usually quiet and soft-spoken, but when she thinks someone's wrong?

Good night.

"The Crusades were a wicked war, and they brought back nothing useful," she says. "But think about it. If Cormac McCarthy really did supply Robert the Bruce with four thousand of the sixty-five hundred troops he needed to win the Battle of Bannockburn, then *he* was the reason the Bruce could hold up against the close to twenty thousand troops Edward sent. Cormac McCarthy would have been the man who won Scotland its freedom. It makes sense that Robert would've sent him half the Stone of Scone if it broke, and that stone really might have some kind of powers."

"But the stone of Jacob for the book of Genesis was found during the Crusades, and—"

"Pah," Vanessa says. "The McCarthys built it. It was a gift from Robert the Bruce. It's the only story that makes sense."

The rest of the tour goes about the same, with Vanessa suddenly an expert on all things Irish and old. Once it's finally over, and we're walking toward the old stables—home to the International Horse Trials in the past —I can't help asking. "What on earth was all that?"

"You were arguing with the guide!" Natalie's lips are twitching, and she leans closer and squints. "What did you do with the real Vanessa?"

Vanessa's shoulders slump a bit. "The thing is. . ." She snorts. "When you came up with our itinerary, I was determined to know something about the places we were visiting before we came. I bought half a dozen books on Ireland from Amazon, but the only one I read. . ." She bites her lip.

"Was a book on Blarney Castle?" Natalie asks.

Vanessa shrugs.

"And you read it on the plane, didn't you?" I saw her tucking something into her backpack at the airport.

She huffs. "You two always know *everything*, and this time, I wanted to be the expert."

We're all laughing as we grab a quick lunch at the Coach House Cafe.

"I could eat here every day," Natalie says, staring off at the stables beyond.

Three horses are in the front paddock, and half a dozen gorgeous heads are hanging over their stall doors, too. It's tranquil. It's green. The wind's a little brisk, but otherwise, it's been a perfect day. On our way out, we stop at the poison garden.

Natalie reads the sign. "A garden to celebrate and warn of the poison that lives in our daily lives and yards." She chuckles. "I suppose we can all relate to that. Flowers. Fruit. Bees. Birds. And a little bit of deadly hiding among it all."

"It's been growing beside us all along, and we didn't even know it," I say. "Just like Brent's brother, Jason's brother, and your best friend."

"Look at this," Vanessa says. "It says that *Ricinus communis*, the castor oil plant, is deadly even in the tiniest amounts." She scowls at it in true Vanessa fashion, as if looks really could kill. "Look how pretty it is, with its fuzzy red flowers and seven-pointed star leaves."

"Lots of these plants are pretty. This one's deadly nightshade," Natalie crouches beside it. "The purply flowers and the black berries are lovely. They look edible."

"But none of these things become problematic until humans do something with them," I say. "I wonder where that puts the blame."

Even after stopping to eat, we reach the Fortwilliam Estate ahead of schedule.

"We have plenty of time to change before we need to meet Rían," Natalie says. But when she pulls down the drive and the great stone house comes into view, I notice there's another car parked out front already. Natalie parks, a little farther from the front of the house than we have

B. E. BAKER

been, her gaze fixed, just like mine, on the blue sedan with the Budget rental car license plate. As soon as we stop, the driver's side door opens.

I haven't met her many times, but even so, I recognize the woman who steps out and straightens.

It's Tiffany, Natalie's 'friend.'

Here in Ireland.

And she looks upset.

But not *nearly* as upset as I am.

CHAPTER 16
Natalie

On the day I almost walked in on my husband, on the day I saw the hot pink stilettos the first time, I was shaky.

All day long.

If I sat down, my hands trembled. When I walked around, I felt jittery, like I'd had too many cups of coffee. The saleslady at the mall where I went to angry-shop asked me whether I was alright. She said I looked pale and jumpy. It took a very long flight and days spent with my friends to relax enough that I didn't feel like I was dangerously stressed.

Tiffany undid all that decompression in one second flat.

All the jumpy, jittery, nervous feelings rush back.

What on earth is she doing here? How did she even know where to come? When I kill the car engine and climb out of the right side of the car, I'm not sure what to say. I feel unsteady and unsafe.

As if she can sense my unease, Vanessa practically jogs around the car to stand beside me.

"Surprise," Tiffany says with a forced smile.

"How did you know where I was?" I ask. "I don't think I shared our itinerary."

"That's all you have to say to me?" Tiffany's staring right at me, her big, wide brown eyes entirely innocent. "You've been badgering me to join you on one of these trips for years, and I finally got away."

Samantha doesn't jog around the car. She doesn't race. She moves like a panther, utterly sure in her own skin. By the time she finally reaches my side, Tiffany's not looking at me anymore. "You must think Natalie's really stupid." Samantha folds her arms.

"You know." Tiffany swallows, and then she arches one eyebrow. "All of you know."

"I never liked you, you know." Samantha wraps an arm around my shoulders. "I thought it was because I was jealous. We knew Natalie first, and you kind of stole her from us. Whenever she said you were her best friend, casually or not, it made me a little angry."

Tiffany frowns, but when she opens her mouth to talk, Samantha cuts her off.

"But now, I think maybe I could tell from the start that you were rotten. There are two kinds of women in this world, after all. There's the kind who are capable of being happy for their friends, the good kind, the healthy kind. Then there's the kind that are so insecure that they're jealous of everything their friends have. Guess which kind you are." Samantha's really on a roll.

Tiffany's entire face is flushed, and her hands are clenched at her side, but she lifts her chin. "I'd like to talk to Natalie alone."

"Sometimes you can't just steal what you want," Samantha snaps. "I do realize that you never learned that lesson, so maybe now's the time for it to settle in."

Tiffany isn't letting go, though. "I've come a long way to see her, and I think—"

Samantha steps closer, releasing me and squaring her shoulders. "I make fifteen hundred pound animals do *just* what I say with a strap of leather and a piece of metal this long." Samantha gestures with her hands. "I'd love to see what I could make you do with the same tools."

I grab Samantha's wrist. "It's fine."

Samantha freezes. "If you want to talk to her, we'll go."

"I don't want to," I say. "But I think I need to."

My dearest friend stares at me for a moment, her eyes intense. I'm not sure what she's looking for, but I guess she finds it. Samantha nods, and then she tosses her head at the car. "We'll wait in the car where we can see you, but we can't hear you." Then she turns back toward Tiffany. "Five minutes and just a crop." She shakes her head and narrows her eyes.

I can't help my snort-laugh. If this weren't such a weird situation, I'd be howling. Samantha's. . .one of a kind.

"Walk with me," I say.

Tiffany nods.

I start moving toward the right side of the house. There's a little inset garden area, and just below it, there's a metal table with some chairs. It's as good a place as any to talk to the friend who screwed me over.

Only, I find that I can't walk patiently quite that far. "Why are you here?" I blurt. "How did you figure out that I know?"

"You were weird on the phone," she says. "And then I remembered that you said your flight was a day later than you thought." She frowns. "It wasn't easy, but I checked the home security footage from the office, and I saw you show up and then leave, and I just knew." She clears her throat. "I knew what you would've seen."

I shake my head. "Hoisted by my own petard."

"Huh?"

"It's from Shakespeare," I say. "*Hamlet*—I'm the one who pushed for the cameras to be put in, because Mason started traveling a lot." It hits me for the first time that he suddenly started traveling about seven years ago. The same time Tiffany started working with him. "Was that—"

My friend's brow furrows. "I came here to explain."

I shake my head. "You know what the worst part of all this is?"

She swallows.

"You're supposed to feel safe with your spouse, with your family, and in your own home. Your friends and your family, they keep you safe. That's their whole point. I do it for my kids, I do it for Mason, and I do it for my friends. You and Mason took that away from me, and that's why I still came on this trip." I realize it—my actions finally make sense. I thought I'd attack my husband if he betrayed me, but I thought that because I always had him at my back. With his help, I *could* attack someone. But finding out he was cheating felt like being cut down at my knees. And finding out it was with Tiffany?

It made it so much worse. I felt like someone whose entire stool of support just toppled underneath her.

"I came on this trip to sort through how I felt so I could return home when I was ready and confront you. But now you've taken that control away from me, too. I don't even get to pick the timing." I shake my head. "So you know what? Go ahead, Tiffany. Say whatever you came here to say." I set my jaw, determined not to say anything else until she's done.

"I—you know my husband." She sighs. "David's so old." She wrings her hands. "You know my parents too. They're disastrous. Mooches. Embarrassing. I knew the most important thing I needed to find in a spouse was financial security, and someone who would never, ever leave me. I found that with David."

She came here to tell me that her sixty-nine-year-old husband's old? I must look as unimpressed as I feel, because she starts talking faster and gesturing bigger.

"If I'd met Mason first—you know we're a perfect match. We both love what we do, so when we started working together, it just. . ." She shrugs. "I'm really sorry. I really do love you, and so does Mason. That's why we've. . ."

The fact that she's here, speaking for both of them, fills me with a fury that I can't even try to contain. "Did you tell him you were coming here? Does he know that I know?"

She steps toward me, but her toe catches in the thick tufts of grass, and she stumbles.

I ought to step forward and make sure she doesn't fall, but I don't. I simply watch as she lands face first on the ground.

"He doesn't know anything," Tiffany says. "This is coming out all wrong."

"I'm sorry," I say. "It must be very hard for you, having difficulty explaining the situation."

Tiffany stands. "It *is* hard. This is the hardest thing I've ever done."

She has got to be kidding.

"No, Natalie, that's not what I'm saying. What I mean is that, I love you even more than I love Mason. It's just that, I needed him more than you did. Or, I needed something from him, too, something I couldn't get anywhere else."

"You flew to Ireland to tell me that. . .what? I shouldn't be upset that you *borrowed* my husband for sex, because yours is old and mine's a better fit for you than he is for me?"

Tiffany makes a strange growling sound—I think she's frustrated. "No, just listen. It was an accident between me and Mason. You were on this same trip, seven years ago, and he was annoyed. He's never taken a boys' trip, you know, not ever. I had just started working there, and he was saying how much it sucked that he had to work such long hours and then watch the kids all alone while you went off with your friends, and then I said it was dumb, too. I said you had me—what did you need these trips for?"

"So it's my fault?" Is that really what she's saying?

"No, but you were gone, and we were both missing you and. . ." She shrugs. "It was a one-time mistake. We both agreed we'd never do anything like that ever again, and Natalie, we didn't."

"You want me to believe that seven years ago and last week were the only times—"

Tiffany groans. "That was our plan, and you would never have known or been hurt. But then, the next year, on the night you left, we had this big project at work, and we were the last ones to leave, and, well." She cringes. "But the thing is, we agreed *again* that it would only be while you were gone."

"You made a pact to only hook up while I was away having fun of my own? Seriously?" In her mind, did that make it okay?

"No. Look, we knew it was wrong." She looks up at the sky like she's entreating God for his help in having patience with me or something. "It wasn't until three years ago that it *ever* happened when you were in town."

"Are you saying you first slept with Mason seven years ago, but you've been having a full-blown, ongoing *affair* with my husband for three years, now? I'm so stupid that I had no idea?"

"Because we both love you," Tiffany says. "That's why it worked. It's really kind of like one of those throuple relationships. You read about them all over these days. They're actually really healthy. In fact, I think Mason would be fine with—"

"Please stop," I say.

Tiffany's mouth closes, her eyes tightening.

"Do not *ever* suggest anything like that to me again, and if you so much as think about saying you love me again, you'll wish I'd let Samantha tear you into shreds."

Tiffany nods. "He'll pick you," she says. "When you go home, and you confront him, he'll pick you. He loves you more than he loves me." She bows her head. "And so do I."

"Then how—"

Her head snaps back up. "Have you ever been on a diet, and you know you shouldn't have any chocolate, but then you just find yourself standing in the pantry, pounding a chocolate bar?" Her eyes are wide, pleading.

The sad thing is that I *have.* Not a chocolate bar, but a sleeve of Oreos. Same thing. I know what she's trying to say, but. . . "Mason's not a candy bar, and you're not violating a self-imposed diet to try and lose three pounds. You *slept* with my husband. You helped him violate our wedding vows, not to mention your own."

She shakes her head. "I haven't slept with David in *years.* He's not even capable anymore, and—"

"You chose to marry him," I say. "Stop acting like you're some kind of victim of abuse."

"So you're just going to leave him?" Tiffany asks. "When? After you get home?"

"I didn't come to the decision easily."

Her lips compress. She nods slowly. "I thought you might."

"I can't—I'll never get that memory to disappear," I whisper. "I saw your shoes. That's how I knew it was you."

She sighs. "Then I have something else for you."

I want to tell her that I don't want anything from her. I want to tell her where she can jump, but I don't. At least she cared enough to come all the way out here.

At least she cares.

It's not enough, but it's something.

She holds out her hand, her carefully manicured fingers wrapped tightly around something small.

"What's this?"

"Mason started to worry a few years ago that you might find out about us. He's got some money he's been keeping separate." She swallows. "I thought you should know about it. Stealing from you just didn't sit right with me—I never needed your money. That's the one thing David has plenty of."

Stealing from me didn't sit right with her? "Am I supposed to thank you?"

"No, you can hate me." Tiffany steps closer. "I understand, and if I were you, I might hate me, too. But I really do love you. I hope you'll understand that one day. I feel as guilty as you can possibly imagine, and I'm also sorry. I thought all I needed was money, and I'd be fine, but I discovered that I wanted more."

"You wanted what I had."

She shrugs.

"I think it's time for you to go." I turn toward the car, where Vanessa and Samantha are finally climbing out. They're clearly done waiting patiently.

"I'm sorry I showed up in the middle of your trip," Tiffany says. "I'm —I guess I got greedy. I was hoping there was some way I might not lose you."

I'm sad to lose her, too.

But seeing her here, finding out just how bad this all was? I can't see any way out of this that leaves us friends. I can't see any path where Mason and I stay married, either. The betrayal's just too big. It's too painful.

It's way too much.

"I'll—I won't tell Mason, alright? I'll let you handle that."

She'll let me tell my own husband that I've found out about their affair. Everything she says pisses me off, but I try to remember that in her mind, she's trying to do me a favor. By all counts, I suppose I should've expected her to scurry to him with the revelation right away.

She's trying to show me she's loyal to me, but it's far too late.

I trudge back to the car slowly, watching Tiffany as she picks her way across the lawn in the most impractical shoes ever selected for a trip to the Irish countryside—stiletto heels. Probably some expensive designer brand.

At least they aren't pink.

"Heading home already?" Samantha's arms are crossed, and her right finger's tapping against her left forearm. Her eyebrow's about as quirked as it can be. "What a devastating shame."

Vanessa giggles, and her eyes widen. She's like the world's cutest mouse. But she's *my* mouse, and I love her for trying to bare her tiny teeth in my defense.

Tiffany straightens by her car door and opens her mouth, but then she closes it. I have no idea what else she wanted to say, and that's okay with me. I'm not sure I'll ever care what she has to say again.

"We better get changed quick," Samantha says. "Or we'll be late for our ride."

I forgot about the ride. I think about begging off—I'm sure they'd understand—but there are times when you just need to feel a massive, fuzzy beast taking orders from you. "Oh, man. Drew's *just* the man I want to see right now."

Samantha smiles. "I thought he might be. I may switch with Rían and try Conor today."

"You could try one of the cobs," I say. "That palomino's spectacular, and the red roan's pretty cute, too."

"You know who I really want to ride," Samantha says.

"That thoroughbred, Liam," I say. "I knew the second I saw him."

"Well, that's true," Samantha says. "But I also want to swing my leg over that shining black lunatic in the pasture. What was his name again?"

"Scout," Vanessa says. "I imagine you'd be the perfect match for him. He looked completely bonkers."

I can't help my chuckle. "You did seem a little crazy just now, but in the best way."

"I'm sorry if I went too far," Samantha says, "but if you knew how much I restrained myself." She shakes all over like a wet terrier. "I've never wanted to punch a human more."

"You threatened to tear her up with a riding crop." My lip twitches. "I wish I'd gotten that on video."

"Hey, do you guys think Rían would let me ride Foxy?" Vanessa asks.

Samantha and I both freeze, and then we smile at each other.

"Yes," I say.

"I'm sure he would," Samantha says.

It's exactly the kind of good news I needed today.

CHAPTER 17

Vanessa

My husband Jason was in the army reserve, and I told someone he was in the military once, and he looked like I'd stabbed him. After that, he explained the concept of stolen valor.

"I'm in the reserves," he said. "I never saw active combat, and I never say that I did or even imply it."

Technically, the rules for stolen valor only really apply to claiming medals or awards you didn't receive, but I never forgot that it's a crime the military actively prosecutes.

Today, I saw both of my friends being the bravest versions of themselves. Samantha roared like a leashed lion. She listened to Natalie, but she leapt forward to protect her fearlessly with slavering fangs bared. She would've done anything, said anything, to keep our friend safe. Natalie was just as impressive. She was calm, polite, and sophisticated when other women would have leapt forward and pulled that woman's styled and blown-out hair.

Tiffany knew what she'd lost, at least. That satisfied me a little.

But I didn't feel like I belonged beside these two women. I'm not someone who fights. When the grocery store overcharges me, I don't say a word. When my order from Amazon has just one item instead of two, I just order another. When my kids get an unfair grade, I teach them about how life isn't always fair, and tell them that we should work harder.

172

In my experience, fighting just leaves you bruised and tired.

But today, these two women fought fiercely. It made me wonder whether I should be suing Jeremy. He knows what he did was wrong. I know it was, too. But can I really bring a legal claim against Jeremy? Would Jason even want me to?

That's not an issue I have to tackle today.

But riding a horse again?

That I can do.

If my friends can be brave, and if they can be strong when faced with their enemies, then so can I. Or at least, it feels like I can until I'm walking down the stairs and back out into the front courtyard. The green grass seems to stretch out for *miles*, and there are hardly any fences. If my horse decided to take off, where could I wind up? Drowned in the Blackwater? Broken and mangled beside an overgrown hedge? Halfway to Scotland?

Each breath I draw feels unsteady, and I start to rethink my rash proclamation. I don't know Foxy. I'm not the kind of rider who just hops on an unknown horse, even if she is small. Even if she did let me graze her, perfectly politely, for over an hour.

Grazing isn't riding.

Riding isn't safe.

I've lost my mind.

And that's that.

When I finally reach the corner where Samantha and Natalie are standing, I open my mouth to tell them that I've rethought things, but before I can say a single word, Natalie grabs my right arm, and Samantha grabs my left.

"Oh no, you don't," Natalie says. "You wanted to ride, and you're going to get on that little mare's back before you change your mind."

"You know it only gets harder to get back on the longer you put it off, so of course you're going to be scared." Samantha doesn't even look at me. She just starts walking, the two of them dragging my expensive and barely-used riding boots through the thick green grass.

"Hey," I shout. "Let me go."

"You're a grown woman," Natalie says.

"That's my line," I grump.

"It should be," Natalie says. "But we're overriding you this time. You have a desire to ride, and we're going to force you to see that through."

"What if the horse chucks me off." I hate how panicky I sound.

"We'll toss you up on her back on a nice, thick patch of grass," Samantha says. "It'll barely hurt if you fall."

"That's not reassuring at all," I say.

"It is soft grass," Natalie says. "But it won't matter, because. . ."

"You won't fall," Samantha says. "That mare doesn't have crazy eyes or a double whirl on her forehead. I checked. Plus, all three of us will be right beside you to walk you through it."

In the end, they aren't kidding. Once we reach the barn, I'm too embarrassed to throw a big fit in front of Rían, and I think they counted on that. Samantha picks out most of my gear and half-tacks up my horse for me. She's so fast with her own preparation that we're all ready to go at about the same time.

It helps that Foxy keeps looking at me like a puppy and intermittently bumping my hand with her soft nose. For a moment, it feels like old times. We're chatting. The horses are stomping and head-tossing, and they're making familiar horsey noises. The ones who aren't coming start to call to the ones who are. And then the three of them are all walking outside, ready to mount, and the panic hits me like a brick wall.

I *cannot* get on this horse.

I don't even know her.

I don't know the area.

If I get on, I could fall off. And since I haven't ridden in forever, let's be honest. I probably will. All Samantha's dumb stuff about soft grass was just that—dumb. No matter where you fall at forty-one years old, your booty *hurts*. If I'm unlucky, much more than that will hurt.

"What?" Samantha circles back around toward me. "Do you need help walking over to the mounting block?" She tosses her head at it. "I'm not getting on until you do."

She may have just found out that I'm not riding anymore, but she knows me well enough to know that I'll have no problems with circling around with Foxy and tacking her down once they're all up and ready to go. "I can't do it." I try to speak the words firmly, but they come out tenuous and small. "I—I can't. I wanted to, but I'm not like you two."

Samantha shakes her head. "You're wrong. You're just like us. You've just forgotten that temporarily." She thrusts Conor's reins at me. "Hold him while I ride her."

"What? Why? I'm not riding him." But she's ignoring me, already swinging up onto Foxy's back, and then withdrawing her boosting foot from the much-too-short stirrups on my saddle.

As if he can sense that I'm less powerful, less reliable, and less competent, Conor's nostrils flare at me. I'm suddenly staring at a much larger and a much stronger horse than Foxy the friendly Connemara pony. But again, Samantha's not taking any time for explanations. She's already shifting Foxy back and forth, her heels down perfectly, even without stirrups.

"It'd be a shame to put this cute little girl back without riding her at all. Let's see how broke this little pre-broke pony is." Samantha's smiling. One moment later, Foxy's trotting off, head up, eyes wide.

We all follow them into the paddock beside the barn, the empty one with the open gate. It's as close to an arena as they have here, apparently. A moment later, Foxy's head has dropped, her neck's curving in, and she's half-passing to the right.

"Does Samantha do dressage too?" Rían asks.

Natalie shakes her head, patting Drew's neck. "She did for a few years, but not for quite a while. She just values equitation more than most jumpers."

"What a cute little pony." Samantha's beaming every time she and Foxy circle close to us. "I like her."

That's hardly a surprise—Samantha likes virtually *every* horse we've ever encountered. She's always insisted that almost all horse problems are really rider problems that the horse is sick of dealing with. If I was paid a dollar every time I heard her rant, I'd be able to buy the Fortwilliam Estate and move here.

Conor sighs and drops his head, clearly looking longingly at the grass. "Not in your bridle, sir," I say. "You obviously already know that, from your forlorn sigh."

Five minutes later, when Samantha's still riding Foxy, I'm almost bored. Conor is for *sure* bored as the pair of them canter in a perfect little circle, and Natalie and Drew have taken to riding in a circle at the trot more or less in the same small area as Foxy and Samantha. Rían and Dara should probably join them, because she's dancing around like a pop star that drank one too many Vitamin Waters.

"I can go tack Conor down," I say.

Samantha stops then, near the gate. "This little mare's a delight. There's not an ounce of stinker in her." She walks her toward me. "Are you sure you don't want to get on, just here in the paddock?"

I knew it.

She's pushing me now—she didn't just want to ride her. "I already told you," I say.

Natalie interrupts. "What would you tell your kids right now? What if Bryce was having some kind of computer problem he couldn't solve? Should he just quit because he's stressed out?"

She didn't say Trace, which I appreciate, but I can't help thinking about him. He's definitely been faced with some terribly hard problems, but this isn't the same. "I don't need to ride," I say. "I'm fine without it."

"I disagree." Samantha swings down and leads Foxy toward me. "You're saying that now, but your soul needs it."

I'm not like them. It's never been more clear. I'm just *fine* not riding. I don't need it like they do. Am I brave enough to confess that?

"Vanessa Littlefield," Natalie says, "I have seen you do things that would break most people. I've watched you support your husband through his father's death. You held your family together after your own husband died shortly after. You went back into the workforce, and you have been a phenomenal mother in spite of challenges that would have defeated most of us normal humans. You *can* get on this horse." She shifts Drew closer. "Stop thinking about it and just do it."

Samantha holds out her hands, Conor's reins looped around her shoulder, and without thinking about it, I swing my foot into her hands and she boosts me up.

I barely need a boost. Foxy's just fourteen hands.

When my backside settles against the smooth leather of the saddle, when my hands grasp the reins, the leather sliding between my pinkie and ring fingers and flowing upward, pinched between my thumbs and my forefinger, I take a big breath.

Then I let it out.

Foxy exhales at the same time, turning her head to the left just enough that her eye meets mine. Then she nods just an inch. It's the strangest thing, but it really feels like she can tell. It feels like she wants me to know that she senses that I'm scared. She knows I'm broken, but she's got me.

Samantha doesn't wait for me to burst into tears. She doesn't make a big thing out of it. She just hops upward, almost flying into Conor's saddle without a mounting block, and positions her hands on the reins, and then she says, "Let's go."

My heart leaps into my throat, and I want to haul back on the reins and protest. Sitting in the saddle was enough for one day. But it's too late. The horses are already moving, Foxy along with them, and I'm balancing, my toes sliding into the stirrups in just the right place, my weight balanced on the balls of my feet, heels down, and I'm rocking along at a nice, energetic walk.

Drew and Natalie swing around and take up the place behind me, with Samantha just ahead, and it feels like my friends have taken up an honor guard to keep me safe. Now I really do start to cry, but softly. One tear slides down my right cheek, and then another leaves a wet track on my left.

"Are you alright?" Natalie whispers. Her horse, the big, solid grey who's so bright he's nearly white, whickers. "If it's really too much, we can go back."

"No." I can barely say the word, but I feel it when I do. "I'm glad I'm riding." I'm surprised to find that it's true.

I'm not sure whether I was lying to myself out of fear, or if I just forgot how good it felt to ride, but my heart soars as we walk along the path toward the Blackwater River. It feels like. . .it feels like I'm finally *me*. It's like, for the past few years, I was drowning slowly, and I'm finally coming up to take a big, ragged breath.

After my father-in-law died, we could barely make ends meet with the loan we were repaying for the money we gave to Jeremy for his half of the company. Then Jason had a heart attack, and the pandemic slammed us, and I thought the company was going under, and then Trace had shoulder surgery and started having his substance abuse problems, and then he fell off the deep end, and the hits just kept coming. Riding wasn't even a possibility, and I was scared.

Not just about horses.

About the future.

About who I was without Jason.

About whether I'd ever be me again, if I could ever be happy.

It hits me then, like a hammer to a lightbulb, that I haven't been happy in a very long time. I've been tired, and I've been stressed, and I've been scared, but I haven't been *happy*.

I'd almost forgotten how it felt.

I was still trying every day, but nothing I did was ever enough.

I'd become a female Sisyphus, constantly trying to get that stupid boulder up the hill, and watching in despair as it tumbles back down again. As we head to the left, and as the girls chatter about the nuns who live to the left of the estate, I can't help thinking about how much I needed this trip. Jeremy may have sold a company that wasn't his to sell, and he may have kept half the money that wasn't his to keep, but he was right to send me out here.

I don't even regret coming.

Maybe I should regret it. The boulder definitely crashed at the bottom of the mountain when I left to come play with my friends. But I needed to let go of the rock for a few days. I needed to look out at the sunshine from the back of a horse.

I needed to feed my starving, emaciated, nutrient-deficient soul.

The rest of the ride is *delightful*. The sun shines. The birds trill, even in the pre-spring weather. The horses are all excellent, and Foxy's transcendent. She does just what I ask and nothing more, and I'm utterly shocked that Natalie was right. It does all come back.

I'll be sore tomorrow, but I remember how to move her off my leg. I can turn her around. I shift the reins a little bit when there's a distraction, just to remind her to pay attention to me, so she remembers that I'm the boss. It's all as easy as, well, as riding a bike. If that bike was likely to spook at a car backfiring and chuck you in a ditch.

Even so, this little bike acts like she'd feel bad if she dumped me.

When we get back, after we tack down, I check my clock. It's late enough in the day, and he's been there long enough that the rehab facility might let Trace take my call. I'll tell them I've had an epiphany. I'll tell them how badly I need to talk to him. Even if it's a day early, they should make an exception for a parent who's out of the country, right?

I dial the main line.

"Northstar Drug Rehabilitation Center of Boulder," the perky woman says.

"Uh, yes, this is Vanessa Littlefield. My son Trace checked in six days ago. His uncle brought him, because I'm in Ireland, but I filled out all the paperwork online."

The woman clucks.

"I know you usually won't allow calls until they've been there a week, and I understand the importance of them being able to focus." Though, now that I'm saying the words, I realize that the typical process of these rehab facilities seems to sort of fly in the face of what Natalie was saying about connections. Why do they cut the kids off from their own mother? Cutting them off from other druggies, sure, but why his parents?

"Ma'am, the problem—"

"I really need to talk to him." I say. "I know you have those protocols for a reason, but I'm in Ireland right now, and I left right before he checked in, so I haven't seen him in a week, and I have something important to tell him. Can you just make an exception this one time?"

"Ma'am, if you'll just listen," the woman says, "I can explain. Your son, Trace Littlefield?"

"Right."

"We received the paperwork, but no one ever checked in here under that name."

"That can't be right," I say. "I gave you my credit card."

"Yes, ma'am. We received that information as well, but Trace never physically showed up."

I can hardly believe what she's saying. Trace *isn't* at Northstar? Where did Jeremy take him instead? "Okay, thanks." I hang up, and I call Jeremy.

I should call Trace, probably, but I'm too upset. If he answers his cell phone, if he's not in rehab at all, I might kill someone.

"What's wrong?" Natalie's at my side, her eyes intent.

Samantha pops up on the other side. "Yeah, what's going on?"

Jeremy answers at that moment, of course. "Hey, Sis. Calmed down yet?"

"Have I calmed down?" I ask. "Hm, let me think. I'd say the answer to that's no. I just called Northstar, and they said the most fascinating thing."

"Ah, about that," Jeremy says. "You really needed to get away—"

"So you could rob me blind," I say. "I remember."

He clears his throat. "The company grew from *my* work, Vanessa. It makes sense that I should get some of the increased value that came after Jason died."

"And if you'd come to me and asked me to give it to you," I say, "I'd have figured it out."

"Yeah, I know what that means, though. 'Figuring it out' means, 'sorry, it's too complicated.'"

"And what does, 'I'll put your son in rehab for you,' mean?" I ask. "Or was it just too *hard*, what with all the papers you had to sign to screw me and the kids out of what we owned?"

"I like the new and improved Irish version of Vanessa," Jeremy says. "You're fiery. I wonder how you'd look with red hair."

"That's not something you'll see anytime soon," I say. "But when I get home, you're going to find out just how fiery I am. I'm not sure you'll like the new me, because the first thing I'm going to do when my plane lands is sue you."

CHAPTER 18
Samantha

The day I met Vanessa and Natalie, I was wearing cowboy boots. I'd been begging my parents to let me ride for years and years, and for my seventh birthday, they signed me up for a horseback camp. I was *giddy*. My mom and dad had read all the requirements, and they had dutifully packed my lunch, signed all the releases and waivers, bought me a helmet, and found me a pair of boots.

Unfortunately, the paperwork hadn't specified what *kind* of boot.

I was the only kid at the entire camp wearing cowboy boots. I guess all the other parents knew that, since it was an English barn, they needed little black boots called *paddock* boots. I had plastic brown and pink cowboy boots with the word "yeehaw" printed across the shaft.

Whoops.

Most of the kids thought my novelty boots were funny.

"Where'd you get those?" a girl with black-framed glasses asked. "Boot Barn?"

"More like Goodwill," a little girl with a purple helmet said. "No one has made boots that tacky in a decade."

"Clearly she's never been on a real horse before," a girl with a bob said.

But one girl was frowning instead of laughing. She was smallish, and her hair was plaited in two long, blonde braids that hung past her shoulders. She had cute little pink flowers woven into the braids, which the other girls had been cooing over moments before.

I wasn't sure why she was frowning, but I worried she was about to come up with a doozy, making everyone laugh twice as hard. I didn't have a cell phone—no one had them back then. But if I'd had one, I'd already have called my mom to beg her to come pick me up.

That little girl didn't zing me, though. Instead, she said loudly, "I love those boots. In fact, would you trade with me?" She sat on the bench near the wall and unzipped the back of her shiny paddock boots and slid them off. "I could use those for dresses on Sunday, and I could wear them to cowboy day at school." She's smiling at me, and I think she's serious.

"She won't really trade?" purple helmet said.

"No way." Black-framed glasses snorted.

Blonde braids squared her shoulders and picked up her boots, standing as she held them out to me. "Please?"

"Won't your mom get mad?" I asked.

She shrugged. "She won't even notice."

Another little girl who kept her soft brown eyes down on the floor most of the time looked up. "You should do it. She wants them." She smiled at me, but it wasn't mean. It was kind. The girl's little brown curls were already wisping away from the ponytail her mother probably put in that morning.

"I do. They're the coolest boots I've ever seen." Blonde braids marched my direction. "Will you do it?"

I blinked—I had no idea what to say. Before I could even sit to see if our feet were the same size, the trainer walked into the tack room.

"What's going on?" Grace asked. "Why are your shoes off?"

Blonde braids lifted her chin. "She doesn't have paddock boots, and I really want her cowboy boots. We were about to trade."

Grace must have been wise. She looked between us and then at the other girls. Then she nodded. "You can't trade, sadly. It's against camp rules, but I do have some boots with a smaller toe you can borrow for camp. Those very cute cowboy boots might get stuck in the stirrups, and that could be dangerous."

After that, no one else made fun of me.

Blonde braids was Natalie, of course, and eyes-on-the-floor was Vanessa, whom she'd already taken under her wing when the other girls mocked her for never meeting their eyes. She defended both of us fiercely, and no one dared to question her.

After that, I'd have followed Natalie anywhere. She turned what could have been a very embarrassing week into something that set me apart. Vanessa, clearly not quite the firecracker Natalie was, nevertheless extended her support to me in smaller, quieter ways from the start. When my lunch got swiped by the large yellow lab with the big mouth and the long tongue, she handed me half her tuna sandwich without a single word. When I wasn't sure how to hold my hands on the reins, she showed me.

By the end of that week, the three of us were already fast friends.

A year and a half later, Natalie's parents bought her a horse. Vanessa's parents found one a month after that. It was the *only* thing I wanted, back then. I was leasing one from the trainer, but after my two best friends bought one of their own, I just *had* to get one too.

"You only want one because they have one," my dad complained. "If they were leasing still, you'd be fine with the lease."

He was right, of course. When your friends move on, you want to go with them. Otherwise, you might get left behind. Over the years, that wasn't the only thing they did that I had to do too. And sometimes it went the other way. I'd do something—like moving from hunter to jumper—and they'd follow along behind me like little ducks as well.

As I stare at my email, reading over Brent's proposed settlement offer, I can't help wondering whether I'm agreeing to this for the right reasons. He's not being nasty in this email. He's not being mean about the settlement terms, either. He's being. . .almost generous. His proposed settlement for our divorce is just like Brent has always been for the whole of our marriage, right up until that unfortunate business with the house for his brother.

Fair.

Measured.

Entirely cordial.

He's offering me a perfect split down the middle of our assets, without asking for any allocations for the money I've spent on horses, or the extra time I was in grad school to earn my nurse practitioner's license. He's even offering to give me my horse, Varius, without a corresponding value allocation on his side. I mean, sure, my warmblood warrior's pretty old. I doubt

I could sell him for much at his age, but he could still be sold off to pretty much any jump barn with a lesson program. He's capable of packing around most anyone on a two foot six course without any sort of training or maintenance. I could get fifteen out of him, maybe. Brent knows enough to know that. Plus, he's always acted like he almost resented all the time and money I spent on horses, so. . .

Honestly, I expected much worse.

Which makes me wonder whether I might be doing the equivalent of demanding my parents buy me a horse of my own when I could save money by leasing. Am I just agreeing to a divorce right now because one of my friends lost her husband and the other's leaving hers? Am I throwing away a perfectly good marriage instead of working through the snags because my friends are all about to be single again too?

Instead of replying to the email, I close my laptop and slide it into the bag. I'll think about it while we're out today, so I can have a little time to figure out how best to respond.

Has Brent had second thoughts?

This isn't the kind of decision I should be making on a vacation, probably. And if there's any chance I'm being influenced by Natalie and Vanessa, I should make sure that's not my impetus. They wouldn't want me to do something like this because of them either.

I hear the door next to me open, and I grab my bag and jacket. When I duck out, Natalie and Vanessa are already waiting.

"Okay." Natalie's clearly recovered from her run-in with Tiffany. She's dressed as cute as I've ever seen her, including the cutest little bright red coat that must also be new. "Who's ready to tour some farms?"

"I'm looking forward to the cheese tour," Vanessa says. "Not sure about the honey one."

"We know." Natalie shakes her head and chuckles. "But what will you do if they don't have cheese sticks?"

Vanessa swats her arm. "Stop. I've evolved."

"Thank goodness," Natalie says.

"I'm more excited about the honey," I say. "Always have liked sweets more. But which one's first? I can't remember."

"The cheese tour's pretty finicky on the time," Natalie says. "Only on Tuesday at noon. So we're doing the honey tour first, and then on to the cheese-tasting."

"I don't really know much about bees," I say, "but I do hate being stung."

"I imagine most people agree with you," Vanessa says. "Being stung. . .not fun."

Once we're on the road, I can't help asking how Natalie's doing. "You still feel okay?"

Natalie's brow furrows. "Okay?"

"About Tiffany showing up," Vanessa asks. "I was wondering, too."

"Oh." Natalie nods. "I guess I just keep expecting to hear from Mason. She's got to tell him she came and that I know, right?"

I'm not sure.

Clearly, Vanessa has no idea, either. Natalie's the one among us who always knows what's going to happen and how to fix it. I understand horses, but people are often a mystery.

"What did she hand you at the end?" I wanted to know yesterday, but I didn't want to pry.

"A jump drive," she says. "It's got all of Mason's financial information on it. He's been saving money in accounts that aren't linked to our joint account and retirement fund. They're actually at a completely different bank." She shakes her head. "It's a lot of money, actually. I'm kind of embarrassed I didn't notice."

"Why?" I ask. "How would you have noticed? He was intentionally hiding it from you. Don't ever be embarrassed for trusting the people you're supposed to trust."

Natalie sighs. "I guess. . .I feel like I was an idiot for just believing we were fine. I should've noticed something." Her hands tighten on the steering wheel. "Seven *years*," she says. "Seven years he and Tiffany have. . ."

"You are a good person," Vanessa says. "You didn't see that in them because that kind of ugliness doesn't exist in you." My quiet friend sometimes hits me in the face with these straight up *brilliant* insights.

"She's right," I say. "You can't think of yourself as being stupid. You were *pure*, and there's not a lot of that out there anymore. Don't feel small because you're good."

"The sad thing is, I'm not sure whether I am anymore." Natalie's eyes are dark, and I can't blame her for losing faith. It sucks when we have to carry around the scars from other people's terrible behavior.

When we reach the bee place, I can't help smiling. Even in April, there are flowers blooming all over. It's such a cliché, and I kind of love it.

"I'm Aoife," she says. "You must be here for the tour." Her eyes crinkle near the edges when she smiles, and her reddish brown hair forms a beautiful, curly halo around her head.

"We are," Natalie says. "And we're excited to learn all about Irish beekeeping."

"Then you're in the right place," Aoife says. "My father started this business before I was even born, and I think my parents passed down a passion for bees, wildflowers, and honey in the womb."

After we introduce ourselves, explain that we know nothing about bees, and that we're from the United States, she leads us across a large field where she shows us their beehives. "We have just over two hundred hives here," she says. "And all of our bees are native Irish Black Honey Bees."

"Does their honey taste different than honey in the United States?"

"Well, the taste of the honey has more to do with where the bees are collecting the pollen," she says. "So honey made from dandelion or clover blossoms will taste different than honey made from cherry blossoms or sycamore trees. I don't think there's a lot of difference between Irish Black Bees and Italian ones, but the Italian ones are killing off our native bees, and we're fighting to keep them safe."

"That's terrible," Vanessa says. "I'm sorry."

Aoife shrugs. "We try to focus on the good parts of our work, though. And what's sweeter than honey?" She smiles.

"You know, horses have favorite things to eat that sound an awful lot like what the bees use," Natalie says. "I had a horse that hated clover, but another one that would preferentially eat it all."

"That's funny," Aoife says.

"What does your favorite flavor of honey come from?" I ask. "Clover? Dandelions?"

She shrugs. "I like it all, but my favorite's probably the ivy blossom honey, made in the autumn and winter." She winks. "We don't sell that, in part because we let the bees keep most of it for the winter, and in part because it's the best flavor."

As we look at the hives, made up of shelves they call "supers," Natalie asks, "How do you know how much honey to leave them, and how much you can take?"

Aoife clearly loves what she does—she's been smiling almost the entire time we've been here. "Well, like with most things, it's a bit of a balance. We let the newer colonies keep it all, but as they're more established, you can get a pretty good feel for how much you can take. Most years, with our healthy, strong colonies, I can take almost a hundred pounds of honey in two or three different rounds. I try to leave around ninety pounds of honey for each colony to last through the winter, because I don't like feeding mine sugar water. In some places, they need to, but Ireland's green year round. When it gets cold, the bees need extra honey to stay warm, but as long as we leave them enough, they're just fine."

"How does a bee keep warm?" I ask. "Do they swim in it or something?"

Aoife laughs. "They consume it and use the energy to shiver—the movement of their muscles warms them up, and they all kind of pile on top of each other in a big pile to share heat. It's ingenious, really. They're always connected in a way that humans just aren't."

"But sometimes, maybe we should be," Natalie says. "It's interesting how carefully you balance what you can take and what they need."

I think about what Natalie's saying. She's been putting efforts and love and support *in* to her family for years, and Mason's been hiding money and taking out everything he can at the same time. We don't have beekeepers to make sure we're all getting enough. Some people just take and take and take, leaving us nothing to keep warm over the winter—we need to eliminate those takers or we might wind up frozen or starved in spite of our best efforts.

Next, Aoife shows us their processing area, including their honey extractors. They're large metal machines where they put all the honey they've collected, and it runs through these large rectangular bevels to filter out the parts of the honey humans don't need. It does preserve the honeycomb, because they can use that for other things like candles.

By the time we leave, we're all a little sad. The bees aren't nearly as aggressive as I expected. "Do you get stung often?" I ask.

"I'm lazy about smoking or wearing the protective clothing." Aoife shrugs. "And I'm still almost never stung, but keep in mind that I'm around the bees a lot, and they recognize human faces. They know I'm not a threat."

"Bees recognize humans?" Natalie sounds shocked. "Seriously?"

"They do, and like most things, they give back what they get."

When we get back into the car, each of us leaving with a bag of candles and honey, I can't help thinking that we should all be as fair as the bees, giving back what we get.

Luckily, the next stop, the Cashel Blue Cheesemakers, isn't too far, because we're running late.

"It's hard to make up time on these back country roads," Natalie grumbles. The winding paths, the narrow lanes, and the hedges that nearly brush the side of the car make it impossible to speed safely. . .unless you're Natalie, I guess. She's a terror, I swear, but we do finally swing around a corner and shoot down the small drive and we're all still alive when we do.

When I see the sign that says "Cashel Farmhouse Irish Cheesemakers," I breathe a sigh of relief. Then I take in the beautiful collection of buildings. They have a full dairy farm here, clearly, but they also have several large buildings clustered together where I'm guessing they make the cheese.

We make it with one minute to spare.

"From the tone of the emails, I was afraid if we got here late, they'd cancel on us," Natalie says.

When we open our car doors, there's already a woman walking toward us with a pleasant expression and shoulder-length brown hair. "I'm Sarah," she says. "You must be the holiday guests who emailed about a special cheese-tasting."

Natalie nods. "Thank you so much for accommodating us. I know you don't always do tours during the early spring."

"It's a busy season for us, with most of our cows either having their calves or settling in with them." She waves us forward. "But this is my very favorite part of my job—sharing our story and our cheese with new people."

"How long have you been doing this?" I ask.

"My entire life," Sarah says. "My parents started this company quite some time ago, and it's been more than thirty years now since we put Ireland on the map with our famous Cashel blue."

We follow her into a small, stone converted barn that's weathered very well. Everything inside's bright and white, but all the trim is appropriately painted blue.

"I'm going to be honest," Vanessa says. "I'm excited to learn about what you do here, and I love most cheese. . .but I don't really like blue cheese."

Sarah circles around behind a small farm table, so I can't see her expression to guess how she's responded to that proclamation. Various things are spread out across the large wooden farm table. There are small white paper cups, a cheese plate with a wedge on it, wrapped cheeses, and even a tray with crackers, jam, and other snacks decoratively arranged. "Then you haven't had the right stuff yet." She doesn't look worried at all. "I know blue cheese gets a bad rap, but hear me out, and give it one small try, and I think we might change your mind."

"Doubtful," Vanessa whispers, but she doesn't argue.

Sarah looks totally unconcerned. "If you had any idea how often people start their visit here with exactly that sentiment, you'd be far less dubious." She points at the cups. "First though, we'll try some cheese curds. Do you know what those are?"

"It's some part of the cheese?" Natalie asks. "And I think it comes from the start of the process."

"Very good," Sarah says. "We take all our fresh milk first and process it. It's mostly from our own Fresian cows, but everything that we don't produce comes from our neighbor's cows. All our products come from somewhere that's within a five-minute drive of our farm. First we pasteurize it, and then we put the milk in great, large vats, which I'll let you see through windows. We can't go inside for sanitation reasons. We add some special ingredients, like rennet and blue mold, and within an hour, it's already begun to form into clumps, and those clumps are fresh cheese curds." She shifts three small white paper cups toward us. "You won't taste the signature blue cheese flavor in these." She arches one eyebrow. "So go ahead and try it. It's safe and quite mild."

I'm not as nervous as Vanessa, but the small whitish blobs in the cup don't exactly look appetizing.

"You didn't come all the way to Ireland to stare into a cup." Natalie tosses hers back and chews the contents.

That's enough to get Vanessa and me to follow, and I don't regret it at all. The cheese curds are soft, as mild as Sarah said they'd be, and frankly, delicious. "Oh, that's good," I say.

Sarah smiles. "Here's a spoiler for you. It's all going to be good."

A few moments later, I believe her. She walks us through their process, one day at a time. They remove the whey through stirring, shifting, and then flipping. Then once they form the cheese curds into cheese rounds, they pierce the whole thing with needles so the mold can breathe.

It's aged then, and that allows the mold to form in the right quantities. "Since I'm a partial owner now, and since I'm kind of taking over from my parents," Sarah says, "I get the job of tasting all the batches so we can determine exactly how long they should be aged. We want our blue cheese to be mild, and we want to convert people who are a little leery of harsher or spicier blue cheeses that they've tried." She leans closer. "Now that you tried our Cashel Blue, if you're convinced I'm not speaking lies, you might be ready to try our Crozier Blue."

"Crozier?" Natalie asks.

"It's one of the only blue sheepsmilk cheeses in Ireland, and it's named after St. Patrick's Crozier, which is a very special piece of silver that can be found in the Rock of Cashel, around the corner from here."

"I wonder if we have time to go by," I say. "That would be fun."

"Oh, you should," Sarah tells us.

After sampling the Crozier Blue, only Natalie really likes it. "Though it's much creamier than I expected," I admit. "It's just a little too strong for me."

We all buy some cheese, even me, and then we head out as quickly as possible in the hopes of being able to go by the Rock of Cashel. We do make it to the stunning castle, but we're running a tad late.

"It closes at 3:45?" Vanessa asks. "What a stupid time to close. Why would anything close so early, and not even at a normal break like four or five?"

I throw my door closed and we all start to jog. It's three-thirty-two, and we're not at all sure we'll make it to the front in time. I'm out of breath and heaving by the time we reach the front desk, and the ticket-taker doesn't look very friendly. "Hello," I call. "Is there any chance we can grab a ticket and just take a quick peek? We promise we won't be long."

The man's frowning, and I'm not sure we have much chance, when Natalie's phone rings. Her face goes entirely white. "It's a Texas number. I think it might be Mason."

"Never mind," Vanessa says. "We'll just take some photos from over here." She points.

And Natalie answers.

CHAPTER 19
Natalie

The first day I was gone, when Mason thought I was traveling, I was really shopping in rage and despair, binging Netflix and crying, or sleeping at the Holiday Inn near the airport. Tiffany may have thought it was a lousy place to stay, but I happen to like Holiday Inns. They're reliably clean, and they have free breakfast. Mason didn't message or call me that day, and I'm pretty sure he didn't even think about it. Once I was gone, he was *free* to do as he pleased, and he clearly did.

The second day, when I was actually traveling, he tried calling, but I didn't answer. I texted and told him the reception was bad.

Every day since, I've managed to fob him off with some kind of lame excuse whenever he calls and either avoid talking to him or get off the phone quickly. I've also sent a sequence of generic photos of scenery from some of the places we've visited. I'm not in a single one, and even on my social media posts, I'm not showing my face. I'm not sure why I decided to deny him so much as a glance at my face, but it felt like I was making a tiny, pathetic sort of stand.

He's not loyal? He can't even see my face, then.

I doubt he even noticed.

Mostly on these trips, I just hear from the kids. That's always been true, and Mason's explanation is that he wants me to enjoy myself. He usually just calls if there's an emergency or some task he isn't sure how to

191

complete. I always thought it was sweet that he gave me space. But two days ago, Clara, our oldest daughter, notified me that Mason 'lost' his cell phone. I'm not sure whether he really lost it, or whether Tiffany told him I know and he's using that as an excuse to come up with some kind of plan.

Either way, he hasn't texted or called since.

I've been dreading the moment that I have to actually talk to him on the phone, now that he might know that I know. I'm not sure I can hold it together.

When I see the area code for Austin—512—I just know.

It must be him.

Tiffany has come clean, and now it's time for me to actually talk to my husband about all this. Ugh. My stomach isn't in knots. It's way past that. It's tied into a hammock, basically. Samantha's about to start arguing with the poor tour clerk when I finally answer.

"Hello?"

I brace myself for the voice I always thought was the epitome of sexy.

Low.

Husky.

Nonchalant.

"Mrs. Cleary?" The high, nasal voice on the other line is most definitely *not* Mason.

It's a relief, but it's also a shock.

"Uh, yes," I say. "This is Natalie Cleary. Can I help you?"

"This is Mr. Showalter."

Showalter. It's a weird name, and he's saying it like I ought to recognize it. I wrack my brain, and it finally comes to me. "Ah, Mr. Showalter—you're handling my father's estate."

He clears his throat. "Indeed, I am. I'm calling you with good news."

"Did you finally work something out with the ex-wife?"

"Which one?" he asks.

I can't keep track of which ones have already settled or given up. "Umm, all of them? Any of them?"

"It's actually quite a long story," he says. "But if you'll recall, Mrs. Hellesbore—"

"I'm actually in Ireland right now," I say. "And I'm paying about forty cents a minute to talk to you." That's probably nothing to his hourly rate, which if I recall is closer to something like ten dollars a minute.

"Right, well, I'll give you the short version."

"I appreciate it."

"We had a hearing—impromptu, really, but the judge assigned to the case is handling something else, and he ruled on the motion I made for—" He cuts off. "Sometimes lawyers struggle with keeping things short."

I can't help chuckling. Now that I know it's not Mason calling, I'm in a surprisingly good mood. "It's fine."

"All the claims made by the ex-wives, as well as the alleged other children, have been closed. The DNA tests came back exonerating your father from paternity on any of them, and the wives' claims were considered spurious. That means we finally have the green light from the judge to distribute your father's estate."

"Oh, well, that's great." Dad was hardly chaste, but apparently he managed not to sire any more kids. That was for the best, honestly. He never cared about me. I doubt there's much left, but I still worry about the timing. "I'm actually about to be going through a divorce, I think. Could receiving the funds now complicate things? Maybe this could be delayed just a little longer."

"Nothing you receive as an inheritance is considered community property," Mr. Showalter says. "As long as you keep the property entirely separate, there's no way your soon-to-be ex-husband can try to claim any part of it."

"That's good news," I say. "So if I just set up a checking account in my name, will that be enough?"

"You might want more than a simple checking account," Mr. Showalter says. "I know you've been pretty hands off so far. . ." He coughs. "In the nearly two years we've been dealing with this case, you have never once asked me the size of the estate. It's not very typical, if I'm being honest."

"It's fine," I say. "I know Dad spent a lot while he was alive, and I knew it would take forever to sort through the whole thing. And honestly, I just didn't want to get my hopes up. It's kind of been my coping strategy with my dad since I was five."

"Well, now we have final numbers. After our legal fees have been fully paid, which were rather extensive, thanks to the variety of claims pending against the estate, you should still wind up with close to three million dollars."

I choke.

"Miss Cleary?"

"Yes," I say. "I'm here."

Apparently, I'm freaking rich.

For the first time in my life, I'm actually grateful to my dad. When I hang up, Samantha and Vanessa are looking at me with careful concern. I'm a little tired of always seeing that expression on their faces. It makes me feel pretty pathetic.

"I take it that wasn't Mason?" Samantha asks.

"It was my dad's lawyer," I say. "He just called to tell me that he's finally going to distribute my dad's estate—right around three *million* dollars."

Samantha uses a word—loudly—that our mothers would have spanked us with our own crops for using, and Vanessa's jaw drops.

"We need to go out for drinks," I say. "Tonight, it's on me." I can't seem to stop beaming.

Ever since I saw those hot pink stilettos, I've been a little scared. I'm a smart person, and I'm a good mother, but I haven't really prioritized developing my ability to earn money over the past twenty years, and I'm about to be in charge of supporting myself. My dad may not have taught me much over the years he spent on this earth, and he certainly never showered me with gifts, but apparently he made decent money as a dentist, and his vulture-spouses didn't steal all of it.

"Thanks, Dad," I whisper, as I climb into my rental car. "I'm not quite as mad at you as I was."

"What?" Vanessa asks.

I shake my head. "Nothing. Just muttering."

"What are you going to do with it?" Samantha asks.

On the drive back, it's all we talk about.

"You could buy a beach house and never work again," Vanessa says. "Sip mai tais all day and make Mason raise the kids."

"Then they'd be total brats," I say. "But good idea. Keep them coming."

"Buy a massive barndominium and do nothing but ride all day." Predictably, that's Samantha's suggestion.

"Ooh, or you could buy a barn and teach little rich brats how to ride horses," Vanessa says. "You'd be the new Miss Grace."

"Grace's still training," I say. "I'd be the new Miss Natalie."

"Wait, I have a better idea," Vanessa says. "Move up to Colorado and help me with my kids. We can tell people we're sister-wives and our husband died and freak them right out." She snorts. "That would be so funny."

Samantha's laughing as she says, "Or you can move back to Florida, and we can get a big house together. I'll handle all the flower beds, since I know how much you hate them, and you can clean all the toilets."

"We can get four dogs," I say. "Since Mason wouldn't let me have any at all."

"Yes," Samantha says. "You have an army of children to help potty train them—let's just make it five."

"My kids would help," I say, "but they'd do it badly, so the dogs would probably go all over the house." I groan. "Maybe just one dog."

"One dog's just sad," Vanessa says. "You need at least two so they have a buddy."

"It's like horses," Samantha says. "Once you get a dog, you wind up with like five."

By the time we get back to Fortwilliam, I'm in pretty good spirits. All the remaining stress from the moment when I thought Mason was calling is almost entirely gone. But yet again, there's a car parked in the drive as we pull up.

This time, it's not a rental car. It's a car we've seen before. It takes a moment, but I place the fancy Audi. "It's that Ciril guy," I say.

"Cillian," Samantha says. "The guy who owns Fortwilliam."

"And who's trying to *sell* it," Vanessa says. "Hey, one thing no one said is that you could buy this place, almost." She's smiling, but. . .

It's not a horrible idea.

In fact, it might be the best idea yet.

If I moved all the way to Ireland, I'd basically never see Mason. Or Tiffany. It would feel like starting over entirely. Maybe the kids would be excited to experience something totally new. Or, you know, my kids might hate it. I'd be forcing them away from everything they know. They'd have to start over in every way. Plus, even if I have a big chunk of money, it's not like I can afford a place that costs seven million bucks—we looked up the price the second we realized it was for sale. I'm sure a place like this costs a mint to maintain as well.

As cool as it would be, it's not at all realistic.

But as I look at the amazing, beautiful estate, I *wish* I could buy it.

Ireland's been a place of healing for me, and I'll forever think of it as the escape from my life I desperately needed. Fortwilliam was even more of an escape than the rest of the country, because it was another instance of me making a bad decision—getting scammed—and yet, the country, or one man and his very kind housekeeper, decided to take us in.

They cared for me when I was stuck.

They took care of me when my own husband didn't.

It restored my faith in humanity, honestly, and my trust in myself. I can never thank them enough. But when we get out of the car and Cillian heads our way, I try. "Thank you so much," I say. "Staying here has been like a dream, and I know you didn't owe us anything, but you should know that it meant a lot to us."

"Did it mean enough that you would be willing to get up a little early tomorrow?" He looks a little pained.

"What's wrong?" I ask.

"We have a request for a showing," he says. "The buyer's on a tight timetable, so it needs to be at eight in the morning tomorrow."

I blink. "A buyer?"

He nods. "A solid one. They want to turn the place into a hotel, which makes sense. A lot of the large places like this are being repurposed for the hospitality industry. The only sad part is that they want to tear down the barn and cottages and build a lodge in their place, but it makes sense. There's also plenty of space for it. I think they're planning a golf course too, with views of the River Blackwater."

"Oh, no," Samantha says. "With all this space, do they really have to demolish the barn?"

"It'll become a carpark, probably," Cillian says. "Or possibly they'll repurpose and refurbish parts of the outbuildings to be a place for the staff to stay."

A hotel.

If I bought it, I could keep the barn for horses, and I could turn it into a hotel with horseback rides. Two sources of revenue, and I could have the house and barn of my dreams. Although, not quite, if I'm renting out the house.

"What's that big building by the barn?" I ask.

"Actually, there are four houses on property other than the main house," Cillian says. "I'm not sure, but I think they want to turn the gardener's cottage into a storage shed, so at least some of the old buildings would stay."

"How would you feel about showing us around right now?" I ask. "I just came into an unexpected inheritance, and I'm trying to figure out what to do with it."

Cillian laughs.

But a moment later, when I don't join him, he realizes that I'm serious. "You mean it?"

Samantha nods. "She did, and I think it's a brilliant idea."

"Oh." Cillian chuckles. "Well, sure. Why not? You've already seen the barn."

He's right about that. It's one of the main selling points. "And what about the horses? If I bought it. . ."

"You could keep them for sure," Cillian says. "Getting rid of them's just another chore on my list. But you may not have noticed all the buildings around here. There's the Steward's Cottage beside the barn. It's one of the largest of the outbuildings."

We look at it first—and it's more than I even imagined it could be.

"My aunt plastered over the exterior stone," Cillian says. "It brightened it up quite a bit. Then she painted it the same blue as the barn trim. I think it managed to preserve the look while also updating it."

The rooms inside aren't large, but they've all been updated. The tile in the kitchen and bathrooms, and the carpet in the other rooms is all pretty new. Even the kitchen's cute, with a vintage look to the appliances that matches instead of fighting with the old world feel.

"Blue roan with dapples," Samantha says. "This place is so nice! Your aunt must've updated it, right?"

Cillian shoots her a strange look, but then he nods. "She liked redoing old places—that's one of the reasons she bought this to begin with."

"Where did her money come from?" I ask. "Clearly she wasn't hurting if she could maintain all this."

"Her grandfather—my great-grandfather—started a pretty famous brewery," Cillian says. "Since she never married, she found other ways to occupy herself, and restoring older homes that had been neglected and saving donkeys were her two main passions."

"Well, thank goodness for that," Vanessa says. "Four bedrooms, great light from all the windows, and it overlooks the barn."

"I'd move in tomorrow," Samantha says.

"You would?" I spin on my heel and grab her hands. "Why don't you? You were kidding before, about me moving to Florida, but you *could* totally buy this with me."

"You should," Cillian says, his eyes dancing. "You do like the barn."

"I *love* the barn," Samantha says. "But I have a horse back home, and—"

"They transport horses," I say. "I'm sure of it—think of all those warmbloods they bring to America every year. You'd just be hauling one back."

"But he's older," Samantha says. "I wouldn't want to stress him like that."

"We have lovely horses here," Cillian says.

"Spoken like someone who does not understand horse girls *at all*," I say. But I can't give up on it just yet. I slide my arm through hers. "Just think about it as we walk." I snap a bunch of photos and a few videos with my phone, because if we *did* do something crazy, like move to Ireland, a cottage with four bedrooms that's right by the barn would be *just* the place for a single mom with five kids to stay while renting the posh, main home.

"While the steward's cottage's nice, the coach house is even nicer— twice as large—and was renovated in the past two years." He frowns. "It's on the other side of all the farm stuff, whereas the stable cottage is right here, but I don't have keys for that—Rían has them."

"We can look at the coach house first," I say. "That's fine. We don't mind a little extra walking."

As we head around the stable, past the herb garden, and through two small paddocks, fenced on one side with a living hedge, the double pointed roof of the coach house comes into view.

"I can see why it's the coach house," I say. "It's near the main house, but also has a lot of cobblestone areas in front."

"Most of it's been paved now," Cillian says. "But Clara left some of the cobblestone for history's sake." He points. "It's got five bedrooms and three bathrooms. It also has the most modern kitchen of all the outbuildings, and I think you'll like the flooring." Cillian's quite good at his job, showing us all the features that are modern and the charming elements that have been preserved.

"I love that two of the bedrooms overlook the small paddocks," I say. "And two more overlook the garden and the big stone gate with the green doors."

"It does have the nicest views, other than the main house," Cillian says.

"But I think Cillian's right," Samantha says. "If you *did* buy it, your family should fit fine here in the coach house." She winks at me. "And I think Vanessa's entire brood might fit in the steward's cottage. . ." She lifts both her eyebrows.

"Don't pull me into this crazy scheme," Vanessa says.

"What about you?" Cillian's paying more attention to Samantha than he is to me. "I think you might like the smaller stable cottage, which connects to the stables themselves. Once we kick Rían out. . ."

"Does he have somewhere else to go?" I feel kind of horrible talking about kicking out the man who's been so kind to us.

"He stays with his mother at least half the week," Cillian says. "He usually just sleeps here when he's hungover."

"Well, I can't wait to see it," Samantha says. "A smaller place that's attached to the stable and right next to the steward's cottage sounds *perfect.*"

"He was out lunging one of the ponies when I called earlier." Cillian frowns. "Hopefully he's back now to show us around, but prepare yourself. He's not neat and tidy."

Samantha shrugs. "What twenty-something male is?"

"I always was," Cillian says. "But I suppose most aren't."

We check the stable house, but no one answers, and Rían doesn't answer his phone, either. "That's irritating," Cillian says. "But pretty typical with him."

"Most people who work outside aren't great at checking their phones," Samantha says. "Sometimes people get irritated with me for the same reason."

"Did you say there were four outbuildings?" Vanessa asks. "What's the other one?"

He points. "On the far side of the barn, there's an old stone building that hasn't been re-plastered. It's bigger than the stable house, but the gardener's cottage would have to be renovated," Cillian says. "It's a lot of work, I should warn you, and I'd say it's not very habitable right now."

"How bad is it?" Samantha asks.

"Girlfriend remodels houses as her job back home," I say.

"You do?" Cillian looks impressed. "Well, the plumbing needs some work. The kitchen has a leak, and the water pressure in the bathroom's terrible. Both bedrooms need new windows. They leak a little during every large storm. Clara sort of stopped working on it, because she was storing all the furniture she didn't use in the main house in there. There wasn't really any way to work on the place while it's stuffed to the gills, and I couldn't get her to actually toss any of the old stuff prior residents of Fortwilliam had saved."

"Maybe we keep it as a shed," I say. "It's probably hard to look at, stuffed with things."

"Do you know how big the steward's cottage is?" Vanessa taps her lip with one finger. "It's a four bedroom with. . .more than two thousand square feet of living space? Does that sound right?"

Cillian's brow furrows. "I'm accustomed to thinking of things in square meters, but I think that's close. It's just under two hundred square meters."

"And the gardener's cottage, which is not currently habitable," I say. "That's about the same as the stable cottage?"

"Yes, they're both a hundred square meters or so, with just one bathroom, a small kitchen, two bedrooms, and a sitting room."

Samantha's whipped out her phone. "A hundred square meters is eleven hundred square feet, and that's just fine with me." She chuckles. "If we're really considering this."

"The coach house is about 300 square meters." Cillian's brow is furrowed. "*Are* you really considering it?"

"That's three thousand and three hundred square feet," Samantha says. "Not too bad, even for a family with five kids."

"Do you really have five kids?" Cillian looks flabbergasted, which is how most new people I meet in Austin look when I tell them.

"That's why she needs a lot of space," Vanessa says. "But a paltry two thousand square feet's okay with me. I just have three kids."

"Just three?" Cillian's smiling. "And what about you?" He's trying to be smooth, I think, but it's not subtle at all.

"I don't have any kids," Samantha says.

"You don't like them?" He frowns. "Or you just. . ."

"We haven't really snooped around in the main house," I say. "Why don't you fill us in on how big it is."

"Right, of course." Cillian straightens. "There's technically a home called the fisherman's cottage that was built alongside the main house, but last year, Clara had contractors connect the house fully. That brings the house square meters to a thousand. It also has ten bedrooms, nine full bathrooms and two that just hold the jacks."

"The what?" I blink.

"Ah, I'm sorry. A toilet, in America."

"Jacks?" I ask. "Really?"

He shrugs. "I've heard you call it the John. Is that so different?"

I guess not.

Vanessa clears her throat. "So there are five separate houses, plus the barn and more than two hundred acres?" She whistles. "Maybe we *should* buy this."

"We?" I raise both my eyebrows. "Now that would be an adventure. All of us together again. . .in Ireland?" I can hardly believe it might even be possible. It *wasn't* possible last week. But with Heavy Lifting sold for Vanessa, albeit against her will, my dad's inheritance, and Samantha contemplating divorce. . . "This has been a vacation to end all vacations—and now we're thinking of making this our home. It's wild."

It only takes us half an hour to see what we can of the gardener's cottage, which Cillian's right about—it's stuffed to the rafters. It's good we're quick, because the main home's just as beautiful throughout as it was in the rooms we've seen.

"Though I hate the peach in the entryway," Samantha says. "And the weird lime green carpet *has* to go too."

Cillian laughs. "Some of Clara's color choices were. . .interesting, to be sure."

"But it's cool there's a billiard's room," I say. "And that kitchen she rebuilt." I can't help whistling a little. "It's magnificent."

"The woodwork is perfect," Samantha says, "but the colors are masterful. They're as good as the detail in the sitting room by the front door."

"That room was left almost entirely as it already was," Cillian says. "The Duke of Westminster brought all the moldings and fireplace and whatnot from one of his palaces. All Aunt Clara did was refurnish it."

"Well, she has an eye," I say. "It's such a lovely room."

"Hey, does the furniture come with it?" Samantha asks. "The listing doesn't say."

"Not all of it, no," Cillian says. "Or at least, I hadn't meant to pass it all along, but if you ladies want it, I'd include it."

"If there are some pieces you want," I say, "especially the art, I'd understand."

"I don't want any of the art." He glances at a strange painting of a black horse that is shaped in a way no horse has ever been shaped, and has eyes on the front of its head, and then he shudders.

I laugh. "I understand that. We may have to rehome some of it."

"Can we see the kitchen one more time?" Vanessa asks.

She's the most talented cook among us.

"Sure," Cillian says.

"It's my favorite room in the house, and that's saying something," Vanessa says as we walk back into it. "I could put a couch down and just sleep right here. I *love* the actual wood burning oven."

"I'm surprised the kitchen feels so bright and light—and the counters." I run my hand across the smooth, light wood. "I love the look of half wood and half granite."

"I googled the oven," Samantha says. "It's a local manufacturer that combines wood firing with the benefits of electric thermoregulation."

"And it's beautiful," Vanessa says.

"Mrs. Murphy commands in this kitchen like a drill sergeant," Cillian says. "When I was younger, before my aunt stopped hosting parties, you should have seen it fully staffed."

"It would be an amazing place for weddings," I say. "Can you just see it?"

"Ooh," Samantha says. "And for an equestrian-themed wedding?" She shivers. "I wish I could get married all over again, just so I could do it here."

"Oh, you're married?" Cillian is *so* not coming off as nonchalant, even though he's clearly trying.

"Well, not for long. Her husband turned out to be a total jerk," Vanessa says. "She deserves a do-over."

Samantha's blushing now, so I decide to save her.

"It almost feels like this whole thing was designed to be a hotel," I say. "I mean, sure, there's some work to do to make it more open and to make the lower floor more usable, but. . ." I spin around. "I could totally make this work."

"It's a little complicated," Cillian says, "getting permission to just move to Ireland. I think you'd need a work visa."

I can't help frowning at that. "Which I know nothing about." I sigh. "And of course, my kids will have opinions, too."

Samantha's asking about the utilities costs as we walk back down to the front entrance. From the front windows, I see Rían leading a horse out of the barn and into the courtyard.

"Ho!" he calls. "You're still here? Fancy one more ride?"

Cillian laughs. "When they leave, you'll have to actually do all your work on your own again."

"I'm not looking forward to it," Rían says.

"Do we have time to go change?" Samantha asks.

"Of course." Rían shifts so we can see his horse easier—it's the little bog pony. "Just working this one for a few moments." She's not even saddled. He must be planning to lunge her.

"What about you?" Rían's looking at Cillian now. "You could join us."

"Do you ride?" Samantha asks.

Cillian shrugs. "Not very well, but I used to enjoy it when I was younger."

"You should come," Samantha says. "You can keep selling us on the stunning property we probably shouldn't even be considering."

Cillian laughs. "I certainly can't ride out in this." He glances down at his fancy black suit. There's already a smudge on the shoulder from when he tried to shift things over in the gardener's cottage so we could get past the main living room and into the kitchen.

"Change into one of my jumpers," Rían says.

"If I can tolerate the smell, that might work." Cillian starts moving down the path to the farm buildings.

"He's borrowing a *jumper*?" We're moving back up the stairs already, so I'm not sure whether he even heard me. If he does, he doesn't respond.

"Cillian in coveralls?" Samantha asks. "I'm more excited than ever for one last ride."

"I think you might have a crush on him," I say.

"Stop." Samantha rolls her eyes.

But when your husband's planning to divorce you without a second thought, it might feel at least a little bit nice that someone handsome thinks you're pretty. At least, from my perspective, it's hard to imagine that *anyone* would ever like me again. That may be one of the scariest parts about leaving Mason.

I'm forty-one.

Am I really ready to walk away from my husband, my life, and everything I've ever known? What will I find on the other side? I'm a middle-aged woman without much about me to impress anyone. No one else is going to think my five kids are much of a prize. But if I moved here, and if I turned this beautiful estate into a business...

Would I be doing something impressive?

Maybe I'd be happy enough doing that, that it wouldn't matter if I'm alone for the rest of my life. When we walk back downstairs, I notice that Vanessa's dressed to ride. Again. Samantha catches my eye and widens hers. I widen mine in response and toss my head.

"You two don't have to act like I'm a flighty bird you mustn't startle."

Samantha and I both chuckle—nervously.

"We're just happy to see you changed," I say. "It makes us feel. . .whole again, somehow."

"Me too." Vanessa's words are small, but they feel genuine.

No one even asks which horse for Vanessa. Samantha saddles her own horse in two minutes—I have no idea how she's so fast—and immediately starts helping with Foxy. Moments later, we're all mounting. That's the first time I notice Cillian, to be honest, and I'm surprised.

He's not wearing a jumpsuit at all. "Oh," I say. "Thank goodness you're not wearing coveralls."

Cillian frowns.

Rían quirks an eyebrow. "Why would he be wearing coveralls?"

"That's a very nice navy *sweater* you loaned him," I clarify. "And you two wear, surprisingly, about the same size in pants."

Cillian's eyes widen. "Trousers?"

"Uh, sure," I say.

"And this is a jumper." Cillian pulls the sweater away from his chest an inch or two. "What's the other word you used? Coverall?"

"Jumper means sweater in Ireland. Got it." I laugh. "Never mind about the other thing."

Samantha and Vanessa are laughing. "Yes, that's better than what we thought you'd be wearing."

"What kind of clothing did you think I'd own?" Rían looks a little offended.

"Who knows?" I ask. "You Irish men wear different things than we do back home."

"And you play different sports," Vanessa says. "I can't stop thinking about that game from before—hurling?"

Rían grins. "Yes, my friend was sad you didn't come to our next game, even though we still won. He asked about his lucky charm."

"Oooh," I say. "Vanessa has an admirer."

Vanessa inhales sharply and looks at her feet. "Not because of that," she mumbles. "But I was looking at the movements they make, with the sticks." She lifts her head back up at the end, thankfully.

"Hurleys," Rían says. "The sticks are called hurleys."

"My son was a football champion," Vanessa says. "Not your football, but American football. But he can't do what he used to anymore, after he had a surgery. I mean, he *could*, but he's not good enough to play for his team now. But watching what they do, I think he might be able to do that reasonably well."

"How serious are you ladies about possibly moving here?" Cillian asks, glancing from Vanessa to me and then to Samantha. "I thought it was mostly just a lark."

"I'm entirely serious," I say, realizing that it's true.

CHAPTER 20
Natalie

This time, instead of heading to the left and the nunnery, Vanessa wants to ride by the castle. "I haven't seen it yet," she says. "I hear it's a nice ride."

The look she exchanges with Samantha has me a little suspicious. "You can't go inside," I say. "Even the gardens are by admission only—you need a ticket."

"But we can walk down the river bank, no?" Vanessa looks entirely innocent now, wide eyes and raised eyebrows.

I roll my eyes. "Sure, fine."

Even though I'm mildly annoyed, I keep a careful watch on the under-brush. Around every green turn, my heart accelerates a little. I don't want to admit it, not even to myself, but I'm kind of hoping I'll bump into Richard.

Which is really stupid.

In a random dream I had last night, we ran into him while we were out for a ride, and he invited us back to see the inside of Lismore Castle. It was ridiculous. I'm not a child. I don't have secret aspirations to wear a crown and be a pretty princess. I've cleaned too many toilets, changed too many diapers, and mucked too many stalls to suffer from any delusions that I might one day be royalty in any circumstance other than on Mother's Day. Even then, I get a crown made of construction paper.

Thinking about my dumb dream just makes me think about Mason and Tiffany again, and it puts me in a horrible mood.

Unsurprisingly, no prince, duke, or earl makes an appearance to cheer me up. No birds clean up my dishes. No squirrels make my bed. Because I don't live in a fairy tale. I have a boring, old, regular life.

Of course I do.

But Vanessa does really well on her second ride—even better than the first. She stays on Foxy's back, which is always a win on a trail ride, and the sweet little mare's a model citizen. She doesn't spook, yank, or race. And when Lismore Castle comes into view, I can't help my gasp. The large square turret and the smaller, round tower beside it, rising up into the blue, cloud-streaked sky, are a breathtaking sight.

Of course anyone would be impressed. "It really is too bad we can't go inside," I say. "It's a lovely castle."

"It sure is." I hate Samantha's smirk, but I know she's doing it because she loves me.

We've all just turned around when a voice calls out. "Natalie?"

My heart races as we wheel around.

Richard's riding the same blood bay with the striking, perfect socks that he was on before, but this time he looks like he's barely been ridden. His sides aren't heaving, and there's no sweat on his neck. "I hoped I might run into you out here." He trots up to the rest of us, our horses all sniffing the air and shuffling around. "Would you mind if I rode back with you?"

"We'd rather see your grounds," Samantha says. "We tried to get a tour of your fancy castle, but they said that plebeians like us aren't allowed inside."

Richard blinks, and then he laughs—it's almost a bellow, really. "I would happily show you around, but the whole castle's rented out starting tomorrow for a wedding, and I've been kicked out myself. The staff's currently working feverishly to make it sparkle."

"How big's the group this time?" Cillian asks.

"It's some kind of tech billionaire's daughter—from California," Richard says. "Though if you saw their list of demands, you'd think she was a famous Hollywood starlet."

"Not all of us Americans are quite so high strung, I swear," Vanessa says.

"Most of us drink water from the tap and muck our own stalls," Samantha says.

"Like a good plebeian should." He's smirking, so at least Richard knows a joke when he hears one.

The ride back to Fortwilliam's quick, or maybe it just seems that way. I can't think of anything to say for most of the way. Samantha and Vanessa pelt Richard with questions, and I try not to cringe too much.

"Give us a virtual tour," Samantha says. "Since we're to be denied the pleasure of seeing your massive castle ourselves."

"Lismore was actually first built as a battlement," he says. "That's why it's positioned along the river. It actually began its life as Lismore Abbey and only later got upgraded to a castle."

"But your family has always owned it?" Vanessa asks. "Since the time it was an abbey?"

Richard shakes his head. "No, and in fact, when you look into most of the great houses and castles, you'll find that most of them changed hands many times over the years. Lismore belonged to the earls of Cork for a long time, but in the mid 1700s, when the last one died, it passed to the last earl's descendant, Charlotte, who happened to be wed to the fourth Duke of Devonshire—William Cavendish. It's been in our family ever since."

"You'll need to learn all the history of the places around here," Cillian says. "They're all draws to the tourists you want to bring over."

"Bring over?" Richard glances my way.

I hate the feeling of my cheeks turning pink. "Um, we're thinking of buying the Fortwilliam Estate and making it a hotel."

"You don't say." The corners of Richard's mouth curl upward. "Who is *we*?"

"I'm thinking of coming with her," Samantha says. "We could live in the cottages on the property and rent out the rooms of the main home."

"I'm not sure we can really afford it," I say. "But we're looking into it. I have five children I'd need to convince, plus there's a lot of paperwork in moving to another country that I know nothing about."

"I have a friend from Cambridge who specializes in that sort of thing," Richard says. "I'm happy to refer you."

"That would be amazing," I say.

"If you email info at Lismore Castle," he says, "Helen can get you Archie's info. I'll let her know you need it. She runs everything for me at the castle."

Email his Irish assistant—at first I'm disappointed that he's not giving me his number. But then, the more I think about it, the better I feel. We're acquaintances, and he's keeping things proper. No guilt is exactly what I need.

Even if a little voice is telling me I was stupid to think he might like me at all. He's just a charming British man. That's all. I'm the delusional one.

"If you don't have other plans, we should all go to dinner," Richard says. "We can talk more about your plans—plus, my cook will be far less stressed if I don't try to eat back home."

"Dinner?" Rían smiles. "Are you paying?"

Richard laughs. "Of course I am. How about Foley's?"

It takes us a moment to work out the details, but Rían and Cillian are quite keen on the invite, which tells me it's as exciting for them to spend more time with the Earl of Burlington as it is for us.

Once we get back to Fortwilliam and we're tacking down the horses, Vanessa squeals. "An actual duke invited us to dinner because of you."

I roll my eyes. "Not because of me."

"Totally because of you," Rían says. "I've known him for years now, after bumping into him on a ride just after starting to work here, and he's never once invited me to so much as a single drink."

"And, he's not a duke, remember?" I ask. "His *father's* a duke."

"Same thing," Samantha says.

"No, she's right," Rían says.

"I can't believe this happened," Cillian says. "And while I was wearing borrowed clothing." He sighs. "At least at dinner I'll be dressed appropriately."

"Oh, no," Vanessa says.

"What?" I ask.

"What on earth do you wear to go to dinner with a duke?" Vanessa looks truly distressed.

We all laugh, but I'm actually worried. None of us brought nice clothing.

"Foley's isn't fine dining," Cillian says. "Not like any place in London, or even Cork. Whatever you brought with you will be fine, I'm sure." His reassurance would carry more weight if he hadn't just told us with relief that he'd be wearing a designer suit.

An hour later we're all, more or less, ready to go.

I'm wearing the new boots I got on my shopping binge, cleaned of all traces of mud. I'm also wearing my mostly-clean, new Mackage coat, and a brilliant blue, cashmere sweater I bought in Dublin on our first real day here. When I pass the mirror, I pause, and I don't feel *too* bad about what I see.

Samantha's coming out of her doorway when I walk into the upstairs landing. "That color totally makes your eyes pop," she insists. "And you curled your hair!" Her squeal makes me laugh. "I swear, you look just like Meg Ryan—a young Meg Ryan."

One time, ten years ago, someone said I reminded them of Meg Ryan. It was the nicest compliment I've ever gotten, and I've clung to it like a wisteria vine on a brick wall ever since. When you have the quintessential girl-next-door look, you take any compliment you get.

"How much younger than her can I really look?" I ask. "I'm forty-one."

"She's probably sixty now." Samantha shrugs. "Right?"

That's depressing. "And please don't act like this is a date or something," I say. "It's not."

B. E. BAKER

"Well," Samantha says. "It's three hot ladies and three single men."

"We don't actually know whether any of them are single," Vanessa says, finally emerging from her room. "And if you're calling this a date?" She pulls a face. "I should stay home, because I'm *not* going out with twenty-something-year-old Rían. So just, stop."

"See? We agree," I say. "Just a group of friends."

Samantha rolls her eyes. "Fine. It's not a date—obviously. I'm still married, and so are you." She arches one eyebrow at me. "But I may as well tell you. . .I sent an email to Brent today, agreeing to the terms he laid out for our property division."

"You did?" I'm floored. "It's been less than a week. He's already spoken with a lawyer?"

She shrugs, but I notice that her eyes are welling with tears. "I guess he wasn't wishy washy about this at all." It must sting that he's *so* keen.

"I'm sorry," I say.

She shakes her head. "Nope, we're not doing that. Not right now." She waves her hands in front of her face. "I didn't bring waterproof mascara."

Cillian's pacing outside the house, but he stops when we join him.

"Ready?" I ask.

"Where's that idiot, Rían?" he asks. "If he makes us late—"

"I'm here." Rían's jogging down the path between the barn and the house. "Ready to go."

"Are you wearing the same jumper you loaned me?" Cillian arches one eyebrow.

Rían snorts. "No way. I just have a lot that look the same—I like blue."

Now that Cillian mentions it, it *does* look similar, but paired with weathered jeans, Rían the horse-guy actually looks pretty handsome. Is he trendy? I wouldn't have guessed it from the past few days, but maybe that's just his work ensemble.

The drive from Fortwilliam to Foley's in downtown Lismore takes about five minutes, and I notice Richard walking across the street as we pull into a parking space. Only then do I realize that I can see the outline of Lismore Castle behind the buildings on this seemingly main street of town.

"The castle's right next to the town," I say.

212

"It's actually the town that's close to the castle." Cillian puts the car in park. "It sprang up around the castle, many centuries ago. It was the castle occupants who employed and provided for all the townspeople."

Of course. "The feudal stuff is a strange concept for Americans," I admit. "We don't have any castles."

"Which is a strange concept to us Irish," Cillian says.

Foley's is a cute place—with what looks an awful lot like a Texas flag out front. I want to ask about it, but after Richard joins us, I can't get a word in edgewise. Everyone who was invited seems to have a list of questions they want to ask. The hostess seats us in an outdoor room that's not really fully exposed to the elements. It has a clear plastic ceiling and walls, and is apparently called the Stone Room. Or at least, that's what a plaque on the outside wall of the main building says. Richard orders a handful of appetizers, and most of them sound great. Bruschetta, garlic mushrooms, prawn 'pil-pil,' whatever that is, and calamari.

Cillian's focused on details of the Lismore real estate market, and Rían keeps interrupting him with horse-racing questions. They sit on either side of Richard, leaving the girls and me to settle across from them. It *definitely* doesn't feel like a date. It almost feels like we're at some kind of business networking dinner.

"I didn't realize he was into racehorses," I whisper to Samantha, just as the waitress arrives to take our order.

"All the Cavendishes love racehorses," Richard says. "I didn't have much choice in the matter."

I startle a bit, surprised that he heard me.

Cillian frowns—apparently I've interrupted some information he was in the process of getting from Richard. Thankfully, Richard doesn't seem to notice.

"The very first Duke of Cavendish had to leave England after Charles the First died—a long story." He smiles. "While William was hiding abroad, he became obsessed with a new sort of riding he discovered in Paris, and when he returned, his obsession transformed the method of riding in England. That method of riding you would now know as dressage."

"You're kidding," Samantha says. "I think I've heard of him—he left a handwritten list of his fifty-something horses when he died."

Richard smiles. "That's definitely William, but we've all been obsessed with horses, and I suppose I'm no exception."

"That's how the three of us know each other," Vanessa says. "We all rode together as little girls. Our obsession turned into a lifelong friendship."

"That's a special connection," Richard says. "I hope you don't take it for granted."

"I think we have in the past," I say. "But I definitely don't now."

"How serious are you about moving here?" Richard asks. "Buying Fortwilliam is a big commitment."

"I know it seems kind of crazy, but I think we're pretty serious."

"You know, there's a romantic story that connects Fortwilliam and Lismore," Cillian says. "Have you heard of Fred Astaire?"

"The dancer?" I ask. "My grandmother was obsessed with him."

"Along with the rest of the world back in the 1930s and 40s," Richard says. "But what a lot of people don't recall is that when he first began dancing, he was overshadowed by his enormously talented sister."

"Adele," Cillian says. "She and Fred did every production together, and England fell in love with them both. They'd put on every new production on Broadway first, and then they'd bring it over to the UK and it would run nearly as long here."

"Sometimes longer," Richard says. "But unlike her brother, Adele didn't love show business. She disliked it, actually. She loved dancing, but she hated the other things that went along with it."

"So when, after one of their shows, she met a man named Charles. . ." Cillian smiles. "A man who was ten years younger than her, and was dashingly handsome, she decided to take some time off from performing."

"She leased the Fortwilliam Estate," Richard says, "to be closer to Charles Cavendish, who was staying at Lismore Castle at the time. His father owned it, the ninth Duke of Devonshire. After they decided to marry, Victor gifted Lismore to his son, my great-great-uncle Charlie. Unfortunately, he was an alcoholic, and he didn't live to be happily married for very long. Their love story was passionate, but it was also turbulent and tragic."

"Did you ever meet them?" I ask.

Richard shakes his head. "Adele far outlived my great-great-uncle, but even she died right after I was born—she wasn't in good enough health to even come to Lismore in the last few years of her life. They do say she was in love with the castle and came for decades after Charles died."

"It's a beautiful story," Samantha says. "I love it, and I bet it helps us bring tourists to Fortwilliam."

"If only Lismore Castle was open to the public," Cillian says, "instead of just the gardens and the art exhibit. That could really revitalize the whole area."

"About that," Richard says.

"About what?" I can't help my frown.

"Do you recall our conversation at Dunluce?"

"You mean when we met less than a week ago?" I can't help my smirk. "I'd have to be addlebrained not to recall it."

"I don't think I'll ever be able to forget seeing you sitting in the mud next to Natalie," Samantha says. "It's an image that's burned into my brain."

"I was headed out here, but I made a few stops along the way. See, my father's getting along in years," Richard says. "We're not sure how much longer he'll be with us." He looks almost resigned about it. Typical Brit. "We have some big decisions to make. Even with most of the family's real property held in trust, estate taxes will have to be paid."

Cillian coughs. "Oh, no."

"We're considering selling Lismore," Richard says. "Although we are looking into some other options too."

"That would be a huge change," Cillian says.

"And I'd be sad if you didn't come back again," Rían says.

"But it might be better for everyone here, especially if it becomes a tourist draw," Cillian says. "How confidential is this?"

Richard arches one eyebrow. "Pretty confidential at this stage. I haven't made any decisions yet. I'm gathering information."

I'm only really considering Fortwilliam for the first time as of a few hours ago, and I barely know Richard.

So why do I feel gutted?

The appetizers arrive then, and I dive in. "This bruschetta's to die for." As I reach for the second to last piece of ciabatta, my hand brushes against Richard's. A tiny thrill races up my arm. "Oh, sorry." I pull my arm back, not even touching the bread.

"Take it," he says. "I'll take this one." He picks up the one on the far end. "I'm glad you like it."

"Natalie barely touches calamari," Samantha says. "Not much of a seafood fan, so it's good for her that you got the mushrooms and bruschetta."

"It's a shame, close to the coast like this. The seafood's amazing." Richard leans a bit closer. "Or at least, that's what they say. I'm not much for seafood either, to my father's great dismay."

When the food comes, I notice that Richard ordered the open-faced steak sandwich. "The carbonara's my second favorite," he says, eyeing my meal. "Good call."

"I like this place," I say. "Everything's been good."

"Is Mrs. Murphy still running Fortwilliam?" Richard asks.

Cillian nods.

"Then you sort of know the chef," he says. "This restaurant's run by her daughter and son-in-law."

"Small towns," I say. "I love it."

After we've had dinner, I excuse myself to go to the restroom—too much water—and when I return, they're debating the merits of the meringue, the cheesecake, and the brownie.

"Not to throw a wrench into things," I say. "But sticky toffee pudding will always be my favorite."

"Pudding?" Vanessa grimaces. "I'm not eight."

"But this pudding's a cake," I say. "You'll love it."

Richard orders one of each, but he adds. "We'll take two orders of the sticky toffee pudding. Natalie needs her own."

I shake my head. "I can't possibly. I'm on a diet."

He laughs. "Women are always on diets, but as far as I can tell, they rarely need to be on them." He nods. "She'll have the pudding."

When the desserts come, they all try the various types and weigh in on what they like. Richard slides one of the puddings over to me. "This one's for you."

"You know, you can't do stuff like this," I say. "I really am on a diet."

"And I meant it when I said you shouldn't be," he says.

"Are you really going to sell Lismore?"

He shrugs. "Are you really going to buy Fortwilliam?"

I shrug back.

"Then we might be at an impasse."

"Impasse?" I blink. "How so?"

"How can I decide whether to sell the Irish castle I almost never visit when I'm not sure who might move into the neighborhood?"

My heart picks up. "You know, I'm still married."

"I do know." He smiles. "You keep reminding me, but I doubt you will be for very long."

"I—" I take a bite of my sticky toffee pudding, which is just as good as I remember it being. It's warm, it's soft, and it's just a little chewy. Rich, dark, and delicious.

Kind of like the man paying for our dinner.

"We should get a photo," Samantha says, "to document the dinner we all had before the duke sells his castle."

"The duke is my father," Richard says. "And if Lismore's sold, it won't be his fault unless you can blame someone for dying."

"Sometimes I do," Vanessa says. "But I know it's not fair."

After we all smile for the photo that our waitress takes, I find myself on the far side, next to Richard. For the first time all night, he can probably hear me, but no one else can. "I understand why you'd want to sell Lismore," I say. "It's really the same reason I want to buy Fortwilliam."

"Oh?" His eyes are bright, and his expression pleasant. He's wearing modern clothing, but I swear, it almost feels like Mr. Darcy has stepped off the pages of *Pride and Prejudice* and joined us.

"When the misery caused by something is greater than the cost of having it, it's time to let go." I sigh. "That's why I've decided to let go of my marriage, and maybe even my home."

"I think that's a smart decision," he says. "But only you can make it."

He's right, and I think I already have. Knowing that I have options available to me, fun and exciting new vistas I can pursue even without a husband, helps me make the decision with a lot less fear.

Even if I never see Richard again, I'll always be grateful to him for showing me that the whole world isn't full of Masons. Good men do exist after all.

CHAPTER 21

Vanessa

I shouldn't have come on this trip.

My son didn't get checked into rehab, when he clearly needed to.

My dishonest brother-in-law took advantage of my absence to steal a company my husband built and paid for.

I should've been at home, managing my life and keeping my kids safe, but instead, I was in Ireland, playing with my friends. I rode a horse for the first time in years, and it was. . .at the risk of sounding like a hippy, it was therapeutic. I should be frantic right now at all the things that went wrong thanks to my selfish girls' trip. Instead, I almost feel happy.

Calm.

Peaceful.

I'm also a believer that things usually happen for a reason.

Would I ever have sold Jason's company? No. Never. Would I have considered any treatment for Trace that wasn't the official, established plans set out by a licensed drug rehab facility? No. I'd have kept enrolling him in the various approved and vetted programs forever. And maybe that *is* the best method to help him.

But after talking to Natalie, I looked up some of the information she mentioned. I watched the Ted Talk she referred to, notably given by a Brit, and I researched the impact of connections on addicts.

The data supports what Natalie said.

I might have been approaching things all wrong before now.

So, for just a moment, I consider the insane thing Natalie's thinking of doing. It's nuts to buy a massive, gorgeous, expansive estate in Ireland, of all places. Riding horses with tourists on holiday and running a hotel? It's utter madness.

But I'm an accountant.

It's what I do—keep track of money. Right now, I mostly manage things for other people. But why not do it for my friends? Why not go into this with them? I can't get the company back, and if I can't. . .what am I doing in Colorado? For the first time, while my friends are getting ready to leave, I'm running numbers in earnest.

With what I just got from the sale of Jason's company, and with what I could get from the sale of our home, I could afford to contribute to this crazy idea in an amount *almost* equal to Natalie, and I could move my family to Ireland. I'm researching the various visa laws when someone knocks on my door.

"Mrs. Murphy has breakfast ready. They have that possible buyer taking a look in an hour, remember?" Natalie asks.

"I'm awake." I fling the door open.

Natalie stumbles back a step. "Yes, you are."

"But I'm not sure we should leave." I fold my arms. "I don't want that other buyer to get this place." I huff. "I want it."

Natalie beams. "Are you serious?"

I nod. "Would it be insane?" I laugh. "Probably, but it's the first thing I've been excited about in a very, very long time, and I never do anything crazy. I think I'm overdue."

Natalie grabs my hand. "Me, too."

We manage to clear out in time for the buyers to take a look, but only just. A sleek black sedan that I suspect is the potential buyer passes us on the mile-long, tree-lined drive out of Fortwilliam and back to the main road.

As we pass the last pasture, the one with the stunning, flowering tree in the center of it, I must be thinking the exact same thing as everyone else, because Samantha squeals. "I can't believe we're considering this. We came here for vacation."

"I know," Natalie says. "And my kids may immediately freak out. Clara's going into her senior year, after all."

"And Hannah's what? A freshman?" Samantha asks.

"She'll be a sophomore next year," Natalie says.

"Bryce too, but he has no friends. He'll probably be excited to leave. I'm sure Trace will hate the idea," I say. "But I don't really care much what he wants."

"If the two of you are really serious," Samantha says, "then maybe I am, too."

We spend the rest of the drive talking over details. "It's seven million for the property, but I bet we can get Cillian to come down a little," I say. "I ran some numbers."

"I don't want to lose it to the hotel people because we're trying to save a bit," Natalie says.

"You two are such nerds," Samantha says, "and I love it."

"It would be best if we can afford to pay for it with what we have saved. Maintenance on a place like that," I say, "will be painfully high. We'll need one gardener at least—maybe two. Someone will have to help with horses. I'm not sure what Rían charges, but maybe him. We'd need to keep Mrs. Murphy and have at least one other woman to clean full time to run it as a hotel. We'll need weekend coverage. We could wind up tied to it, especially if it's hard to find reliable help."

"It would become a lifestyle," Samantha says. "And our busiest times are probably the times most people don't want to work. Summer and holidays."

"Getting visas and moving will be a mess," Natalie says. "But I'm not going to lie. Even with all that, it sounds like the adventure I need."

"Do you really want five dogs?" I ask. "Because that's a lot."

Samantha laughs. "Maybe we could start with just one."

"I call the coach house," Natalie says. "Five kids."

"The steward's cottage would be great for us," I say. "All my kids could even have their own room, and the kitchen's small, but honestly, I'd probably sneak over to the main house when I want to make something fancy anyway."

"I like the idea of having a small house," Samantha says. "Less to clean. I'm sure the stable cottage will be fine, but I'm also not afraid of refurbishing the gardener's cottage if Rían really needs somewhere to live."

"You can be in charge of all the horse training," Natalie says. "You might not even need him."

"Unless I'm out giving tours," she says. "And we have enough horses we might sometimes do two tour groups."

"True," I say.

"Either way, I'll work on redoing the gardener's cottage," Samantha says. "If I don't need to live there, we can rent it out separately to parties who want more privacy. We could rename it the fisherman's cottage since the actual fisherman's cottage was assimilated into the house."

"Other members of our staff might use it," Vanessa says. "Then their board would be part of their pay."

"Good ideas," Samantha says. "Natalie can manage the bookings and all our social media."

"And help run the horseback ride tours," Natalie says. "Hello. That's half the reason I want to do this."

"Same." Samantha laughs.

We fill up most of our three-hour drive with possibilities, and I'm not sure time has ever flown quite so fast. When we finally reach the famed Cliffs of Moher, I'm more than ready to stretch my legs. From the very second we open the door of the car, the wind attacks my hair, whipping it around my head like a turban and practically choking me.

"I'd heard the wind here was something else," Natalie says. "But I had no idea it weaponized your hair." She ducks back in the car to tie her hair back and stuff it all under a cap.

"I hope that's tight," Samantha shouts when she re-emerges, "or you'll lose it."

We all walk quickly up the path to the ticket office. The wind's brisk, and it's chilly, but the countryside's still bright green. As we draw near, we can already tell the scenery from the Cliffs themselves is going to be breathtaking.

The visitor's center's well done, and the gift shop has lovely things like hand knit scarves with delicate lace trim. I buy a nice, pink scarf and wrap it around my neck in anticipation of a very cold walk to the overlook. I don't regret having bought it, especially when the wind howls all around us. It's quite a climb to the top, even if the path steps are paved and quite solid, and I'm not cold when we finally reach the overlook. The wind tears at my new scarf, my face, and my hands. The waves crash below, and there's a mist resting over everything, in spite of the ceaseless wind.

But the Cliffs of Moher weren't overhyped.

They're spectacular.

"Ireland—" Natalie shakes her head. "Somehow it's both old and new. It's bright and brilliant and also steeped in history. I love it here."

She's right.

There's something I can't quite articulate, but it feels like Ireland has a depth, a past to it that I've never felt anywhere else. Maybe that's why, when my history back home feels so full of sorrow, that I can see a future for myself here. I see a verdant, green, welcoming place for us all.

"I think Bryce would love this," I say. "And I know Trina would. She's always making fairy circles and braiding clover and flowers into crowns."

"Ah, to be seven again," Natalie says. "I have no doubt Paul would be trying to fling himself over the edge right here." She reaches out and shakes the guard rail. "It's good these are sturdy."

"Young boys aren't for the faint of heart," I say.

That's when I notice Samantha's crying. I wrap an arm around her shoulders.

"I—I wish I'd adopted a child." The wind snatches her whispered words away almost as quickly as she says them. "I should've ignored Brent and just done it."

"You know, our kids are basically your kids," Natalie says. "You'll probably be sick of them within a few weeks."

Samantha doesn't say anything, but she wipes her tears, and she bravely forces a smile. "I know."

As I stand with my two best friends, looking out over the Cliffs, I can't help thinking about how some things change in a blink, but other things last. Years have passed since we were kids, and many friends have come and gone. Even Jason, who changed my life in so many ways, was here, and now he's not.

But Samantha and Natalie are like these cliffs. They've weathered storms with me, and they're still by my side. I feel. . .at peace with the idea of trying to make a new life, supported by these two women. People I can rely on. People who would never steal from me. People who chivvy and push and cajole me to get back on the horse, literally and figuratively, just so I can move ahead in my life. Nothing in it for them.

It's rare and it's beautiful, what we have.

"I think we should make an offer on that place," I say. "And I have plenty of cash to contribute, and no business to run back home anymore. All I have to do now is give notice to my job."

"Well," Natalie says. "That and get visas, sell your house, pack and move. You know." She rolls her eyes. "Details."

I laugh. "Sure. A *few* other things." But strangely, it seems doable. Very, very doable. And I'm looking forward to tomorrow instead of dreading it.

On my flight home the next day, I start making lists of things I hope my kids would enjoy about Lismore, because my next sell job will be a big one. I need to get my kids on board with this out-of-the-blue move so I can change all our lives. . .forever.

CHAPTER 22

Samantha

Planning to buy a stunning estate in Ireland feels like a dream. So when I get on the plane, *of course* I wonder whether I've lost my mind. I've been married to Brent for a long time. He's been with me through a lot of things, and he's far from perfect.

But he's not a villain.

Is this all some kind of crazy, insane lark? Am I making a huge mistake to let Brent just walk away? Should I fight to stay with him, convincing him to give 'us' another chance?

When I think about buying Fortwilliam and walking away from my life in Florida, the only place I've ever lived, I feel surprisingly good about it. The only thing that really gives me pause is being so far from my sister, my nieces, and my nephews. I'll miss my brothers, but it's not quite the same as leaving my sister.

Five years ago, I'd never have considered it.

But now they're all so busy with their kids' activities that I hardly see them. I do make it to virtually every 'thing' the kids do. Dance recitals. Karate tournaments. Before my niece Kylie quit doing them, horse shows. But none of that's something they *need* me for, and my siblings are all out of the 'please rush over and watch my babies during this emergency' stage. They mostly used my mom for that anyway.

I suppose that's the thing about *not* having kids.

It makes it way easier for me to upend my life and move.

But Varius.

He's my biggest concern, really. I've been doing some research—lots of horses come and go from the Ocala area, clearly, but it's still a daunting process. The biggest question mark is quarantine. There's no way to know how long they'll hold him in Ireland, or what circumstances he'll be kept in during that time. A lot of horses lose weight, and he's old. It'll be harder for him to regain whatever he loses.

I feel like one of those clicking metal balls on a wire during my long trip back. One minute I feel good about moving on. Brent's been toxic. I'm not happy. I should let him go. But the next, I worry about throwing away something decent and think I should work harder on what I have. I still can't decide how much of what I'm feeling is fear, and how much is another emotion, and if so, what?

I have realized one thing by the time I land: I'm a mess.

As I'm deplaning, I turn my phone on, and I'm bombarded by messages. Typical long-flight nonsense. I have a message from my schedule coordinator asking me to cover for a co-worker with a funeral. There's a message from our investment guy wanting to set up a sit-down. Not going to happen. There're also about five messages from local businesses I never should have given my number.

But then I see my vet called. Six times.

My trainer called too, three times.

I whip out my phone and start listening to the messages.

The first one's from the trainer at my barn. "Hey, Sam, it's me. Listen, it's early, but it looks like Varius is colicking. He's rolling, and I've given him banamine, but I'm going to go ahead and call the vet. I know you're out of town."

My heart rate skyrockets. That was minutes after I went through security.

The next message is from my vet, Amy. "Hi, Samantha, it's me. I started giving Varius oil, but it won't stay down. I think we're dealing with a twist in the intestines, and I'm recommending surgery as soon as possible. Call me back."

Another one from her, an hour later. "It's been an hour, and he looks worse. I think we need to get him to the hospital right away," Amy says. "Call me back immediately."

The next message is also from Amy, and I'm feeling sick—very, very sick when I click play. "Hey, Samantha. I don't feel good about this. I wish you'd pick up. Since I hadn't heard from you, I called your husband. He's listed as your emergency contact, and he said since Varius is older, and since you're already worried about stepping him down, and since the colic surgery would be risky, you'd want to wait and see if he'll improve without costly intervention, but I have to tell you, I don't see how he possibly could. I see the obstructive lesion on ultrasound, and it's strangulating. I think we need to act immediately, unless you're ready to put him down."

Brent said to wait and see.

There's absolutely *no way* he could possibly think I would want to wait. He's known me for decades. I would *never* hold off on an emergency surgery, no matter my horse's age.

It's five in the morning when I dial my vet, and I'm worried she won't answer. Given that she was awake at eleven p.m. leaving me voicemails from my barn, I'm hoping she doesn't jump through the phone and kill me when she does pick up.

"Samantha?"

"I'm so sorry, Amy, I was flying home from Ireland."

"I'm the one who's sorry," Amy says, clearly groggy. She clears her throat. "Varius. . .we should've trailered him over for surgery right away."

"Do it now," I say. "I'll call Kim and see if she can do it." I'm panicking. "I'm still at least an hour and a half away, and I have to go through customs."

"There's nothing you can do now," Amy says. "I'm so sorry, Samantha, but Varius died around midnight."

My hands were shaking already, but now all of me starts to shake.

He *died*?

How could he have died? He was *fine* when I left. He was. . .*fine*. I'm breathing too fast. My heart's racing. "I—oh my word, Amy. He *died*?" Tears roll down my cheeks and splash on my jacket. "He *died*?" People are looking at me strangely. They're walking farther and farther away from me. One mother puts her arm around her little girl and speed-walks her to the far wall.

"I know it's not your fault, but I just. . ." Horses die. They just do. I've lost three already, but I was prepared for it. I never had it all hit me in a three-minute period before.

No warning.

"I am so sorry, but your husband was so adamant that you wouldn't want to spend the money on an emergency colic surgery for an older horse that—"

"He wasn't that old," I wail.

A man with a black jacket with the word **SECURITY** printed on the front left is walking toward me, murmuring into a headpiece.

"I tried to tell him that I thought you *would* want the surgery, but he insisted." Amy's voice cracks. "I'm so sorry."

I can't hear anything else she says, and I can't see what anyone around me is doing. Not anymore. Rage rises up inside of me, hot and red.

I'm going to kill Brent.

Forget a divorce.

I'm going to wring his neck with my bare hands. And when I'm done, I'm going to burn him to ash in the firepit behind our house. The authorities won't have any trouble figuring out it's me, but I *dare* a jury to convict me.

How could he do that?

Varius was just a horse—he couldn't speak for himself. He couldn't protect himself. He relied on me to protect him, and I failed him.

I'm sobbing now, my whole body shaking.

He's only a horse—I know that. But I don't have kids—he's my child. He's *all I have*, and now, because of *Brent,* he's gone.

I hate him.

Any mixed feelings I had, any desire to reconcile, it's vapor.

I can never forgive Brent for this.

Not ever.

When I get out of the airport, I don't even drive home. I drive straight to the barn, and I practically sprint from my car to the stall where Varius has always waited for me. Where he's still waiting for me. I can barely see for all the crying, and for a brief moment, I imagine he's just lying down. Maybe he's sleeping. He loves to sleep in his stall.

But he's not asleep.

When I pass through the door, his body's already cool.

And now that I've seen him, now that I know it's real, I'm equal parts fury and misery. I cry for a very, very long time before I finally leave my sweet, beautiful, devoted Varius behind and drive home. When I get there, Brent must be leaving for a meeting or something. He's all dressed up.

"I guess you heard." His voice is flat.

He knows how I'll react. He did it. . .did he do it to make sure I wouldn't have second thoughts? Was he trying to hurt me? Did he really take out his anger at me on Varius? What kind of monster would do that?

Every happy memory we shared, every little victory, every celebration, they're ash now. As I stand on my own front porch, staring at my husband, I feel *nothing*.

My hatred's gone.

My anger has evaporated.

Love and hate are opposites, you see, and what he did, it burned all of that out of me forever. When I look at Brent now, I just see a sad, middle-aged man with whom I share nothing.

"Let's list the house this week," I say. "I want to get this all done as soon as possible. I'm moving to Ireland."

His brow furrows, and he inhales sharply, but he doesn't argue with me. He just nods. "Sure. If that's what you want."

"It is," I say.

Then I push past my husband, and I walk inside my house to pack my things. I spend most of the rest of the day crying, but at least I'm not swinging back and forth. Not anymore.

I call Natalie that afternoon. "Hey girl," I say. "You made it back okay?"

"I did," Natalie says. "But it's not the best time for me to chat right now."

"I just wanted to say—I'm in. I saw Brent today, and I can't stay here. I'm ready to move when you are. Let me know what you need."

"Really?" Natalie says.

"I'm completely and totally serious. If the other people who looked at the place didn't put an offer down, I'm ready to start talking actual numbers."

"What did you decide about Varius?"

I inhale deeply and draw in a ragged breath. I can't start bawling now, not again. I only barely stopped. "Let's talk about it later. He won't be a problem."

"Okay," Natalie says. "Well, that's exciting. I'll call you tomorrow."

For the first time today, I have something to smile about. Our Irish escape is officially underway.

CHAPTER 23
Natalie

I've imagined the moment when I see Mason again dozens of times, now. Sometimes he knows I know. Others, he doesn't. Sometimes he acts like he doesn't know I know, but I can tell he does.

In every single instance, he's somehow villainous.

A mustache-curling, dagger-hiding, horn-wearing demon. But that's not the man I've spent the last twenty-one years with. I thought I was married to a kind, caring, considerate husband I've relied upon in basically every circumstance. Somehow, on that day I saw the pink stilettos, I disassociated him with everything that went before.

He became just a villain.

As the plane lands and the moment I've been putting off approaches, I'm virtually certain that he knows I know. Tiffany *flew to Ireland*, for heaven's sake, and she tried to convince me that we could still be friends. I turned her down, so there's no way she didn't head home and tell him what happened.

Right?

Right.

I'm sure they've been working on the details of their Evil Plan ever since she left Fortwilliam. Maybe Mason hid even more money than she told me about. Maybe they're working to somehow defraud me at this very moment. Or perhaps they spent all night last night together, laughing at what an idiot I am. I feel like I don't know my own husband *at all*, but I do know he won't be taken aback when I accuse him of cheating on me. He must be expecting it.

He won't be shocked when I ask for a divorce.

I'm half expecting him to have preliminary papers in the car when he pulls up on the curb to pick me up. I am *not* expecting Mason to show up with all five kids, a bouquet of roses, and a sign that says "Welcome Home Mom!"

I've gone on a lot of girls' trips, and nothing like *this* has ever happened. It's got to be evidence that he knows I know.

"Hey, guys." My eyes dart to Mason's—which look surprisingly non-villainous—and he shrugs.

"We missed you," Clara says. "And Hannah had to do a project for art class, so we figured, why not make it this?" She gestures at their sign, and I realize that they've illustrated the inside of all the block letters. Horses. Social media. Photography. Disney World. Cookies. All the things they, apparently, associate with me.

"Yeah, Dad said I couldn't watch Ben Ten at all," Paul says. "He said until I can read at level two, no television shows of any kind." His bottom lip juts out.

"Clearly it was a traumatic week for everyone." I can't help my smile, and in spite of myself, I somehow slip into what feels like a very normal morning. "Hey, wait." I look around. "Don't you guys have school?"

"Inservice day," Hannah says. "Long weekend."

How perfect for me.

"I can't believe you forgot that," Mason says. "That's not like you."

I blink. Does he really have no idea that I know? Or is he a much better actor than I had any idea he might be? That idea makes me extremely uncomfortable, because he's been cheating on me for seven years, and I had no idea. He *must* be a great actor.

Or I'm a monumental moron.

The rest of the way to the car, and then for the entire drive home, I find myself analyzing every single thing he says, trying to read between the lines. But it all seems so *normal*. So mundane.

It makes my idea of moving to Ireland seem preposterous.

How could I ever have considered blowing my entire inheritance on a mansion in Ireland where I'd be starting and running a hotel, which I know nothing about? I'd be moving to a country I've never lived in, with absolutely not a single soul I know or trust. But even stranger, how can I be sitting here, making small talk with my family as if nothing at all is wrong? How can things feel so. . .unbroken when I know they're wrecked?

The kids kind of carry the conversation the whole way home. Clara, Hannah, and Amelia tell me about their horseback riding lesson. Blaine tells me about piano and choir. Paul tells me about a dog that followed him all the way home from the school bus, and how Mason broke his heart when he told him he couldn't keep it.

"It probably belonged to someone else," I say. "Stray dogs would smell, and they'd be dirty and super skinny. I'm pretty sure Dad was right —it just went back to its real boy."

But finally, we do get home. Clara ordered pizza from an app while we were *en route*, and it arrives moments after we do.

"You promised we could watch the new Spiderman when you got back," Paul reminds me.

It feels like I made that promise a year ago. "Sure," I say. "That's fine."

But when the twins start clamoring for popcorn, I stand up immediately. "Dad and I can get it. We'll be right back."

I just need one minute without the kids, so I can see whether he knows I know. Just one minute. But the second we walk alone into the kitchen. . .it's clear.

He has no idea.

Tiffany hasn't told him anything.

I'm not sure how that could be, but he literally grabs my waist, a move I always loved, and drags me toward him. "I've missed you."

I've been acting like I really am Meg friggin' Ryan since we got home. The kids helped, shoving me right into a role I'd been unwittingly playing for years, apparently. But now that they're not here, I can't do it.

I can't hide my revulsion.

"What's wrong?" Mason's hands release me, but his eyes show his confusion. Even now, he doesn't look the slightest bit guilty. It's unbeliev-able. If I didn't *know*, I might think I was making it all up.

"You're mad I didn't call much while you were gone—I get it. But Tiffany completely *bailed* on me at work with *no* explanation. She just didn't show up, and my phone was either stolen, or. . ." He throws his hands into the air. "I don't know. It just disappeared. Then we had two big meetings that almost fell apart. It was a total disaster of a week." He sighs, shaking his head at the same time. "I'm so glad you're home."

"That's unlike her, isn't it?" I arch one eyebrow.

"Tiffany?" He frowns. "She's always been extremely self-centered. She's flaky sometimes, too, but not like this. Not when you're gone, or in a way that harms the business." He sighs. "I know you handle things with the kids effortlessly, but I'm telling you, we almost died without you here. The kids were trying to be sweet, but they put that sign together because they were about ready to burn me at the stake." His half-smile pains me.

That's another of the things I always loved about him.

His cocky arrogance.

His half-smile and the dimples that show up with it.

He shoves his hands in the pockets of his jeans, and I remember how I swooned the first time he did that. "Speaking of—they'll come for us if we don't get them that popcorn, stat. I think they've already made a Mason-sized noose."

"I know the truth." I feel tired as I say the words, like I've aged one hundred years.

He looks totally befuddled. He's going to make me spell it out.

I take a big breath. "Tiffany realized I knew, and she came to see me in Ireland. That's why she flaked on you."

He frowns, and it's another familiar expression. He looks genuinely puzzled, like what I'm saying still makes no sense. "You know what?"

"I had my days wrong," I say, softly. "On the day I left, I took an Uber back, and I saw you two. *Together.*" I don't look away, but I don't yell either. All my rage, all my pain, it has somehow drained away, and the only thing that remains in this moment, a moment I've dreamed about, obsessed over, and dreaded. . .is a deep and abiding sorrow, a soul-deep ache of loss and betrayal.

His eyes widen, finally.

He gasps. "You mean. . ."

I nod. "Yes, that's what I mean. You and I?" I shove a bag of popcorn into the microwave and hit the popcorn button. "We're through."

"Look." Mason straightens. "I'm not sure what Tiffany told you, but it was all her. That woman's not your friend. She's basically one part she-devil and nine parts jealous-of-you. Plus, it was a one-time thing. You can't really mean that our *family*'s over because I was tricked into making a mistake."

"Really?" It's funny, how now that my anger's gone. . .I just don't care. I'm so unimpressed with everything he says that he can't hurt me. "At least Tiffany was honest after she got caught. She told me it's been going on for seven years." I lean against the counter. "In fact, she told me you'd be into a throuple."

Mason's eyes bug. "A—what?"

"You know," I say. "You. Me. And her." I grimace. "I have to tell you, I wasn't impressed, not with either of you. And luckily, it all happened when I had a week to myself to think about everything." I wave my bare left hand at him. "I threw my ring in a lake." I frown. "Actually, no. I think it was the ocean." I grimace. "Probably never getting that one back."

"Natalie," Mason says. "You have to at least let me explain."

"I think you lost the chance to do that when I caught you, but just in case you hadn't, the first words out of your mouth when I told you I knew were a lie. A *lie*," I say. "After cheating on me repeatedly for seven years with my best friend, your *employee*, when I called you on it, you lied."

Mason closes his eyes and covers them with his hand. "This—you just took me by surprise. I need a minute to catch up."

"Oh, you're surprised?" My laughter sounds a little unhinged, but I can't seem to stop it. "When I walked into my own house that day, and I saw you with another woman, I was *shocked*," I say. "But everything since has just been one indignity after another." I shake my head. "I'm sorry if you're having trouble processing."

"Mom?" Paul's standing in the doorway. "Is the popcorn done?"

The microwave dings then, as if it was just waiting to be inquired after. When I open it, smoke billows out, because the popcorn button on our microwave results in burned popcorn one hundred percent of the time. "Oh, bud, I'm sorry. I forgot to pull it out early."

"It's okay," Paul says. "I've done that, too."

I crouch down, and I pull him close, and I stroke my hand over his hair. "I love you, sweetie. I've missed you a *lot*."

"I missed you, too. Dad kept making me peanut butter and grape jelly sandwiches."

"Ah," I say. "He tried to poison you. How could he not know you only eat peanut butter and nutella?"

"Exactly." Paul's smiling as he heads back into the movie room.

"For their sake," Mason says. "Won't you try to forgive me?"

"You don't get to do that," I say. "It's not on *me* to forgive you for them. You did what you did, and you lied about it, and you covered it up, and I will never trust you again. Not ever, not even for them."

Mason balls his hands into fists, and he glares. "You won't even hear me out? Is that really the kind of woman I married?"

"I'm not the woman you married anymore," I say. "Now I'm the woman you cheated on, and let me tell you something." I step closer. "I let myself have *lot* more fun without feeling guilty about it, and I think you'll find me far less accommodating."

"You—she—"

"Tiffany also gave me some files she'd been keeping track of. Money you didn't want me to know about, but also. . ." I pause for dramatic effect. I had no idea being villainous was this fun. Maybe that's why they all do it. "It feels like the government doesn't know about it either, because I've seen all our tax returns, and none of this was on there, either."

Mason's face goes white.

"You have two ways to play this. We can drag this through the court, both of us hiring lawyers, and I can hand mine the files Tiffany shared with me, and I can tell her to do her worst. The evidence I have will be entered in the record, of course, and I'll be sure to send a copy to the IRS, you know, to get my part of our taxes square, *or* you and I can agree to a very generous split of *all* the money, and you can promise to pay a reasonable amount of both child support and alimony. Then I'll take that money and move to Ireland, where I'll raise our children. You can see them once a year, over the summer, for a full month."

"What?"

I shrug. "Unless you choose to forgo that month, which is also totally fine."

"Once a year?" Mason explodes. "You're kidding, right? *Ireland*?" He slams his hand down on the counter.

All the kids shoot out of the movie room like his hand released a latch or something. Their eyes are large and round as they stare at Mason and me.

"What's going on?" Clara asks.

"Your father and I are getting a divorce," I say. "This isn't quite how I wanted to let you guys know about it, but don't worry. He and I will work hard to keep things civil, and we'll make sure that all of you are well cared for."

"I'm living with you," Clara says.

"Me too," Amelia, Blaine, and Hannah say, at virtually the same time.

"We have to pick?" Paul asks. His lower lip wobbles.

"Yes," Clara says. "You have to pick."

"No," Mason says. "That's not right. You can split time between me and your mom, and I'm not even sure we will get a divorce. We have some talking to do. For now, go finish the movie." He points.

"It's because of Tiffany, isn't it?" Clara asks.

My jaw nearly hits the floor.

"You mean because she comes over a lot when Mom's not home?" Hannah asks. "Is that why?"

"How do they—" I feel sick. How could the girls *possibly* know?

"I saw her once when you weren't here," Clara says. "Coming out of your room with her hair in a towel. She said her water wasn't working, but it seemed weird."

"And I saw her here, too," Hannah says. "When you were on your trip last year. She was sleeping in your room, but she said it's because they were remodeling her bathroom." She scowls. "It was early in the morning, and her kids weren't here. It made no sense."

"I should've told you," Clara says. "But she begged me not to, and I was worried. . ." She looks at the floor.

She was worried I'd leave their dad.

Just like I'm doing.

But I can't stay for them.

I'd resent them.

I'd never be able to forgive Mason, and I'd slowly shrink and shrivel until there was nothing left.

I know myself. "Well, you girls are very smart. I just found out about this, and I'm. . ." My voice's trembling too much, so I just stop talking.

"If we have to pick, I pick Mom, too. I'm sorry you'll be all alone, Dad, but maybe you'll like it." Paul's nodding and smiling at Mason. "You yell a lot when Mom's not around."

"No one has to pick anything right now," I say. "Let's try and finish the movie."

"I want Dad to go," Clara says. "I think he should stay at a hotel."

"Or to Tiffany's house," Hannah says. "Tell her he's her problem."

"I don't want Dad to go." Paul starts to cry. "Does he have to leave?"

I pull Paul in for a hug. "No. He doesn't have to go right now. Let's all go in and watch *Spiderman*."

The movie's ruined, and the only person who doesn't know it is Paul. He snuggles up next to Mason and acts like everything's fine. It feels a little like watching a burning building collapse.

Once the movie's over, Mason packs a bag. "I'm going to stay at the apartment at the office for a few days," he says. "I'll give you some space to think this all through."

"It won't change anything," I say.

"You never know," Mason says. "Maybe being home will make you rethink."

It won't, but it actually feels almost good that he wants me to. I figured he'd be relieved that I know and he can move on with Tiffany. She's smarter, makes more money, and she's way, way hotter. I'm just the pudgy girl next door. She's the bombshell home wrecker whom everyone chooses over the tired, sad homemaker.

Literal moments after he leaves, my phone rings. It's Samantha. "Hey girl," she says. "You made it back okay?"

"I did," I say. "But it's not the best time for me to chat right now." All my girls have come into the kitchen, and they're circling me like a pack of wolves, determined to get information.

"I just wanted to say—I'm in. I saw Brent today, and I can't stay here. I'm ready to move when you are. Let me know what you need."

"Really?" I thought for sure once she got home Brent would convince her to give him another chance. People don't let women who look like Samantha walk away, especially not blah nobodies like Brent North. He's about to lose the *best* thing that ever happened to him. Surely he knows that.

"I'm completely and totally serious. If the other people who looked at the place didn't put an offer down, I'm ready to start talking actual numbers."

But what about her horse? She was worried about him making that long trip. "What did you decide about Varius?"

She sighs dramatically, which worries me. "Let's talk about it later. He won't be a problem."

She must have talked to a vet. Maybe the trip's not really that hard on horses. A few hours on a plane, and a few days in quarantine, and done? That would be nice. "Okay," I say. "Well, that's exciting. I'll call you tomorrow."

"What's exciting?" Clara asks. "I'd like to hear something exciting." She looks very close to tears.

"I loved Ireland," I say.

The other girls filter into the family room, too. I guess I'm telling them all now.

"While I was there, I fell in love with a place. A really big, really pretty property. It has a stable that fits quite a few horses, and there are several different, very cute Irish cottages on the same piece of property."

Clara looks confused.

Hannah heard horses and her eyes brightened. Apparently, that's already enough for her.

Amelia's the one who asks. "Why are you talking about it? Are you going to buy it? Are we moving to Ireland?"

I smile. "A lawyer called—I finally got my inheritance from your grandfather, and I thought I might spend it to buy this farm in Ireland."

"Is Ireland where the leprechauns are?" Blaine asks. "The little people who have pots of gold hidden under rainbows?"

"That's not real," Amelia says. "There aren't tiny people who grant wishes. Right, Mom?"

"It's true that the leprechaun legends are Irish," I say. "But Amelia's right that they aren't real."

"Do people speak English there?" Clara asks. "Because I got a C in Spanish. Remember?"

"They all speak English," I say, "but they do have their own language —Gaelic. It might be fun to learn some of that, but you wouldn't have to."

"Maybe." Even Hannah looks unconvinced.

"I thought we could turn the big, fancy house I was looking at into a hotel, and then we could offer horseback tours to people who come to visit."

"Could we help you?" Amelia's eyes are huge.

"And can we get a pet pig?" Blaine asks. "But not one that we'll eat."

"And goats," Amelia says. "Or maybe sheep."

"Why not both?" Hannah asks. "And some chickens."

"She didn't say she bought a farm," Clara says. "She said it's going to be a posh hotel."

"It's just a nice house that I'd like to turn into a posh hotel," I say. "But it has a farm area. I don't see a reason why we couldn't get a few other animals."

"I'm in," Clara says. "Anything that gets you away from Tiffany and Dad."

"I want you guys to be able to see your father," I say. "I won't be upset that you spend time with him. He's been a good dad, at least."

Clara shakes her head. "No, he hasn't. You've been a good mom, and you've made excuses for him, but Mom, he's always been pretty checked out."

"He's at work too much," Amelia says.

"And when he's home, he's always looking at his phone," Blaine says.

"He's not perfect," I say. "But he does love you, and I want you to spend time with him, still."

"If we do move to Ireland, can we still come visit him?" Hannah asks.

I drop a hand on her shoulder. "Of course you can."

"Then I'm in, too." Hannah smiles. "I love you, Mom. I want you to be happy."

"I think we can all be happy there," I say. "But I want to talk about all the details, and I want you guys to be as happy as I am about the move."

"I still think there might be leprechauns," Blaine says, "and I mean to catch one."

There may never be leprechauns for her to catch, but I think the move might still be magical. I hope, very much, that it is.

CHAPTER 24

I n the years before Jason died, we made lots of plans for the future.

We sold our small, starter home, and we bought a larger place. The kids were getting bigger, and we just felt like we needed more room. After he died, it felt like we'd been stupid to get a bigger note and have more things to maintain. I lamented the upgrade.

We started putting money into a retirement plan, so that when it was time to cut back work hours, we'd have money to fall back on. That money's still there, but I couldn't touch it when I needed it, or I'd have had to pay a big penalty. I cursed the IRA rules and our idiocy in dumping money there.

We cut out all the fried food we'd been eating, and we started eating whole grains. We reduced our red meat intake and started integrating fish instead. Both of us started to work out, together. Jason lost almost forty pounds, and I lost nine. I don't regret the changes, but it felt like a joke—Jason died of a heart attack at forty-two. A *heart attack*, two years after we totally changed our lifestyle to be healthier. Why?

The biggest change we made was paying off the loan we'd taken out to pay Jeremy for his half of the family business. We could have said we'd come up with it after his dad died. We could have tried to pay him off more slowly, too. But we wanted to get out from under what we saw as a debt, and we did it as fast as we could. It meant that when Jason's friends were hurting, when their businesses were going under, and we bought a lot of their practically-new equipment so they didn't default on their loans and ruin their credit, we *really* struggled to make all our payments.

I actually picked up part-time work doing tax returns so we didn't default on anything.

Jason was adamant that when the economy surged back, he'd have what we needed to really make a big profit. That part was true enough, but because we had a lot more debt, I couldn't try to muddle through things myself.

I needed help.

All that equipment absolutely had to be serviced and used regularly.

In spite of my part-time work, we burned through all our non-retirement savings to make the payments in the months that people were shut down for COVID. If Jeremy hadn't stepped in when he did, if he hadn't shown up and taken over after Jason's death, I would've gone under. At the very least, I'd have been forced to sell the equipment back to the friends we'd bought it from in the first place.

Because Jeremy was here when Jason wasn't, the business grew.

How much of that growth was from my and Jason's work? How much was from Jeremy's?

I can't be sure.

Some was Jason's vision. Some of the growth was from me as well. After Jason died, I started doing lots of things for the business I hadn't done before. After the kids were in bed, I did all the books. I emailed accounts. I prepared invoices. I did my job all day, I cared for the children each afternoon and evening, and then late into the night, I worked on Heavy Lifting.

Hard.

But Jeremy did a lot, too.

Maybe he's entitled to his share of the profits, even though he didn't technically own any part of the company anymore. Most of my anger might have been related to how he handled it, and not really related to my frustration that he walked away with part of the sale proceeds.

It wasn't his to sell.

But maybe he felt like that was the only way he'd get what he deserved. Maybe Jeremy didn't trust me, and this was his poor way of dealing with that.

On my way home, I start walking through possible scenarios in my mind. I'll talk to Jeremy, giving him the benefit of the doubt, and I'll ask him why he did what he did. If he's the least bit apologetic, I'll just let him keep his share of the money. It wasn't a business I wanted to sell, but it wasn't something I could run without him either, and I can't expect him to keep doing that until my sixteen-year-old son can take over.

I wasn't being fair, either.

When I get home, I'm not as tired as I could be. I managed a few hours of sleep on the flight, at least. A flight home from a vacation. I remind myself that Jeremy *did* send me on a girls' trip. More than one. He's been trying to watch the kids, and hopefully he has some kind of explanation for why he didn't put Trace in the rehab facility like we discussed.

I'm sure he does.

For Jason's sake, I need to make sure I keep the peace with his family. He's not here to advocate for them, so I have to make sure I'm doing my part.

When I walk through the door at home, I expect the kids to be at school. Trace certainly isn't—he's flipping through channels on the television like he's playing a game of hot potato with the remote.

"What are you doing here?"

Trace spins around, shocked, and I realize he's stoned. There's a big bag of potato chips in front of him, but it looks almost empty.

"Where's your uncle?"

Trace stands up. "Shoot, I thought you were coming home tomorrow."

"If you had known it was today, would you be at school?"

Trace smiles. "Well, I wouldn't have been here."

"You should be in rehab," I say. "Jeremy said—"

"Look, gang, don't go at him, okay?" Trace shakes his head. "Uncle Jeremy gets it, because he smokes too. He knows it's not a big deal. He's been managing his life just fine."

He smokes too? "He—what?"

He slaps his forehead. "Shoot. He didn't want to tell you, but only because he knew you'd act like that, but it's not a big deal, okay? Plenty of adults smoke, Mom, especially here."

Plenty of adults smoke. "So in your mind, and in your uncle's, *I'm* the problem? I'm just not 'chill' enough?"

"Exactly." Trace smiles again, and this time, he sits down. "See? Like, my life isn't over just because I'm not a slave to the teachers and the man."

"The man?"

"You work too hard, Mom. Your whole life can't be work."

"Actually." I walk across the room, drop my bag on the ground, and snatch the remote. "Your whole life doesn't have to be work *because* I work so hard. Your uncle the smoker's also a sponger. See any kind of correlation there?"

Trace shakes his head. "He works as hard as he needs to work, and no harder. That's what we should all do. The world provides." He nods slowly, his eyes glazed over.

I slap him across the face.

Hard.

"You're a complete idiot for listening to him."

Trace reels back, his hand flying to his cheek. In his entire life, I've never once raised a hand to him. Not once. Never.

Maybe that's part of the problem.

There have never been any real consequences to anything in his life.

I step closer. "While I was gone, your 'the world provides' uncle stole two million dollars from us. *Two million dollars.* Are you 'chill' with that? Because it would have been your money someday. You won't have that money now, the money your dad worked so hard to earn, because your super chill uncle stole it so he can fund his laid-back lifestyle."

Trace blinks, still pressing one hand to his cheek. "He would never do that."

"No?" I clench my hands at my side to avoid doing anything horrible again. Tears are rolling down my face now, and I hate how emotional it makes me look. "You may not believe me, but I already talked to him about it. He didn't deny it. While I was gone, he took my power of attorney, which he procured under false pretenses, and he sold your dad's company, keeping half the proceeds for himself."

Trace's eyes flash. "You must have misunderstood. Uncle Jeremy would never do that."

"I did do it." Jeremy's at the top of the stairs. "I didn't steal it though, like your mom says. I did take half of the sale proceeds, and I did sell the company while she was gone with her power of attorney, because I knew she'd try to keep me from taking my fair share."

Trace's jaw drops.

So much for the apology I was hoping he'd make. "You said you wanted nothing to do with the company years ago, and Jason and I took out a loan and gave you four hundred thousand dollars. We nearly killed ourselves paying off that loan, and you weren't even working."

"But then after Jason died, *I* had to step in and save the company. I recharacterized your payments into a loan," Jeremy says, "because I deserved what I got."

"You really did that?" Trace asks. "Seriously?"

"If your mother wasn't so greedy and unreasonable, I wouldn't have had to do it. She should've asked me whether I wanted to sell it back when the offers first came in. Did she even tell you about either of the purchase offers we got? One was a year ago, and the other was six months ago."

"Trace is sixteen. I told you I wanted him to have the chance to take over his dad's company when he graduates, so you know why I didn't consider selling."

"And that's when I knew what I had to do to get my share," Jeremy says. "I'm not the villain here. She is." He points.

Trace looks confused.

But I'm not. Not anymore. "You know, when I was on my flight home, I felt like maybe I'd overreacted. I was going to talk to you and if you felt bad about how you handled things, I was going to let go of my anger." I snort. "But now? I think I didn't do enough. I wasn't *mad enough.*"

"Drop it?" Jeremy jogs down the stairs. "I almost hope you do try to do something about it. What are you going to say? All the paperwork supports my position, that it's half mine."

"That's not true," I say. "I have the loan paperwork Jason and I took out, and I have the emails from your parents about the valuation and the amount that constituted half of the business at that time."

"And my testimony will clarify that I changed my mind, and you guys agreed to make it a loan to me instead, a loan that I couldn't get at the time because I wasn't employed. You did me a solid, as family should."

"Why on earth would we make you a loan when no bank would?"

"Family affection." Jeremy's smile is diabolical. "It'll be your word against mine, and who do you think looks better to a jury?"

"Your mother's on my side," I say. "She'll testify for me. She called me to tell me that she thinks what you did is wrong."

"Mom thinks up is down and black is white. She's old, she's confused, and asking her to testify is pretty grasping of you, really." Jeremy smiles. "You'll put her through a lot of misery, and I promise, it won't help you."

"Ah, but your parents' wills say that they're leaving the entire business to us, because you got paid already—"

"They never executed those." Jeremy drops his voice. "That makes their first will controlling."

"They *did* execute them," I say. "I saw them—"

Jeremy shrugs. "You know, it's the strangest thing. I checked their fire safe, and you know, the only ones I could find were the ones leaving their Heavy Lifting shares to us equally."

"You destroyed them," I say. "You're disgusting—how do you think Jason feels about you doing this?"

"I got his widow two million bucks, so I'd say he's pretty happy with me."

Trace's eyes widen. "You got two million dollars?"

"Yep," I say. "Half of what we should have gotten, and now you have no future here anymore." I straighten my shoulders. "And frankly, I can't trust that you'll be safe here, either."

"Safe?" Trace tilts his head. "What does that mean?"

"I think your uncle's a bad influence, so I'm selling our house and moving our entire family to Ireland."

Trace splutters.

The bus stops on the corner, letting Bryce out. That means Trina should be home soon, too.

"But for now, since you're a person I really can't trust, I'd thank you to gather your bags and leave." I stare pointedly at Jeremy.

"Ireland?" Jeremy shakes his head. "You've lost your mind. What on earth would you even do there?"

"My friends and I are starting a hotel," I say. "And we've already found the perfect place."

"Who's going to help you with the kids?" Jeremy asks. "You can barely go three days without calling me."

"Did I mention I have friends going there with me?" I ask. "People I trust."

"I don't want to move to Ireland," Trace says. "I don't know anyone there, and my friends are all here."

"I'm not overly impressed with your friends," I say. "And I think it's high time you made some new ones."

"I won't go," Trace says.

"Well, it's really too bad that you're a minor," I say. "Because minors don't get to choose what they do or where they go."

"Yeah, Jason would be really proud of you. You're a *wonderful* mother," Jeremy says.

"Hey," Trace says. "She is a good mom."

"She's ordering you around like she's the queen, and she thinks the pot's a problem, when you and I both know it's fine. You shouldn't have to live such a miserable life just because that's what her generation was taught."

Trace frowns. "I'm not sure about all that."

"All what?" Jeremy looks seriously annoyed.

Bryce walks through the door, and I find myself wondering why it took him so long to come inside. "Hey, Mom." He smiles. "Welcome back." He hugs me.

As hard as Trace has been to handle, his brother Bryce has been correspondingly easy. He's kind, he's generous, and he's hard-working. He always does the right thing, and watching Trace make bad decisions over and over hurts him almost as much as it does me. I think of Bryce as my teddy bear, because he's so sweet, so kind, and so heart-warming. "I pulled those weeds in the front flowerbed—sorry I forgot to do them before. I meant to have it done when you got home."

The snow melted early this year, and we've already got sprouts out front. The trouble is, most of them are volunteers—I meant to pull them before *I* left. Bryce noticed.

Tears well up in my eyes. "Thank you." I kiss his cheek. "And I have some exciting news."

Trina bursts through the door then, and I notice the elementary bus swinging around the corner. "Hey, Mom!!" She flings her bookbag on the floor and practically knocks me over when she hugs me. She's my little hurricane. Everything she does gets all her attention, always. "I'm so glad you're home. I can't eat any more pizza." She laughs. "I never thought I'd say that, but I mean it."

"I don't know how to make anything else," Bryce says, "and Uncle Jeremy and Trace were. . ." He coughs. "Anyway, we're out of frozen pizzas."

"Out?" I bought *eight* before I left. They really must have eaten it almost every day. "Look you two, I have some news." I force a smile. "You know that I went to Ireland for my trip, and while I was there, I found an awesome property that your Aunts Samantha and Natalie want to turn into a hotel. We're moving there this summer."

"Ireland?" Trina asks. "Is that the place with pots of gold?"

Bryce rolls his eyes.

"We aren't going." Trace folds his arms. "Mom's just being weird because she's mad at Uncle Jeremy."

"Honestly, maybe it's a good idea." Bryce frowns. "You could meet some new people."

"And get away from some bad influences." I glance at Uncle Jeremy. "Speaking of, thanks for watching the kids, but please go now."

"Are you mad at him?" Trina asks. "Because he and Trace smoked a *lot* while you were gone. I even got mad."

Together?

Even for Jeremy, that's *way* over the line. "We can talk about all this later." I point at the door. "Thanks for your help. I really do appreciate it."

The way I can't get him to leave and I keep thanking him, but we both know I'm really ordering him out, makes me think about horse shows, strangely. When you're doing schooling shows, if your horse refuses, you can circle around and take him over the jump again.

If he refuses again, you can try one more time.

But if your horse refuses a third time, you're through.

The announcer will literally say, 'thank you, rider.' But what they mean is, 'please get out. You're done.'

I refuse to drag the kids into this whole mess any more than I already have, so I'm stuck thanking him out. At least the horse show memory leaves me laughing instead of fuming about it.

Jeremy finally leaves, but he looks uneasy for some reason. I can't decide whether he's upset about Ireland, or whether he's mad I'm kicking him out. He had to expect I'd be upset about the business sale and his theft, even if he's justified it to himself until it feels like the just move.

After I get the kids started on their homework, or at least Bryce and Trina, I check the fridge. They weren't kidding—nothing in there other than condiments. It looks like they did eat nothing but pizza while I was gone. I pop one of the lasagnas I left in the freezer into the oven.

"Hey, why don't you come with me to the grocery store," I say.

Trace doesn't look excited.

"I think you need to spend more time with me, not less." I grab my purse. "Come on." On our way out the door, I call out. "Bryce, you're in charge for a bit."

"Okay," he says. "Can you get some Life cereal? We're out."

"Oh, and strawberries," Trina says. "I haven't had those in like a *year*."

"Got it," I say.

On the way to the grocery store, I'm quiet. I would prefer Trace to initiate conversation with me. But after ten minutes of silence, still no luck with that. Once we reach the store, I put the car in park, and I shift sideways. "I know it's been a hard few years. Dad died, you messed up your shoulder, and you must feel lost. I know those are generalizations, but they're pretty obvious issues."

It probably doesn't help that he's at least a little high, but he seems to mostly be listening. "Yeah."

"You do have a lot of things in your life that are good. You have me and your brother and sister. You have a brilliant brain in your head, if you haven't fried it entirely. You have a healthy body, mostly, and you could do a lot of things still—"

"Mom, I don't want to play baseball or tennis. We've talked about this —I liked football. I can't play anymore, so just leave me alone about it. You can't fix me by finding me a new hobby."

"I'm not trying to fix you," I say softly. "Because I can't. No matter how much I may want to, in this life, we either fix ourselves, or we stay broken." I lean closer. "But I want you to want to get better, and until we get there. . ." I shrug. "I'm going to have to start slowly removing things that are blocking your path to happiness. If you thought I was kidding about Ireland, think again. We're selling this house, and we're moving there. You're going to have to get okay with it."

Trace sulks the entire time we're at the store, or maybe he's just mad that I ruined his buzz. Either way, when we get home, I go through his room, like any good mom would, and I find not one, and not even two, but three stashes. I worry that it might stop up the plumbing, but I flush them. Usually he yells, argues with me, and tells me how much money I'm throwing away.

This time, he just watches me.

I'm not sure why there aren't any fireworks, and I don't press for an explanation as to why he's staying calm. I do, however, text Natalie and tell her I'm in. I'm ready for a big change.

I think maybe this is just what we all need.

While I'm unpacking, Bryce taps on my door. "Can I come in?"

"Sure." I shove my stuff off the edge of the sofa and up against my back wall. "Sit."

At first, he just watches me unpack. But after a moment, he says, "Are we really moving?"

I nod.

"We're leaving the house we lived in with Dad?" When his eyes meet mine, they're wide.

"That's one of the reasons I'd never considered it before." I sigh. "But to be honest, this house is expensive, and it's been hard to maintain it alone since your dad died."

"I know."

"You know?" I feel my eyebrows shoot up.

"I've heard you muttering while you pay bills."

So much for thinking I'd kept my stress from the kids. "At least money won't be as tight now. Jeremy did us that small favor."

"Trace says he stole from us. Is that true?"

I'm surprised Trace told him. I nod, reluctantly. "I didn't want to drag you kids into it, but yes." I explain as quickly and simply as I can. "It's another reason I won't be sad to leave."

"No kidding." Bryce slumps a little into the corner of the sofa. "He's not a very good uncle, and I'm not really shocked he stole from us, but he's kind of all we had."

"I know you don't know Aunt Samantha very well, and that's a real shame. You're going to love her. And you might remember Aunt Natalie from when Trina was born, but you'll love her kids when you meet them."

Bryce looks unconvinced. "You can call them aunts, but they aren't even really related to us."

"People you chose are sometimes more precious to you than your own family." I don't mention that Jeremy isn't related to me anyway. "I know you'll miss your friends."

"Not really."

"You can be honest with me," I say. "I'm listening."

Bryce grunts. "I don't really have any, but I am. . .nervous to move."

"I know." I cross the room and drop a hand on his shoulder. "You'll see a lot more of me there, and that's going to be good."

He smiles up at me and nods. "And for what it's worth, I think getting Trace away from Uncle Jeremy and his friends is smart." He leans against my hand, and then he stands. "Tell me what you need me to do, and I'll do it."

"I'm going to talk to my bosses tomorrow, and then we'll go from there."

Bryce pauses on his way out, and then he turns. "And if you can, I think you should sue Uncle Jeremy. Dad would want you to do it."

That makes my heart contract.

I guess even adults need some validation sometimes. I pick up my phone to call Trish and tell her she might need to testify after all, but an unknown Colorado number's calling me already.

"Vanessa Littlefield?"

"That's me," I say.

"I'm Doctor Hesslup at St. Joe's emergency room."

My hand tightens on the phone. "Okay."

"I'm calling because you're listed as the emergency contact for Trisha Littlefield."

No. No, no, no. "Is she alright?"

"It appears she's had a stroke. I'm afraid she's not doing very well, but I think she's trying to ask for you."

Sometimes, I think God has a sense of humor. The only thing in the world that had the power to keep me from moving. . .is helping my darling, supportive warrior of a mother-in-law. I can't leave her alone—Jason would never forgive me. I'd never forgive myself.

All three kids want to come with me, so we drive to the hospital together. While we're waiting by Trish's bedside, I text Natalie again.

Trish is sick. I'm sorry, but I don't think I can move after all. I hope you and Sam can make it work without me.

CHAPTER 25

Natalie

W hen I'm in my pilates class and they say to hold the plank position for ten more seconds, I *swear* it feels like an hour. And when I'm running late for Paul's school drop-off line, I swear the streetlight sits at red for five minutes.

The moment in time when I saw Tiffany's heels s t r e t c h e d.

My one-week pause, taken in Ireland with my best friends by my side, lasted just exactly as long as it needed to. I think someone upstairs knew I needed that trip, maybe more than any other vacation I've ever taken in my life. I needed time to get my head on straight. I needed the support I couldn't have found anywhere else.

I needed *nine* days instead of eight, so I could discover the truth.

Then I needed Samantha and Vanessa to keep me upright when two of the support legs of my life stool were yanked out from under me all at once. No best friend. No husband. Just my kids and my job, and nothing else. Until Samantha and Vanessa stepped into the breach.

Even as we grew apart, I always loved them.

But some people, when they're needed, are strong enough to grow into what you require. It's like that room of need or whatever in the wizard books. Only, this isn't made up. It's very, very real.

I think true friends are the ones who will do anything you need when you need them, and they'll also step back carefully and with love when you're too busy for them. Knowing they'll be with me, it's what I had to have to survive this massive bump in Natalie's Road of Life.

They're part of the reason that the ten weeks between when I arrived home and when I pulled up in front of the lawyer's office today fly by so very quickly.

"Natalie." My lawyer, Matt, waves me back. "Come. Sit."

"Thanks for helping with this," I say. "I know it's a little outside of your comfort zone. You don't usually handle divorces."

"It was new and exciting." Matt straightens, and then he leans closer, his brow furrowed. "Are you *sure* this is what you want? Because when you sign these papers, it's done. The only reason we could process this whole thing in ten weeks is that Mason hasn't argued with you about anything. As an independent party, I can tell you this isn't an equitable split. Even in cases of infidelity, the property is usually split down the middle in Texas."

I don't tell him that Mason's only being so accommodating because I'm blackmailing him. "I know it's fast," I say. "But believe me. I'm not going to change my mind."

Matt hands me the pen. "Let's get started, then."

"And after I sign?"

Matt smiles. "I got these papers from Mason's lawyer, so he's already approved all of it. And he's signed." He points, and I see it.

Mason Cleary.

"In another few days?"

"You'll officially be single," Matt says. "And you'll have full custody of the kids. He gets one month over the summer, though."

"I really appreciate you helping me," I say. "I know you don't do these usually, but all the divorce lawyers I talked to seemed to want to blow it way out of proportion. I didn't want a big fight."

"What do your kids think?" Matt asks. "Are they excited or nervous?"

"Both," I say. "Well, Paul blows hot and cold. He's five, though, so that's always been true."

"Was that investigator useful?" Matt asks. "She came highly recommended, but you never know."

I exhale. "You know, when you said I should hire someone—"

"If someone's lying about an affair, I think you just need peace of

253

mind that's all they're covering up." Matt shakes his head. "I hope she didn't find anything."

After Tiffany disclosed Mason's accounts, I thought for sure that was everything. But Matt's private investigator found two more women and another half million in hidden offshore accounts that even Tiffany didn't know about. "Nothing that shocked me," I say.

"My wife will miss you," Matt says.

I think that's true, but I imagine they won't miss me for very long. None of my friends here feel very real. They were all surface friends. I appreciate Matt's help, and they're good people, but I need new family.

And that's what I'll soon have.

"Do you think he and Tiffany will—"

I snort. "I don't even care."

"For your children's sake, I hope not."

"I just hope he doesn't go to jail. Some of his business stuff. . ." I shrug. "Let's just say that I don't care, except for how it affects the kiddos."

"You can't get child support from in there." Matt's smirking. "So I hope the same thing."

It's *freeing*, not to be tied to the consequences of what he does—or doesn't do—anymore. I still struggle with feeling stupid for not noticing any of it before it was staring me in the face.

"Well, sign here." He hands me another form. "And you'll officially be through."

I want to celebrate.

And I want to bawl.

So I do neither. I FaceTime Samantha.

She's not struggling in the same way I am. She's just squealing. "Girl." She holds up a paper. "*Divorced!*" She jumps up and down and her screen shakes.

"Both of us free on the same day," I say. "I would never, in a million years, have expected this back when we were riding together."

"We're about to be doing it again." Her impossibly wide smile gets even broader. "Two weeks to close!!"

I still pinch myself, sometimes. "My house sale closed last week. Let me tell you, living in an extended stay hotel with five kids is not for the faint of heart."

"At least school is out," Samantha says.

"No, that makes it worse!" I chuckle. "They're all bored. They're around in the two tiny rooms we have, all the time."

"Just two more weeks," Samantha says. "And then our little Irish escape's turning into a whole new life."

"Oh, wait," I say. "I'm getting a call from *Ireland* on the other line."

Samantha pumps a fist in the air. "Go us! Tell Cilly I said 'Wahoo!'"

I roll my eyes. *Cilly?* For the love. I click to change over to the other line. "Hello?"

"Hey, Natalie. I heard your divorce was supposed to be finalized today." They've been pushing back the close for us, so we can buy the property after all our Ts are crossed and our Is dotted.

"Yes," I say. "The ink's not dry, but the papers are all signed."

"For both of you?" He is so awkward when he asks about Samantha. It's kind of cute.

"Yes," I say. "Both me and Samantha are now free. Everything is right on track. We've really appreciated your patience."

"Rían did want me to update you about something, too. Last night, Drew got stuck in his stall. Rían was staying there and heard him screaming, and he did finally get him freed, but he's pretty banged up. We had to call a vet."

I can't help my laugh.

"It's funny?" Cillian asks. "Rían said he was your favorite horse."

"He is," I say, "but he is still a horse. This is just what they do. Did he need stitches?"

"He did," Cillian says. "But I think he'll heal up just fine."

Now I'm laughing again. "Sorry." I stop. "I'm just laughing now, because you're the one stuck paying his vet bills until we close."

Cillian's swearing when he hangs up.

The transfer of funds from Mason's business accounts are delayed by six days, and Samantha's job loses another physician assistant and begs her to stay for another week. It feels like the world's conspiring to keep me in a hotel forever, but *finally* the preliminary visas clear, and I head for the airport in an Uber.

This time, I arrive on the right day.

And I have all five of my children with me. "You guys have everything? Two bags each?"

"You're sure that stuff we put in that big box is going to get there?" Amelia believes only what she sees with her own eyes, and sometimes she even doubts that.

"I'm sure it will get there," I say. "But not for two or three weeks. Remember? It should arrive just in time for school."

I hope.

I didn't tell them we only have a window. They're already nervous enough.

"Are the boys there cute?" Clara asks for the third time. Today. "Tell me they're cute."

"I googled it. They have accents," Hannah says. "But probably bad teeth."

"Stop googling things," Clara says. "You're almost always wrong."

"You're just saying that because you failed that Spanish test when she used Google Translate to help you cheat," Blaine says.

Hannah glares at Blaine. So does Clara.

"We do *not* use Google Translate for schoolwork," I say. "That's cheating, and it sounds like you knew it."

"It was only one time," Clara mutters. "And everyone else uses it, and I hated Spanish."

"You're all done with it now, in any case," I say. "And when we get on this plane, I want to leave all the bad things from our past where they belong."

"Where's that?" Amelia asks.

"In the past." I smile.

"But not Dad, right?" Paul clutches my hand. "You're not saying we have to leave him behind."

I shake my head. "Not at all. Next summer, you'll come back to Austin and spend all summer with him." The mere thought strikes dread into my heart, but I'll face that when the time comes. "But for now, we're going on an adventure with horses, and castles, and—"

"Dragons!" Paul drops his bag and thrusts his hand out as if he's holding a sword.

"There aren't dragons, you idiot," Blaine says. "Mom said there aren't leprechauns either."

"But there are castles," Paul says. "Why are there castles if there aren't dragons?"

The flight attendant's laughing as we pass her, and I just shake my head. It's going to be a very long flight, but in the end, I think it'll be worth it. In fact, I'm downright excited about our Irish Escape.

Dragons or no.

****

I hope this book felt like an escape for you as well! I loved writing it. The second book in the series, The Creaky Old Barn, will be out sometime before November of 2025. You can preorder it in ebook now.

If you loved this, but you haven't tried my books before, you might like my Birch Creek Ranch Series. There are EIGHT books out already. (It's complete!) And you can download the first one here for free... OR you can buy the whole series in a bundle for more than 40% off!

Traditional Irish Apple Cake Recipe

I like to bake things I read about in my research for books that aren't set in my area. One of the things I found and liked best for Ireland was a traditional Irish Apple Cake. Because I changed some things to make the recipe more "American friendly," I'm sharing it here instead of a simple link to download. My family loved this so much that I've found myself making it once or twice a week for months now. You've been warned.

SPECIAL EQUIPMENT: A springform pan, spatula(s), and if you have one, a double boiler makes this much simpler. You can use a pot on the bottom with water and a metal bowl above it as well.

INGREDIENTS:

CAKE:

1/2 cup unsalted butter at room temperature

1/2 cup sugar

2 large eggs

3 Tbsp whole milk or cream

1.25 cups all purpose flour

1 tsp baking powder

1 tsp cinnamon

1/8 tsp salt

confectioner's sugar for dusting on top

3 honey crisp or other crisp apples, peeled and thinly sliced. (usually just over a pound once sliced, if you're worried; slice them very, very thin or they will be crunchy when you're done baking.

STREUSEL TOPPING

3/4 cup flour (all purpose)

1/3 cup oats (I prefer rolled)

7 Tbsp unsalted cold butter, cut in small pieces

1/2 cup sugar

CUSTARD

(I had to make this THREE TIMES before I got it just right, and I found that using a double boiler made it WAY easier to get right. I make custard somewhat frequently, but this is a difficult custard sauce recipe, in my opinion. It's delicious, though, so I thought it was worth it. My family doesn't like the cake nearly as well without the sauce.)

6 large egg yolks

6 Tbsp sugar

1.5 cups whole milk

(or! I used 1 cup of 2 percent/1 percent and added 1/2 cream!)

1.5 tsp vanilla

INSTRUCTIONS:

1. PREHEAT the oven to 350.

2. CUSTARD. Make the custard sauce first so you have time to cool it. Bring the milk to a simmer over medium heat. While you're doing that, whisk the egg yolks and sugar until they're well mixed. With a 1/4 cup measure, scoop some of the hot milk and pour it into the egg mixture, whisking it the whole time so it will not cook the eggs. This is called proofing them. Do this TWO MORE TIMES with 1/4 cup or so of the milk

each time. Then combine the egg and sugar mixture with the rest of the milk over the pot, stirring constantly. Keep it over medium heat and stir it until you notice it's thickening. Here's where I screwed up a few times. It will NEVER get super thick. If you're waiting for that, you'll cook the egg! So once it starts to coat the spoon or spatula or whisk you're using, turn it off. I also recommend that you have a tupperware container with a strainer over the top, so when you are done, pour the custard sauce through that and into the container. Add the vanilla and whisk it up, then pop the top on and put it in the fridge to cool while you make the cake. Without a secure top, your custard will form a crust on top while cooling.

3. STREUSEL TOPPING. This one's easy. Literally just blend it all up with a fork. You're going to think it will NEVER come together, but it will. it's not going to be blobs, though. It'll be kind of clingy powder and small clumps with some oatmeal, and that's just what you want, I swear! Leave that bowl on the counter while you do the other two parts.

4. CAKE BASE. I literally just dump everything into a bowl and use beaters to mix it all up. I don't do anything fussy or first, and it's just fine. You will need to then grease the springform pan (I just used Pam) and spread this in the bottom of it. It's a little tricky, because this is sticky. Smooth it out as much as you can.

5. APPLES. Peel and slice your apples here, and I arrange them inside down in little runs. I think it's kind of fun. I suppose you could just dump them in. I think the tiny, thin slices are key to this cooking just right. It's not quite as good when you overcook it, so...

6. ASSEMBLY. Dump the streusel on top of the cake and spread it around. THE ORIGINAL recipe says to bake for 50-60 minutes at 350. This resulted in an overcooked cake on our end. I don't like overcooked things. I also have a "true convection" oven, meaning mine drops the temp by 25 degrees because it moves the air around with fans AND has heating elements on ALL SIDES of the oven. If you simply have an oven with a fan on the back, I'm not sure how it will go. As most bakers know, the baking is the temperamental part. You may have to play with it. All my recipes have little notes on the baking times and temps. (I toy with them until I find a fit for MY oven.) But what worked perfectly for ME was 44 minutes at 325 convection. You can certainly try pulling a toothpick out of the center, but I think with the apples and streusel, it's harder to tell whether it's fully cooked that way.

7. FINAL TOUCHES. Once it comes out, if your house is like my house, you will be swarmed with people. Husband, sons, daughters. All of them want a slice. Make them wait ten minutes while it finishes baking in that springform pan. During the end of that time, use a sieve to sprinkle powdered sugar on the top. Then you can pop the springform off the edges and let them cut a slice. They can spoon on as much or as little custard as they want.

Acknowledgments

My husband is always my number one supporter. He tolerates a LOT when I'm drafting, and no one supports me and this career more. My mom is right behind him, though, carrying a little pom pom.

And my kids can't be left out, either. They're the first to read every book, and when I have questions about what happened in the past books, they always have the answers. From Emmy who reads them over and over, to Tessa who reads them once and listens to the audio on repeat, I am so grateful to have grown myself five little uber-fans.

My editor and my cover artist are magicians, and I love you both.

But the real stars here are my fans. Without you, without your support, without your recommendations to your family and friends, I would have to go back to being a lawyer with a "real job." Thank you. *Truly*, thank you.

About the Author

Bridget's a lawyer, but does as little legal work as possible. She has five kids and soooo many animals that she loses count. There are for sure lots of horses, dogs, cats, and so many chickens. Animals are her great love, after the hubby, the kids, and the books. She makes cookies waaaaay too often and believes they should be their own food group. In an attempt at balancing the scales, she kick boxes daily. So if you don't like her books, maybe don't tell her in person.

Bridget's active on social media, and has a Facebook group she comments in often. (Her husband even gets on there sometimes.) Please feel free to join her there: https://www.facebook.com/groups/750807222376182 She also gives a free book to everyone who joins her newsletter at www.BridgetEBakerWrites.com

Also by B. E. Baker

I write women's fiction and clean romance under B. E. Baker.

The Irish Escape:

The Crumbly Old Castle

The Creaky Old Barn

The Scarsdale Fosters Series (standalone but interconnected romances):

Seed Money (1)

Nouveau Riche (2)

Minted (3)

Loaded (4)

Filthy Rich (5)

Old Money (6)

A standalone historical fiction:

Hungry: The Inspiring Tale of Three Donner Party Survivors

The Finding Home Series (standalone but interconnected romances):

Finding Grace (1)

Finding Faith (2)

Finding Cupid (3)

Finding Spring (4)

Finding Liberty (5)

Finding Holly (6)

Finding Home (7)

Finding Balance (8)

Finding Peace (9)

The Finding Home Series Boxset Books 1-3

The Finding Home Series Boxset Books 4-6

The Finding Home Series Boxset Books 7-9

The Birch Creek Ranch Series (women's fiction series with romance for each character that spans the series):

The Bequest

The Vow

The Ranch

The Retreat

The Reboot

The Surprise

The Setback

The Lookback

Children's Picture Book

Yuck! What's for Dinner?

I also write romantasy and end of the world fiction under Bridget E. Baker.

The Dragon Captured Series: (dragon shifter romance!)

Ensnared

Entwined

Embroiled

Embattled

The Russian Witch's Curse: (horse shifter romance!)

My Queendom for a Horse

My Dark Horse Prince

My High Horse Czar

My Wild Horse King

My Trojan Horse Majesty

My Death Horse Overlord

The Magical Misfits Series: (paranormal humor!)

My Pigeon Familiar

My Mongrel Pack

My Itching Scales

The Birthright Series (urban fantasy romance):

Displaced (1)

unForgiven (2)

Disillusioned (3)

misUnderstood (4)

Disavowed (5)

unRepentant (6)

Destroyed (7)

The Birthright Series Collection, Books 1-3

The Anchored Series (urban fantasy romance):

Anchored (1)

Adrift (2)

Awoken (3)

Capsized (4)

The Sins of Our Ancestors Series (end of the world romance):

Marked (1)

Suppressed (2)

Redeemed (3)

Renounced (4)

Reclaimed (5) a novella!

A stand alone YA romantic suspense:

Already Gone

Made in United States
North Haven, CT
11 January 2026

86539626R00153